THE
JAGUAR
KNIGHTS

THE
JAGUAR
KNIGHTS

A Chronicle of the King's Blades

DAVE DUNCAN

An Imprint of HarperCollinsPublishers

HarperCollins books may be purchased for educational, business, or sales promotional use. For information please write: Special Markets Department, HarperCollins Publishers Inc., 10 East 53rd Street, New York, NY 10022.

FIRST EDITION

Designed by Jeffrey Pennington

Printed on acid-free paper

Library of Congress Cataloging-in-Publication Data

Duncan, Dave, 1933–
   The Jaguar Knights: a chronicle of the King's blades /
Dave Duncan.— 1st ed.
     p. cm.
   ISBN 0-06-055511-4
   1. King's Blades (Fictitious characters)—Fiction. 2. Knights and knighthood—Fiction. 3. Quests (Expeditions)—Fiction.
4. Swordsmen—Fiction. I. Title.

PR9199.3.D847J34 2004
813'.54—dc22   2004046989

04 05 06 07 08 JTC/QW 10 9 8 7 6 5 4 3 2 1

This book is dedicated to all the wonderful people who still buy books and so make books possible; and especially to the band of faithful who have journeyed through the years with Rap, Wallie, Durendal, and the rest of my imaginary friends.

AUTHOR'S NOTE

Historically, the eagle knights and jaguar knights were the elite troops in the armies of Montezuma, but that is the last history you will find here.

SOME SIGNIFICANT DATES

351, Thirdmoon   Sir Durendal bound *(The Gilded Chain)*

357, Thirdmoon   Sir Wasp bound *(Lord of the Fire Lands)*

367, Twelfthmoon   Sir Eagle bound *(Sky of Swords)*

390, Thirdmoon   Queen Malinda abdicates, King Athelgar succeeds

390, Fourthmoon   Sir Wolf bound *(The Jaguar Knights)*

392, Fifthmoon   Lord Wassail exposes the Thencaster Conspiracy

394, Fourthmoon   Death of Sir Parsewood, Durendal elected Grand Master

395, Secondmoon   Massacre at Quondam

400, Fourthmoon   Sir Beaumont bound *(Paragon Lost)*

405, Thirdmoon   Sir Ringwood bound *(Impossible Odds)*

Contents

Contents

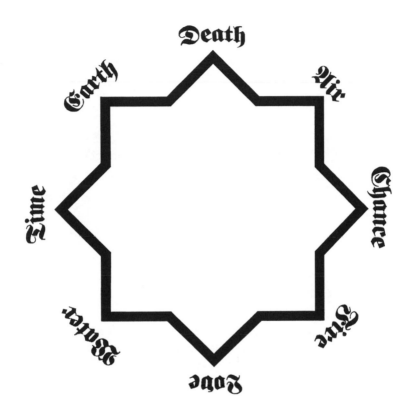

I

The master first lets slip his best hounds

1

Something was up. The Royal Guard liked to think it knew all the news and heard it before anyone else did, but that day it had been shut out. The morning watch had been on duty for two hours already, but Commander Vicious had not arrived to hold the daily inspection and the graveyard shift had not yet been stood down. They were supposedly attending the King, who was meeting with senior advisors in the council chamber. Absurd! Even during the worst panics of the Thencaster Conspiracy, three years ago, Athelgar had never summoned his cabinet in the middle of the night.

Deputy Commander Lyon must have some idea what was going on, but he refused to admit it. Infuriatingly, he just sat behind his desk in the guardroom, reading a book of poetry—Lyon not only read poetry, he wrote it too, yet he was a fine swordsman, subtle and unpredictable. The half-dozen Blades sustaining the permanent dice game under the window were doing so halfheartedly, grumbling more than gambling. Sir

Wolf was polishing his boots in a corner—Wolf never read poetry, was never invited into the games, and cared not a fig what folly the King was pursuing this time.

The park beyond the frost-spangled panes was all pen-and-ink, stark white-and-black, sun-bright snow and cadaver trees under a sky of anemic blue, for this was Secondmoon of 395, the coldest winter in memory. Nocare, with its high ceilings and huge windows, was a summer palace, impossible to heat in cold weather. The King had moved the court there on some inexplicable whim and could not return it to poky old Greymere as long as the roads were blocked by snowdrifts. Courtiers slunk around unhappily, huddled in furs and muttering under their smoky breath.

Innumerable feet shuffled past the guardroom door: gentry, heralds, pages, porters, stewards, White Sisters, Household Yeomen. No one paid any heed until a rapid tattoo of heel taps raised every head. Blades knew the sound of Guard boots, and these were in a hurry.

Wolf went on polishing his left one.

In marched Sir Damon, still wearing his sash as officer in charge of the night watch. The kibitzers by the window exchanged shocked glances. The matter was much more than routine if Sir Vicious had sent a senior Blade as messenger, instead of a junior or just a page.

Damon glanced around the room, then bent to whisper something to Lyon. Lyon turned to Wolf.

"Leader wants you."

Wolf put foot in boot and stamped. "Where?"

Damon said, "Council Chamber. He's still with the Pirate's Son."

At the dice table, eyebrows rose even higher. The Pirate's Son was King Athelgar. It was common knowledge that Vicious preferred to keep Sir Wolf out of the King's sight, so if Wolf was wanted now, it was because the King had called for him by name.

Wolf was the King's Killer.

Ignoring the rabble's surprise, Wolf strode across to the mirror and looked himself over with care. Like all Blades he was of middle height, slim and athletic, but he was invariably the best-turned-out man in the Guard—boots and sword belt gleaming like glass, not a wrinkle in his hose nor speck of dust marring his jerkin. He adjusted the feather in his bonnet an imperceptible amount and turned away. He did not examine his face. No one looked at that horror unless they must.

Exchanging nods with a lip-chewing Lyon, he strode out into the corridor, and Damon fell into step beside him. Together they marched along marble corridors, past statuary and tapestries. Courtiers stared with interest at two senior members of the Royal Guard moving at an urgent clip. Word that the King had sent for the infamous Sir Wolf would spread like fire in dry grass.

So what was up? The last time Wolf had been summoned to the royal presence, Athelgar had named him—over Leader's objections—to lead the Elboro mission, which had required him to kill two brother Blades. It had not been the first such filthy job the Pirate's Son had given him, either, and Wolf's written report afterwards had let Athelgar Radgaring know exactly what he thought of his liege lord. Moreover, since Leader had not ordered him to rewrite it, it had warned His Majesty that others shared those opinions. The Guard had been short-handed back then, else Wolf might have been thrown in a dungeon for some of the comments in that report. In the two years since, Vicious had kept him well away from the King.

What had changed? Well, the Guard was up to strength now, so one possibility was that Athelgar was going to award him the Order of the Royal Boot. That was highly unlikely. Knowing how Wolf felt about him, Athelgar was more likely to keep the King's Killer bound to absolute loyalty forever—safer that way.

Another possibility was that the Pirate's Son wanted someone murdered. Blades were bound by oath and conjuration to defend their ward from his enemies, not to commit crimes on royal whims, but defense could cover a multitude of nasty situations.

Wolf saw anger in Damon's tightly clenched jaw. Damon was a decent man, not one of those who carried grudges against the King's Killer.

"Any hints, brother?"

"Dunno anything. Huntley and Flint rode in about four hours ago."

"Ah! And Leader wakened the Pirate's Son?"

"They've been in council ever since. No one's allowed in or out except inquisitors. A *plague* of inquisitors!"

That news merely deepened the mystery. Sir Flint and Sir Huntley were typical examples of Blades who failed to find a real life after being knighted and discharged from the Guard. Both men were in their fifties, idling away years at Ironhall, instructing boys in fencing and horsemanship, yet still hankering after the sins of the city. Whenever Grand Master needed a dispatch taken to Court, men like Flint or Huntley would accept couriers' wages, knowing that the skilled young pimps of the Guard would always find them some of what Ironhall lacked.

So whatever had provoked this emergency had originated at, or near to, Ironhall. Although it was officially headquarters of the Loyal and Ancient Order of the King's Blades, in practical terms it was only a school and orphanage, a factory for turning unwanted rebellious boys into the world's finest swordsmen. Wolf could imagine nothing whatsoever that could happen there to provoke a middle-of-the-night meeting of the King in Council.

He could guess why he had been summoned, though. When the weather was this bad near Grandon, it must be mean as belly worms up on Starkmoor. Grand Master would not have sent anyone on such a journey unless the matter was supremely urgent, and he had thought the trek perilous enough to send two of them. Most likely his despatch required an answer, and Athelgar had decided to give his least favorite Blade the putrid job of riding posthaste to Ironhall over snowbound roads in this appalling cold. That would be a typical piece of royal spite.

There were Blades on duty even outside the anteroom, which was not usual. The rest of the graveyard shift was sprawled around on the chairs inside it, sulky and unshaven. They looked shocked when they saw the man Damon had fetched. Damon halted, Wolf kept going. Sir Sewald had the inner door; he tapped and opened it so the newcomer could march straight in without having to break stride.

The Cabinet Chamber was large but gloomy, newly repaneled in wood like molasses and furnished with spindly chairs from some lady's boudoir. Athelgar had terrible taste and his expensive renovations were methodically ruining every palace he owned.

Since his summons had officially come from Commander Vicious, Wolf could go straight to him and ignore the King, always a pleasure. He stamped boots and tapped sword hilt in salute. Dark and menacing as one of the bronze memorials along Rose Parade in Grandon, the Commander was standing well inside the chamber, so he had been taking part in the talk, not just being an ornamental doorstop. Vicious was notoriously taciturn, but had not always been so. The facial scar that made speech physically painful for him was a memento of the Garbeald Affair, another of the King's follies. His vitriolic hatred of inquisitors dated from that same disaster.

Maps, papers, and dirty dishes littered the central table. Lord Chancellor Sparrow stood on one side of the crackling fire, the Earl Marshal sat bundled in his wheeled chair on the other, and Grand Inquisitor were by the window, being extra-inscrutable. Grand Inquisitor were twins, indistinguishable. All inquisitors seemed foreboding, with their black robes, sinister reputation, and unblinking stare, but to have two of them doing it at you was twice as bad. The Guard called them the Gruesome Twosome.

Sparrow was a perky, beak-nosed little man, more of a pompous robin than a cheeky sparrow, but rated a better-than-average chancellor. He feared Athelgar not at all and often quashed his mad notions before they did too much harm. The Earl Marshal, old as the ocean and crippled with gout, was asleep. A spidery clerk crouched over a writing desk, busily wielding a quill.

Flint and Huntley were slumped on chairs in a far corner. They looked exhausted and were probably chilled to the bone over there, too. They had earned some sleep, and keeping them from it was carrying security to absurd lengths.

And the Pirate's Son . . . as always, Athelgar was wandering, restless as a dog with fleas. He was not his usual splendid self. His hose were rumpled, he wore no jewelry, and his hair—dyed a respectable Chivian brown—was badly in need of brushing. Even his goatee, which he left its original Baelish red, looked somehow bedraggled. He had just turned twenty-five and was about to celebrate the fifth anniversary of his accession.

"Sir Wolf, sire," Vicious said.

Wolf turned and performed the gymnastics of a full court bow.

"Ah, Wolf." Athelgar headed to the fire. "We have bad news. Your brother has been seriously injured. We are distressed to impart such dire tidings."

That could not explain the emergency. The King had no interest whatsoever in the well-being of an obscure private Blade, whom he had not seen for years, who was not even a member of his Guard.

I know how you weep for him, Wolf did not say, *since you've kept him locked him up on Whinmoor all these years.* "Your Majesty is kind. Injured by whom?" Blades did not meet with accidents.

The uninvited query made the King spin around and glare. "That remains to be discovered. Three nights ago, Quondam was attacked by persons unknown. Sir Fell and Sir Mandeville are slain."

Wolf gaped, shocked into silence. Lynx wounded, two other Blades dead—there should be a dozen corpses lying around as evidence, so why was the criminals' identity in doubt? And *Quondam*? Quondam, on Whinmoor, was absolutely impregnable, a fortress that had never been taken by storm or siege. If this was not a bizarre joke, it must be the start of an invasion. Or armed rebellion. The emergency snapped into focus.

Moreover, the King was *scared*. Wolf's studied opinion, most people could lie to ears, but not to eyes. If you knew how to look, you could learn a man's feelings more truly from the way he held his chin and moved his eyes than you ever could from his words. All really good swordsmen had some of this skill, even if they were unaware that they were reacting to the twitch of an eyelid flagging a lunge before their opponent's foot began to move; it was why Ironhall discouraged dueling masks during training. Grand Inquisitor were unreadable, of course, but the Lord Chancellor was usually fairly legible and Athelgar displayed his feelings like heraldic banners. With shoulders hunched, wrists crossed low, and teeth set, he was proclaiming worry in fanfares. Sparrow was chewing his lip. Even Vicious was not standing with his hands confidently behind his back as usual, but looking rather as if he were poised to leap to his ward's defense. If this tale was a hoax, the King and his most senior advisors were not in on it.

"A sizable force," Athelgar said. "Gone already. Their tracks led to the beach."

"Raiders, sire? Baels?"

"Not Baels!" snapped the royal Bael. "These were definitely not Baels!"

Wolf bowed and waited to hear why the King was so sure and who else could have pulled off such a feat.

The King did not explain. "Baron Dupend was seriously wounded. At least a score of his men were killed, and Grand Master thinks about as many of the attackers. The Baroness was abducted." He paused to stare out the window. "That appears to have been the sole motive for the assault—to kidnap the lady."

Wolf resisted an urge to tell his sovereign lord he was out of his mind. Why should anyone storm one of the most formidable strongholds in all Eurania to carry off a woman guarded by three Blades and a garrison of men-at-arms, knowing the loss of life this must entail? Even if Celeste's stunning beauty had survived four years of imprisonment, that would be carrying rape to improbable extremes, and why else should anyone want that trollop? She had no land, no rich relatives, no importance. Nevertheless, the report had come from Grand Master, and for almost a year now Grand Master had been Durendal, Lord Roland. Any Blade would accept Durendal's testimony if he said the sea was wine.

"My brother's ward was kidnapped, yet he is still alive?" That was truly incredible.

"I said so!" Athelgar was staring at him very hard. "Does this news surprise you?"

Wolf hastily adjusted to the idea that he had been summoned to answer a charge of treason. He looked to Vicious for support and saw suspicion there, too. His path and Celeste's had crossed in the past; his brother shared her captivity at Quondam. He struggled to view the grotesque news through Athelgar's snaky eyes.

Fortunately he need only speak the truth. "It amazes me. Your Majesty, I swear that I had no prior knowledge of any plan or plot to rescue Lady"—he saw warning signs—"I mean *abduct* Lady Celeste. The news dumbfounds me. I do not know who could, or would want to, remove her from Quondam, nor who could achieve it. Surely Your Grace cannot question my loyalty? Even if my binding would allow me to engage in armed rebellion against your royal peace—which I do not believe it would—I should never involve my own brother in so dastardly a plot."

"The evidence is not yet clear," the King said narrowly. "We are not certain who injured your brother, nor which side he was supporting."

"I swear I know nothing about this, sire!"

"Grand Inquisitor?"

The one on the right said, "The witness speaks the truth." They never hesitated and never spoke at the same time, but nobody knew how they did it. They did not just take turns.

The weather in the chamber changed for the better.

"We are relieved to hear it," the King said, without looking much pleased. "Then you will wish to hurry to your brother's side, Sir Wolf, and we will have you investigate this crime for us."

The shocks were coming too fast. Promoted in a blink from chief suspect to chief inspector, Wolf mumbled something about being honored.

"Your first destination must be Ironhall," Athelgar said. "The casualties were taken there, for it has the nearest octogram where they might be healed. Grand Master thinks Sir Lynx will live."

Not *will make a complete recovery*? Wolf nodded, distrusting himself to speak. Outlawed at twelve, imprisoned five years in Ironhall and four more at Quondam—his brother had never known freedom. Now this.

"And that is about all we know," Athelgar said, pacing again. "Everything else is hearsay. Go and find out the facts! The news must be kept secret, until we know who and what and why. Is that understood, Sir Wolf? Extreme secrecy! Premature disclosure will cause panic and talk of a foreign invasion. It may *be* a foreign invasion for all we presently know. The Commander recommends you as the best man to investigate. We know," he added sourly, "that you can be discreet."

And ruthless, but no doubt he was hinting that any other investigator might uncover secrets Wolf had known and kept for years. Those would make stale news now, no longer capable of raising the epic scandal they would have stirred up once, yet Athelgar would certainly prefer that his youthful follies remain unmentioned. Spirits knew he had enough others to satisfy anyone. Wolf bowed and murmured gratitude for the royal compliment.

"You will be granted all the powers you require. Go and see to your brother and then proceed to Quondam."

"Your Majesty does me honor." Wolf wondered if he was being appointed royal scapegoat for something. The King thought of him as a killer, but Vicious knew he did any job as thoroughly as possible, whether it involved killing or not.

"To expedite matters, Commander," Lord Sparrow said primly, "pray advance Sir Wolf adequate funds from the Guard's coffers and apply to Chancery for reimbursement. A representative of the Office of General Inquiry will accompany you, Sir Wolf."

"But I will be in charge?" Wolf's query created an angry pause. It should go without saying that a Blade would not and could not take orders from a Dark Chamber snoop. It also went without saying that the snoop would feel free to ignore, subvert, or misunderstand any orders from a brainless sword twirler like Wolf. Especially Wolf.

"You will report to the Lord Chancellor," the King decreed, "and the inquisitor to Grand Inquisitor."

"Your Grace is setting up two inquiries?"

More glares.

"I do believe, sire," Sparrow twittered, "that Sir Wolf should be given overall authority."

Athelgar nodded grumpily.

Wolf said, "I will also need the help of a sniffer, my lord." This business reeked of conjuration.

"The nearest White Sisters' priory," the Chancellor said, "is in Lomouth. Your commission will give you all the authority you need. The Council expects frequent reports, Sir Wolf, but should you conclude that additional assaults are likely, you will issue a general alarm directly to the authorities concerned."

"Who keeps the King's Peace on Whinmoor, my lord?"

Sparrow pursed lips. "The sheriff is Baron Dupend himself, but you will speak with the King's voice."

"How soon can you leave?" the King barked.

"The moment I receive my writ and the funds, sire." Wolf looked to the Gruesome Twosome. "And my assistant?"

"Inquisitor Hogwood will meet you at the stable, Sir Wolf," said the one on the left.

"We will send your commission there also," said the Chancellor, peering over the clerk's shoulder at what he was writing. "Momentarily."

"By your leave, sire?" Wolf bowed to the King and was dismissed.

2

Vicious stepped out to the anteroom with him. Wolf turned, expecting some sort of explanation, but the Commander just snapped, "Move!" and went back in again.

So Wolf moved. Heads turned as he streaked along the endless marble floors of Nocare, skidding around corners. He paused at the guardroom door long enough to shout, "Modred, pick me out a horse!" and resumed running. He reached his quarters, dressed in two of everything topped off with a heavy fur robe, and was down at the Guard's stable with a pack on his shoulder before the groom had finished saddling up under Sir Modred's needle eye. The yard outside was heaped with dirty snow, and the horses' breath was icing up their stalls.

The haste was unseemly but necessary if he were to leave before Inquisitor Hogwood appeared, which is what Vicious had meant. Nobody liked the way inquisitors spied, lied, and pried, but the mutual dislike between the snoops and the Blades ran especially deep, and Vicious morbidly detested them. Wolf, moreover, was the Dark Chamber's least favorite Blade.

Modred had chosen well, a powerful bay Wolf knew of old, which seemed to know him also, snorting puffs of steam at him and stamping a roughshod hoof on the flags. Young Florian arrived, panting, with a weighty purse from Vicious. A few moments later a mousy clerk minced carefully across the yard to hand Wolf his warrant, signed and sealed. He read it through carefully, disentangling complex prose to establish that he was granted authority to go anywhere, requisition anything, question, detain, or conscript anyone, even suspend civil liberties. It was an astonishing delegation of power, but then he was the government's first response to an act of war, either foreign or civil. Answering Modred's frustrated glare with a smile of thanks, he swung into the saddle and adjusted his sword.

As he rode across the yard, another horse emerged from an adjacent stable and moved alongside, its hooves making muffled thuds instead of the usual clatter. The rider was well wrapped in black fur, with little more than his eyes visible inside the hood of his cloak, but their glassy stare told Wolf his assistant had arrived.

The snoop said, "Trying to sneak away without me, Sir Wolf?"

The little of him that was visible suggested he was too young to be much help, even in a fight, but Wolf would prefer an incompetent rookie to an older man deliberately blocking him.

"I was tired of waiting for you, Inquisitor Hogwood."

The boy held out a black glove. "Your commission, please."

Unable to think of a reason to refuse, Wolf fished out the scroll and handed it over. Junior unrolled it, rolled it up again, and returned it.

"I thought you wanted to read it."

Fishy stare again. "I did read it. Very curious, isn't it?"

That was typical snoop talk, but he sounded even younger than he looked and Wolf clung tight to the remaining shreds of his temper. "Curious in what way, boy?" He put his horse into a saddle-high canyon cut through the drifts to the postern gate.

"In whom it names and whom it does not. The Privy Council is apprised of massacre, either armed insurrection or foreign invasion, and it reacts by sending a twenty-four-year-old swordsman of meager education and repellent reputation."

"It was a birthweek present for me."

"Prudence would suggest dispatching several senior Privy Councillors with an entourage of clerks and attorneys."

Wolf could sneer too. "In this weather, sonny? The poor dears wouldn't last a league." Babyface had made a valid point, though. Wolf would be replaced the moment the roads were passable again.

"Looking to the Royal Guard for brains is still a questionable innovation."

"But I am spiritually bound to absolute loyalty. You are not. Who is not mentioned in the writ who should be?"

By then they were heading for the northern gatehouse, plodding along an avenue flanked by giant beeches, half a century old and barely adolescent.

"Lord Roland, of course. He sent the news. He has gone to Quondam to take charge. As Grand Master of the Blades, he holds one of the senior offices in the realm. He must have been sworn in as a member of the Privy Council before you were born, so why not just send a courier with a warrant to confirm his authority? Of course," young Smartypants added, "Lord Roland is no longer bound and therefore the King may doubt his loyalty. He may see him as being no more trustworthy than an inquisitor."

Fretting at being under Blade authority, no doubt, the kid was trying to make Wolf look like a dumb, pig-sticking swordsman. Doing quite well, too. Obviously he had been better briefed than Wolf had.

"I expect His Majesty wants a second opinion."

"A trained observer, more likely."

"No eyes are sharper than Blades'. Can you use that thing?" Blades had only contempt for the sort of short sword Hogwood was wearing, a gentleman's weapon.

"Not well by your standards, Sir Wolf, but better than most men. I may fare as well as you do against a pack of animals."

The Yeomen at the gatehouse noticed Wolf's cat's-eye hilt and saluted them through. The Great West Road was only a faint trail in the snow. Flakes swirled in the air.

"Animals?"

Hogwood quirked very pretty eyebrows. "The intruders used teeth, claws, and clubs. No swords, no axes. You were not told this?"

Athelgar had been certain the attackers had not been Baels. What sort of injuries had Lynx received? "Animals do not use clubs." Wolf pulled his hood forward. "I hope you can keep up, boy. I won't wait for you."

"You won't have to, Sir Wolf."

"No?" He kicked in his heels and gave the bay its head.

3

In summer Wolf could ride to Ironhall in a single day, but he knew he would be lucky to do it in less than two in that snowy winter. Old Flint and Huntley had done very well to do it at all.

Where there was a visible track, it was rarely wide enough for two horses abreast, so he was spared the need to make conversation. He had time to worry as he rode—worry about Lynx and his injuries, both physical and mental, and worry about the King's motives. Blades notoriously went mad when their ward died by violence, but Wolf could recall no precedent for a ward being kidnapped while his Blade still lived. And why had Athelgar assigned this extraordinary commission to him, of all people? Lynx and he knew things about Celeste that might still embarrass the King if they came out. Now Celeste had vanished, Lynx was at death's door, and the King had sent *him* to investigate the bizarre affair? It made no sense.

The brief winter day was ending in a blood-red smear when the travelers crossed the Gran at Abshurst. With no one else crazy enough to be on the roads, the post house offered a wide choice of well-rested mounts. By law, a Blade could take his pick of the King's horses and Hogwood knew enough to select the second-best. The only reason Wolf had not taken that one was the mean look in its eye.

He would not dare go farther until the moon rose, so he led the way to the dining room, whose stench of bad beer and tallow candles would make a goat gasp. A few locals were drinking in front of the fire, but quickly relinquished that favored space to sword-bearing gentry. Waiters tossed down the usual dirty platters and piled them with winter fare:

salted fish, beans, and pickled pigs' feet. They added fresh loaves, hard cheese, and mugs of small ale.

Hogwood was now revealed as a skinny youth of about Wolf's height, looking no more than fourteen. The mystery thickened—why had the Dark Chamber sent a boy to investigate an act of war or rebellion? Did the assignment seem so hopeless or dangerous that no senior snoop would touch it? The King had been very sparing with information. *Was this a suicide mission?*

"Well, Inquisitor," Wolf said. "Tell me about yourself. You look very young to be . . . you . . . *you're a girl!*"

"So my friends tell me." She smirked.

So much for bragging about the sharp eyes of a Blade! She was tall, but that did not excuse Wolf's folly. He would not knowingly have spoken to a woman so aggressively, and could not mend his manners now without seeming ridiculous.

Male or female, she was absurdly young to be assigned a case of such importance. Nubile, though. Wolf fancied his women well bolstered, with a soft double chin to make them seem more feminine, but Hogwood as a girl was even more of a beanpole than Hogwood the boy. Her hair was as black as her robes, worn in a pageboy cut popular then among youths around court, somehow making her face seem small and boyishly bony, despite full lips and lashes like cortege plumes. In firelight, with winter roses blooming on her cheeks, she was childlike. She would be in grave peril if she ever came within groping range of Athelgar the Randy, who notoriously favored nymphets.

Wolf pulled his wits together. "Tell me about yourself."

"We are forbidden to talk about ourselves."

"Remember you are my subordinate, Inquisitor. How old are you?"

She shook her head, chewing and smirking down at her platter.

"I said, *'How old are you?'*"

She looked up with a sultry glance that would have stopped a knight in a tilting yard. "Old enough for anything you require, Sir Wolf."

He was outmatched. Already he could feel old yearnings wakening. Buxom was not essential. "What grade are you, then?"

She sucked on a bone and waved it in a vague gesture. "Not allowed to tell."

"At least I'm entitled to know your abilities. I have worked with snoops often enough to know they come supplied with various tricks and skills. Some are conjuration, some come from long training, others are gadgets in your pockets."

"My skills will be at your disposal when needed."

Had she been a boy, at that point Wolf would have leaned across the table and belted his ear hard enough to spin his head like a weathercock. "When we set out today you questioned the Privy Council's wisdom in sending a man of my age and background to investigate an act of war or armed rebellion. Tell me why Grand Inquisitor did not assign a senior agent to support me, instead of a flippant sixteen-year-old female apprentice?" That guess could be out three years either way.

"Because I was the best-qualified inquisitor available." The gibe had amused her, which was a warning that the truth might surprise him.

"Qualified how, other than having shapely eyebrows?"

"I am not permitted to answer."

Wolf hurled a bone into the fire. "This is ridiculous!" He studied her for a moment. "I know this fodder would sicken a sewer rat, but it's cold out there, so *eat*. That's an order. You're as frightened as the King was. What do you fear, Hogwood?"

"I am not afraid!" Anger darkened the flush the fire had brought to her cheeks.

"Yes, you are. I know I have the ugliest face in Chivial and they call me the King's Killer, but I rarely kill inquisitors, and never women or children, so you need fear nothing from me, girl. What else scares you? The journey?"

"Nothing!" She glared.

"You're lying," he said and cut a hefty slice of cheese.

Suddenly his assistant was wearing the blank, glassy mask of an inquisitor. Even the flush faded from her cheeks. "This collaboration is not prospering. Start again. You tell me your background and I'll tell you mine."

It was a peace offering, he supposed. They had time to kill, a meal to eat. A job to do. They couldn't fight all the time.

"My history is no secret. I was born Ed Attewell in Westerth."

"In Sheese, to be exact."

"A totally unimportant mining hamlet."

"Is it really?"

He ignored that dangerous invitation to tattle. "My father died in a rock fall, and my mother found another breadwinner. When she died in childbirth, he found another bed mate. When he fell down a shaft . . . and so on. I lost count. They got worse. Worse, they got drunk, and often on money I'd earned in the pits." The last stepfather had given him the start of his face—the smashed nose, crumpled ears, gap teeth. "I had one full brother, Alf. When the current house brute started in on him as well, I decided it was time for us to leave." Wolf had gone for him with a shovel, leaving himself no safe course except flight.

Hogwood had switched expressions, to Dark Chamber Sympathetic Face Number One, perhaps. "So what led you to choose Ironhall?"

He laughed and gulped down some ale. "Crime, of course. Every kid in Ironhall brags of a criminal past. I remember one thirteen-year-old who boasted of being a serial rapist until Prime asked him to explain exactly what a rapist did."

Hogwood did not smile. "But he is one now, of course?"

"He's a Blade in the Royal Guard!"

"The difference escapes me."

Was this insubordination intended to be some sort of flirtation? Hogwood had a very kinky taste in men if she fancied Sir Wolf.

"The difference is that Blades seduce," he said. "If I decided to give you a treat, darling, you would cooperate completely and thank me afterwards." Incredibly, that was true. The legend would overcome even his gargoyle face and macabre reputation if he set his mind to it. It had happened more than once, although he was not proud of the fact.

Hogwood glanced around the dining room. "This is rather public. I hope you will rent a bedroom for your demonstration, Sir Wolf. And explain to me how this legendary side effect of the Blades' binding conjuration differs from a love potion, which is highly illegal."

"It's more fun!" he snapped. Blades were notorious womanizers, but he had never heard of one being accused of rape.

"Then I'm curious to know why you so seldom employ it. But do continue. How did your crimes lead you to Ironhall?" Candlelight danced on the black agates of her eyes.

"Because we had to steal food to survive. They set dogs on us. Eventually we came galloping across Starkmoor, bareback on a stolen horse with a posse hot behind us." Looking back, Wolf could see that the pursuers had let their quarry escape to sanctuary rather than see them hanged.

Two trembling kids were led up the narrow stairs to the stark and forbidding flea room. Sir Parsewood was Grand Master then—stooped and losing his teeth, but well respected. He got the true story out of two waifs easily enough, although he probably did not believe that Alf was thirteen, which is what Ed had told him to say. He talked with them separately, tested their agility by throwing coins for them to catch.

I have room for one," he told Wolf. "If I choose you, will you stay?"

"Not without Alf."

"And if I choose him, will he stay without you?"

"If you'll let me get away before he finds out."

But Parsewood accepted both of them and ordered a skinny boy named Willow to take the horse out to the men waiting on the moor, tell them it had wandered in the gate, and ask if it was theirs. The juniors thought it wonderful to have two Brats to torment instead of one. Wolf they labeled Dog-face, soon shortened to Dog so that Alf could be Cat. Ed took the brunt of the hazing, trying to stand up for Alf as he had at home, but two weeks later another boy was admitted, so Ed and Alf Attewell were promoted to candidates, logically choosing the names of Wolf and Lynx.

"A simple tale, Inquisitor. Tell me yours. What sort of family lets a daughter become a Dark Chamber snoop?"

Hogwood paused in raising a crust to her mouth to give him a very long stare, not the glassy-eyed snoop stare, just a stare. He was annoyed to find himself discomfited by it.

Then she said, "Have you ever heard of Waltham House?"

"There's a Waltham House near the Bastion. It's an orphanage endowed by Queen—"

"Run and financed by HM Office of General Inquiry. That's where inquisitors come from. That's the only home I've ever known, Sir Wolf."

"All of them?" He had never heard this.

"All of us."

"Spirits! No fathers, no mothers?"

Pleasure at shocking him flickered momentarily in her face. "Waifs left on the doorstep, or promising toddlers from other institutions obtained in exchange. The Dark Chamber *is* my family. I have been trained from birth for this work."

He had never wondered where snoops came from. The idea of their black-coated forms emerging from some teeming ants' nest made him squirm. "Time to go. The moon will be up."

She resumed her picky eating. "The groom promised to tell me when it is."

"You can't rely on kids like him."

"I can. He knew I was not a boy and he was not lying. Enough about background, let's discuss qualifications. Why did the King choose you to lead this investigation, Sir Wolf?"

Hoping to shock her in turn, he said, "Probably because he hates me."

She nodded. "Yes. That is curious. It is no secret that you and His Majesty detest each other, which is an absurd situation when you are spiritually bound to defend him to the death. How did this quarrel originate?"

"The Dark Chamber must know. If it matters, why weren't you briefed on it?"

She studied him again, licking her fingers. "I thought we had agreed to cooperate?"

He thought subordinates were expected to be respectful to their superiors, but no doubt inquisitors kept prying from habit, just as Blades had to stay physically active. And the King's motives might turn out to be very significant.

"It's a stupid story." But it had begun in Ironhall, with no witnesses except Blades, so the Dark Chamber might have failed to dig out the facts. "You won't remember King Ambrose. He came to harvest Blades for the Guard only twice in my time at Ironhall—a sick, fat old man, barely able to walk. After that he let ripe seniors pile up like hay before assigning batches of them to courtiers and ministers."

That royal error was later to turn the Thencaster Conspiracy into a Blade tragedy and give the King's Killer his title.

"We all hoped he would die soon, which he did, and one blustery spring day his daughter came riding over the moor with the Royal Guard at her back. It had been many years since a woman had performed the binding ritual, and we juniors noisily laid bets on how many seniors she would kill before she learned how to handle a sword. Fortunately Prime was Hereward, a lad of much more beef than imagination. Amid the chanting and flickering firelight he sat bare-chested on the anvil in the center of the octogram and barely flinched when she rammed his saber through his heart. After that the other bindings were routine.

"Malinda was a staunch woman. I think her husband had taught her fencing. He had certainly tutored their son. We were all puzzled to know why she took only six seniors when there were so many waiting in line. The answer appeared a week later in the form of Crown Prince Athelgar, aged eighteen and as red-haired a Bael in those days as ever earned a dying curse. He insisted on fencing with some of the candidates. I was chosen and made him look foolish. That's all."

Hogwood frowned. "How foolish?"

"Very foolish."

Wolf was only a fuzzy, but a better fencer than most of the seniors. He would have been promoted months ago, had there not been some sad clodhoppers ahead of him. An hour after the Crown Prince arrived, Grand Master sent the current Brat to find him. Parsewood played favorites, and Wolf was one of them.

"His Royal Highness," he mumbled through his awful teeth, "has expressed interest in fencing with some of the candidates."

"That would indeed be an honor, Grand Master."

"I'm glad you think so. You will go first. If you fail to make him look like a paralyzed palsied duck with dropsy, you will find yourself on quadruple stable duties every day until you leave here."

"The prospect forebodes, Grand Master."

"Also flogged raw every morning after breakfast."

"I do comprehend your position, Grand Master."

"Knew I could count on you, sonny."

They grinned together, thinking it was funny, but it did not turn out funny. Give Athelgar his due—one rarely got the chance—he might just have wanted to reassure Prime and the other seniors that he could use a sword, but he was displaying a typical lack of tact by reminding everyone that his father, the current King of Baelmark, had trained at Ironhall. The Blades of the Royal Guard who had been sent along to look after him were especially furious, checking and rechecking foils and padding. The entire school flocked out to the quad to watch.

When they had Athelgar wrapped up like a pudding, anonymous behind a chain mask, Grand Master called forward Candidate Wolf. Assuming he had been chosen for his ogreish looks as much as his ability, Wolf had deliberately mussed up his hair and discarded his shirt, although the day was chilly and everyone else was dressed to the gables for the royal visitor. He was still narrow-shouldered, all wrists and ankles, looking younger than his age, and adolescence had blighted his smashed face with pustules and brown moss he could not shave without bleeding to death.

This eyesore proceeded to make a public spectacle of the Heir Apparent. Wolf planted bare feet on the grass, hooked his left thumb in his belt, and parried every stroke. He scratched. He yawned. When the Prince paused to catch his breath, Wolf switched his foil to his other hand, and still Athelgar could not touch him. To be fair, he would have been judged exceptional by any standards but the Blades', but Wolf made him look like a fretful rabbit attacking an oak tree. Juniors laughed outright. Guardsmen turned purple trying not to.

Hogwood tossed a bone in the fire and licked her fingers. "You were only doing what Grand Master told you."

Wolf shrugged. "Nobody knew then how well our future King could carry a grudge."

"It's a nice story," Hogwood said, licking her fingers. "I can't believe it's the whole truth."

"I also lipped him a few times, but that started it. Now your turn. What makes you qualified for a mission this important?"

Hogwood shrugged. "A doctorate in conjury. I am the highest-ranking spiritualist in the Dark Chamber."

Wolf opened his mouth and no words came out. At *her* age?

A stableboy came to smile worshipfully at Hogwood and tell her the moon was up and he had saddled the horses.

4

Knowing the bare chalk hills that lay ahead, Wolf decided to take a pair of spare mounts, a precaution that would not slow them much. There was no real road there, even in summer, but the wind had cleared away most of the snow and he could steer by the stars. However romantic the combination of moonlight and pretty girls was supposed to be, he could see nothing endearing about that frigid night—breath smoking, horseshoes ringing on frozen ground, relentless cold eating in through his furs. Hogwood had no trouble with her evil-eye horse, so one of them was better than he had expected.

When they slowed the pace to rest the horses, she rode alongside, asking impertinent questions.

"There must be more to the King's dislike of you than you have told me."

"I told you I sauced him, and he's a very petty person." *Not an actual lie, just an incomplete truth.* "Why are you so afraid?"

"What makes you think I am afraid?"

Visual clues—the way she had kept her arms in front of her breasts, for instance, but he did not explain. Blades had professional secrets too. "You know a lot more than you have told me. I still think you were assigned to accompany me because no senior snoop would accept such a hopeless mission. You are worried because you know we are both dispensable and are heading into danger."

"A wild hypothesis! You will be in far greater danger than I, Sir Wolf."

"Why so?"

"Visiting Ironhall." If she curled her pretty lip, it was hidden by her wrappings. "The Blades have a reputation for avenging their own, and no one has ever slain more Blades than you have. I am astonished that you have survived so long."

Hogwood ought to know that he had visited Ironhall a dozen times in the last year, because he was first choice whenever Vicious needed something done out of town—anything to keep him out of the King's sight. Her briefing had been deliberately falsified.

"How many Blades am I alleged to have murdered?"

"At least three, possibly five."

The correct answer was eight, which she should know because the Guard certainly did. "And how many other men?"

"Inquisitor Schlutter for one."

Ah! Schlutter's unpleasant end was the inquisitors' main grudge against Wolf. He wondered whether they had told the girl anything close to the truth; also whether she had been assigned to him as an agent of vengeance. His Majesty's Office of General Inquiry had a very long memory.

"Inquisitor Schlutter committed suicide."

"He was murdered!" she shouted, shaken out of her flippancy at last. "By an outlaw Blade, while you stood by and did absolutely nothing to help him!"

"It is bad manners to interfere in a private quarrel."

"You murder and then joke about it?"

"You expect a serial killer to weep? We were sent to arrest Lord Gosse. He and his Blades had flown, leaving Sir Rodden behind to delay pursuit. Inquisitor Schlutter drew on him—drew on a Blade defending his ward! Coroners usually call that suicide, Hogwood."

"But Schlutter was in charge. You were supposed to defend him. That was what you were there for! Instead, you waited until Rodden killed him and only then did you kill Rodden. You snuffed him like a candle, they said. If he was so easy for you, why did you wait until it was too late to save Schlutter?"

"It was my going-away present for the boy."

She stared at him aghast, knowing that he spoke the truth.

Rodden had been Lynx's best friend at Ironhall, and his death was entirely Schlutter's fault. When Gosse's other two Blades spirited their ward away, they left Rodden to cover their getaway, although he was by far the youngest. That was a breach of the code and Rodden quite rightly resented it. The trail was at least a day old by the time the King's men arrived, so there was time to argue and heroics would do little good. He had understood that. Wolf could have talked him into letting the King's men go past, and that would have saved his life, if not his sanity. But Idiot Schlutter tried to arrest him at swordpoint. Rodden resisted, of course, and after that there was no hope for him.

Wolf's turn. "Give me your professional opinion, Inquisitor. I know you have a golden key to open locked doors. Will it raise a portcullis?"

"No."

"Knowing my brother, I am certain that Quondam was locked up tight three nights ago. Can you suggest any way the murderers could have entered such a fortress?"

"Treachery or conjuration."

"Has the Dark Chamber any theories on who the raiders were?"

"I was told it does not."

"A curious evasion."

Her chin jerked upward. "Agents are told only as much as they need to know. To burden me with theories might bias my investigation."

Her investigation? The child had grand ideas.

"Does the Chamber know why they went to such lengths just to kidnap Celeste?"

"Their purpose is something we have to discover. The Baroness may be irrelevant. My turn: Why did you accept binding to a man you hated?"

Her excessive interest in Wolf's past probably meant that she was after the Celeste story, which he had no intention of sharing with her, relevant or not.

"Stupidity."

"His or yours?"

"Both. By the time Malinda abdicated, I was ripe for binding. One fine spring evening Grand Master summoned us seniors for a little pep talk. The new King was on his way, he said. For five years, he reminded us, Ironhall had given us bed and board, refuge and education. We were rightly proud of what we now were, but Ironhall had made us so. When His Majesty chose to present the bill, it behooved each of us to honor that debt. Of course we all knew that the paradigm ingrate, the one who had refused binding many years before, had been the new King's father, Radgar Æleding. There would be an odor of justice in the air if any of us chose to turn that table on Athelgar himself, but we all promised solemnly not to weasel out.

"Who would be chosen? There were fourteen seniors and Grand Master was sure to hold back four or five to seed the next crop. Lynx and I were eighth and ninth, although we did not know which was officially which. I was privately resigned to being left behind as Prime. It was two years since I had shamed Athelgar at fencing. Judging by the way I had caught him looking at me on subsequent visits, his pride had never healed, so he would not want me lurching around the palace for the next ten years to remind him of that humiliation. I was certain he would assign me to some petty bureaucrat as a private Blade."

Next day Athelgar entered Ironhall for the first time as king. At his side rode a pudgy, red-haired young man. The candidates could not guess who he might be, but they knew where to ask, and the Guard graciously informed them that the popinjay was Garbeald Aylwining, childhood friend of His Majesty, recently come from Baelmark. Neither Ambrose nor Malinda had ever brought spectators along to a binding. Nervous and suspicious, the seniors retired to their dorm to await the ordeal.

Parsewood always sent for the required number plus one, and an hour or so later the Brat arrived with a summons for the top nine, which was about what Wolf had expected. Putting on a brave front, the Blades-elect strode out to meet the monarch, loftily ignoring the excited juniors boiling along beside them.

In the chilly, barren flea room they lined up before Grand Master and the King, while the mysterious Garbeald leaned against the wall with arms folded, watching the proceedings in contemptuous silence. The boys were shocked by their first close look at the two Court dandies. From the plumes on their bonnets to the pointed toes of their buskins, they sparkled and shone. Their polychrome sleeves were puffed and slashed beyond all reason, while their capes and jerkins came down only to their waists, exposing silken hose like paint from ankle to buttocks and gaudy, padded codpieces spangled with jewels. These were the new palace fashions that had appeared since the old Queen departed, featuring the new King's taste. They made Parsewood look like a shabby old crow in his Ironhall patches, and the candidates even shabbier.

"Prime Candidate Viper," Grand Master mumbled, "His Majesty has need of a Blade. Are you ready to serve?"

Viper agreed that he was, paid homage to the King, and was granted a gracious few words of welcome. Then came Second . . . and so on. Wolf had put himself at the end of the line, but when Number Seven, Hengist, had kissed the royal fingers, Parsewood passed over Lynx.

"Candidate Wolf, His Majesty has need of a Blade. Are you ready to serve?"

Wolf snapped back to the beating of hooves, moonlight like crystal, the iron world of winter . . .

"I never expected him to want me," he told Hogwood. "I stared right at him—which is not proper protocol with a king, of course—and he sneered back at me, daring me to let him put a sword through my heart in the binding ritual. If it missed by a hair's-breadth, I would die, and Baels are not known for compassion. But all my friends were watching, so I had no choice. I walked forward and knelt to kiss his fingers."

"The logic escapes me," she said.

"It escapes me now, but I was nineteen then. His Majesty said, 'I do recall Candidate Wolf's skill with steel.' Who was laughing now? Well enough! It was an honor to be remembered by my sovereign and if he had left it there, as his mother would have done, then we could have all smiled and admired His Grace's grace. But Athelgar Radgaring has the tact of a crotch louse."

" 'Ready for a rematch, are you, Wolf?' he said."

"That was gloating. Yes, he was my King and I should have bridled my tongue. I didn't. I said, 'Don't worry, this time I won't be armed.' "

Hogwood gasped. "That was insolence!"

"That was stupidity! I told you it was stupid." Wolf increased the pace, ending the conversation—but not ending the memories.

Parsewood said hastily, "Finally, sire, I have the honor of presenting Candidate Lynx, who will henceforth serve Your Majesty as Prime, here in Ironhall."

Lynx bowed. That should have been that. The candidates waited for dismissal.

"Well, my friend," the King said, "who do you fancy?"

"Viper, I think," Garbeald said in a bored drawl. "I like his taste in names. And that last one. He is so incredibly ugly!"

Athelgar laughed. "He doesn't need a sword—he frightens people to death." He smiled again. "But I want to bind Candidate Wolf personally."

The Bael shrugged and pointed at Hengist. "That one, then."

Athelgar nodded to Parsewood.

"Candidates Viper and Hengist stay a moment," Grand Master said. "The rest of you may go."

He in the Guard, his friend Hengist a private Blade, and Lynx as Prime—all Wolf's predictions had been wrong and he was in shock as he followed the others out. They trooped downstairs to gird on their swords again, then to head out to the quad and the cheers of the assembled juniors. One of the knights was waiting below, congratulating each man in turn, but when it came to Wolf's turn, he added, "A word with you, Candidate."

The others departed, leaving the two of them alone.

Durendal, Lord Roland, former Lord Chancellor, and greatest of all Blades since his legendary namesake who founded the Order—even the cynical seniors held Durendal in awe. Widowed and bored in retirement, he had come to live at Ironhall the previous year, and although he refused any formal title or duties, the entire place soon revolved around him. He could explain anything better than anyone, see farther, say more in fewer words. In fencing, strategy, or statecraft he was the supreme expert. He had a kind or humorous word for everyone and he spoke to the grooms in the stable the same way he spoke to Grand Master.

"You did not spit in the King's eye, I hope?"

"Not quite, my lord."

Roland frowned. "Good. I was a little worried. I just wanted to tell you that it was my idea."

"What was?"

"Separating you and Lynx. Blame me. I suggested it to Grand Master. For Lynx's sake, Wolf."

"I don't understand."

"Yes, you do." Roland's smile took the sting out of the contradiction. "He needs a few months without you. You've been mother and father to him too long."

"He's only seventeen! He can't handle being Prime! Some of those oafs have two years on him!"

The young ones might be worse, though. Lynx was bigger than Wolf, better-looking, much better liked, and potentially a better fencer, although even there he tended to be too easygoing. Wolf told him he lacked the killer instinct, never dreaming how that humor would return to haunt him. Lynx's binding should take care of that weakness in due course, but he would not have binding to help him to handle the junior rat pack. They could make his life one big torment.

Roland laughed. "They'll all stand on their heads for him. Go out there and tell him you're proud of him and expect him to do a great job—which he will."

"Yes, my lord."

"Wolf, Wolf! He needs a chance to prove himself. You proved yourself years ago collecting those scars." He clapped Wolf's shoulder. "Let him wipe his own nose for a while. Understand?"

"I do trust your judgment, my lord."

Durendal just smiled at the sarcasm. "I am flattered! Vicious has been pruning out older men, so the Guard is below strength. Believe me, Lynx will be along to join you by summer."

"And what about this Garbeald?"

Roland glanced at the stair and frowned. "Who's missing?"

"Viper and Hengist."

"Ah. And if His Majesty chooses to assign two Blades to his friend, will you complain to him?"

"Of course not."

"Good. Kings are not always right, Wolf, but they're always kings. And don't you worry about tomorrow night. Athelgar won't miss."

Wolf said, "You're certain of that?" It was his heart they were discussing.

Durendal smiled. "Oh, yes. A monarch must consider his reputation."

The wind was rising, swirling snowflakes over the icy ground in fairy dances. Moonlight shone on corpse-pale clouds piling up in the west, suggested a storm, which at these temperatures would be a killer. They still had two-thirds of the way to go.

The next time they dropped back to a walk, Hogwood said, "Obviously the King did not kill you."

"You snoops are wonderfully observant."

"I cannot imagine how any of you find the courage to sit and let someone drive a sword through your heart."

"There's no real danger," Wolf said. "We've all seen it done a hundred times before we have to do it ourselves."

Expect him. Conjury always gave him a thundering headache, and after four hundred years the Forge was so tainted by spirituality that he had never stayed there long enough to watch a binding completed. That night he had no choice and within the octogram itself the effect was murderously intense. He was barely conscious as he stumbled through the words of the oath. When he sat on the anvil with Lynx and Modred holding his arms, he knew vaguely that the King was taking much longer than usual to line up the stroke, letting the point of the sword wander all around the target chalked on his bare chest, but all he was thinking was that he wanted Athelgar to kill him quickly and put him out of his misery.

"So you won the dare," Hogwood said. "You *won!* Why do you still hate the King?"

She was still fishing for the Celeste story, and Athelgar had ordered him to keep it secret.

"It's my turn to ask questions. Why are you so interested in me, inquisitor? Are you investigating this Quondam mystery, or me?"

"Professional curiosity, Sir Wolf. You are a curious case. You are a perfectionist, the smartest man in the Guard. You named your sword *Diligence* and you polish it about six times a day. You rarely apply the seduction skills that are the main compensation for being a Blade, and when you do form a sexual pairing, it never lasts long. You show no interest in other men. The Guard's confidential file on you describes you as a ready killer who enjoys killing. Understandably, you have no close friends. Is that really all that drives you—a love of killing?"

Had any man asked such a question, Wolf would have blistered his ears, but no man would have dared. Besides, they had long leagues to go yet, and conversation would keep him from brooding on Lynx and his wounds.

"You are good at answering questions with questions, Inquisitor, but you are asking the same thing twice. Do you know what set off the Thencaster affair?" This was a hair-trigger topic, because the treason had come very close to the Dark Chamber itself.

"Lord Wassail walked in on the King's toilet and told him he would be deposed if he didn't act quickly."

"I mean what set off the treason?"

"The King made some bad decisions. The ultimatum from Thergy—"

"You're quoting history books. Athelgar behaved like a maniac, but the last straw was not Thergy. It was Garbeald."

After a moment Hogwood admitted, "I don't know what you mean."

"You know of him as the Duke of Brinton, a Baelish thug who had made even Baelmark too hot to hold him. Athelgar gave that scumbucket a royal dukedom. He also *gave* him two superb young men, like a pair of hunting dogs—Viper and Hengist. They were bound the same night I was. It was when that pissant fustilugs raped Lord Lowbridge's daughter that the Chivian nobility decided they had endured enough. That was when the Thencaster Conspiracy was born."

"Tell me about Viper and Hengist, then."

"No." Wolf nudged his horse to a trot, which made further conversation impossible.

5

He knew the West Road like the damask on his sword, and it had never seemed longer than it did that night. They changed mounts again at New Cinderwich, then went on through the killer dark to Flaskbury. The snowy world lay dead and silent under a moon like a ball of ice. He had to stop repeatedly to attend to the horses' feet.

Teeth, claws, clubs—what was he up against? What opponents fought with such a mix? *Lynx, Lynx! What have they done to you?*

The leg west from Flaskbury was the longest; the eastern sky was brightening by the time they reached Holmgarth. He was determined not to slacken the pace before Hogwood asked him to or fell back, and so far she had done neither. He thundered on the door of the post house until a sleepy hand admitted them.

They waited in the stable itself while the lad led grumpy horses out from their stalls to show. The lamps cast grotesque shadows, the urinous air made eyes sting, but at least there was warmth. Slumped on a bale of straw, Hogwood looked half dead with fatigue, obviously still believing she could keep up with a bound Blade.

"There is no inn between here and Ironhall," Wolf said. "This is your last chance to take a break."

She looked up sourly. "You lead, I'll follow."

"As you please. We won't stay long at Ironhall. As soon as we've heard from the witnesses there, we'll push on to Quondam itself."

"You are in charge, Sir Wolf." She folded her arms and looked down at the floor again, but now she was wearing her dead-fish mask. He suspected she was using it to hide fear, in which case the danger she foresaw must lie at Quondam.

"Did you have any choice when you were detailed to accompany me?"

"We are not allowed to discuss the—"

"I heard. You think I'm going to bungle the most important inquiry in years? The whole Dark Chamber must think so. You were assigned to me as patsy, Hogwood, and you know it. What do they do to inquisitors who fail to get their man? Rack them? Burn them at the stake?"

Glassy stare. "If this mission fails it will be through no fault of mine, Sir Wolf." She could not possibly be old enough to have much experience of major investigations, certainly not as senior inquisitor.

"Nor mine. I always get my man. Perhaps I'll be able to cut a few more notches in my sword belt soon, mm? Think so?"

She turned her face away in silence, as if disgusted by his black humor.

The groom brought another horse and again Wolf told him he did not want one with white hooves. He led it back into the shadows.

After a moment she said, "Tell me."

"Tell you what?"

"What you just remembered."

She was becoming a serious nuisance.

He said, "I know you can detect a falsehood if it is spoken, but I refuse to believe you can read my thoughts."

"Didn't you just remember something significant about this place?"

"No."

"You were pulling faces."

"You're trawling. I've been through here dozens of times. Of course I remember things, but it's nothing that need concern you."

Perhaps it did, because ultimately it concerned Celeste. In that stable, on the very day he was bound, he had heard the first rumble of what was to become the Thencaster thunderstorm. Athelgar had left Ironhall for Grandon at dawn. The rest of the Guard watched in amusement as the eager rookies all tried to ride as close as possible to their new ward. The King ignored them, chatting with Garbeald, who likewise had Hengist and Viper fretting to draw alongside him.

It was there at Holmgarth, when Wolf was choosing a remount in the stable—a place royal feet deigned not to tread—that a heavy hand settled on his shoulder.

"You need some help, brother," Terror said. Sir Terror was an old Ambrose man, likely to receive the Order of the Boot soon.

"That's kind of you, but . . ." Wolf recalled that Terror was one of the finest horsemen in the Guard. "Thanks. This one looks—"

Terror eased him backward into the stall until they were squeezed between rough planks and a piqued stallion. "This one has four white hooves. Always try for black if you can. That wasn't what I had in mind." He spoke more softly. "We all saw what the Pirate's Son did to you last night, toying with you. Nasty, that."

"I survived." Wolf was pleased the incident had been noted.

Terror jabbed him hard in the ribs. "But leave it there, boy! Some might say you earned it by lipping him the day before. Now you've sworn to die for him and he's the King. You can't win that battle. Leader said to pass the word to all the greenhorns, especially you: 'The Pirate's Son has a mean streak, ignore it.' Follow me?"

Wolf shrugged. "I find it contemptible. I'm amused he is so petty."

Poke again. "He can out-petty your amusement any day, kid." The awesome black beard bristled. "Listen! It's not just you. It's not even him personally, just that he was reared in Baelmark and got washed up here in Chivial. He don't know any better. Ever since mommy went home to her pirate, he's been running wild. He insulted the Speaker. He mocked the Lord Mayor and other nobs who came to present loyal addresses. Now he's given that creepy Bael buddy of his a dukedom—a royal dukedom—and that will hit the real nobs like a bucket of vomit. He hasn't been on the throne a month yet. You're nothing, but some people do matter."

This was a jolt of adult reality. Even Wolf was not green enough to miss the point. "You're implying I may have to make good on my oath?"

Terror dropped his voice even lower. "If he keeps on like this, anything may happen."

The novelty of being treated as one of the gang was a heady sensation. "I don't like the look of that Garbeald. Isn't it odd that the Pirate's Son's best friend didn't show up in Chivial until after his mommy had left?"

Poke become punch with an impact that made Wolf gasp.

"Stop it! Vicious said to tell you to keep your jackass mouth shut from now on. Take that chestnut over there, if you're not too proud to ride a mare. She's a little wonder." With that Terror went away.

Of course Wolf had been right about Garbeald, but things might have turned out better if Leader had never sent him that warning. The rest of his conversations with the older guardsmen on that ride had concerned the latest Court scandals, especially the King's new mistress, the exotic Marquesa Celeste, and the way ladies' necklines were plunging to hitherto unseen depths.

At Blackwater, the sky had turned to lead and a bitter wind was lifting the fallen snow and swirling it around the horses' fetlocks. The blur of brightness marking the sun said the hour was not far past noon. There should be time to reach Ironhall before dark.

The small post house there was run by the only fat Blade in the Order, Sir Orvil. Right after his knighting he had married the previous owner's daughter and raised the rates until Ambrose threatened to pass a law to stop him.

Orvil was slack-jawed at seeing an inquisitor riding to Ironhall, and a female one at that. If he had heard of any other raids along the coast he would certainly be babbling of them, but his ignorance of even the Quondam assault showed that news was not traveling as it usually did. He knew about Flint and Huntley, of course, and reported that a second pair of knights, Grady and Godfrey, had followed them the next day. That Wolf and Hogwood had missed them on the road was not surprising. Of course Orvil wanted to know what the fire-and-death was going on to raise so much excitement, and of course nobody was telling him.

"Weather looks bad," he muttered, peering out the stable door at the sky and the snowy folds of the moor. "Starkmoor is death after dark, my lad. We could put you up until it blows over." Again he ogled the inquisitor with disbelief.

"We have to push on," Wolf insisted. "My assistant may have more sense."

She just shook her head, too weary to speak, her face haggard, with dark smears of pain under the eyes, but Wolf knew he might see worse in a mirror. She was certainly using some sort of Dark Chamber conjuration to keep going. Fair's fair—he was drawing stamina from his binding.

"Let me send the boy with you, then," Orvil said, all chubby and sincere. "Tam knows the moor like the back of his head, don't you, Tam?"

The gangling stableboy smiled shyly and continued saddling their mounts. Wolf knew that his dear brother Blade would charge him a month's wages for the loan of his underpaid hand and add as much again for keeping secrets from him, but he also knew how treacherous the moor could be. In his beansprout year, four candidates out riding had been caught in a snap blizzard and died. The locals had an instinct for the moors. He was a Westerther himself, but not from these parts.

"What do you think, Tam? Can you guide us to Ironhall, or is it too dangerous?"

The boy grunted the local equivalent of "Yes" while shaking his head, which meant that he was not frightened and was willing to take them. He also knew that Wolf was a generous tipper. Orvil beamed and prepared to haggle.

Tam turned out to be a wise decision. Wind raged up on the moor, hurling gritty snow in their faces and driving a fog that hid all the landmarks. He took a couple of shortcuts Wolf would not have risked, across bogs frozen by the long cold, but his main service was just to relieve Wolf of the need to do anything except stay on his horse.

Cold and soaked, every bone throbbing with fatigue, he rode in a stupor, thinking—when he thought at all—about meeting Lynx again, after so long. Although Ironhall to Quondam was not far as the crow flew, Whinmoor and Starkmoor were separated by the Great Bog. Horses, unlike crows, must make a day-long trek around by Newtor. On many of his visits to Ironhall, Wolf could have stolen enough time to go and visit Lynx, but his persnickety conscience would not let him be absent from his ward on a personal whim. In four years they had exchanged a dozen or so letters. Lynx would have changed.

Wolf was taken by surprise when the fairytale fake battlements of Ironhall emerged from the whirling murk. There was respite from the wind in the lee of the walls, and he urged his sad horse forward alongside Hogwood's.

"We're here. You've done well, for a woman."

She peered blearily out of her snow-caked hood. "And you, for an old man."

"Are you ready to begin your investigation?"

"Your investigation, Sir Wolf."

"No. Finding out what happened is your job. Report to me everything you discover—who is lying, who is holding back, all your theories and suspicions. If I notice or suspect anything, I will be equally open with you, I promise. I will decide what we do about it all in the end. Meanwhile I want everyone to believe you are in charge and I am just muscle sent along to protect you." He did not feel capable of fighting a dead frog.

"Why?" she demanded suspiciously.

"Do you always question orders? Are you too tired to start work at once?"

"No."

"Then do as I say. I promise you all the credit or blame you deserve. My reputation is already made. Make yours."

"Thank you." She was puzzled, but she was supposed to be.

"Just do a good job." He eased his horse back to the rear again as they turned into the gateway.

Both the King and the Dark Chamber bore grudges against him.

Somewhere on the road he had decided that this affair must eventually result in an inquiry into his inquiry, so he would find himself testifying before inquisitors. The snoops looked after their own and any restriction he placed on Hogwood would damn him, if he wasn't damned already.

When they reined in at the Main House steps, she threw back her hood and stared at him with red-rimmed eyes. "Whom do you suspect at the moment, Sir Wolf?"

"Athelgar, but I don't know what he's up to."

For the first time ever, he saw an inquisitor's smile. It was thin and transient. "Because he sends one of his own Blades to investigate?"

"Partly. Also because I can't think of anyone else with resources to storm Quondam or reason to abduct Celeste. I can't even see that the King has that. If he wanted her back he could just send for her."

"But if we discover that your ward did cause so many needless deaths, you will suppress the truth?"

"You know I will have no choice. How about you, if it turns out that the Dark Chamber is guilty?"

"That is an outrageous suggestion!" Apparently the girl had not even thought of that possibility.

"Why? Don't try to tell me the Chamber never arranges assassinations!" Wolf slid painfully from the saddle.

6

Predictable as roosters at dawn, a dozen boys had come running out to see who these snowmen visitors were. When they recognized the infamous Sir Wolf they stood back and stared, solemn and silent as a forestful of owls. None of them would have seen an inquisitor before or would guess what Hogwood's black robes meant, but they knew the King's Killer, the worst villain in the Guard.

The young swordsman who came loping down after them was Rivers, a smarmy, unpleasant youth, but currently Second and hence a voice of authority with power to punish. He yapped out commands, sending guides off with Tam and the horses to see that they were all cared for, delegating other boys to bring the saddlebags, telling off one to inform Master of Rituals, and dismissing everyone else with dire threats.

He led the visitors indoors. "Sir Wolf, your brother is much improved. No, he's this way, in the guardroom. The infirmary is full of Lord Dupend's men."

"This is Second Candidate Rivers—Inquisitor Hogwood."

Rivers nodded as they walked. "Master Inquisitor, you are . . ."

Wolf was amused to watch "welcome" change to "a woman" and then disappear entirely as Rivers's jaw dropped. How long since a woman of her age had visited Ironhall?

"Is Grand Master still at Quondam, Candidate?" she asked.

"Yes, um, my lady." Walking sideways, Rivers continued to stare at her. "He left Master of Rituals in charge here, and he's done wonders with the healings! The Baron, Sir Lynx, and another dozen. Of course, not all . . . I mean, some of them had very terrible wounds." He pulled a face. "This is a very strange and frightening event."

"When did you hear the news?"

"Just before dawn on the fifteenth, er, mistress. When the raiders left, Sir Alden sent a rider, then loaded the worst of the wounded in a wagon and drove it over here himself. There was a full moon, of course, and the Great Bog is frozen this year."

So Lynx owed his life to the weather? "Who is Sir Alden?"

"Not a Blade, sir. Lord Dupend's knight banneret. Very quick-witted for his years."

Rivers narrowly avoided walking into a red-haired swordsman waiting in the corridor to First House, already beaming at Hogwood.

"Dolores!"

Hogwood said formally, "Good chance to you, Sir Intrepid." She was wearing her working face, all stone and glass.

"And to you. What a wonderful surprise! Welcome to Ironhall, Inquisitor. And brother Wolf, of course."

Intrepid was unpopular in the Order. He had an abrasive manner and was reputed to have deliberately galled Ambrose until the old man booted him out of the Guard several years short of a normal term. Thereupon he had enrolled in the Royal College of Conjury and done so well there that one of Lord Roland's first acts as Grand Master had been to call him back to Ironhall to be Master of Rituals. That had shocked the Blades, but Durendal's opinion carried such weight that Intrepid was now on a sort of unspoken probation. Wolf was willing to overlook a mountain of gall if he had done so well ministering to Lynx and the other Quondam wounded.

"And where did you two meet?" Wolf demanded.

"Dolores was the most rewarding student I ever had," Intrepid proclaimed. "I take it Grand Master's letter reached the court?" He glanced inquiringly from Blade to inquisitor, wondering which was in charge.

"Yes," she said. "The Privy Council sent us to look into things." Subtly, her reply misled him.

"A commendable choice and a very impressive testimonial, Inquisitor. Congratulations! This business may require all your genius. There was undoubtedly some novel conjury involved." He glanced at Wolf to see how he enjoyed being nursemaid.

Wolf just shrugged, confirming the deception.

"Sir Wolf is anxious to see his brother. We will begin with him."

"Of course." Intrepid had brought them to the guardroom. "Thank you, boys. Get them out of here, Second. Leave the bags."

"How is he?" Wolf asked as the helpers reluctantly departed.

Intrepid flashed an annoying smirk. "He looks as if he tried to break up a bear-baiting. If he offers to show you his scars, decline politely. To say that his guts were delivered in a separate container would be an exaggeration, but not much of one, and of course he was almost exsanguinated. It is only because Quondam keeps a generous stock of conjured bandages on hand that he lived long enough to leave the castle, let alone reach Ironhall. Even the healing rituals my predecessors used would have been useless against injury on that scale. We pieced him together as best we could and I tried some new Isilondian chants I brought with me last fall."

"The Guilliane Hortations?" Hogwood asked.

"No, I went straight to Barbuse's Variation of the Sidonia Catabolism. After all, we had almost nothing to lose! It worked better than I had dared hope. We cannot relax for a few days yet, of course. The internal healing may not have been complete and I have a few more things to try, but I do have hope that he will be back to his old self, or should I say young self, in a week or two. Sir Wolf need not give up hope of some nephews and nieces yet."

Much tempted to give Intrepid some injuries of his own to experiment on, Wolf said, "And his state of mind? He has lost his ward."

For the first time Master of Rituals lost his air of infallibility. "He may not have quite realized that yet. He seems sane enough. It may be that the trauma of his injuries somehow compensated . . . there have been cases . . . still somewhat dazed, of course . . . takes time to recover from spirituality on that scale. And loss of blood and shock." He reached for the handle.

"Wait," Hogwood said. "Baron Dupend?"

"Ah. I've kept him alive so far, but at his age . . ." Shaking his head sadly, Intrepid opened the door.

Next to the Seniors' Tower, the guardroom was Ironhall's closest approach to an indoor midden. Every Blade in four centuries seemed to have left something behind as a souvenir: clothes, tack, books, even unpaired boots. The average guardsman visited it about once a year and did not care. Wolf cared, and whenever he came by on one of his courier trips and had time to kill, waiting for day to dawn or someone to finish a letter, he tried to tidy up. The mess always returned before he did.

This time it was better. Someone had shoveled the litter into a corner and installed decent furniture. On one side of an amiably crackling fire a dark-haired boy sat at a table with quills, paper, and a silver inkwell. On the other, Lynx leaned back against heaped pillows on a bed. He stared at the visitors and for a gut-wrenching moment nothing happened.

Then he said, "Wolfie! What by the eight are you doing here? Wolf, you old scoundrel!" He tried to laugh, sit up, and hold out his hands, all at once. The result was a wild spasm and a grimace of pain. He sank back, cursing, and by that time Wolf was there to embrace him.

He had changed in four years, of course. He was all-over huskier and hairier than before, and had grown a beard, brown and curly. He also bore the pallor of a very narrow escape and the bewildered look that followed massive healing conjuration. Purple-and-yellow swellings marred the right side of his face, with traces of dried blood showing in his hair.

"Still a bit tender," he muttered. Sweat gleamed on his forehead. His attempt to sit up had dropped the blankets and exposed a nightmare of rose-red scars on his arms, chest, and shoulders.

Wolf said, "Take it easy, then, you great idiot! Flames, man! *What* were you fighting?"

Lynx smiled ruefully. "Dunno. It wasn't human and I never want to meet it again!"

"It? Just one?"

"One was enough."

Wolf mumbled manly, no-nonsense condolences, grateful that Hogwood's presence saved them from becoming maudlin. Lynx, always the sentimental one, began blurting out mawkish gush about how long it had been and how much he had missed him, and so on. Wolf stepped back and introduced the inquisitor as a warning that he must guard his tongue.

Intrepid indicated the boy now standing uneasily beside the table. "Inquisitor, this is Prime Candidate Tancred, a swordsman of great future renown."

"Good chance to you, Prime."

"Mistress!" Tancred tapped his sword hilt. He had infinitely more poise than Rivers. He was probably a couple of years older than Hogwood.

"Prime has been taking dictation, Inquisitor," Intrepid said. "I asked Sir Lynx to relate as much of what happened as he could remember, considering it important to catch his testimony as soon as possible." He preened at his own brilliance.

"Very wise," Hogwood said. "How many other witnesses are here?"

"Eighteen, of whom eleven are capable of testifying. I set seniors to take statements from all of them."

"Excellent. Prime, the Council has declared this matter a state secret. We require your oath of secrecy regarding everything Sir Lynx has said. Repeat after me . . ." Hogwood's eyes were caves of fatigue in a chalk cliff and yet she radiated confidence and authority. That was how she was trained to act, of course, but Wolf was impressed by her sheer physical toughness, steel sword in silk scabbard.

Tancred was a solemn youth who looked vaguely worried at the best of times, but he spoke up bravely as he swore the oath. "I think Sir Lynx had finished, Inquisitor," he added. "I had just finished reading his testimony back to him when you arrived."

"Very well. I can see that your handwriting is as stylish as your swordsmanship, and for that I am already grateful."

Tancred saluted again. Skilled fencer that he was, he read the signs and headed for the door without needing to be told.

Lynx called, "Thanks, lad. Big help. Always knew you'd turn out to be one of the good ones."

Beaming at this tribute from a hero, Tancred departed.

Hogwood turned to Intrepid and swore him to silence also, which tweaked his beard. She said, "About security, Master . . . has anyone left Ironhall since the news arrived?"

His pout deepened. "Grand Master, of course. Sir Alden and his man went back to Quondam. Grady, Flint, Huntley, and Godfrey to Court. The carters come and go. I gave strict orders not to gossip to them, but it's hard to make that stick. They can tell that we have more mouths to fill. Is there anything else you need right away?" He wanted to leave before he was ordered out.

"Food and rest, a hot bath if one is available. I should be finished here in an hour or so. Sir Wolf?"

"I'll wait here, if I may, Inquisitor. Naturally I am interested to hear my brother's story."

Intrepid saw a chance to flaunt authority. "No more than twenty minutes! I do not want my patient overtired and we have another healing scheduled to treat the adhesions." He paused at the door. "I hope you will be our guest at the evening meal, Inquisitor?" His eyes gleamed at the thought of displaying her at high table. "And your escort, of course."

After the long hours of cold, warmth was making Wolf's head spin and he was sure Hogwood would collapse if she did not sleep soon.

She surprised him yet again. "Sir Wolf and I will be honored. If you will send me those other statements right away, Master, I will get to work."

As soon as Intrepid had gone, Hogwood went to the table and flipped through the pages Tancred had written. Wolf pulled a stool up to the bed and regarded his wounded brother, who smiled vaguely back. Anger began to beat like a pulse in Wolf's temple. Would Lynx ever recover his wits properly? Whoever or whatever had done this to him must be hunted down and dealt with.

"You been doing some fighting yourself, Wolfie," Lynx said. "Who cut the bits out of your face?"

"It's a long story. You feel well enough to answer questions?"

"I'll try. The world's still fuzzy at the edges."

"You understand I'm here as the King's servant? You will be testifying as if in a court of law and that Inquisitor Hogwood's account of your answers may be entered in evidence at some other time and place?"

Lynx glanced at her and pitched a magnificent Cute Little Boy smile. "I'll try to impress her with my innocence."

He probably did not realize he was doing it, but Wolf had seen the Blades' legendary seduction powers in action often enough, although rarely as blatantly—or as potently, so far as another man could judge. He wondered how resilient dear Dolores's defenses would be if Lynx really tested them. The hero's honest, open face was unmarked; even when visible, his battle scars lacked the grotesque horror of Wolf's mutilation.

If Hogwood noticed, she gave no sign. "I will summarize for you what your brother has already said, Sir Wolf." She marched over to the fire, turned her back on it, and proceeded to rattle off a concise account of Lynx's deposition.

7

estimony of Sir Lynx, companion in the Loyal and Ancient Order of the King's Blades, as dictated to Prime Candidate Tancred at Ironhall, this 18th day of Secondmoon, 395:

I was accepted as a candidate in Ninthmoon of 385 and bound on the 13th of Fifthmoon, 390, by Marquesa Celeste. At that time she also bound Sir Fell and Sir Mandeville, and she appointed me commander of her guard. We escorted her to Grandon and thereafter resided at Court until four years ago . . . almost exactly. Firstmoon of 391. Anyway, then she married Baron Dupend and moved to Quondam Castle, on Whinmoor.

Is this going to be on oath?

Then I'd better tell the truth. Celeste was never a real marquesa. She was the King's mistress. He tired of her and ordered her to marry old Dupend, but she didn't. The notary kept asking her those "Do you?" questions and she kept saying, "No, I don't!" and in the end he just shut his book and declared them man and wife. I carried her out of the palace over my shoulder, screaming. Yes, really. No, she was screaming, I was just angry, but I was bound to defend her and I'd been told very clearly that much worse would happen to her if she didn't do as she was told.

So Quondam was a jail for her. An awful place—bleak and cold and drafty, perched on the edge of the sea cliffs. Nothing ever happens there, but it is the strongest keep in Chivial and Dupend would rant for hours how it had withstood assaults by Baelish raiders, turned back rebels during the Fatherland War, and so on. Quondam holds the land road to Westerth and the sea approach to the Straits, and has never fallen to storm or siege or treachery. So he says. Or used to say. He can't say it now, because it certainly fell to something four nights ago. Funny he should brag, because it belongs to the King, not him. He's no rich landowner, just a paid employee who never set eyes on the place until four years ago.

He's listened to too many minstrels. On the night of the raid, he was feasting in his mead hall like an olden-times hero—rushlights flickering through wood smoke, walls hung with ancient weapons, flushed faces at the tables as knights gorged and quaffed, a harpist twanging and warbling up in the minstrel gallery. All that. Don't forget greasy odors of roast pig still wafting from charred remains on the spit above the hearth. Yes, absolutely crazy!

I know I took a clang on the noddle and am foggy on some details, but I will swear to this feast nonsense. It happened two or three times a week, all year long. This was how the Baron celebrated the anniversary of every battle his ancestors had fought in (or run from), the fall of every town they'd sacked, and every siege Quondam had withstood. His dates were skittish, so that the Battle of Arbor might fall in Thirdmoon one year and Sixthmoon the next, but it's the spirit that counts, they say.

Dupend was far too deaf to hear the music, which was no great loss, and had no teeth for the roast boar, which was a hog from his sties. The wenches were serving watery cider because he couldn't afford mead, and the brawny heroes were just his men-at-arms plus a few local farmers acting out the farce in return for a free meal. Their ancestors might have owed knight's service to the lord of Quondam, but those days are long gone, even on Whinmoor.

The old fool is . . . was? Well, I hope he makes it. Where was I? . . .

Lynx was as near the hearth as anyone and he was still cold. He stood behind his ward, but slightly to her left, so he could toast his buns without keeping the heat off her. She and the Baron were seated at the center of the long table, their backs to the blaze. Beauty and the beast were not speaking to each other, but that was normal. They never did. Fell was on the right side of the fireplace. Only the turnspit was closer to the flames than they.

Dupend hated his wife's Blades almost as much as he hated her, because they would not take his orders. It did no good to explain that Blades never took orders from anybody. He screamed if he caught them questioning visitors or searching the baronial bedchamber. Sometimes he would decree that they were not to be fed, so they had to pretend to take food from the cooks at swordpoint. He never let them dine in the great hall with his pretend knights, so they stood guard at mealtimes and ate later in the kitchen.

Long ago they had agreed to rotate the leadership, just to ease the appalling tedium, and this was Fell's month to wear the sash. Mandeville was off patrolling the rest of the fortress. No one could remember a winter so bleak, even on Whinmoor. Sheep had been freezing to death on the hills and cottagers in their beds. Even Celeste, who normally flaunted a king's ransom of jewels on large areas of bare skin, was muffled to the eyebrows.

She was chatting with Sir Alden, Dupend's knight banneret, the one genuine warrior in the castle, a boiled-leather veteran of the Wylderland campaigns. He took his duties seriously. Even in that weather he posted sentries on the battlements, but they would certainly have headed indoors to find a brazier as soon as his back was turned, so Fell had warned Mandeville to be especially vigilant and make doubly sure the gates were locked and barred. Nowadays it seemed insane to raise a drawbridge and drop a portcullis, but they did so every night without fail; that was the one thing on which Baron Dupend and his wife's Blades agreed.

As the remains of the mock boar were being carried out to feed the kitchen staff, Lynx drew *Ratter* and deftly detached a slice of pork. He chewed happily, unnoticed by the Baron, provoking sly grins from the servants. The harpist was coughing his lungs out, up there in his smoke cloud.

Sir Mandeville came running in by the pantry door, yelling, "To arms! The castle is under attack!"

The drunks howled jeers and catcalls. Lynx hurled the meat in the fire and wiped grease from his hands, while exchanging shocked glances with Fell. Blades did *not* make jokes about danger to their wards! The deaf old Baron was yelling hysterically, wanting to know what all the commotion was about.

Mandeville arrived at the fireplace, panting. "Men coming in the gates," he said. "They've killed Dogget and Treb."

Then the hounds sprang up, growling. Thunder, the leader, started her terrible baying and charged out the door Mandeville had left open, vanishing with the rest of the pack on her tail. Men who would not believe a Blade would trust a dog, and in the sudden silence everyone heard what they had heard, a drum beating. Sir Alden had a voice like a harbor seal—not beautiful, but audible for miles—and he began roaring at everyone to start stripping weapons from the wall displays. In moments crashes of crockery announced that the tables were being tipped up and dragged over to the corner he had designated for the redoubt.

Lynx and Mandeville waited for Fell to issue orders. Normally a Blade guard prepared plans to deal with any conceivable emergency, but an armed invasion of Quondam was unthinkable. Even a lifelong worrywart like Wolf would not take that idea seriously. The keep was the Great Tower, but it was not provisioned for siege, so they would freeze to death in there before dawn, and to reach it, they would have to cross the bailey, which the enemy already held. Fell had no choice—although the hall had four entrances and was therefore not truly defensible, the Blades must remain there with the others and defend their ward as best they could.

"The corner!" Fell shouted. Lynx and Mandeville grabbed their ward's arm and rushed her, almost carried her, across to Alden's makeshift fortress.

Other women might have screamed, but Celeste was a tough gosling. Her only protest was a calm "Put me down, you bullocks! I'm perfectly capable of walking."

Now servants were pouring in from the buttery, yelling about raiders. The main door flew wide and intruders appeared en masse, bringing an icy gale with them. Half the rushlights blew out and the smoke billowed worse than ever. At first Lynx did not believe what he was seeing. Apparently Quondam was being assaulted by the grand parade from one of those masquerade balls King Athelgar fancied. The newcomers wore bizarre headdresses and swirling cloaks, some had elaborate masks, and some bore strange basket structures on their shoulders. Others were close to naked. Their eyes glinted in the rushlight, but their faces did not show up well enough for them to be fair-skinned Baels.

And he saw no glint of metal, neither weapons nor armor. He relaxed, convinced that this was some absurd joke. Then he remembered the dogs. What had happened to the hounds? With even some of the women armed, they were about fifty defenders facing at least six times that number.

Drums boomed out a signal and the enemy charged. Lynx drew *Ratter* and barely had time to raise her in mocking salute before the nightmare army was pouring over the barricade. About six of the illusions came straight for him.

Next thing he knew, he was down on the floor in a jumble of bodies and shattered furniture. His head rang carillons of pain and when he touched it, his hand came away bloody. He was lying on the corpse of a hefty, dark-skinned youngster wearing a loincloth and sandals. This was madness. *It was colder than death out there!*

Even in that hubbub, he could hear his ward's screams. She needed him. Fell was shouting his name, too. He struggled to his feet and headed in their direction, stumbling over the confusion of dead and wounded. The invaders were leaving by the same door they had come in, carrying their wounded, abandoning their dead. Fell was hobbling after them, carrying *Widowmaker* in his right hand. His left arm hung limp and he was a southpaw, almost useless that way. Beside him went one of the farmers, a solid yokel armed with sword and shield. Lynx managed a wobbly sprint and the three of them were almost together when they reached the hearth and caught up with the rearmost invader.

He had to be important because he was screeching incomprehensible orders in a discordant, inhuman voice. He loomed so grotesquely tall, at least seven feet, that he must be on stilts, and his streaming cloak swirled in iridescence—an impressive masquerade costume, but not warrior garb by any stretch of the mind. His head was hidden inside a bizarre furry helmet and Lynx saw no indication of a weapon under the cloak.

Somehow the giant sensed the threat behind him, for he spun around only just too late to avoid a wild haymaker overarm stroke by Fell. *Widowmaker* slammed down on his right shoulder. Had Fell been fighting southpaw he would have slashed the freak's head off, helmet and all, slick as cutting berries. As it was, he almost severed the man's arm. The giant yowled in rage, struck the farmer's matching stroke aside with his left hand, and kicked the man like a mule, sending him sprawling. Then Lynx was there, thrusting *Ratter* into his heart.

That's what he meant to do. He underestimated his opponent. Despite his size, that tree-high monstrosity was so incredibly nimble that he dodged Lynx's thrust at zero range. *Ratter* sliced along his chest and tangled briefly in his cloak. His left hand smashed down on Lynx's arm.

Lynx registered the clang of his sword hitting the flags and stooped to snatch her up. His fingers refused to obey him. He stared in bewilderment at his forearm, which had been macerated into raspberry puree and slivers of bone. The lower half hung at right angles, as if he had grown a new wrist. One blow had done that?

So Fell and the raider and he were all one-handed. Fell was now behind the giant, though, and this time he slashed at kidney level, cutting through the cloak. Blood burst out. The giant should have dropped to the floor and died, but he didn't. He rounded on Fell with a massive, deadly blow to the face. He was wearing gloves armed with knives, and one blow did to Fell's face what he had done to Lynx's arm.

The farmer closed again, with even less success. He was game, but he was nothing compared to the Blade-killing monster. The *thing* parried the man's sword aside like a straw and kicked again, but this time up, under the older man's shield. Its boots were toothed, too. The farmer screamed. The thing finished him off with another punch.

By then Lynx had retrieved *Ratter.* He was not quite as inept with his offside hand as Fell was, and this time he made certain of the freak with a cut on its good shoulder, severing the tendons it needed to raise that arm. One-arm was now no-arms.

"That fixed you, swine!" he roared.

No. It was spilling blood in rivers, but it leaped on Lynx, crunching his shoulder in its jaws. He heard bones crack as they hit the floor together, with the invader on top. Lynx tried to grab the thing's throat to choke it, but he had only one useful hand. The monster had no usable hands anymore, but it had knives on its feet, and it proceeded to rip Lynx apart with those.

8

$\mathcal{H}$ogwood said, "Do you, Lynx, warrant that what you dictated to Candidate Tancred is the truth as you know it?"

"Wait!" Wolf barked. "He's not himself." Naked savages in midwinter, superhuman warriors, unknown conjurations, insurrection for unknown purposes?

Lynx tried to laugh and grimaced in agony. "I know it sounds mad, Wolfie, but the others will back me up."

"It agrees with Grand Master's report," the inquisitor snapped.

Small wonder the Council was confused and the King so worried! When the Thencaster Rebellion exploded, Athelgar had followed age-old tradition and fled to the safety of Grandon Bastion. The Bastion would be no haven if conjury could now take even a major fortress like Quondam so easily.

Wolf parried and riposted. "Pray note, Inquisitor, that the bite marks on my brother's shoulder were made by jaws larger than those of any hound I ever saw. The King speculated that he might have been injured while fighting for the wrong team, so for the record, Lynx, did you fight to prevent the abduction of the Baroness?"

"I did."

Had there been a fleabite of hesitation there?

"You were wounded by the invaders?"

"I was."

"While fighting alongside the Baron's men, the defenders?"

"Yes."

If dear King Athelgar had been hoping Wolf would have to arrest his own brother and charge him with murder, he would be disappointed. Relieved, he turned to Hogwood. "Is the witness telling the truth?"

She regarded Lynx glassily. "He has not lied yet. Pray do not interrupt while I am questioning the witness, Sir Wolf. Sir Lynx, you describe the intruders as dark-skinned. Black or dark brown skin is found in southern lands, where the sun is closer to the earth. Were these such men, or had they dyed themselves to be less visible at night?"

Lynx tried to shrug and winced again. "I don't know. They seemed about the color of ripe chestnuts, but the light was very poor."

"Describe the helmet your assailant was wearing."

This time his pause was longer. "I'm not sure now that it was a helmet. A sort of spotted mask covering his whole head . . . but it bit me . . ." He peered down at his ravaged shoulder.

"You described the Baroness as wearing 'rags and jewels.' What did you mean by that?"

"What I said," Lynx retorted grumpily. "She had no decent clothes and if she hadn't worn her jewelry all the time, it would have been stolen."

"By whom?"

"The Baron."

"Who is her current lover?"

"Mind your own business." Lynx set his teeth. For all his amiability, he could be stubborn as moorland granite.

But so could an inquisitor, and this one was very eager to prove her competence in an investigation of historic importance. "You are required by law to answer my question. Did she have a lover?"

"Baroness Celeste is my ward and I will not—"

"Wait!" Wolf was willing to keep Hogwood on a slack rein, but browbeating his invalid brother went too far. "Lynx, we're trying to find her. You want her found, don't you? We need your help. The only reason to kidnap Celeste is to free her from captivity and only a lover would care enough to risk this. Were you or Fell or Mandeville swiving Celeste?" Seeing another refusal coming, he tried to forestall it. "Specifically—within the last year, did you or Fell or Mandeville have carnal relations with Baroness Celeste?"

Lynx glowered. "No. None of us."

"She had no lovers?"

"If by lovers you mean admirers, then everyone who pees standing up. If you mean who slept with her, then nobody."

Knowing Celeste, Wolf found this statement as incredible as the assault itself. He sighed and returned the witness to Hogwood.

"The Baron is a very old man," she prompted.

"And smelly." Lynx bared his teeth. "Celeste would not have him in her chamber. She slept alone and we stood guard outside the door. Dupend loathes her. He has grandsons older than she is and she will inherit everything he has left, through dower rights. He wanted nothing more in the world than to catch her with a man so he could divorce her and spit in the King's eye. That would be dangerous for her, and we made certain no other man got near her!" Anger had raised pink roses on his ashen pallor. His voice was as taut as a bowstring. "To the best of my knowledge, Celeste has balled no man or boy since the day she left Greymere. I don't pretend she enjoyed chastity, but we weren't bound to keep her happy, only safe, so we saw to it."

"Not easy?"

Lynx conceded, "Like herding wasps!" with a shamefaced grin.

Hogwood took off after another scent. She was literally steaming, standing there before the fire. "So you have no idea who might have plotted to rescue Celeste from her captivity?"

"Not like that," Lynx muttered.

Flames! Wolf bit back another interruption. He was growing very uneasy.

She pounced. "Like what?"

"Not killing and violence."

"Who was plotting to free her, and how?"

"Me." Lynx spoke unhappily to his own toes. "Us. Least, we'd talked some about it. We worried about her sanity. Lately she'd taken to weeping and moaning for days on end. She'd stand on the high battlements, staring down at the surf, brooding. We stayed very close to her when she did that. We searched her room every day for knives or rope. That sort of thing."

"She was always a wonderful actress," Wolf said, earning another brotherly glare.

"A few months after Baroness Dupend was sent to Quondam," Hogwood said, "she bore a child."

"Athelgar's, not Dupend's!" Lynx shouted. "Everyone knew that."

"It died within a few days?"

"Everyone celebrated! The Baron celebrated. Celeste was the only one who mourned."

"Did you not mourn it?"

That was an unfair question, but Lynx answered before Wolf could object.

"No. No, we celebrated, too, thinking she might be released then, that the King might let her go and live somewhere better." He stared down at his thick, scarred arms on the cover. "Even her Blades!"

"If the death of her child did not make her suicidal, then why this sudden concern for her sanity now?"

"How much cruelty can a woman take? Four years in jail? Four years of that awful climate? Four years of that awful husband? No ladies-in-waiting for company, no lady's maids to dress her hair? All her gowns—remember, Wolf, she had three wagons with her when she left Grandon? All that stuff disappeared. She wore her jewels all day long and probably in bed, too, for all I knew. Everything else got pilfered—clothes, silverware, even furniture. All gone."

"What did the Baron do about that?"

"He was behind it. He stole whatever he could and sold it. It was part of the deal, I think."

"What deal?"

Lynx sighed. "We thought Athelgar threw in her jewels when he gave her to Dupend. Dupend seemed to think he had a right to them."

That was reasonable, because if Athelgar felt an unwanted mistress was his to dispose of as he pleased, he would not scruple to deal off the finery he had given her.

The snoop said, "So what were you Blades planning?"

"We talked," Lynx said grumpily, "*just* talked, about one of us riding into Lomouth to pawn a bracelet or something and hire a ship. Then the other two would bring her. We hadn't gotten very far."

And never would have, if the Baron had sent his men after them. But he might just have shouted, "Good riddance!" Wolf made a mental note to ask Hogwood about dower rights.

"So," she said, "her Blades were plotting rescue but had not taken action?"

"That's right."

"And you know of no other plots?"

"None."

"Could the Baron have faked this attack himself?"

Lynx snorted. "Never."

This had gone far enough. "Can't my brother be allowed to rest now? It would seem that he has cleared himself of any complicity in this affair."

"Not necessarily." Hogwood continued to stare snakily at her victim. "Sir Lynx, have you deceived me or tried to deceive me in any way, by omission or equivocation, misdirection or evasion?"

That catchall invitation to self-incrimination was a hoary inquisitorial trick, repeatedly denounced by the courts and repeatedly resurrected. Fortunately Lynx was aware of it. "I refuse to answer that."

Intrepid walked in, ending the interrogation. If Wolf was not satisfied with Lynx's story, he could not expect Hogwood to be.

9

"The statements you wanted, Dolores," Master of Rituals proclaimed breezily, handing her a sheaf of paper. "Also some evidence for your, um, weapons expert. Sir Alden brought this along when he ferried over the wounded."

Intrepid enjoyed annoying people, especially people with any trace of authority. He handed Wolf a club as long as a man's arm, carved from some dark wood. It was not too heavy to swing with one hand, although the leather-bound grip had space for two. The shaft was an intricate tangle of fanciful birds, beasts, and vegetation, flaring out like a paddle at the working end, which was inset with teeth of black stone. Three of the original four had broken off, no doubt when that part acquired its ominous bloodstains.

"It impresses me more as a work of art than a weapon," Wolf said, "but it could obviously damage people." He tried it for size against the wounds on Lynx's scalp. "I've never seen its like. Have you any idea where it came from?"

"No," Intrepid said, "but Grand Master thought he did. We did not have time to discuss it before he left for Quondam."

"No metal? Black stone, sharp as razors."

"Allow me." Hogwood took the weapon, giving Wolf in return the thick wad of eyewitness accounts, which she had already read. "This stone is volcanic glass, called obsidian. It fractures to extremely sharp edges. You will note that the design represents an animal's paw, probably a cat's—four operational claws and a smaller one set back so it is not engaged."

"Dogs have feet like that." Wolf hated being lectured.

"But dogs do not fight with their feet. And there are no dogs shown." She was peering at the carvings. "Cats and birds—raptors, probably accipiters, and possibly buteos." Know-it-all smartyskirts!

Intrepid was amused. "Send it to the Privy Council and let the royal falconers worry about it. I have put you in the Queen's Tower, Dolores, since Baron Dupend has the Royal Suite. You will find a hot tub ready for you there. You, brother, will have the honor of sleeping in Grand Master's bed."

"No!" Wolf said. "I am not worthy."

"We have nowhere else to put you."

"I'll bed down in his study."

"I wish you a comfortable night there."

Wolf understood the sneer a little later, when he reached the study and found it in chaos: floorboards missing, half a fireplace, stacks of building materials everywhere. Ironhall had been already crowded. With Vicious anxious to replace all the old Ambrose and Malinda men, enrollment had been raised to record numbers and more knights had been brought in to instruct. The Quondam wounded had filled the infirmary.

Wolf picked his way across to the tower door and went up to Grand Master's chamber. Unlike other knights who moldered away in Ironhall, Durendal was a wealthy man, and he had already refurbished the turret with opulent rugs and elegant furniture, very unlike the school's usual relics. A hearty fire was driving off the chill and illuminating down-filled quilts and silken sheets, shelves of leather-bound books, golden candlesticks, a carved alabaster inkstand on the escritoire. Three oil paintings—a strikingly beautiful young woman, a boy, and a girl—were clearly from some master's brush. Wolf felt like a trespasser.

When he had made himself presentable, he headed down to the inevitable pre-dinner assembly, aware that he would be made to feel like a trespasser there, too. Except for Grand Master and a few others, the knights spurned Wolf the Blade-killer.

Eight or ten knights were already present, as were Inquisitor Hogwood and Master of Rituals Intrepid, who was obviously enjoying the sensation she caused. A few fogeys sulked in the background, shocked to see a Dark Chamber snoop allowed inside Ironhall, but the rest had crowded in to enjoy rare female company. Some would not have seen a woman in years. She wore inquisitorial robes of plain black, without adornments, her sable hair was gathered in a caul, yet adulation converted her into a reigning monarch and her perfectly ordinary chair into a throne. No one could have told from her looks that she had ridden almost thirty hours over winter roads.

Wolf entered unnoticed and accepted his usual goblet of well-watered wine from old Hurley. Sir Bowman, the new Master of Sabers, made him welcome with his usual wry humor and they stood back to watch as each newcomer reacted to the situation by drifting into one party or the other. The pro-Hogwood faction was ahead by about twelve to seven when a voice like a very rusty trumpet screeched out at their backs.

"Even inquisitors are better than murderers."

"Even female inquisitors are!" croaked another.

The room stilled. Wolf glanced across at Intrepid, who just shrugged. He turned to face the withered remains of Sir Etienne and Sir Kane, Ironhall's oldest inhabitants. Kane had been bound by Ambrose III and bore the unwelcome title of Father of the Order, being over ninety. Etienne could not be far behind, and neither seemed capable of supporting the weight of the cat's-eye swords they still had the audacity to wear. They had gummed Wolf before, but always Grand Master—

whether Parsewood or Durendal—had snapped them back to heel. Tonight Grand Master was in Quondam and his stand-in did not want to spoil the fun.

"Arundel he slaughtered!" Etienne quavered. "And young Rodden."

"And Hotspur!" Kane yelled. He was as deaf as a rock and almost toothless. "And Cedric! And Warren!"

There was no way to deal with this horrible pair except to remain silent. Normally Wolf never cared what they said, but tonight Hogwood was listening.

"I don't think Cedric was one of mine," he said. "He died of old age years ago." He wished certain others would, and soon.

"What's he say?" Kane demanded.

"Jared, then! Your brother in the Order and you murdered him!"

Bowman intervened. "They wanted to die, you old fools. Their wards were plotting treason! They were torn between their binding and their loyalty to the King. If not Wolf it would have been the entire Order coming after them or the Household Yeomen or gangs of thugs with nets and clubs. That meant arrest and trial and madness. Wolf gave them an honorable way out, one last glorious duel to the death with a brother Blade. Wouldn't you have chosen that, a fair fight?"

Kane sprayed anger. "Shameless slayer! Apostate!" He hadn't heard a word.

"Quintus!" Etienne quavered. "What about Sir Quintus, eh? Quintus won the Cup two years in a row and you'll not convince me you were ever good enough to kill Quintus! Not in a fair fight."

Wolf shuddered at the memory. Why did they have to drag up that one? Quintus had been a senior when he was admitted to Ironhall. Quintus had been his hero. Seeming to lose his temper was easy.

"You besmirch my honor, you foulmouthed old stinkard?" he roared. "Draw and defend yourself." He slapped the dotard's face, less gently than he intended.

Etienne staggered back, bewildered. Some of the onlookers howled in horror at a mass murderer challenging so old a man. A few others guffawed, but Wolf had driven the game beyond reason, as he intended.

Intrepid jumped forward to steady the tottering ruin. "Very droll, brother, but not seemly when we have a lady guest. Brothers, shall we go in to dinner?"

Playing his role as Acting Grand Master, he led the procession into the hall with Hogwood on his arm. Wolf attached himself to the end of the line, although a member of the Guard should have been given precedence; indeed, as bearer of the king's writ, he could have claimed the throne itself, but that was traditionally reserved for Grand Master or the sovereign. Intrepid ignored tradition by planting his hindquarters on it and then smirking around at the angry glares of the other knights. Why had Roland, with his astoundingly keen eye for people, left this popinjay in charge during his absence? Life was beset with mysteries.

The meal dragged interminably. A fair storm blew outside, making the myriad blades dangling overhead thrum a restless jingle. Newcomers were supposed to stare up at the sky of swords in terror when that happened, but Hogwood ignored it and chattered instead to her neighbors, Intrepid and Master of Sabers. That night the seniors ate their meal without ever taking their eyes off her. Wolf was mostly concerned with trying not to yawn.

The meal was followed, as always, by a reading from the *Litany of Heroes*. Intrepid did not invite the visiting guardsman to do the honors, as was customary. Typically, he chose one of the most recent entries, but it was at least brief and gave no details.

"Number 301, Sir Reynard, who on 14th Fifthmoon, 392, died defending his ward. Let us pay tribute to our fallen brother."

Wolf stared out over the hall but no one met his eye.

Then Intrepid presented Inquisitor Hogwood, sent by His Majesty to investigate the atrocity at Quondam, and asked if she would care to say a few words. Wolf was sure she had not been forewarned, but she never hesitated.

"It would be more appropriate for a Blade to address Blades and future Blades. Sir Wolf?"

Wolf rose to face angry silence. He gave them four sentences. He mentioned the King's decree of secrecy and paid tribute to the gallant defenders who had died at Quondam, especially the two Blades, who had been true to the ancient traditions of their Order. "I swear to you all," he concluded, "that Inquisitor Hogwood and I will fulfill His Majesty's solemn command. We *will* discover the culprits and we *will* see them brought to justice!"

The moment he sat down old Bowman was on his feet, applauding. Tancred picked up the cue. The boys followed Prime's lead. Then everyone had to join in the standing ovation, even Etienne and Kane, who could not have a clue who was being cheered. The King's Killer sat in angry silence as the hall rang and the sky of swords overhead thrummed in approval. He had never been given a standing ovation before. He was sure he would never get another, and this one was for a foolish boast he had no hope of ever carrying out.

10

A single candle flame danced nervously to the shutters' castanets and the wailing flutes of wind in the eaves. Wolf had reports to read, but even that slight activity must wait upon some rest. His body dropped gratefully onto Grand Master's bed and went to sleep at once, eager to do whatever it is bodies do to repair extreme exhaustion. His mind remained alert. At such times he tended to worry about his ward and whether the sex-crazed halfwits of the Guard were keeping proper care of him in his absence. He forced it to consider the Quondam problems instead. Why had the King chosen him, why had the Dark Chamber chosen Hogwood, why had the intruders squandered so many lives to so little purpose? Strangest question of all—why Celeste?

It was several days after his binding that he first set eyes on the King's exotic mistress. Rookie guardsmen must be outfitted with livery before they could be seen around Court. They needed specific Guard training, not the least of which was just learning their way around whatever palace was currently the royal residence. They must endure lectures on the latest politics and court scandals—Baron This can be violent when drunk, Lord That spies for the Isilondians, and so on. They were offered certain initiation rites.

Celeste's title of King's Courtesan was unofficial but no secret. Her quarters were located directly below the Royal Suite, and Greymere Palace was riddled with secret passages and concealed stairways. Vicious was too tactful to post men outside her door, but any intruder breaking in during the night would have greatly brightened the lives of half a dozen Blades dying of boredom in her antechamber.

Her path and Wolf's first converged one evening when he was on guard at the entrance to the West Hall and she was dancing with the King. Even at that distance, a naive country lad was impressed by her red-gold hair, her incredible body—invariably clad in a scandalously revealing gown—and the ripples of excitement that always marked her location in a crowd, but he was still gawking at every chandelier and cleavage in sight, and not as impressed as he should have been. A day or two later he stole a closer look at her and was very impressed indeed. She did not notice him.

The Marquesa de Sierra Crudeza was rumored to be an illegitimate daughter of King Diego of Distlain. Her husband, the Marqués, was by then in Clag Street debtors' prison and destined to remain so until he died of jail fever, which he did with tactful dispatch. An uncanny air of danger and mystery hung about Celeste, adding to her attraction. She had been the belle of the court of Isilond until the queen poisoned the king in a fit of jealous fury, so Chivial was almost a letdown for her. Court gossips twittered that the White Sisters could smell conjuration on her and she had bespelled Athelgar. The Blades knew that this was not true; her hold over him was not spiritual at all. The Guard called her the Hag.

About two weeks after Wolf's binding, a rumor swept through the Court that the Marquesa was with child. The news rolled on to echo in all the courts of Eurania, but in fact it was mere speculation, which passage of time disproved. She had experienced a mild dizzy spell, no more.

Bloodhand and Wolf were on ornamental duty outside the ballroom door, required to stand there like candelabra until the palace burned down or rabid Baels came foaming along the corridor, smiting bystanders with axes. The clotted cream of Chivian society swept through between them in jewels and finery without a glance. Except, for some fateful reason, Celeste, who arrived like an empress regnant, leading her train of ladies-in-waiting. Her overskirt was a wonder of scarlet-and-gold brocade, rich and weighty, as were her puffed and slashed sleeves. Those were tasteful and respectable, but her lace bodice was fine as gossamer and virtually transparent. Athelgar encouraged her to flaunt what he could enjoy and other men could not.

As she swept past Wolf, he winked. She carried on into the hall as if nothing had happened, trailing attendants and a faint scent of lilac. The babble hushed for a moment, which was normal and predictable. Suddenly women screamed. The two Blades ran to investigate. The lady had fainted, that was all.

It had taken her a moment to make the connection. Boys change much more than girls do, and she had not seen him before in that context. Wolf was sorry he had startled her so badly, but that, he thought, was that.

Wrong.

How could the King's mistress possibly snatch a private word with the most junior member of the Royal Guard? For Celeste this was no problem at all. She was at the height of her powers then, able to manipulate Athelgar like a silken glove on her subtle little hand. She began by persuading him to declare that the annual Apple Blossom Night festivities would include a masked ball, thus throwing the Court into panic and canceling sleeping time for every tailor and seamstress in the city. The Guard detested nothing in the world more than a masked ball. Leader canceled all leave for that evening.

Celeste was more than a perfect body driven by a lust for power. She also had an incomparable sense of humor, and that evening she chose to dress in Guard livery. Needless to say, no Blade had ever revealed so much of his chest in public, nor had such a chest. Never had silken hose looked as good on their legs as it did on hers. At an appropriate moment, she excused herself and in the powder room concealed her costume under a white domino, which one of her maids had brought for her. With the hood raised to hide her resplendent hair and a white mask in place of her former blue one, she returned to the ball anonymous.

Wolf was on duty beside a table of comfits, although spirits know what good he was supposed to be doing. He caught a whiff of lilac and looked around to see familiar sea-green eyes peering out at him. He knew every gold fleck in them.

"Hello, Amy," he said. "Congratulations."

"I think you have made a mistake, Sir Blade."

"Really? How are Tim and Sarah and Eli and all the other Sprats? How are things in Sheese anyway?"

She sighed. "Much duller after you left, Ed." Amy Sprat was a realist. A ghost of a smile played over the rose petal lips. "And what is the price of your silence?"

"That smile is ample reward, my lady." He could smile too. "I didn't talk then and I won't talk now."

"You swear?"

"I swear on my soul and on the happiest of memories. Your secret is safe with me. Take him for all you can get."

She moved closer to the table to sample the sweetmeats. She reached for some treat; her breast touched his arm. The Guard's orgying lessons had not yet expunged all his innocence, but he knew enough to see that she was searching for a solution, testing his susceptibility. Memories made his head swim and his flesh throb. Everything he knew about sex he had discovered with her.

"Don't," he murmured, edging away.

"I'd like to, you know? I never met a lover better than you, Ed."

"Thanks, but I'll wait until you retire, if you don't mind."

"What's your name, Sir Blade?"

"Wolf, my lady."

"Very fitting"—she raked him with a smile—"wild beast of the moors. What happened to Alf?"

"He's still at Ironhall. Don't worry about him, either. I'll warn him to keep his mouth shut."

Moorland green shone in her eyes again. "You're a good friend, Ed Attewell. I have influence, you know. Anything I can do for you?"

Wolf chuckled, wondering if she could see how he was sweating. "You owe me nothing, Amy. I am always in your debt."

She floated away, and a few moments later he saw her back in among the bluebloods, laughing at some jest of the King's.

Amy Sprat had learned what she wanted, and she needed less than a week to get it out of Athelgar. She began by going riding with her ladies in Sycamore Market to be booed. The good people of Grandon were grudging in their support of a foreigner King and had no love at all for a foreigner mistress. There were scores of buxom Chivian girls willing to do anything a Marquesa could do. Booed she was.

Wolf learned of her success late one night when he was fencing in the gym, being coached in sabers by Martin. Having spent all day on an orientation tour of the city, he had not heard the news. Bram put his head around the door and yelled over all the clattering, "Anyone seen Lyon?"

Willow, practicing in another corner, shouted back, "He led the Ironhall party—King's orders."

Blades went back and forth to Ironhall all the time. It was a welcome perk, a break from routine. But not the Deputy Leader. Wolf howled, "What?" and had the breath knocked out of him for his lack of attention. "Why?"

"The binding," Willow said. The company groaned in disapproval.

"Who's binding?" The King wasn't, because Wolf had watched him retire.

"The Hag."

Wolf was out the door before his foil hit the boards.

Being recently married, Vicious was spending much more time in his quarters than Blades normally did. He did not appreciate fists thundering on his door in the middle of the night. He was even less impressed when he opened it a crack and saw the most junior of his men stripped down to his hose and an unlaced, sweat-soaked shirt, unarmed, out of breath, hair all awry.

He stepped aside to let Wolf into his reception room. The bedchamber door was closed. He was heated and sweaty himself, wearing only a shirt wrapped around his loins. Wolf had probably arrived at the most inopportune time possible.

"Keep your voice down and be very convincing." Vicious's voice was soft and his stare hard.

"The Pirate's Son's assigning Blades to the Hag?"

"What business is that—" Vicious recalled who was Prime, and his eyes flashed like razors. "What if he is?"

"I knew her before the King did!"

Vicious stared at him for a long time. He was a dark-skinned man, showing surprising muscle when he had his shirt off, as he did then, and extreme menace when he had a naked sword in his hand, as he did then.

"When?"

"Before Ironhall. Her name is Amy Sprat. We were kids together in a hamlet called Sheese, in Westerth."

"Guardsman, you are being misled by a chance likeness."

Wolf shook his head. "We've spoken. She's Amy. She has a birthmark on her thigh. About here. She claims it's shaped like a heart, but that depends which way you're looking at it."

Leader's eyes shone brighter in the candlelight. "Spirits, man! She's only fif-
teen now! When was this?"

"Fifteen bullfeathers! She's eighteen, ten months younger than me. I was
fourteen then . . . I wasn't the only one! Every boy on the moor was a close friend
of Amy Sprat."

"Death!" Vicious advanced a pace. "Why didn't you tell me this sooner?"

Wolf retreated. "You told me . . . told Sir Terror to tell me . . . to keep my
mouth shut."

"Not to me, you idiot!" Vicious muttered a curse. "It's too late to catch them.
Have you told anyone else of this?"

"No, Leader."

"Then don't, as you value your neck. If His Majesty assigns Blades to a
friend, that is absolutely none of your business, Sir Wolf, brother or not. Is that
clear?"

Wolf could do nothing but mutter, "Yes, Leader." Lynx was to be bound to
a harlot.

"You are telling me that His Majesty's concubine is an imposter, vulnerable
to blackmail?"

"Er . . . I suppose so."

"Which means you withheld information relevant to His Majesty's safety?"
Gulp! "Yes, Leader."

Vicious looked him up and down. "And you ran all the way here from the
gym looking like that?"

"Yes, Leader."

"Present yourself after the morning muster with a written list of the regula-
tions you have broken and a recommendation for punishment. Now get out."

Wolf got out.

He had been thinking only of Lynx. Vicious could see not one but three men
betrayed and must have been even angrier than Wolf was. Furthermore, Wolf had
presented him with the ghastly problem of telling the King his paramour was a
fraud and a potential traitor. If he didn't, sooner or later the Dark Chamber cer-
tainly would, and even in those days Vicious hated inquisitors.

He dropped a hint of his feelings the next morning. It was Guard tradition
to have a malefactor recommend his own punishment, which Leader would then
either accept, halve, or double. Like any man in this predicament, Wolf consulted

experts and then set his penance unfairly high, as he thought, in the hope of hav-ing it halved.

Vicious tripled it and added two five-league runs.

11

$\mathcal{I}$nquisitor Hogwood slept the sleep of the innocent, no doubt, but Wolf must spend half the night in snail-pace reading, snug in Grand Master's bed, working through reports by flickering candlelight. The other witnesses confirmed Lynx's incredible story. One veteran man-at-arms had even witnessed his fight with the giant in the spotted helmet, if that is what the monster had been, and swore he'd never seen a man move so fast. Wolf read everything three times, wishing the other seniors had matched Tancred's superb handwriting.

But none of it made any sense. Why attack Quondam? Why the at-tackers' bizarre costumes and weapons? Why Celeste? If her Blade said she had no lover, then she had no lover. She was no missing heiress; her father and grandfather had been shepherds, her mother a sister of one of Wolf's stepmothers. Any secrets she knew would be years old. Celeste had been a stunning woman, but she was not worth scores of lives.

She was not worth what she had done to Lynx, Fell, and Mande-ville, either. Wolf had been sincere when he promised not to betray her, but how could a strumpet trust a man, any man? She had taken Lynx hostage for Wolf's good behavior, turning up at the palace a few days later with three bewildered young Blades at heel.

A week or so after that, when Wolf was alone in the junior Blade dormitory, changing to go on duty, Lynx entered silently, having always had a creepy ability to move quietly. Wolf looked up from straightening his hose and was startled to see his brother's familiar grin overhead. He was arrayed in a bizarre livery of purple and gold, with Celeste's arms outlined in seed pearls all over his chest.

Wolf jumped up and hugged him. "Congratulations!" This was their first chance for a private talk.

Lynx squeezed him till his ribs creaked, then chuckled and settled on the edge of Ivor's bed. "Not commiserations?"

"There are advantages to being a private Blade."

"Tell me about them some time." Lynx normally took life as it came, so from him that remark was a scream of frustration. "Like not being thrown out to starve after a mere ten years?"

"Like not having time to die of boredom. And I hear she appointed you Leader. Congratulations again!" Wolf had a low opinion of both Fell and Mandeville, and assumed Grand Master had guided Celeste's choice.

Lynx hesitated, glanced at the door as if you to confirm that they were not being overheard, then muttered, "She said I was the best. Almost as good as you, she said."

Wolf stared at him aghast, eventually whispered, "You didn't!"

Lynx bit his lip and nodded, still studying Wolf's boots.

"When? I mean where . . . I mean . . . Lynx, you mustn't!"

"Ironhall. The same night."

"Don't you remember what happened to Sian and her Blades?"

"Sian was Queen."

Wolf wanted to scream and could only whisper. "You think that would matter to the Pirate's Son?"

Blades bragged that their binding made them irresistible to women and rarely mentioned that the reverse was also true. They were the randiest of men and a Blade bound to a woman was notoriously prone to do his guarding at unseemly close quarters. Celeste was lusty, a skilled seductress, and Athelgar had let her bind three teenage virgins. It was easy to guess what had happened right after the binding, while they were still dizzy from the ritual, the excitement, the aftermath of danger. Likely Celeste was as inflamed herself, having just stabbed them all through their hearts, but even if she had been her usual calculating self, it would have been out of character for her to resist such a temptation. Of course she would have pled exhaustion and a need to rest after such an ordeal. Of course her Blades would have escorted her to her quarters, and of course she would then have sampled them. They would have been child's play for her, mere nibbles.

"He'll kill you all," Wolf said. "Who else have you told about this?"

"Just you . . ." Lynx laughed sheepishly and forced himself to look up. "I'm *only kidding, Wolfie! You really think we'd be such idiots as to bed the King's private harlot? Just joking, Wolf."*

"That sort of joke will laugh your head off."

They never discussed that subject again. From then on Wolf never saw Celeste without at least two of her Blades in attendance. He could always count on a smile whenever she caught his eye and a fiery glare when the King did. Vicious had passed on Wolf's revelations, of course. The quarrel that had started with juvenile mockery would never heal now—Athelgar had made Wolf's brother slave to a harlot, Wolf had enjoyed the favors of the King's mistress.

Yet Celeste was so skilled at her work that she kept her royal lover enraptured for months longer. Only as summer faded did Athelgar's attention start to stray. In her desperation, Amy abandoned whatever conjuration she had used to block conception. By Long Night she was with child, royal child. No monarch wanted bastards complicating the succession, and by then Athelgar's fancy was set on the shamelessly underage daughter of the Duke of Finemont. Celeste had become a bore.

As the King cast around to find a father for his spawn, into view tottered ancient Baron Dupend, a man with more ancestors than teeth, a widower whose purse was as lean as his shanks. He had come to Court seeking permission to sell off the last of his entailed estates, a desperate solution that would leave his sons paupers without totally banishing the threat of debtors' prison for him. His Gracious Majesty was amused to offer the noble lord the wardenship of Quondam, which was located conveniently far away, plus the slightly used, visibly pregnant, but witty and lusty Marquesa Celeste, supported by a bribe handsome enough to save the old fool from bankruptcy. In Firstmoon of 391, the marriage was announced—not the betrothal, but the accomplished deed. After that day the Attewell brothers did not meet for four long years.

Typical of Athelgar! He simultaneously infuriated the nobility by insulting one of the oldest houses in the land and the burghers by squandering a fortune in tax revenue to dispose of a doxy he could have given to a gardener. There never was a man with such a gift for making enemies.

But none of this ancient history explained Quondam.

Someone rattled the latch, trying to open the bedroom door. Wolf was off the bed in a flash of steel, *Diligence* in hand. He flipped the bolt and kicked the door wide. It hit someone.

Lynx swore in the darkness. He came limping into the light, swaddled in a fleece bedcover that made him look like some huge half-melted bear, wearing the bemused smile of an amiable drunk.

"Stubbed my toe," he muttered. "Need talk . . . like old times."

"Sit and be welcome." Wolf closed and bolted the door again, saw him settled on the hob, poked up the fire. Lynx had no shoes, no lantern. "How did you get through the study?"

"Mm? Painfully. This like old times, middle of the night?"

"It is." Wolf pulled up a chair and beamed at him happily. "Spirits, it's good to see you again! Had another healing?" Lynx had not been drinking. Intrepid had scrambled his brains with a blizzard of elementals.

He nodded vaguely. "Shoulder's better." He demonstrated moving his left arm, flexed his right hand, and then tugged the rug around him again. He was wearing nothing under it. "Swordsman needs his arms, Wolf."

"Hard to hold a sword with your teeth."

"Got no sword. Lost *Ratter*!" His face crumpled like a child's.

"You dropped her in the fight. We'll get her back for you. Listen, I need your help. Can you think of any reason at all why anyone at all would want to kidnap Celeste?"

Lynx was incapable of serious thought just then, but if he'd worked out an answer earlier he ought to remember doing so. He sniffed. "Lost my ward, too. What sort of Blade loses his ward? Oh, Wolfie! What am I going to do, Wolfie? Wander the world forever looking for her?"

"Start by working out who took her. Tell me about her missing years."

"Huh?"

Wolf sighed. "How did Amy Sprat become the Marquesa Celeste? When did she leave Sheese?"

"Week after we did," Lynx said, as if that was obvious.

His wits would return by morning, but Wolf could never be patient when a job needed doing. In four years of captivity, the languishing Baroness must have rehearsed her troubles to her Blades, drunk or sober, and Wolf set to work to drag her story out of Lynx, phrase by phrase. It took an hour.

A lecherous old chapman peddling pots in Sheese had discovered Amy Sprat, flower of the moors. Recognizing her burgeoning beauty and natural skills, he had taken her away with him and set her up in Lomouth as a source of revenue for him and a benefaction to the young men of the city. Seeing how she was being exploited, she had run off with a ship captain, who took her across the Straits to Isilond. From there, somehow, she found her way farther south, to Distlain. For the next five years or so, while Lynx and Wolf studied swordsmanship at Ironhall, Amy had learned a different trade. Her story, as told to and by Lynx, involved a huge cast of villains, johns, pimps, sugar daddies, blackmail victims, crooked officials, and outright suckers, with herself always the persecuted heroine. Wolf inferred that she had been more puppeteer than puppet, deliberately scaling the social ladder until she could pass for nobly born.

A few months before Malinda's abdication, Amy had returned to Chivial with the express intent, so she claimed, of snaring Crown Prince Athelgar. She had acquired a husband for respectability and appropriated the name of Celeste from the notorious seductress in the Isilondian murder scandal. Whoever the supposed Marqués was, it had been child's play for Amy to dump him in Clag Street, out of her way, as soon as the Prince nibbled her bait. She claimed that the first thing Athelgar had done to celebrate his mother's departure had been to head straight from the docks to the palace and try out the royal bed, even before sitting on the royal throne. The royal bed with Celeste in it, of course.

Clearly the spurious Marquesa had been absent from Chivial for years, which explained why she had been so shocked when Wolf recognized her. Secondly, her associates had been sailors, small-town doctors, younger sons of minor aristocracy—none of whom could have found the resources to storm Quondam. There had been no mastermind behind Celeste except Celeste herself, and Wolf had still not found a credible suspect.

"Gone!" Lynx sniffed. "Lost my ward. No Blade's ever lost his ward before, Archives says. I'll go crazy!"

"I think you'd have . . ." Wolf caught a spark of an idea before it could emerge in words. Playing for time to think, he said, "I don't think

Hogwood was completely satisfied with your testimony. Did you hold back anything? Is there anything you can tell me that you didn't want to put on the record?"

"Just that I loved her."

"You said she'd kept her legs together at Quondam."

Lynx sighed and a tear trickled down into his beard. "I don't mean that sort of love. Oh, we had to be so cruel! I love her, Wolf! We all loved her."

"She's a harlot!"

"I know. But I love her."

"That's your binding talking, chump!"

"It's my binding feeling it." A tear trickled from the other eye. "The most beautiful woman in the world."

"No doubt," Wolf agreed with a shudder. "You still say you didn't swinge her when she was at Quondam?"

"No," Lynx said grumpily. "But not from want of longing."

"She'd have agreed?"

Lynx just scowled. Stupid question.

Wolf said, "I still can't understand anyone sacrificing so many lives to carry her off. Have you thought of any sane reason why anyone should? Or any other reason for the attack on Quondam?"

"Jewels?" Lynx muttered. "I told you she used to wear all her jewels. That's what I'm afraid of, Wolf. It was easier to carry her away decorated than to strip her there. They took her to their boats, kept the jewels, and dropped her overboard." He put his face in his hands and started weeping in earnest.

"You've been conjured out of your wits. You want to lie down and get some sleep?"

He grunted. "Can't sleep."

Wolf said, "Good." The spark of an idea was glowing nicely now. "You remember Quintus?"

Lynx looked up with a sad smile. "Remember his fencing. He won the Cup twice, didn't he? Remember his laugh. Always laughing. You could hear Quintus laugh right across Starkmoor."

Wolf would certainly never forget that laugh. "Ambrose gave him to Baron Elboro, him and Warren."

"And you killed them," Lynx said, starting to show more interest. "Intrepid was telling me. Why d'you kill so many brothers, Wolfie? Why you, always? Why not let some of the others do some of the King's dirty work? Or why not catch them in nets or something and revert them?"

"Because reversion spells almost never work and you can't catch a Blade with nets or anything else if he knows you're coming for him, and they all knew. As soon as the Thencaster Plot crawled out of the midden they all knew we'd be coming for their wards."

Lynx said, "Oh. Right."

"They were all half crazy from divided loyalty anyway. Elboro was the last. The King put me in charge . . ." There were details Wolf had never told anyone, not even including them in the infamous report he had filed after he'd done Athelgar's filthy work for him.

"Three Blades and two snoops," he said, "but by that time I was wearing the sash on these excursions. We discovered a possible escape route over the rooftops and if we knew of it, we could be certain that Elboro's Blades did. I set a trap. I thought it would be better to herd Elboro into the chokey than try a frontal assault."

Leaving his helpers to wait in ambush, he beat on the door in the middle of the night, the traditional hour for Death to come calling. He waited a minute, then opened it with an inquisitor's golden key and went in. Elboro House was very opulent, all marble and thick rugs and gilt-framed mirrors. Warren and Quintus stood foursquare in the great entrance hall, barely visible in the moonlight. He had not expected both of them.

"Look who's come!" Warren said. "Your reputation has preceded you, brother."

Wolf gave them the speech he had ready. "We shall not be disturbed. You know you cannot escape and I know you cannot give up, any more than I can. I offer you a clean, quick end, or you can kill me and endure what follows. The choice is yours."

Warren laughed shrilly. "You plan to take us on together? My Leader is a dueler of renown and I certainly intend to defend myself."

"That is your right," Wolf said, hoping they did not mean it. He drew Diligence. Two more swords flashed from their scabbards. He was gambling, of course, that their ward was already fleeing between the chimney pots and they would play for time, rather than fight seriously.

He was wrong. Quintus stayed out, but Warren was recently married, un-willing to die, and a deadly fencer. The rugs made for tricky footwork and ab-sorbed the sound, so only clattering metal broke the silence, just panting breath and starry gleams from the steel. They worked their way around the hall, with Wolf doing most of the recovering, but in the end he got his back to the light and used that advantage to find an opening.

As he stood in bitter triumph over the body, sobbing for breath and bleeding like a pig from what Warren had done to him, he heard Quintus chuckle in a soft, macabre mockery of his boisterous mirth back in the days of their innocence.

"That was the easy part," he said. "Try your teeth on me, Sir Wolf."

He came forward in a whirl of rapier and the King's Killer had no chance at all. Quintus drove him into a corner, pricking and jabbing without mercy, adding scars to his face with a surgeon's precision, and all the time cackling.

"You don't need all that much ear. . . . A little more leer . . ." Conjury could heal cuts, but not replace missing flesh. Soon Wolf was fighting with an arm over his forehead to keep the blood out of his eyes. Repeatedly Quintus cornered him, cut him some more, then let him break free, just to drive him back the other way. No swordsman in creation could have held him off and Wolf was convinced that Diligence was on her way to the sky of swords when his opponent suddenly hurled his rapier down and ripped his doublet open. And laughed.

"Oh, Lynx! You think he had a laugh when he was at Ironhall, you should have heard him then. The Yeomen two streets away heard him."

Lynx's eyes were still not back to normal, but he was interested enough to forget his own plight for a moment. "What happened?"

"I killed him. The point is that his ward was dead, Lynx. Elboro fell off the roof and saved Athelgar the headsman's hire. Quintus's binding snapped and he knew it right away."

"So?"

"You still can't sleep."

Lynx shrugged stupidly, still bemused. "I fainted from lack of blood."

"I said *sleep*. Your binding's intact. Your ward's still alive."

Lynx's eyes seemed to shine like a cat's then. "Celeste? Alive?"

"She has to be. You're still bound!"

She had not been taken for the sake of her jewels and dropped over-board. That was not the explanation.

12

$\mathcal{B}$y the time the morning bell began its clamor, Wolf had finished writing a full report of his progress so far, little as that was. He had wrapped the bizarre wooden mace for shipment to the Privy Council and copied out parts of Lynx's testimony for Master of Archives, so that Fell and Mandeville would receive due honor in the *Litany*. He had also raided the kitchens for a quick breakfast. Snow was falling but the wind was veering to the south, which on Starkmoor usually meant a break in the weather.

He found Hogwood in a hallway, cornered by Tancred and Rivers, both of them smiling inanely as they practiced making conversation to a female person. Other boys slunk by at a safe distance, young ones smirking, others pouting enviously but knowing better than to intrude. She looked more exhausted than she had the previous evening, but if she had been using some sort of conjured stamina on the journey, she would almost certainly suffer aftereffects.

Wolf himself was still one huge ache, but he beamed cheerily and saluted. "Good chance, Inquisitor! Any instructions for me this fine morning?"

"Ride out in the blizzard and freeze to death," she said sourly.

Rivers guffawed. Tancred frowned warily, trying to work out the play.

"I would, but I have to defend you from these lecherous characters."

Tancred took Rivers by the elbow and led him away.

"Why do you pretend I'm in charge?" Hogwood said. "Wouldn't Ironhall be pleased to know that the King had chosen a Blade in such an emergency?"

Wolf shrugged. "Just habit. A dagger up my sleeve. And I care nothing at all what Ironhall thinks. We must ride to Quondam today."

She glanced at the white nothing beyond the windows. "When the weather improves." The fear was back, suddenly.

"Come plague, earthquake, or tidal wave, I ride to Quondam today."

"Let me know when you leave so I can testify at the inquest."

"Soon. I'm on my way to interview the Baron."

"I just tried." Her eyes glinted at scoring a point. "He's still unconscious. One casualty died in the night—"

"Which one?"

"The cook. One of the grooms is capable of answering simple questions now, but can add nothing new."

"Good work," Wolf conceded. "I'll go and try my hand. If I'm not in the infirmary, you'll probably find me in the gym."

An hour later he was little wiser. The witnesses' estimates of the invaders' numbers ranged from eighty to a thousand, so he was inclined to trust Lynx's guess of three hundred. There had been at least two of the cat-masked warriors on stilts, and the farmer who had witnessed Lynx's fight with one of them confirmed that the freak had singlehandedly felled two Blades and another swordsman. He also insisted that the monster had managed to get back on its feet afterwards. That sounded impossible, but others had seen its corpse in the bailey later.

Wolf's need to reach Quondam was urgent, for this was the fifth day since the attack. The wind was definitely dropping, though, and he could wait a little longer.

He went across to the gym and learned that Tancred could now beat him black and blue at sabers, as he had been able to do with a rapier for the last half year. The lad was a wonder. Bowman swore he was the best since Durendal, and certain to start winning the King's Cup as soon as he joined the Guard. Some of the lesser lights ventured to try out against the killer, too, and a couple gave him a worthy workout. Aware that he lacked patience to be a good instructor, Wolf tendered what advice he could, and those who could recognize the gulf between fencing as a sport and real-blood sword fighting were eager to learn from a man with so many scars.

But noon was approaching and he must leave soon to reach Quondam before dark. He found Hogwood in the library, going over incantation scrolls with Intrepid, who was sitting very close to her. They looked up at the newcomer as if he ought to kneel.

"A clear need for Veriano's Excoriation," Intrepid said.

"Don't bother, I'm leaving anyway," Wolf retorted. "It's a fine after-noon for a ride."

"You can't see your nose in front of your face out there, man. I know that you wouldn't want to, but even you can't be crazy enough to risk the moor in this weather."

"Watch me. Have I left out anything, Inquisitor?" Wolf handed his report to Hogwood, who performed her usual instantaneous reading and returned it.

"The pattern of injuries," she said. "I have seen no wounds except your brother's that could not have been caused by clubs like the one Sir Intrepid gave us. Broken bones and cracked skulls are commonest. Cuts and puncture wounds are largely confined to the men-at-arms, and a couple of male servants, both large men."

Annoyed that he had not seen that, Wolf sat down at the next table and reached for a quill and inkwell. "So the teeth were reserved for se-rious opponents? Why?"

"It would seem that the invaders hoped to disable rather than kill, but I cannot suggest a reason. Sir Intrepid, I need a few words with Sir Wolf."

Intrepid's face flushed to match the red in his hair. He sprang up and strode out the door, slamming it loudly behind him.

Wolf signed the report and sealed it. "The snow's stopped, almost."

Hogwood said, "You do not seriously intend to set out across the moors in this fog?"

"I have a compass."

Her mouth and neck were tense with fear, but he could not tell whether she dreaded the journey or something waiting at Quondam.

"Sir Wolf," she said with unusual respect, "will you answer a question?"

"Ask it and see."

"This is not just nosiness. It is relevant to your mission today. Ac-cording to Sir Intrepid, you have slain more Blades than I was informed. Eight, he says."

"You are surprised that your bosses tell lies?"

"And I have also learned that the very first of your victims, Sir Hengist, was your closest friend here at Ironhall."

The sort of friend a man finds only once or twice in his lifetime; the sort of friend a man would die for. Wolf just nodded. Words to an inquisitor must be carefully dispensed.

Hogwood said, "There were witnesses when he died, including inquisitors. Deliberate cold-blooded murder, I was told."

"An indiscretion. But Hengist was the first, and once a man develops a taste for blood it soon becomes a habit. It really is time to leave now. I'll have Intrepid send a courier—"

Her eyes were very large and very dark. "Candidates Hengist and Viper were bound as Blades to the Duke of—"

"Don't call him that! Garbeald was *trash*! And when even the King had to admit it and sign the warrant, someone had to arrest him."

Only Blades could hope to arrest Blades, so Vicious went in person, taking twenty of the Guard. His scar and his hatred of inquisitors dated from that night. That was the start of the slaughter, although they hadn't known then that the Thencaster Plot was coming and there would have to be many more arrests.

"Garbeald fled, with his Blades," Hogwood persisted.

"Of course. But I fail to see what this has to do with—"

"They were cornered at Hobril. Garbeald was taken into custody, but only after Sir Viper had been killed and Sir Hengist gravely wounded."

"Don't forget the other casualties, Inquisitor. Be exact. Four guardsmen, two inquisitors, and six men-at-arms. Commander Vicious almost lost half his face that night." *Oh, how those two fought! The entry in the Litany did not do them justice.*

She grimaced. "The fighting was over, the Duke in custody. An inquisitor was applying conjured bandages to Sir Hengist, trying to save his life. You pushed him aside and ran your sword through the prisoner's heart. It was cold-blooded murder."

"Was that what happened? The witnesses disagreed."

"The Blades all lied, yes. You escaped without even a reprimand."

Not true. Vicious upbraided Wolf for being so public, but he was harder on Florian and Sewald for not doing their work properly earlier.

"Your best friend, and you murdered him!"

"When you are older, you will learn not to listen to gossip."

"Don't you dare patronize me like that!"

"Grow up. It's time to go." Wolf headed for the door.

He must not, would *not, remember Hengist drenched in his own blood—gasping in agony, yet tortured even more by the intolerable shame of having betrayed his king and failed his faithless ward. He and Viper had fought like legends against impossible odds and now he faced certain madness when Garbeald was hanged, as he was. Cruelest of all memories was the dawn of hope in his eye when he saw his old friend arrive and the relief when Wolf reached for Diligence. . . . The nod.*

"Wait!" Hogwood shouted, jumping up and slamming her hands on the table. "Then Sir Jared, Sir Warren. And *Quintus!* The champion! You actually went in alone against two—"

Wolf turned in the doorway. "I am going to Quondam now, Inquisitor. If you prefer to remain here and jabber with all the old women, I will quite understand."

"Listen to me! Those Blades wanted to die, yes?"

"Definitely irrelevant."

"So do you!" she yelled. "Don't you understand? Right now, you're setting off across the most treacherous ground in Chivial in dense fog. That's suicide! Ever since you killed Hengist you've been trying to kill *yourself.*"

"If you believe such nonsense, girl, you're in the wrong profession. See that report gets sent to the Council."

Wolf slammed the door on her.

II

Skilled huntsmen knowing all forms of spoor . . .

1

Tam and two Ironhall hands were perched on kegs around a crate, playing a game of straws. They had three layers on top of the bottle and matters were getting interesting, with six copper groats at stake. Wolf waited until the next straw was in place. Nothing collapsed.

"Tam, good chance to you."

Tam looked up warily. "And to you, Sir Wolf."

"Can you guide me to Quondam in this?"

The boy glanced out the window, pushed hair out of his eyes, and said, "Naw, sir. Not today."

Wolf flipped a golden crown, flashing like sunlight in the gloom. The men exchanged wondering glances. Stable hands never saw gold.

"Naw, sir. Too dangerous." It was Tam's turn to play. He added a coin to the stakes and chose a straw.

Wolf said, "Two crowns."

"Stop it!" Hogwood said at his back. "Only an idiot would go out on the moor in this weather."

"All men are fools for gold." Wolf was conscious of other hands closing in to listen. "Not for two?"

Tam licked his lips, shook his head.

"How about four?" Wolf counted them from one hand to the other. "Four gold crowns to guide me to Quondam. That'll buy you a fair wife and a share in two oxen."

"Stop it!" Hogwood yelled. "You are tempting the boy to kill himself."

"Six, then? Six crowns will rent a farm, buy a fishing boat." Clinking coins, Wolf looked at the others and was surprised that none of them spoke up. "No takers on six? Then I'll go by myself. Greg, saddle me a horse."

"I won't!" the hostler said harshly.

"Then I'll do that myself, too. Come, Tam, you'll feel guilty all your life if I die and stupid if I don't. Name a price."

Tam was sickly pale. He licked his lips. "Make it ten, Sir Wolf?"

Was that the biggest fortune he could imagine? "Ten it is. To be paid at Quondam gate."

Tam touched a finger to the heap of straws, dropping them all. He stood up. Wolf surprised him by offering a hand to shake.

"Courage becomes a man. Brains are for cowards. Follow when you dare, Inquisitor."

"Burn you!" Hogwood said. "Burn your guts for tinder! Saddle one for me, too, hostler." She wheeled on Wolf. "And we'll take a spare saddle horse in case one goes lame, and a packhorse with food and bedding, you hear?"

Wolf said, "If you insist." He had been planning to do so. "See to it please, Greg." He went into the stable office to wait by the fire. Hogwood followed.

"Finding the grownups' league a little scary, Inquisitor?"

"*Stop babying me!* I find your condescension as repellent as your morbid pursuit of danger."

"You must have done well in vocabulary class." He liked her glares. Other inquisitors he had worked with had kept their corpse faces in place all the time, and she rarely used hers. He must not start thinking of her as a desirable woman, though. That road would be scarier than the moor.

"Tomorrow morning would be safer," she said. "We'd only lose a few hours."

"Any job worth doing must be done right, which means losing no hours in this case." He risked a smile, a real smile, not the permanent fanged leer that Quintus had given him. "It really isn't that dangerous! The fog is not thick enough for us to fall off a cliff and the bogs are frozen. Tell me about dower rights."

"The baron's debts swallowed everything the King gave him to marry Celeste. If he died, his widow could claim all of whatever pittance was left. If he'd caught her in adultery, he could have divorced her and she'd have lost her dower rights. That's what kept your brother out of her bed."

Aha! "So his sons had motive to make sure she died first." There had to be a sane reason somewhere behind the madness.

Sweet Dolores gave him a look worthy of Vicious in one of his well-named moods. "Two middle-aged farmers struggling to keep their households fed hire a few hundred cutthroats to paint themselves brown, run half-naked through a Secondmoon freeze, break into a fortress, kill dozens of innocent bystanders, and abduct a baroness? And they keep it all secret? His Majesty's Office of General Inquiry had no forewarning of this atrocity at all, Sir Wolf!"

"The raiders departed in ships, so the cutthroats were hired abroad."

More eye-rolling. "And where did the money come from to do that?"

"Her jewels!" he said. "They took her jewelry as well!"

"Surely it have been cheaper just to poison her? And you are overlooking the club, or mace. It makes your theory absolutely untenable, Sir Wolf."

"What about the mace?"

At that point old Greg came to say the horses were ready.

Starkmoor weather could change in minutes. Compared to what had gone before, the fog was merely damp, not frigid. It seeped inside clothes like cold sweat and beaded the horses' manes. They rode in single file, with Wolf in the rear sneaking glances at his compass and growing steadily more impressed by young Tam's performance. He found the

Newtor turnoff easily enough, lost the road once, found it again, and brought them safely to the Great Bog. From then on there were no trails and no landmarks. He began veering to the west.

"Hold!" Wolf said, riding forward. "You're going in circles. I'll lead now."

Tam's face was white as milk, his eyes wide with terror. "I'm gone lost, sir!" He knew every rock and bush on Starkmoor and had never seen a map in his life.

"No, we're not lost. We'll head southwest until we reach the coast road, then cut back east again and come to either Quondam or Newtor."

It would not be quite that simple, of course, but the only really serious risk was that of the weather changing. The bog was actually easier going than the uplands, because the reeds and moss and general flatness had held the snow better, so there were no thick drifts hiding sudden hollows or rocks.

In a little while Hogwood rode up alongside him.

"If I'm trying to kill us," he said, "why are you here?"

She glanced sideways at him, studied the fog ahead for a moment, and finally said, "It's true, you know. You fit a pattern—your perfectionism, like polishing your boots all the time, your lack of close friends, your deliberate courting of danger. Quintus and Warren cut you in ribbons, I heard. You could have served your ward without having to endure that. People are not always aware of their own motives."

"My only motive is to guard the King. I was asking about yours."

Again a hesitation, but shorter than before. "Ambition."

"Grand Inquisitor Hogwood?"

"It's possible!" she said indignantly.

"I know. Women have been Grand Inquisitor in the past."

She seemed mollified, perhaps surprised that he knew that. "If I make a success of this assignment, I can expect to be promoted at least two grades. Maybe even *three*, Grand Inquisitor said."

They had started a conversation, which was promising. "So your family will be proud of you?"

"That remark is insulting! You are no gentleman."

"I never claim to be. Spare me girlish tears. You're doing a man's job, so I treat you like a man. You want compliments? Very well. Few men could have kept up with me on that ride from Grandon. You're tougher than most Blades I've known."

"How sweet of you to say so, Sir Wolf! Your honeyed words will completely turn my foolish head."

Wolf laughed. "If you can discover who abducted the baroness and why, you very likely will be in line to become Grand Inquisitor. You will certainly have a wonderful future in the Dark Chamber."

"Now you know my dark secret," she said, studying him under the winnowing-fan lashes. "I know your past. What of your future, your ambition? What will you do when you are knighted?"

If Athelgar ever dared release him. "Find a job. Men do not become rich in the Guard."

"That's not much of an ambition. What sort of job?"

What had she expected him to say? That he would marry and breed children? What woman would have him? "Assassin. I'm good at killing people and it probably pays well. My turn now. Why did Grand Inquisitor choose you for this mission?"

"I told you! I'm an expert conjurer. A major stronghold fell without even a warning. *How* it was done matters even more than *who* did it or *why, Sir Wolf.* Tell me why you stabbed Sir Reynard in the back."

"Tell me why it matters." That ended the conversation.

2

$\mathcal{A}$s daylight was fading, the travelers heard sounds of surf and crying seabirds, and soon arrived at a cliff top. By then the fog was so thick that the sea below was totally obscured, but they headed east, following tracks in the snow, until the towering ashlar walls of Quondam solidified out of the murk. The battlements overhead were invisible, and the great, gloomy pile seemed big as a mountain.

"Half an hour later and we'd have been spending the night in a snowbank," Hogwood complained.

Wolf thought he'd done quite well, all things considered. "Do so if you want to."

The drawbridge over the dry moat was down and the outer gates stood open, but he was not surprised to see the far end of the barbican blocked. Any garrison would be vigilant so soon after a massacre, even more so if the great Durendal was in charge. A voice called down a challenge.

It amused Wolf to answer with "Open in the King's name!" While he waited, he pulled out his purse. "Tam, your wages."

The boy shook his head wildly, making hair flap. "Didn't earn him, Sir Wolf. 'Twere you guided me."

"Take it."

"No, sir. Didn't earn 'im. You'd been finding th' place swifter enough witharn me."

"I wouldn't even have found the Great Bog before dark," Wolf said. *"Take it!"*

Tam flinched and held out a large and grubby hand, into which Wolf counted ten gold crowns. "This is for courage. The King has lots more where it came from."

Hogwood sniffed. "You are liberal with your sovereign's gold, Sir Wolf."

Wolf did not reply. Did she think they were not being watched? The story would loosen tongues and speed feet in his service.

The great gate creaked open far enough to admit a horse and rider. Wolf led the way through, into a bailey so depressingly huge that no end to it was visible, just towers and ramparts fading away into murky Secondmoon dusk. Men-at-arms in leather and steel closed in around. Resenting their suspicious glares, he dropped flatfooted into the slush to splatter them, then turned to see if Dolores needed help.

"Oh, an excellent choice!" Grand Master pushed through the throng and thumped his shoulder. "Welcome, brother Wolf! You bear the king's writ?"

Lord Roland was still tall for a Blade and bore his years as if he had thrown away a score of them. Age had not withered him. He wore an opulent sable cloak and a wide hat with osprey plumes, both of which would have attracted admiration in Greymere itself, and yet he made such garb seem totally appropriate even in that remote medieval stronghold. He had moved fast to be there and greet the newcomers, for he was noticeably dry in a company well wetted by the fog.

Wolf saluted. "Grand Master, may I present Inquisitor Hogwood? She was sent to investigate these odd events you report. Regard me as senior henchman."

Lord Roland bade her welcome, doffing his fine hat to bow, but his eyes were as bright as a pigeon's. "Before I turn over my highly questionable, self-proclaimed command here, Inquisitor, I should probably inspect your commission."

Hogwood gave Wolf a what-do-you-expect look. He produced the warrant, which Grand Master unrolled just far enough to read the name on it. He returned it with a knowing smile.

"As I said, an excellent choice. And young Tam Trevelyan! In this fog? Laddie, I never believed your dad when he bragged you could find your way over the moors blindfold and backward. Well done, Tam! Walt, see he is made welcome." He glanced up at the gloom, then at Wolf and Hogwood. "You have earned a fireside carouse, both of you, but there is one thing you should see as soon as possible."

Hogwood said, "Then lead on, my lord."

Lord Roland guided them through muddy slush, between decrepit sheds and paddock fences. They passed the looming mass of the Great Tower that Lynx had mentioned and the glazed windows of the baronial living quarters, slate-roofed, quaint, and shabby. Quondam had stood guard on its cliff for centuries, but the world was passing it by. However massive the great curtain wall, Athelgar's Destroyer General could batter a breach in it now in a few days. That was not what the intruders had done, though. They had known a better way.

"What news of Lynx, Wolf?"

"He is well, Grand Master, thanks to Master of Rituals's skill at commanding elementals. He seems likely to recover completely."

"I am joyfully moved to hear that. I did not dare to hope. The Baron?"

"Intrepid has not conceded the battle yet."

"He is a wonder." Roland chuckled and led the way up a long stair to the top of the wall, where only a low and rickety railing separated them from a forty-foot drop to the courtyard. On the outer side, two steps led up to the battlements. Wolf went up and leaned out between merlons, but saw nothing but fog. Surf rumbled very far below him. He followed the other two, walking along the rampart, noting that the slush had been well trodden.

In places the walls were capped by outlook turrets, crenellated and corbeled outward like swallows' nests to give the defenders an unobstructed field of fire. Grand Master halted when he reached the nearest.

"I don't suppose you can see, but the invaders came up the cliffs just below here. Their tracks were obvious when I arrived, straight up from a small beach called Short Cove. It would be a hard climb even on a dry summer afternoon, a path to tax goats."

Hogwood said, "Then straight up the walls, too? Human flies?"

"No. From here they went around to the gates and in through the barbican. There is a narrow path around the base of the walls, not one I should care to try at night."

"So treachery opened the gates?"

"Perhaps."

"Someone must have lowered the drawbridge and raised the portcullis," she insisted.

Grand Master nodded. "But one picket was killed up here on the battlements. He was thrown off, or fell over the rail—or jumped, perhaps—and died when he hit the courtyard. So the matter is not that simple. When the invaders withdrew, taking the Baroness, they very sensibly followed the main shore road down, which is much easier. And that was that. They took all their boats away, despite the men they had lost."

"How many men?" Wolf demanded. "How many boats?"

"I do not know. Normally you can see Short Cove from this turret, but no one has ventured down to the beach to look for traces, so far as I know. There were no boats in sight when the sun rose."

"What was the state of the tide during the attack?" Hogwood asked.

"I did not think to ask, I am ashamed to say." Roland was clearly annoyed at displaying human failings.

"Doesn't matter," Wolf said. "The question is, who opened the gate?"

The older man shivered and pulled his cloak tighter. "Let us discuss that when we go inside. What I really want you to see, Wolf—and you, Inquisitor—is up on that lookout."

He gestured again at the turret. It was unroofed and higher than the rampart, reached by a short flight of steps. Wolf went up them carefully, for there was no handrail and they still bore enough snow to make them treacherous. A hurdle had been stood across the top, as if to bar entry to the turret itself. It was a semicircular space surrounded by a crenelated wall, and at first glance it was totally empty. Most of the snow in it had melted to slush, and even before that the tracks would have been overlain and unreadable by anyone but a skilled woodsman. But in a few places he made out single, distinct impressions, and then he could only stare in disbelief.

A gasp at his shoulder confirmed that Hogwood was seeing what he saw. How could they possibly report *this* evidence to the Council?

Grand Master chuckled below them. "From your reactions, I infer that the prints have not all melted?"

With anyone else at all, Wolf would have suspected a joke in very bad taste. Hogwood did not know Lord Roland as he did.

"Who found these marks and when?" she shouted.

"They were pointed out to me as soon as I arrived." Grand Master sounded more amused than angered by her suspicion. "I have taken statements from the men who discovered them. I do not believe they are faked, Inquisitor."

Three toes forward, one behind. Here and there, in the most sheltered examples, imprints of great talons also. The brutes must be as big as ponies. Their feet were larger than human.

Hogwood's voice was shriller than an inquisitor's should ever be. "You are testifying that the gates were opened by invaders who flew up to this turret mounted on giant birds?"

"No." Roland's tone sharpened, bringing echoes of the authority he had borne for a generation as Lord Chancellor of Chivial. "I merely show you evidence I believe to be genuine. Draw your own conclusions. You can interview everyone in the castle at your convenience. Shall we go indoors now?"

3

Worrying about those monstrous bird tracks, Wolf followed Hogwood and Grand Master back down to the bailey. Chivian conjury was supposed to be the best in the world. So he had always been told. But flying horses were something very new. As they reached the bailey, he caught Hogwood grinning to herself. If the fortress had fallen to treachery, she would have faced a straightforward inquisitorial investigation, probably solvable with her skill at truth-sounding. Instead she faced a major problem in conjury, so she was gleeful. She was showing no signs of her former fears, although now she was in Quondam—discard one more theory.

In the hall where so many had died, the only signs of the battle were fresh rushes on the floor and two carpenters noisily repairing furniture. Lord Roland beckoned a passing servant to order fires lit in the guests' rooms, water heated, hot bricks piled in their beds, then led the way up a creaking staircase to what was obviously the baronial bedchamber, for a massive four-poster occupied most of it. If that been Celeste's bed for the last four years, there was nothing of her in the room, nor of the Baron either—no fine mirrors, no sumptuous robes discarded over chairs, no lingering scent, no silver toiletries arrayed on gilded furniture. Old and cramped and shabby like the rest of the castle living quarters, the room was as impersonal as an icehouse, although it was warmed by a huge fire of driftwood roaring welcome on the hearth. The only noteworthy object it contained was a rickety table bearing papers, ink, wax, and pens.

"I have been working in here," Grand Master said, "because the solar is colder than the ocean and the hall is too public. Pray make yourselves at home. So, Inquisitor—this maniac did not kill you on the way here?"

"But not for want of trying, my lord." She was giving him her professional haddock stare, which was a reminder that she almost never used it on Wolf.

Roland was untroubled. "He drives himself hard, which is why the King sends him out when lions prowl. May I suggest, brother, that you proclaim your commission tonight in the hall? Then, if the weather permits, I can return to my duties in Ironhall tomorrow. Another day of this thaw and the Great Bog will be its deadly old self again."

"It cannot melt so soon, my lord."

"It will flood and be more dangerous than ever."

"Well, I will read myself in if you think it necessary, Grand Master, but I have no intention of letting you escape so easily. I hereby appoint you acting warden of Quondam until His Majesty's pleasure be known."

An aging servant brought in a steaming copper jug and three tankards. Lord Roland poured, and they began sipping the fragrant brew. It burned Wolf's mouth and raised every hair on his chilled body.

Grand Master said, "I will serve as needed, but is that altogether wise, brother?"

"It is the smartest thing I can think of. My charge is to find out who did this terrible thing, not to wait around here in case they try to do it again. I cannot understand why the Council did not send the writ directly to you."

"I am sure the inquisitor can tell you that."

"I am somewhat puzzled by His Majesty's decision," Hogwood said.

He feigned surprise. "It is simple, surely? Ever since Thencaster, the royal buttocks rest uneasy on the throne. I am not Athelgar's man, I am an Ambrose leftover. He did not appoint me Grand Master, he approved my election. Now I send in a lurid dispatch, raving of improbable superhuman invaders at a time of year when no sane warrior leaves his fireside. I describe a massacre and announce that I am taking charge. I am the last man he would trust to investigate, Mistress Hogwood."

Or believe, if he began babbling about pony-sized birds.

"To question your loyalty after such a lifetime of service is blatant insanity, Grand Master," Wolf said. "But I have no wish to jaundice the royal eye against you. If you wish to suggest a substitute warden, I will accept your recommendation."

"I am sure you will find an excellent candidate close at hand." Roland's refusal was accompanied by just enough smile to take the sting out of it.

"You have been here four days, my lord. You have had time to query, investigate, and ponder. Tell us what happened."

Grand Master sighed. "Oh, I wish I could!" He scooped a sheaf of papers from the table. "Let's see . . . Sir Alden loaded twenty-five seriously wounded, including himself, into a wagon, and brought them to Ironhall. Seven of them died on the journey."

"And one since," Hogwood said. "A cook."

Roland made a note. "The dead he left here totaled twenty—that is two Blades, seven men-at-arms, two visitors, eight male servants, and a page. The invaders killed off any of their own wounded who could not walk, leaving fifty-four corpses behind. I have details here . . . and some drawings of those tracks you saw. I discovered that one of the grooms is an excellent artist. . . . An inventory of the enemy dead and their weapons. . . . Statements from everyone who was present, including a former forester. He read the invaders' tracks for me."

Hogwood had the grace to look impressed. "You have been diligent, my lord! You said, 'everyone'?"

"Everyone I could get. Some witnesses had fled by the time I arrived, but I had them brought back. Except . . ." He thumbed through the sheets. "This one . . . 'Nathaniel Dogget, his mark.' A page serving in the hall. His father was slain in the assault, so I let him return to his family. And two young pikemen—Rolf Twidale and Cam Obmouth. They were on watch, so they may have been slain and thrown over the battlements. Or they may still be running, somewhere very far away."

"Or they were abducted along with the Baroness?"

Roland shrugged, as if to say that anything was possible in a nightmare. "Everyone else awaits your pleasure, Inquisitor. I certify that my own account is the truth as I know it." He passed her the papers.

While Dolores flipped through them in her infuriating show-off fashion, Wolf said, "What I want to know is: Who were they?"

"Ah." Grand Master smiled. "There I can show you some evidence. I made a collection of the best examples." He rose and went around the four-poster to unlock an ironbound chest, returning bearing a familiar-looking wooden billet. "You have seen these? Sir Alden brought one to Ironhall, and we gathered up dozens here. We call them 'cats' paws' because they always have the same five claws, four on the top edge and one so far back as to be useless. The carving on the shaft varies, within narrow limits—cats, birds, flowers, serpents, other symbols I cannot decipher."

"If a rebel chief wanted to arm his men without attracting notice," Wolf said, "then he might dream up something like these and have them carved for him in any forest hut. The Dark Chamber keeps track of standard weapon manufacture and importation, does it not, Hogwood?"

She groaned. "Will you explain art to him, Lord Roland, or must I?"

"No need," Grand Master said, with more tact than truth. "Wolf knows that no Chivian artist could have carved these. They are too unlike any craft he would have ever seen. They are alien, strange. All artists work within their own tradition. This style is enormously different, exotic to our eyes. The invaders came from no nation in Eurania, I am certain."

"Their weapons did not, you mean?" Wolf asked.

"They did not. Their skin color is wrong. Their features are wrong."

"So they were not painted? Have you kept some of their dead for us to see?"

"I have kept all of them, because they do not decay in the sort of cold we have been having, and also the balefires for our own dead consumed all the firewood Quondam can spare. The ground is too hard to bury them. If this thaw persists, we may have to give them back to the sea. It brought them here, after all, and from very far away."

"You cannot say from where?" Hogwood asked.

Roland smiled inscrutably. "I cannot, but wiser men than I will be able to identify the clothes and chattels. Their dead wore strange garments and decorations. None of their weapons were metal, but they would be baneful enough. For example . . ."

He rose and went back to the chest in the corner, returning with what was obviously a wooden sword, its edges inlaid with obsidian teeth. "Be careful! These are as sharp as razors!"

Wolf took the hilt. "Impractical for battle, surely?"

"You could not parry with it, but two of our dead were decapitated by such weapons, each with a single stroke. No, that is a dangerous thing."

"But consider the numbers, my lord! Estimates vary but most witnesses thought there were between two and four hundred invaders. And they had the advantage of surprise. Against how many defenders?"

"About fifty men, plus a score of women and children."

"Yet the invaders' losses were more than ours, even if you include our wounded. Militarily the result was an upset and that can only mean that our weapons were superior!"

"Or their fighting technique was inferior," Hogwood said, taking the sword.

"Possibly." Grand Master handed Wolf a matching stone-toothed dagger from his chest of wonders. He was enjoying displaying the bizarre hoard. "Darts, glass-tipped, and this hooked stick is a thrower for them, called an atlatl, if memory serves. This one is decorated with gold leaf and shell, but most were plainer. They are about as deadly as bows in practiced hands, I'm told. About as many shields as corpses . . . look at this shield. Made of woven reeds, covered in fur and trimmed with feathers. And this one, of cane with a flower design made entirely of feathers. I wonder what Griffin King of Arms would say to this heraldry, mm?"

"They are superb work," Wolf admitted, "very light. They might block obsidian teeth, but a rapier would go straight through them. What beast sports this spotted fur?"

"Ah! Perhaps an ounce?" Grand Master smiled as if enjoying a secret joke. "When I was about the age you are now, brother, King Ambrose sent me on a very long journey to a land called Altain, far to the east of Eurania. In the mountains of Altain lives a very large, much feared, spotted cat called the ounce. It is twice the length of the lynx we find in northern Eurania, and is either related to the pard or a highland variety of it. I saw the skin of one and it looked just like that shield."

"You think the invaders came from Altain?" Hogwood demanded sharply.

"No, I don't. I still have much to show you. Headdresses, now. Fit for the palace ball. Like this. You would look sweet in this, Wolf."

He handed over a crown of feathers, brilliant blue and green, trimmed around the headband with gold. He followed it with dozens of extraordinary garments and artifacts, chuckling at his audience's amazement—a full-length cloak of iridescent feathers, sewn on what seemed to be very delicate cotton, sandals of some mysterious flexible stuff, fabrics of various dimensions and dazzling colors, displaying bizarre images of beings with multiple heads, human or otherwise.

"This is not just stranger than I expected," Wolf admitted. "It is stranger than I could have imagined." Athelgar was going to have a thousand fits.

"Now for treasures." Grinning, Grand Master brought a leather bag and returned to his seat to open it. "A disc of gold, inscribed in unknown glyphs. This bracelet seems to be pure gold, as are these two earrings. These other trinkets are copper. But what of this ornate pin? It held a man's cloak. Or these?" He passed over three carvings about the size of thumb joints, one of crystal and two of lustrous green stone. "Bizarre, are they not, but have you ever seen such delicate workmanship? A bird of prey and two cats?"

Hogwood and Wolf duly admired the little carvings but were puzzled by their backs, where each bore a stud like a small mushroom.

"What are they for?" he asked, just as she said, "What are they?"

"Why, those are labrets, of course!" Grand Master laughed. "Lip ornaments. The green stone is jade, I believe. I must report, Inquisitor, that I noted many corpses with pierced earlobes or lower lips and some with pierced noses, so I assume that much evidence was stolen before I arrived. Excepting one more item, these are the only true valuables I found."

"I will give you a receipt for them," Wolf promised, for they both knew how suspicious the officials in Chancery could be. "And I'll offer reasonable payment for any more turned in."

"Lips?" Hogwood tossed one of the labrets and caught it. "Surely, such a weight would drag down the lower lip and expose the teeth? Wouldn't that look ugly?"

"I'm told it does," Grand Master said solemnly.

"Told by whom?" she snapped.

"Where in the world has this stuff come from?" Wolf asked.

Hogwood frowned at his clumsy interruption.

"That is for you to determine." Lord Roland reached to the bottom of the bag. "This, finally. This is my favorite." He produced a flat package.

Holding it so Hogwood could watch, Wolf opened the cloth wrapping to reveal a roughly pentagonal plate about the size of a man's outspread hand. Its front surface was a mosaic of innumerable tiny fragments of greenish-blue stone, depicting the face of a cat with lips open to reveal the double row of fangs. The image would have seemed fiercer and more impressive had its eyes not been closed and its color not so improbably non-cat. The backing was a thin sheet of dark wood, which protruded slightly beside each ear and was pierced to take a thin leather thong.

"Curious thing," he said. "It would not be popular as a pendant, though. Most ladies would object to the weight. It would anchor a small boat."

"No woman would be allowed to wear that." Hogwood disentangled the thongs and extended them. "The right is shorter than the other. Both seem to be bloodstained. Was this cut by Sir Fell?"

Inscrutable, Roland sipped his drink. "Why do you ask?"

"Sir Lynx described a battle with a giant masked warrior. Sir Fell struck him on the shoulder, the right shoulder. The pendant fell to the floor?"

Grand Master smiled and nodded. "Correct. I admire your reasoning. We found it not far from Sir Fell's body, near the hearth. The giant's corpse lay just outside the door, and there was a fragment of thong embedded in the wound. It has a sinister beauty, this feline, wouldn't you say?"

"It is the emblem of a chief," Hogwood said, "like the cat's-eye swords you both wear."

Wolf resented that comparison. "Why are its eyes closed?"

"I'm sure that is significant," Roland said, "but again you must seek wisdom elsewhere. The stone is turquoise and the fangs seem to be seashell. Exquisite workmanship, you agree? It obviously belongs to the same artistic tradition as the cats on the clubs."

"It has that same strangeness," Hogwood agreed. "But surprisingly naturalistic, too."

"Like the labrets." That was Wolf's contribution to the learned confabulation.

"You will observe," said Grand Master, who had had several days to observe, "that the stones suggest the spotted rosettes of ounce fur."

"My lord," Hogwood said in her iciest inquisitor voice, "you are keeping information from us. Who told you those sticks were called at-latls? Who described labrets to you? Where have you seen these things before?"

Former Lord Chancellors were not easily browbeaten. "I am withholding no facts, inquisitor." His voice was tempered steel. "To burden you with guesswork would not advance your search."

"By law, you are required—"

"By law my Privy Councillor's oath takes precedence. I will answer to His Majesty."

"You told me yourself, Hogwood," Wolf said, "that your superiors withheld information from you to avoid biasing your thinking."

"I did not! What I said was—"

"Come, now!" Grand Master said easily. "I suggest you both leave your cares for another day and attend to your personal needs."

"First I will see these corpses you have collected," Hogwood snapped.

"Then I hope you have a strong stomach. Pray come this way."

Wolf followed the two of them down the creaking stairs, even more deeply troubled than he had been on the way up. He had never met the word *labret* before, but he had seen one the previous day. At Ironhall, among Grand Master's personal treasures in his bedchamber, he had noticed a thumb-sized golden stud bearing a serpent's head; he had admired its workmanship and assumed it was some sort of foreign decoration—the Order of the Golden Snake, perhaps. Now he knew what it was and why Lord Roland had known that excessively obscure word meaning "lip plug." He must know where his own labret had come from, and therefore what people had attacked Quondam. So why not say? He was withholding vital information from the King's inquiry. But to doubt Lord Roland's loyalty was blatant insanity. Wolf had said so himself only a few minutes earlier.

4

The Great Tower is no longer in use," Roland explained as they trudged through the bailey's slush, "except to stable bats and rats. The floors are unsafe."

He unlocked the door with a key as big as a boot. Having no windows, the lowermost room had taken on a foul smell of death, like a badly maintained outhouse. It echoed creepily. As Wolf's eyes adjusted, the wan beams of the lanterns reached out into the darkness to reveal row after row of corpses on the floor.

"First look at these two." Grand Master led the visitors to a pair of shrouded bundles on makeshift tables. "I had these wrapped in the hope of keeping rats away from them. I shall have to move . . . you may wish to have them moved to the icehouse, Sir Wolf."

"Good idea," Wolf said. "Others will want to see them after us." He opened the flaps of heavy oiled canvas and uncovered one of the mysterious raiders.

He was young, stocky, and certainly darker than any Chivian, perhaps chestnut color as Lynx had suggested, although it was hard to judge corpse pallor in that light. His only garment was a loincloth consisting of back-and-front flaps hung on a cord, but what he had lacked in clothes he made up in decoration, being painted in gaudy stripes of red, black, and yellow.

"His feet are muddy," Grand Master said, "so he came barefoot. The breechclout is universal, but most of the others wore more—tunics, capes, cloaks, feathered headdresses. Some had greaves on their legs and a few wore a sort of padding, like cotton armor. I wonder if this lad was of low rank or just demonstrating his courage?"

Hogwood peered at an obscene clot like a blackberry over his heart.

"Unlucky enough to encounter Sir Mandeville, I fancy," Roland said, "since he was the only one sporting a rapier. But physically this man is typical. No sign of beard stubble and only traces of a mustache, although he seems quite adult. Note that his lower lip has been pierced. He wore the crystal labret I showed you. You would think he would have preferred to invest in better armor instead."

"Noble birth and low rank?" Hogwood suggested. "Or lowborn and high rank?"

Wolf said, "The poor devil was even uglier than I am."

Grand Master shook his head. "Beauty is largely habit, Wolf. By our standards, his nose may be too long and his lips too thick. His eyes are not quite the shape ours are, but his companions all look much like him, so I expect his sweetheart considered him handsome enough. He was a husky chap, you must admit."

"Well, we can discard any notion that these men are Chivian, or even Euranian."

"Indeed you can. Look at the other one. He was certainly a leader."

Roland led the way to the other table, and Wolf guessed what they would find there from the length of the bundle—and he no longer expected stilts, although Lynx's estimate of seven feet tall seemed reasonable. This corpse's skin was the same color as the other man's, and at first glance he seemed lean, almost slender, but that was an illusion caused by his height, for his limbs were meaty. He had not been slain with rapier finesse. The corpse was black with dried blood; fragments of white bone shone in the gaping shoulder wounds. Lynx's cut along his ribs was trivial, but Fell's slash at his loins must have cleaved his liver in two. Yet still he had fought, this giant warrior, overcoming even Blades.

Ripped remains of a feathered cloak were glued to his body by caked blood, as was his breechcloth, but Wolf began his inspection by bringing his lantern close to the boots with claws on them that Lynx had mentioned and so nearly died from. They seemed strangely misshapen—too long and lacking a proper heel—and each bore four black, curved talons, which were not at all fragile. Those and the spotted fur itself were coated in clotted blood and fragments of flesh. Realizing whose that was, Wolf turned away in revulsion.

Or else just in refusal to accept an impossible conclusion.

"The claws seem to be retractable," Hogwood announced, studying the right hand. Hand, not glove.

Wolf forced himself back to the great feet, and this time saw them as they were—enormous furred paws. As a man, the monster had been a giant; judged as a cat walking on its toes, its proportions were more understandable. Legs, arms, and torso were human; hands and feet were not.

He and Hogwood converged on its head, which still bore a golden circlet supporting a plume of feathers. The helmet was no helmet, any more than the gloves were gloves or the boots, boots. Its eyes were closed, but the great jaws hung open, its huge fangs still bloody. No human mouth could have crushed Lynx's shoulder.

"Fire and death! Is it man or brute?"

"Man," Hogwood said. "It gave orders, remember?"

Lord Roland chuckled. "Would you argue with them?"

"Or both?" said Hogwood. "Man and pard combined? Or did he die while changing from one to the other?"

Wolf raised his lantern, its flame dancing as his hand trembled. His questions spilled out too loud, echoing in that sepulcher. "What do you know that you are not telling us, Grand Master? Did you not meet with such creatures back in the Monster War?"

"Not like this, I think. The chimeras we faced then were animals— unstable, short-lived, and no smarter than dogs. This big fellow was described as giving orders. He was in charge."

"Is he a shape-shifter, then? Did he fly up to the lookout as a bird, and change into a pard for the assault? Was he changing back when he died?"

"I know no more about it that you do, Wolf."

Hogwood's voice was calmer than Wolf's. "But you know where he came from, this half-man, half-cat. You know whose foul conjurations produced such a monster."

"I do not know, Inquisitor." After a moment Roland added, "The witnesses claim that he slaughtered three men singlehanded and two of those men were Blades. Does not a warrior so mighty deserve a better name than *monster?*"

"It will do until we find a better," Wolf said.

During dinner, Wolf talked with Sir Alden—peppery, bristle-bearded, and much weathered—who regarded him and his fancy writ with the contempt due to an upstart court jester. Yet this was the man who had ignored a badly broken arm to drive a wagon all the way to Ironhall through the rigors of a Secondmoon night. Many men were living now only because of that feat, notably Lynx. The old campaigner was a very impressive man, and Grand Master's smile in the background confirmed that Alden was the candidate he had in mind for acting warden.

Later the inhabitants of Quondam were assembled to hear the King's writ read out and give three cheers for Athelgar. This time Wolf dared not brag about bringing the culprits to justice. No one would believe him. He explained that everyone would be required to make a statement to Inquisitor Hogwood. He also warned that all booty belonged to the King.

"However," he added, "I will accept any souvenirs you turn in, with no questions asked. Gold I will buy for its weight in crowns, and I will pay fairly for anything else."

The hall being the only warm place outside of the kitchens, Wolf settled there to read through the statements Grand Master had provided. Others seeking warmth or company spread themselves around adjacent tables or just sat on the rushes to gossip and ignore the minstrel wailing up in the gallery.

Soon a nervous youth shuffled up to Wolf, watched by many eyes.

He laughed. "Drew short straw, did you? What have you got?"

Shyly the boy produced a massive thumb ring, intricately carved and too heavy to be anything but solid gold.

"Now here's a jewel fit for a king," Wolf said. "The castellan would have had money scales around somewhere?"

The lad returned in a few moments with scales and an eager, relieved grin. It took seven crowns from Wolf's expense pouch to outweigh his ring, but the boy strutted off with a negotiable fortune in place of stolen property that he would never have disposed of otherwise for anywhere near its true value.

Half the hall promptly stampeded in Wolf's direction. He bought a chain and a pair of silver anklets, but the fourth man produced a gold duck as big as a plum, in itself heavier than all his remaining coins. Obviously Wolf had bitten off far more than his purse could chew. He offered the man an IOU, written in a fair hand on parchment, payable on demand by any of the royal coiners and slathered with an imposing wax seal. The hard-bitten Westerther farmer just scowled and clung tight to his loot. The treasure-buying project had apparently sunk at the dock.

"May I assist?" Grand Master inquired, joining the meeting. "I have every confidence in Sir Wolf and will be happy to countersign his notes, if you wish. Then, even if His Majesty refuses payment, you can collect from me." He sat down and added his signet and signature.

That was good enough for the farmers and men-at-arms. They all knew of the great Lord Roland, both by reputation and now personally. With his help Wolf went on to buy earrings, bracelets, jeweled pins, necklaces, gem-studded sandals, labrets, ornate belts, deer, bees, monsters, birds, chains, bells, daggers, headdresses, cloak pins, and odd symmetrical plugs he was told had been extracted from noses. Steadily the pile grew. Gold and silver were easy to value by weight. For jade, crystal, turquoise, feather-work, and so on, he just set a price in consultation with Grand Master, refusing to haggle but trying to be generous without drawing the noose any tighter around his neck than it was already. He was convinced that he was doing his duty, yet he could almost feel the rough hemp against his skin. His authority did not extend to ransoming stolen property, for that was itself a felony, so there was a chance that Athelgar would simply seize the loot as his by right and charge Wolf with embezzlement of crown funds. He would enjoy doing that. It might even amuse him to leave Grand Master to pay the tally, but that was unlikely, because every Blade in the country except the Guard itself would rise against him. Still, Roland was taking a risk in helping Wolf, and they both knew it.

Eventually the flow of loot slackened. Some latecomers admitted that they had already smuggled their booty out of the castle, so Wolf promised them time to recover it and turn it in. Only after they had gone was he left alone with Grand Master and able to thank him.

Roland stood up, chuckling. "I don't think you're taking much of a risk, brother."

"I am guessing at the purity, remember."

"You have usually proved to be a very sound guesser, Wolf! Let's talk later." His smile implied *after your assistant has gone to bed*.

He strolled back to the hearth to resume his previous conversation with Hogwood. Wolf demanded a stout satchel and manhandled his loot upstairs, wondering what those two were discussing so earnestly.

5

Refusing Grand Master's offer of the baronial bedchamber, Wolf had selected a room in the attic. It was a poky cubicle, so small that the door opened outward like a cupboard's, and it held only a cot, a chair, and a clothes hamper, but the chair was much more comfortable than the lumpy bed, a strong hint that this was a Blade's lair. In the basket he found some items he recognized as Lynx's.

He poked up the fire and settled down to make an inventory of the booty he had just incurred for the royal treasury. The total cost came to a staggering thirty thousand crowns. The greatest part of that had been spent on actual bullion and he was gambling on his childhood experience in the mines, which made him fairly certain that the foreigners' gold was very close to pure metal, twenty-four carats. King Athelgar's coinage was not, for he had been debasing it, as the Guard knew, even if Parliament had not yet caught on. That meant that the beloved monarch could clear a profit of at least a hundred percent just by melting down the entire heap and coining it. Wolf considered that prospect the downside of an otherwise enjoyable evening's work.

The mystery of Celeste's abduction now seemed even deeper, for her jewelry had certainly not been the motive. What sort of raiding party came to battle dressed like a king's court? Even Baelish pirates, who loved to flaunt their ill-gotten finery, never risked it in actual combat.

Before morning he must complete yet another report, but what in the world could it say? And what could he do next? He was certain that the answers were not going to be found there at Quondam. Having seen the awful place, he could even find it in him to pity Celeste, imprisoned there for the crime of conceiving a child no one wanted— likely not even she at first, although Lynx had insisted she had mourned it as any mother would. Rescuing her from this captivity had cost the lives of almost ninety men, women, and boys.

Why?

The question waited for an answer.

Other people came upstairs and closed their doors and the attic grew quiet again. His accounts completed, he stoked up the fire and struggled down the ladder with his precious satchel. He found Grand Master still fully dressed, leaning back against piled cushions on the big bed, but he came alert at once.

"Make yourself at home, brother. Leave your cloak and dagger on the table and poke up the fire."

"I want to add my loot to yours," Wolf said. He did so and doublelocked the chest with a golden key, a conjury only inquisitors were supposed to possess. He declined Grand Master's offer of refreshment, and the two of them settled before the hearth with the air of men getting down to business.

"I did not wish to gossip in front of the inquisitor," Roland said, showing anxiety he had concealed formerly, "but tell me truly how Ironhall fares. Rituals is coping, you said, but how about the rest?"

"I think he may have rubbed some fur the wrong way."

Grand Master smiled. "Very likely. Most of them are terrified by novelty. He is not, and I wanted him to have a free hand to work on the wounded. But I should dearly like to return to my post and smooth that fur, Wolf, as soon as the fog lifts."

Wolf was horrified to hear the head of his Order pleading with him. "Of course! I will send an escort with you."

"I'm sure Tam will suffice. Thank you. Now, brother, a question. This is only old man's nosiness, I fear, but your companion puzzles me. Did you choose her?"

Wolf laughed at the thought of a Blade having carnal designs on an inquisitor. "I thought she was a boy."

Lord Roland shook his head, frowning. "Then what are Grand Inquisitor thinking of, sending a child on a man's job? They must have dozens of experienced agents who could have kept up with you on the journey. If she bungles the investigation, His Majesty will be much displeased."

"It puzzles me, too. She claims to have a doctorate in conjury, but I expect the snoops are up to something underhand, as usual."

"Now, now!" Grand Master waggled a finger. "They will have their reasons. Inquisitors spy excessively on the innocent, but they serve the same king we do, if in different ways. Once in a while they may satisfy what they see as His Majesty's needs rather than his expressed wishes, so the royal hands are not soiled."

"As in the case of Lord Musthorpe?" Musthorpe had been another Thencaster suspect, but had succumbed to a very convenient fever before the warrant for his arrest could be delivered. The Guard was convinced the Dark Chamber had poisoned him.

Grand Master shot Wolf a dark glance. "There are such things as coincidences." He could have pointed out that the Musthorpe's death had been so ambiguous that his Blades had eventually recovered from their bereavement, which was more than could be said of those the King's Killer had taken off the roll. "I want to tell you two things, Wolf. Firstly, I sent an appeal for help to Mother Fire Rose, prioress of the White Sisters at Lomouth. You know the lady?"

"No, Grand Master."

"Do not be deceived by her homely manner. She has a mind like a rapier. But she is old now and will probably send someone else."

"The cat-man was obviously conjured. What else do you suspect? His medallion?"

Grand Master took up the tongs and jabbed idly at the fire. "I'd be interested to hear the worthy Sisters' opinion of that, but not at all surprised if they fail to find any conjuration on it. Which brings me to the second thing. I kept secrets from you and the inquisitor, which was a foolish old man's whim. I will confess to you and trust your discretion."

Here came the golden labret. "That won't be—"

"No, please! I should have told you right away. My motives were very trivial. There is no evil secret behind this. It was just that all my life I have refused to involve my family in affairs of state, and I balked at doing so today, stupidly. The person I was shielding was my son."

"Oh?" Wolf had never heard him mention his family before.

"Andy was for many years a sailor, eventually master of his own ship, a trader and explorer of some renown. He always brought back mementos from his travels, and after one voyage he presented his mother with a jade figurine of a somewhat sinister-looking cat. He gave me a labret of gold, depicting a fanged serpent—with an explanation of what it was, of course, and the joking suggestion that I start a new fashion around court by having my lip pierced. Being a loving and dutiful son, you see. Can you imagine what old Ambrose would have said? Both trinkets came from wherever your invaders came from, for they show the same artistic style."

"So the next question is—"

"Where did he acquire it? Somewhere in that newfound world they call the Hence Lands. Exactly where I cannot recall, for he had many tales and it was long ago. Andy's only a farmer now. He lives in my old house, Ivywalls, just west of Grandon. If you wish to consult him, then I am certain he will eagerly provide what help he can." Grand Master glanced at his guest, and some trick of the light on his gaunt features cruelly emphasized the age he so rarely showed. "I did not mention him earlier because the Dark Chamber will—"

"Hassle him mercilessly, of course."

"Exactly. And, knowing Andy, I am sure he will react badly if he is not forewarned. At times he displays a streak of orneriness he claims to have inherited from one of his parents."

Suddenly Wolf had a lead, a light to follow, and his way ahead was clear. "I must return to Grandon very soon—to see tonight's haul of loot delivered safely, if nothing else. Also, I am sure there are no more answers here in Quondam. I do not think your son can be kept out of the matter entirely, but I promise I will not mention him to Hogwood until I have had a chance to speak to him myself."

"Then I am much in your debt, Wolf. Truly I am! I will give you a note of introduction. Once the situation has been explained to him, Andy will gladly help you track down these vicious killers."

"I do not see he need appear in the affair at all," Wolf said.

"Ah, but there is more." Grand Master sighed. "My wife was much attracted to the figurine, but she took a virulent dislike to the labret. She was a White Sister and not given to strange fancies. Although she could detect no trace of spirituality on my little snake head, she would not have it in the house. I took it to my chambers in Greymere, locked it away, and forgot all about it until after I left office. It is presently in Iron-hall. I will be happy to let you have it, if you see the need. I am sorry I kept this tale from you."

Wolf squared mental shoulders and said, "I am sorry for not being quite open with you either. Ironhall is so crowded that Sir Intrepid insisted on billeting me in your chamber last night. I saw your serpent."

Grand Master laughed with no trace of resentment. "As I tell the juniors, honesty is always the best policy! I thank you for not unmasking me before the inquisitor."

"It never occurred to me to."

Knowing that the abduction of Amy Sprat had been effected by men from the far side of the western ocean made the matter more mysterious, not less. Wolf said, "Make one more confession, Grand Master. Have you any notion, any wild wisp of a theory, to explain why these men should sail halfway around the world to this castle merely to abduct Baroness Celeste? At *this* time of year?"

Roland shook his head and went back to staring into the fire. "Not an inkling. It is incomprehensible. They must have traveled for months. Andy spoke once of seeing *naturales* in large canoes on rivers, but they have no seagoing craft, so far as I know. His Majesty has chosen you to solve one of the greatest mysteries of the age. He chose wisely, I believe."

"You never used to flatter."

Grand Master sighed. "You never needed it before. Now you need all the support you can get."

They sat and talked of lesser things until a sudden collapse of the fire warned Wolf that he had lingered too long, because his host needed sleep, even if he did not. He thanked Grand Master again for all his help and set off up the ladder to his garret. He had not bothered to bring a lantern down with him, but he had left the door ajar to let firelight guide him home.

Someone had closed it, and not the wind, because he had propped it with the chair.

Royal guardsmen went armed with a sword only. Standard livery did not include a parrying dagger, any more than it included plate mail, and the average Blade never bothered to wear one unless he was expecting trouble. *Nobody* picked fights with Blades! Wolf was an exception. He always carried a poniard at his belt and Sir Vicious had never told him to get rid of it, although he had blasted a couple of juniors who had tried to copy his example. Wolf also kept a stiletto in his sleeve, but no one knew about that.

Now he drew both dagger and *Diligence*. He took a very long time to raise the latch, and even longer to ease the door back far enough to peer in with even one eye. At that point he sheathed his blades and opened the door the rest of the way, faster but still silently.

The chair stood by the dying fire, and the person sprawled in it was Dolores Hogwood, apparently fast asleep. She was slender, but no one would mistake her for a boy now, and a man would have to be very greedy to complain about her figure. Her flowered robe had fallen open to reveal a shapely leg in its entirety, which hardly mattered because the silk was sheer enough to give him an excellent view of the rest of her as well. Very rich ladies might possess such gauzy, provocative garments, but normally they were only seen in brothels. Why would an inquisitor bring such a thing along on a mission to a wilderness like Whinmoor?

Oh, spirits, he was tempted! It had been a very long time since he had been alone with a pretty girl. Whenever he did find a woman who could tolerate his nightmare face, inevitably someone would soon mention his tally of dead friends—to her or her mother—and that always ended any hint of romance. Hogwood was not merely pretty, she was young, nubile, and gorgeous. She was clearly very much available. He was extremely tempted to provide what she had obviously come looking for.

He was even more tempted to pick her up bodily and hurl her out into the corridor.

He took several deep breaths to bring his mangled emotions under control. Then he quietly collected his baggage and tiptoed across the corridor to Hogwood's room. He gathered up her things—she was a lot less tidy than he was—and took them back to where she slept. When he left, he used his golden key to bolt the door behind him. It felt like a very stupid decision, but he was already a mass murderer. He had no wish to be a convicted rapist also. If the Dark Chamber wanted revenge for the death of Inquisitor Schlutter, it would have to be more subtle than that.

6

Wolf ran into his seductive assistant in the hall at dawn. She favored him with a full inquisitorial dead-fish stare, which was not just a way to intimidate witnesses; it could also be used to mask emotion. She should have been blushing a screaming scarlet. He suspected that he was, and tried to look angry.

"Grand Master is almost ready to leave. Have you anything to send with him?"

"No, Sir Wolf."

That was a relief. If she planned to accuse Lord Roland of withholding information, she was not yet ready to commit her beliefs to paper. Or she did not trust him to deliver the report, perhaps.

Out in the bailey a full spring day was getting itself organized, complete with sunshine and birdsong—just strident gulls and terns, admittedly, but better than nothing. Water was dripping everywhere and the mud was ankle deep already. Grand Master and Tam duly departed, taking with them three cat's-eye swords.

Wolf located Sir Alden in the stable, grooming his horse. "We must dispose of the bodies." *We* meaning *you*.

The old warrior rested an arm on the horse's croup and regarded him without enthusiasm. "Throw 'em in the sea?"

"The King won't want corpses washing up all along his coasts."

"We're short of firewood. If weather turns bad again, we're like to freeze."

"I understand the floors in the Great Tower are unsafe?"

Alden waited a beat before nodding. "Baron won't like it."

"The Baron is past caring and we cannot tolerate fifty rotting carcasses. Use whatever fuel you have on hand to burn them and treat the floors as your emergency store. So ordered in the King's name, if that's how you want it."

For the first time Alden ventured a smile. "Aye, Your Majesty."

Wolf ordered the two sample bodies moved to the icehouse as Grand Master had suggested, and then began making a gruesome inventory of the others as each in turn was carried out—guessing at ages, noting war paint, clothes, body piercings, and so on. They might have dressed like fops, they might be uglies by Chivian standards, but they were an impressive collection of brawn. All were men in their prime with the right calluses for warriors, but curiously few scars. His study had no real purpose. Mostly he just did not know what to do next. He was a swordsman, not an inquisitor.

He had assumed that Hogwood was working her way through the castle, questioning every witness in turn to make sure they were hiding nothing—a procedure likely to be as futile as what he was doing. Not so! When about half the bodies had been loaded on to the wagon that served as hearse, he was startled to see his black-robed assistant disappearing out the postern gate. He caught up with her as she neared the top of the cliff. She was walking blind, her attention entirely on something she held cupped in both hands.

"Fine morning for a stroll," he remarked. "Mind telling me what you're doing?"

She did not look up. "An extreme longshot, Sir Wolf. I have a tracker and I am following the Baroness's trail. It is faint, but I seem to be obtaining consistent results."

She was walking in the muddy track the raiders had left on what Grand Master had called the main shore road. Wolf had watched conjured tracking before, once even trailing a fugitive who had fled by boat, but this particular scent was more than five days old.

"What did you use for a drag?"

"I left it wrapped up in one of her ladyship's dresses overnight."

The trail descended rapidly, more like a slightly less steep strip of cliff than a road, and the footing was greasy as hot butter. Hogwood ignored the terrain, detouring safely around the boulders and chasms as if she trod in the exact prints of the warrior who had carried Celeste down this precipice by moonlight. Poor Celeste! Wolf wondered if she had been still screaming as she came this way.

In places on that death-defying scramble he made out individual prints preserved in mud or slush—marks of shoes, mostly, also bare feet, but no tracks of giant birds, or cats.

"Did you find out about the tide?"

"Yes," Hogwood said vaguely, still staring down at the tracker. "It was at the full. Extraordinary."

Wolf ground teeth in silence for a few moments before giving in and saying, "Why extraordinary?"

"The night of the full moon? The highest tide of the month? Baelish raiders would never beach boats then and risk being stranded for two weeks."

"Two or three hundred strong men could move a few boats a long way down a beach."

At that moment Hogwood slipped and almost fell. He caught her elbow to steady her.

"Don't touch me!" She shook him off, keeping her eyes on the tracker.

He released both her and his temper. "You were ready enough to be manhandled last night."

Here the way crossed a very steep gully. She began edging sideways down the slope. "And evermore I will be remembered as the girl who couldn't even lay a Blade."

He followed. "I'd have been happy to start your education, but I didn't want you waking the entire castle shouting rape."

She stopped abruptly at the bottom, standing in the stream itself so he almost walked into her. She was still bent over the conjurement. He thought she was losing the track, until he realized that her shoulders were shaking.

"What's wrong?"

She gasped. "Please!" She was *laughing*! "Don't say things like that. I have to concentrate."

"Like what?"

"Like the idea of *you* raping *me*. Be quiet. This is important." She started climbing out of the gully.

Wolf followed in furious silence. He was certain now that Grand Inquisitor had sent Hogwood along with the express purpose of compromising him somehow. The doctorate of conjury was a lie or a red herring. There was no other explanation for the negligee or last night's blatant performance. Today's derision was simply another tactic.

When the trail arrived at the beach, he said. "If you weren't trying to stage a rape, what was the reason for that disgusting performance?"

For the first time she looked at him, dark eyes mocking. "Disgusting? Spirits, can't you guess? I fancied a man and a Blade was the obvious choice. Women can enjoy bed sports, too, you know. Or haven't you ever noticed?"

That was absurd. He had not been using Blade charm on her and nothing less would make a pretty girl lust after the ugliest man in Chivial.

"Decent women do not even think that way, let alone talk like that."

"By the seven saving spirits! A Blade lecturing on morality? And how can he know what a woman thinks? Now be quiet, Wolf, or you will make me break the thread."

He was just plain "Wolf" now, was he?

Short Cove was well named, just a scoop out of the cliffs, a hummocky, boulder-strewn meadow with a small stream draining away into a pebble beach. The tide was out, the air pungent with odors of sea-weed, raucous with the screech of seabirds.

"Very tricky harbor," he observed profoundly, staring out at some jagged rocks not far beyond the breaking waves. "And shingle, see? Won't find any marks of boats on that." He looked up at the cliff and a solitary turret of Quondam visible above it. "They did go straight up, as Grand Master said! They didn't find the road in the moonlight, just made a beeline for the fortress, right up the face of the . . ."

He was talking to himself.

Hogwood had not turned toward the sea, but was still following her tracker's guidance, stumbling across the coarse bent grass of the meadow. He went after her. He should have used his eyes to better effect, for the passage of so many men had left an obvious trail there, too. It terminated in a wider trampled area, as if the invaders had milled around for a while. The newcomers' arrival had interrupted birds, which clamored up in a noisy blizzard, screaming protests as they circled overhead.

"No!" He drew his sword, yelling in fury as he ran forward to where they had been feeding. Beyond the trampled area, the invaders' trail ended between two rocks. On the landward side the grass was crushed and flattened; on the other it stood proud, rippling in the cold salt wind. On either boulder . . . things not to be looked at.

"Not the Baroness?" Hogwood said. Her face was almost green, and he doubted his was any better.

"No. The pikemen." They had found the missing Cam Obmouth and Rolf Twidale. The birds had found them first, though. One or two tried to return and he chased them away with more oaths.

"You keep these vermin off and I'll go and fetch some horses," he said. "Or would you rather go?"

"Please." Hogwood was shrunken and huddled, every inch of her con-veying horror and nausea. "I should . . . I ought to look around here first."

She seemed more childlike than ever. If he opened his arms she would fall right into them. And hate herself ever after. She had too much pride. So had he, after the previous night's display. He was tempted, though.

"What is there to see?" he said, deliberately harsh. "The raiders didn't leave by boat. They almost certainly didn't come by boat. They traveled by conjuration." The mystery was becoming ever more bizarre. "You're the expert, Hogwood. Did they come all the way from . . . from, er, wherever they came from . . . by enchantment or just from a ship off-shore? And why take two prisoners and then butcher them in cold blood?"

"Some sort of ritual," she muttered, looking everywhere except at the bodies. "No octogram that I can see, but travelers have reported con-jury performed in other ways in other lands. There was a fire, see?—here, between the rocks."

Wolf shooed birds again. "Go and tell Sir Alden. I'll stand watch."

She nodded gratefully and hurried away.

The victims' clothes lay in the grass. They had been stripped naked and then stretched out faceup on the rocks. Whatever had been done to them after that had left the boulders drenched with blood, but he could make out no details because the birds had picked the corpses almost to bare bones. Then the invaders had disappeared. This was quite clear, for their trail entered the area and no trail departed. The bodies had been left for the gulls and the insects, and somehow that made him angrier than anything else.

He strode up and down for the next hour, warding off the shriek-ing gulls and waiting for the horses, and swore dark vows of vengeance on whatever monsters had perpetrated this horror, whoever they were, and wherever they came from.

7

There was something morbidly fascinating about any very large fire, and especially a funeral pyre on a cliff edge, with yellow flames stream-ing in the sea wind, the harsh lamentation of gulls. Wolf had spoken the eulogy, just a few words in the King's name, thanking the men who had fallen in his service. He had let Sir Alden hurl the brand onto the pile to start them on their way. It seemed wrong to make Twidale and Obmouth share their funeral with their murderers, but there was no other practical solution, so he had made sure that the Chivians' carefully wrapped remains were placed at the top, in the spirit of the old sagas, where slaves and captives were sacrificed on the balefires of warriors.

"Now it is safe to break the news to the families," he said. "Who can guide me?"

"I'll do that," Alden growled. "I knew them, you didn't."

Wolf did not argue very hard. Later, when the pyre began to collapse, the old man rode away into the gathering dusk and the other spectators began wandering back to the castle, for the wind was chill.

Wolf remained, brooding. His mission was complete, as far as he could take it. Now he must return and deliver a very unwelcome report to the Council. He must advise the King that there was still no explanation for the abduction of Celeste and he was powerless to punish the guilty or even to defend his realm against any future attacks. No keep was secure now, no one safe against attack.

Hogwood spoke at his elbow. "You mourn."

He turned with a sigh. "You think a mass murderer can't be a hypocrite too? I just love funerals. I was standing here planning some more."

She shook her head. "You are right to be bitter."

"And you were right to be frightened of me. What exactly did Grand Master tell you last night?"

"We talked a long time. I don't remember exactly."

"Inquisitors forget nothing. He told you something that completely changed your mind. Until then you were scared of me. Right after that little chat you tried to throw yourself into my bed. That's been your mission all along, hasn't it? The massacre was just a sideshow for you. Your real job was to seduce me, and the thought of sleeping with a murderous ogre had you seriously affrighted. Then—behold!—suddenly you were eager. My looks didn't change. What did? What lies did Grand Master tell you?"

Hogwood's unforgettable eyes were brimming over with innocence. Or tears brought on by the wind. "I know he wasn't lying. He said you killed your best friend because he asked you to. Sir Hengist was horribly wounded and fated to go mad if he didn't die first. His death was a mercy. After that you were bearing as much grief as any man could, so when other Blades had to die, you appointed yourself executioner. Whenever possible, you spared your brothers from having to share your guilt."

Wolf clung tight to his temper, but he was furious that Durendal had dared to gossip about him to an outsider. "That's nonsense. I just enjoy killing."

"Not according to Grand Master. The real culprit, he says, was King Ambrose, who gave away so many Blades to the nobility in his old age."

"No! The real culprit was that worthless incompetent Athelgar, who provoked the nobility into rebellion!"

"It was not his fault that they had Blades to defend them! He could not even arrest them for questioning."

Wolf was very close to shouting at the stupid wench now. "He didn't need to arrest them! He could have dealt with them the way he dealt with Celeste—put them under house arrest and use their own Blades as jailers. Then nobody would have had to die!" *And nobody would have had to kill.*

"But in the event," Hogwood said, "those Blades did have to die and you took the guilt on yourself. You never stoop to making excuses, Grand Master said, so fools don't see that. Most Blades just ignore you because they don't even want to think about it, he said. But some knights at Ironhall know better. Sir Bowman, for example, a highly respected former deputy commander. He wasn't shunning you."

"He's a friend."

"You have no friends. Friendship hurts you so much you don't dare to make any more friends."

"We grownups don't believe in fairy tales."

"I am not a child! Didn't your amazing Blade vision notice even that much?"

"You seriously expect me to believe that Roland's homily gave you a sudden impulse for a tumble in bed with a killer?"

She nodded. Perhaps it was a trick of the wind and the sunset, but he could have sworn he was seeing an inquisitor blush. She must have a doctorate in blushing.

"I don't think so," he said. "Then why pack a negligee? I think the Dark Chamber wanted a handy assassin on staff and you were assigned to trap me. What sneaky conjuration can you pull on a man in bed, Inquisitor?"

She said coldly, "No conjuration will work on a bound Blade, Sir Wolf, as you well know."

Certainly no enchantment could warp his loyalty without killing him, so Wolf was not seeing the whole plot yet. "Your technique is not exactly subtle, is it? Did you fail seduction classes?"

"No, my instructors praised me highly." Sarcasm slid off her like rain off a duck. "We were taught how to snare normal men by leading them on and then refusing them satisfaction, but that trick is useless with Blades. Subtlety will not work on them."

He couldn't resist asking, "What does?"

She sighed. "Anything. Just being female. You're the first Blade in history to refuse a chance like that. The negligee was a mistake."

Such brazen vulgarity disgusted him and emphasized how young she really was. "And all this to avenge the late, unlamented Inquisitor Schlutter?"

"No. The purpose was what you said, to enlist you into the Dark Chamber."

He stared at her.

She stared right back. "Truly."

He had suggested that without believing it. The trouble with snoops was that you never knew how many layers there were. Catch other people in a lie and then you'd probably dig out the truth, but with inquisitors you never knew what you were expected to disbelieve and what other lies lay behind the ones you could see, and what lies lay behind them in turn.

"You need an experienced assassin? You expect me to kill for love, not money? Or is there money involved as well? How much a head?"

"There is no point in negotiating."

"But you admit you were assigned to snare me?"

She shrugged. "My mission was to hire you, but I have learned that Grand Inquisitor were mistaken in their assessment of you. You do not kill for pleasure, so you will not accept the offer I was authorized to make."

"I love the smell of fresh blood."

"No," she said sadly. "You are not a violent man at all. The only time I have seen you lose your temper was with the seagulls. You were right when you said I feared your reputation, but now I have come to know you, I am truly sorry for you, a gentle man trapped in a vile job."

"I don't want your pity!"

"Was that what you were demonstrating last night?"

Wolf reminded himself that no man could ever win an argument with an inquisitor. Or a woman. "I am still curious to hear your offer. It will have to wait until after I'm released, though. Commander Vicious will not look kindly on me if I keep asking for weekend passes to go and stiffen someone." Not that Athelgar would ever release him.

"That was to be part of the offer," Hogwood said. "Release."

He stood very still while his mind flailed like a flag in the sea wind. Yes, he had heard her correctly. The wind was stronger and colder, making him shiver desperately. *Release? Freedom?*

"Even the Dark Chamber cannot offer that."

"Yes, it can." Was that triumph glinting now or just mischief?

"Athelgar would never agree."

"He can be persuaded."

"To use conjuration on the King is treason. Even to tamper with my binding is."

"There is another way."

"Wolf!" a voice cried. "Wolfie!"

Two people were riding in from the moor.

He forgot Hogwood. He yelled, "Lynx, you crazy man!" and went bounding over the gorse to meet him. "Did Master of Rituals say you could get out of bed?"

His brother peered down at him, trying to force his usual amiable grin from a face so pale that it shone like ivory in the gloom, a rictus of pain and exhaustion. "Of course not. Haven't made up the rest of my blood yet, is all."

Lynx began to dismount, lost his balance, and cried out in alarm. The mare was already spooked by the fire. Wolf tried to catch him, but Lynx fell like a mountain and flattened him into the heather, while his mount went bucking and kicking off across the moor. It was a humiliating accident to happen to a pair of Blades.

Lynx found Wolf's top end and demanded, "You all right, Wolfie?" Then he collapsed on top of him again, howls of laughter alternating with gasps of pain as his scars pulled. Wolf was so happy to see him better that he began laughing too, still pinned under him.

The other arrival was an angular figure in a practical tweed riding costume, staring bleakly down at them. "Sir Wolf, I presume?" she inquired icily.

Lynx caught his breath with an effort. "Sister Daybreak," he gasped. "Got no sense of humor." He went back to laughing.

8

No, Sister Daybreak could never have laughed at anything in her life. Receiving Grand Master's appeal in the absence of Mother Fire Rose, who had been in Grandon all winter, she had traveled from Lomouth to Ironhall the previous day and been very unamused to discover everyone sworn to secrecy and unable to tell her anything.

The following morning Wolf's crazy brother had insisted on riding over to Quondam to retrieve *Ratter* and had offered to escort her to Lord Roland. Master of Rituals had sworn he would never arrive at Quondam alive, and had been proven unpleasantly close to right. Lynx didn't care. He had his sword back, having met Tam and Grand Master on the way, and he never stopped grinning and joking while they loaded him on a litter and carried him into Quondam.

Sister Daybreak resembled an angular tree trunk washed up on the shore, bleached, scoured, and stripped of its bark. Her voice was a raven's croak, her face bleaker than Starkmoor, slashed into deep lines of disapproval. She especially disapproved of grotesques holding high office and read Wolf's warrant through twice before accepting that His Majesty could have made such an error.

Later, after she had dusted herself off and changed into her White Sister robes—white steeple hat and all—she was able to disapprove of a cramped baronial bedroom as the site of an important meeting. Hogwood was there, of course, applying her fishy stare, and Lynx sprawled back against pillows on the bed, working his way through half a roast goose and three flagons of beer.

Daybreak sipped water and declined further refreshment. "I am starved for information, though. Even Grand Master told me almost nothing. There was a raid, I understand. Men were killed?"

"Between eighty and ninety," Wolf said. "They took greater losses than we did, because they used ineffective weapons. Such as this." He had the chest open by then and began, as Grand Master had, with one of the cat's-paw maces.

Sister Daybreak did not approve of it. She felt it, sniffed at it, and passed it back, shaking her head. "A curious thing, but it bears no trace of spirituality."

He offered a gold labret. She hesitated over that, frowning distastefully. "No. Nothing. What is its purpose?"

She disapproved of that, too. And so it went. Wolf produced only a small fraction of the artifacts in the chest, because if there had been any really serious conjurations there, she would have sensed them from downstairs. Some she seemed to find more distasteful than others; some she examined with extra suspicion—peering, sniffing, touching, even seeming to listen to them—but her conclusion was always the same: None had been conjured in any way.

Wolf did not believe this. The raiders would not have believed it either. Any conjurer would insist that good-luck charms were useless, as likely to summon bad fortune as good, but no soldier would go into battle without one. Even some Blades wore them. Love charms were effective, which was why they were illegal. The status that cat's-eye swords gave their bearers was mostly granted by law, but a White Sister could smell spirituality on them, left over from the binding ritual, and only they could undo that binding, so the swords did have power. The men who attacked Quondam had decked themselves up in gold, body paint, and jewels for some good reason.

Like Grand Master, Wolf left the pard mosaic plaque to the end. Hogwood had compared it to a cat's-eye sword, and on viewing it a second time he could see how its closed-eye arrogance reeked of power. Its owner had certainly not needed any emblem to enhance his stature or fearful aspect, but if the pendant had been the secret of his shape-shifting, its loss had caused him to remain half man and half cat.

Sister Daybreak recoiled from the sight of it and seemed loath to touch. She peered at it quickly, then thrust it back.

"Nothing! Repulsive, but no spirituality."

"Let me see that!" Lynx demanded, licking his fingers and showing interest for the first time. He grabbed it when Wolf held it out. "Whose was this?"

"Your furry friend."

Lynx stared at it sadly for a moment. "Then I claim it by right of conquest!" He knotted the ends of the thong together and hung it around his neck.

"I'm not sure the King will permit that."

"You know where it is when you want it." He unlaced the neck of his doublet so he could tuck the pendant inside. "It's safe on me."

But was he safe from it? Sister Daybreak was staring at him as if he had filled his shirt with pig manure.

Wolf said, "Thank you for your reassurance that we have no evil conjurations to worry about, Sister. There are a couple of bodies down in the icehouse that I would appreciate your looking at also. If you feel up to it, we can attend to that and then go into dinner. Or it can wait until tomorrow."

Was that a wisp of a grin crossing Hogwood's face?

Sister Daybreak's conical hat rose straight up, with her head still in it. "By all means let us get it over with. I have come a long way unnecessarily, but I wish to make an early start homeward tomorrow. Daybreak begins at dawn, I always say!"

"An excellent principle. Inquisitor, if you would be so kind as to lead the lady down to the icehouse, I will follow as soon as I have locked these trinkets safely away."

As the two women trooped out, Lynx yawned and stretched his arms. "For the last four years I've dreamed of sharing this bed. You weren't the one I dreamed of sharing it with, of course, but I'm sure you won't mind . . ." He flashed an arch look. "Unless you have plans to share it with someone else?"

The thought had crossed Wolf's mind less than a hundred times in the last hour, but he said, "No. You're welcome to rest there as long as you don't mind candles burning all night."

"How's that slinky little inquisitor of yours, anyway?"

"She is definitely off-limits as far as you are concerned."

"Ah? Like that?"

"No. Like nothing, but you stay away from her."

Lynx chuckled—knowingly, as he thought. He made no move to put his boots on, so Wolf left him where he was and hurried down the stair after black robes and white robes. He very much wanted to hear Sister Daybreak's assessment of the cat-man.

As it turned out, he knocked her hat off.

She had been warned! The woman was abrasive and arrogant, much too sure of her own opinions, but Wolf repeated that she was about to view a man's corpse; he had been severely wounded and was not a pretty sight.

She knew better. "I have seen cadavers before, Sir Wolf. Pray be speedy lest we freeze."

The icehouse was small and underground, set in the shady south-west corner of the bailey. At that time of the year it was almost completely full, and the two corpses had been dumped in on top of the stock, the big one at the front. There was very little headroom and Sister Daybreak's towering hat was ridiculous. She was bent double, her nose almost touching the tarpaulin that Hogwood and Wolf were attempting to open one-handed. All three held lanterns, which cast an eerie golden light and make the work tricky.

"There!" Hogwood said, as they dragged back the last flap. The corpse lay on its back with its front paws crossed on its belly. Wolf was at the head, Hogwood at the feet. Daybreak stood between them and for a moment she peered back and forth in incomprehension, trying to make sense of the gruesome display.

Then she gave a sort of yowl and leaped back, straightening up and slamming her head against the vaulted roof, dropping her lantern. Wolf and Hogwood let go of theirs in grabbing her, so suddenly they were a Blade and an inquisitor supporting a stunned White Sister between them in total darkness.

Wolf said, "I've got her. Can you make a light?"

The Quondam icehouse was not well kept. The floor was not only wet, as was to be expected, but also muddy, and in the process of hoisting Daybreak over his shoulder he trampled her hat into oblivion. She started coming around as he carried her up the steps to the bailey. She was a tough old slab of driftwood, though. After a rest beside the fire in the hall and a glass of mulled wine, she wanted to go back to work right away. Hogwood bandaged her scalp wound and Wolf ordered her to bed in the King's name.

9

Wolf had hoped to leave the next day, but he knew Lynx would insist on going with him—anything to see the last of Quondam—and was not well enough to travel. Although Wolf's conscience might have rejected that as a reason for delay, he did have legitimate business to finish and morning brought a drumming downpour that was certain to turn snowy roads into quagmires. He found Sir Alden leaning against a door-jamb scowling at the weather.

"Good chance to you, Warden."

The soldier transferred the scowl to him. "You saying I'm to be Acting Warden?"

"I suspect it will be a permanent appointment. Name your stipend and I'll swear you in."

"King'll want a lord."

"He'll have trouble finding a real lord willing to live here. What he needs is a damned good soldier."

"Horseapples! Ought to rip the place down."

Surprised to hear his own opinions coming from such a source, Wolf said, "Why?"

Alden spat into the mud. "If you can't hold a fortress, you raze it so your enemy don't use it against you. I'd need a thousand men to hold this place against what came by a week ago."

Even without the raid, Quondam was an outdated symbol of royal power, serving no purpose to justify its running expenses. Wolf certainly intended to tell the Privy Council so, but kings had strange ideas about symbols and honor.

He wondered how many more insights Alden might have. "That's very valuable advice. Can you tell me why the raiders took the Baroness?"

Alden's leathery scowl softened. "She's just a trophy, poor lass. Always was, I'd say."

"And I'd agree. Why this time, though?"

"Ah!" The old warrior sighed. "If you can storm a stronghold and carry off the lord's woman in all her finery, then you've proved something. Doesn't matter who they were or where they came from. They took her home to show their king what they'd done."

Brilliant! Flaming brilliant! "I should wrap you up and send you to the Council!" Wolf said.

"Try it."

"No thanks."

Alden spat again. "It cost them, of course. They lost more men than we did. They need better weapons. Wonder why they didn't take any of ours with them when they left?"

"They didn't?" The man was a mine of insights!

"Maybe a few. Haven't counted. Could match what's left against the smoke stains on the walls."

"Do that!" Wolf said. "Yes, please do that!"

Later the White Sister appeared, a little whiter than usual, wearing a goodwife's bonnet over her bandage. She insisted on taking a second look at the freak corpse in the icehouse. After staring hard and long at it, she capitulated with better grace than Wolf had expected.

"I cannot detect conjuration on this body."

"You mean he was born like that?"

"Of course not. I mean that my skills are unable to detect this form of enchantment. I sense a dark, ingrained evil that I do not understand. It is alien to everything I know. Everything I told you yesterday may have been wrong." She shut her mouth with a click of disapproval.

"Lord Roland warned me that such might be the case." Wolf caught Hogwood's eyes shining at him in the lantern light. He had promised to share all his information with her, but he had not shared that.

III

The chase is reserved to the lord . . . lesser orders [hunt with] snares and nets

1

The royal standard no longer flew over Nocare. His Majesty, it seemed, had returned to Greymere, in the heart of Grandon. Athelgar rarely stayed in one place for long, but he had been excessively inconsiderate, even for him, in moving Court in such weather. He could travel in his fine waterproof coach, but hundreds of people must have toiled for days in a solid downpour to satisfy his whim, and uncounted wagons had churned the highway to soup.

Having no need to return to Ironhall, Wolf and his companions had followed the coast road through Newtor and Narby, then cut up to Flaskbury from Brimiarde, but they had not had a dry moment the whole way. Three people and five beasts in mortal misery had plodded tracks that were rivers of mud and waded fords that were raging torrents. He had sent no reports ahead, because they could not arrive before he did. The Council would not expect mail in such weather.

Every day Lynx grew visibly stronger. Often he was his amiable old self, blissfully happy to be released from jail at last; at other times he would retreat into sullen despair, remembering that he had lost his ward, the only Blade ever to do so. Wolf had no comfort to give him. Even if Celeste were still alive, the world was too big for one man to search it all.

Wolf avoided Hogwood as much as he decently could, partly because he did not want her asking what else Grand Master had told him, but mainly because he distrusted his own weakness. If she convinced him that she could really arrange his release from the Guard, he might agree to anything—anything short of murder, surely? Yet, would killing strangers for the Dark Chamber be any worse than killing friends for the Blades? He also distrusted the looks he saw her giving him at times. Her childish efforts to appear a woman only made her seem even younger. Grand Master's absurd excuses had transformed the infamous Sir Wolf into some sort of grotesque martyr in her eyes. Dread had become fascination, and an odious duty had been sugar-coated with adolescent infatuation. What could he say or do to make her hate him again, to remove the temptation before it wore him down?

He had intended to drop off Hogwood and the treasure at Nocare and go on to visit Grand Master's sailor son by himself, but Athelgar had foiled him. Wolf happened to be in front, leading the packhorses, when he recognized the turnoff to Ivywalls from Grand Master's directions. He took it.

"Where are you going?" Lynx shouted.

"To see a man who may be able to tell us where your ward went."

"Who?"

"Baron Roland," the inquisitor said.

Wolf turned to glare. She dead-fished back at him.

Lynx repeated, *"Who?"*

Sir Durendal had been created Baron Roland of Waterby on the day he saved King Ambrose's life in a fabled feat of arms. He had been promoted to earl when he became chancellor. Since he could not use both titles, his son was allowed to use the lesser one by courtesy, a favorite trick of the nobility. But how had the inquisitor known?

The way led over a gentle ridge into a snug valley, a haven of fruit trees and well-drained, tidy fields. Countryside rarely looked fair in winter, but that did, combining clean lines of good maintenance with the ramshackle comfort of a place that has had a few centuries to settle into its role. Roland's son might be "only" a farmer, but he was a good one. The house, when it came into view, was ancient, well-kempt, and impressive.

A chorus of barking announced the visitors' approach. When they reined in at the steps, a bulky, white-haired worthy was already awaiting them between the pillars. He seemed too old to be the Baron and too dignified to be a servant. Dismounting, Wolf let his cloak fall away from his sword hilt. The watcher snapped his fingers and men came running from nowhere to take the horses. Had he given some other signal, no doubt the hands would have arrived with hounds and weapons. It was slickly done, suggesting that everything at Ivywalls would be slickly done.

Wolf offered Grand Master's letter. "Wolf of the Guard to see the Baron if he is available."

The old man acknowledged the seal with a smile that would have looked good on anybody's grandfather. "His lordship is always happy to welcome Blades, Sir Wolf. I am Caplin, the butler. If you and your companions would be so kind as to come this way. . . ."

Wolf offered Hogwood his arm and followed. He had no qualms at leaving the raiders' treasure unattended, because she had warded the bags. Anyone trying to open them would receive a memorable surprise.

Their sodden outer garments were taken; they were shown into a snug library where a fire warmed the winter evening and glinted on shiny leather chairs. The paintings on the wall were tasteful yet intriguing. Rugs and tapestries looked exotic and non-Chivian, while the bronze statuette was classic Isilondian; yet everything was of such quality that nothing jarred. This was how the truly rich lived, those who could afford to be comfortable and did not need to flaunt their riches by adhering to the current fashion. Although none of the visitors was in uniform, the admirable Caplin was no doubt already explaining to his employer that a guardsman and a private Blade had come calling with an inquisitor.

Wolf said, "Hogwood, how did you know who we were coming to see?"

She turned from her study of the book titles, wearing her professional corpse mask. "A lucky guess, Sir Wolf."

"Based on?"

"Lord Roland was evasive. He is beyond suspicion himself so he was protecting somebody else, and you cooperated with him, so the problem was probably trivial. A former Blade is unlikely to have family he cares about, other than children. You said we were coming to see a man, so I guessed an eldest son."

"Standard inquisitorial sneakiness!"

"Thank you!" Her glee lit the room.

Lynx guffawed. "She has your measure, Wolfie."

"She needs a good spanking."

"Likes the kinky stuff, does she?"

"Wolf!" Hogwood took two strides to the fireplace and lifted down a small greenish carving. "Look at this!"

The men joined her. Grand Master had called it a "somewhat sinister-looking cat," but it was only a kitten. Yet . . . was that a subtly malign look in its eye? Yes, this might be a very tricky feline when it grew up. The style was by now unmistakable.

"Which of you is Sir Wolf and how may I assist you?" The man in the doorway was no better dressed than his butler and not much less bulky, although he was carrying muscle, not fat. He seemed around forty, weathered and dark, not especially tall, but with a self-assurance that did not appreciate uninvited guests meddling with his possessions. He held Grand Master's letter. Although he did not look like his father, Wolf recognized the glare.

He bowed. "I am Wolf, my lord. Your honored father sent me to ask you where you got this cat."

The scowl darkened.

"May I present Inquisitor Hogwood . . . Sir Lynx of the Blades. We have ridden for four days to ask you this. My commission—"

Roland took the writ, raised his eyebrows at the royal seal, glanced over the text, then returned it with a half-bow. "My father is clearly not the only one who holds you in high regard, Sir Wolf. How may I help you?"

Wolf held up the kitten.

The farmer's laugh had a solid, trustworthy sound. "You were serious? Sigisa. Don't tell my father, but I won it in a dice game in a tavern."

Sigisa? That meant nothing. Wolf said, "Where—"

"But it came originally from Tlixilia."

Hogwood said, "Oh, of *course!*" as if that explained everything.

2

"Ⲧ̄he Hence Lands were discovered about forty years ago by some Distlish sailors blown far to the west by a storm. . . ."

The Baron had suffered no argument—business could wait, the visitors would spend the night at Ivywalls, and his home would be honored by their presence. He offered every comfort, even dry clothes kept on hand for travelers, there being only so much that one could pile on a horse.

Wolf found himself bedecked in a burgundy brocade jerkin finer than anything he had ever worn. Later, enjoying a superb meal, and sipping seductive wine from a crystal goblet, he decided this was how all swordsmen should go adventuring. Hogwood shimmered in a jade silk gown belonging to Baroness Maud herself, who was an ivory figurine, gracious and aristocratic. Small children romped somewhere in the background in the care of servants.

Magnificently fed and dry for the first time in days, three grateful travelers settled down in the library with their host. A couple of their bags had been brought in and set down in a corner to reek of horse. The Baron swore the oath of secrecy without demur, knowing that he would learn nothing at all if he didn't.

"Distlain," he said, "managed to keep the discovery quiet for a few years, long enough for its men to establish that there were scores of islands involved, some of them very large. Finding that the people there were defenseless against properly armed and trained soldiers, the Distliards claimed the territory for their king. Other nations learned what was happening and failed to see why King Diego should own all that territory. Distlain established bases in the area and tried to keep the rest of Eurania away by force. Times got exciting. They still are, from what I hear."

Obviously he was enjoying a ray of excitement in the drab boredom of winter. "Once or twice, I even found myself fighting my King's friends in the company of his foes. Baels, no less! Father never knew that, fortunately."

He stopped to smile inquiringly at Hogwood. Men always smiled at her, but in this case she had indicated by a minute readjustment of an eyebrow that she wanted to ask a question.

"I've often wondered, my lord," she said, "why Baels didn't discover the Hence Lands first."

"I'm sure they did. Many of the spices and dyestuffs they traded that were supposed to be from the distant east had really come from the west, but they kept the secret. The Hence Lands offer little for Baelish tastes, though. Most of the islands are small and have little or no water. When there are *naturales* on those, they're starving primitives, living on fish and roots and any visitors they can get their hands on." He chuckled heavily. "When they say you will stay for dinner, they really mean it. The Distliards take them for slaves, but the Baels never bothered. Slaves don't travel well and Baelmark could always pick up better slaves closer to market.

"Then there's the big islands, and some of them are enormous, bigger than Chivial. They're jungly and mostly mountainous: Fradieno, Mazal, Condridad, and others. Their culture is primitive, better than the small islands had, but producing nothing worth stealing from a Baelish or Distlish point of view. The Distliards have colonized them, setting up plantations for cotton and spices and so on, none of which would have any appeal to a Bael. Baels don't farm. The *naturales* still hold out in the interiors in many places, raiding the Distlish towns.

"Finally there's the mainland. We had several names for it in my day, but now it seems to be one big continent. Leastways, no one's found a way around it yet. It has huge mountains near the coast in places. And it has real cities. The greatest of those is Tlixilia."

Roland paused, studying the wine in his glass. "That's properly the name of the imperial city, but it got applied to its empire, which includes many lesser cities, and sometimes people extend the name for the whole mainland. Now the Distliards have taken to calling the city itself El Dorado, the place of gold. It is reputedly bursting with gold and art and precious things, magnificent buildings. Those who have seen it rave about it, but they're all *naturales* of one tribe or another. I don't think any Euranian has seen Tlixilia City itself and returned to tell of it. The Distliards claimed sovereignty over El Dorado, too, and sent armed expeditions inland to explain to the Emperor that he was now King Diego's vassal. The Tlixilians disagreed then and haven't been convinced yet."

"Good fighters?" Lynx asked, picking his teeth with a fingernail.

"Yes and no. I've never met them. From what I heard, they have no iron, no bronze, just gold, silver, and a little copper, so their weapons are edged with stone. They make armor from cotton padding, and it's more effective in that climate than steel plate, but most of them scorn to wear it. They fight for odd reasons, in odd ways. They try not to kill their opponents. They prefer to take prisoners—for slaves, and also for food, because they have no cattle or other large livestock, and a man tires of beans. That hampers them, because it's harder to overpower a man than it is to kill him. One-on-one in an equal contest, they're fighters as fierce as any in the world, but put fifty Euranians against fifty Tlixilians with their own styles of fighting and the Euranians will win every time. Luckily the odds weren't even. The *naturales* outnumbered the Distliards by a thousand to one, and blotted them. The Distliards regrouped and began organizing the Tlixilians' local foes against them. Things started to get bloody.

"But the Tlixilians are still independent and the Distliards daren't set foot on that part of the mainland. They maintain a few trading posts on offshore islands, notably Sigisa. That's where I picked up the cat. It had come from the mainland, but I don't know how—looting being more likely than honest trade. Battle honors, perhaps. I got a gold lip stud the same way. Did Father mention that?"

"I saw it at Ironhall," Wolf said. "A serpent."

Roland nodded. "Mother had been a White Sister and detested that thing. She couldn't say why, just that it was evil."

"You haven't mentioned Tlixilian conjury, my lord," Hogwood said.

"Sir Wolf hasn't asked me to." He tempered the remark with another not-fatherly smile at her before looking to Wolf. "Relevant?"

"Very."

"I'm no expert." He pulled a face. "I do know it's different from ours. It's reputed to be extremely powerful, but that may be just the Distlish excuse for their battlefield disasters. Tlixilian conjuration is largely or entirely devoted to warfare, and it involves human sacrifice. All their conjurers belong to one or other of two great military orders. You ever heard of the *jaguara*?"

Hogwood frowned; the Blades shook their heads.

"It's a pard, a huge spotted cat, very deadly. That carving represents a *jaguara* cub. The Tlixilians are reputed to name their conjurer-knights after the *jaguara* and the eagle, the night hunter and the day hunter. There are wild stories about feats of conjury in battle. If you believe them, their spiritual power comes from ripping the beating hearts out of sacrificial victims."

Hogwood and Wolf exchanged glances.

Lynx snorted. "Pig wallow! What sort of conjury would that be?"

"Very potent!" Hogwood said. "But limited in scope. I can't see doing a healing that way, because you would be invoking death, not revoking it, but you could summon some of the elementals in immense strength. The heart itself combines five of the eight: earth because it is a solid, water and fire from the blood it pumps, plus time and love. Add deliberate death and you have gathered power to fashion massive conjurations. And chance!" she added quickly. "You said they used captives taken in battle? That supplies the element of chance. Seven out of the eight! Only air is missing."

The Baron chuckled. "They commit their atrocities on top of towers. That would bring in air elementals, wouldn't it?"

"Of course!" Dolores looked pleased.

Wolf shuddered. "But what do they do with this foul ritual?"

"Well," said the Baron, "for example, I've heard tell of an enchantment called 'the Serpent's Eye' that turns whole companies of troops into slobbering idiots—conscious, but unable to use their arms even to defend themselves. There's tales of sentries found impaled with their own pikes and tents full of sleeping men where every second man had his throat cut without the others hearing a sound. And ambushes galore—armies rising out of the dust. I'm just repeating hearsay, you understand. Distlish propaganda."

"Believe it."

Roland raised eyebrows expectantly. It was time to pay the piper.

"Ten days ago," Wolf said, "several hundred Tlixilians came ashore at Quondam Castle. They probably arrived by conjuration, but we can't prove that. They stormed the fortress, carried off the castellan's wife, and then disappeared. We lost thirty dead and about half that wounded; their death toll was over fifty. It took less than an hour. They departed by conjuration, ritually slaying two young men in the process."

Roland's face had gone slack with shock. "*Here?* In *Chivial?*"

"Not far from Ironhall."

"That is incredible. What for?"

"We don't know. A warning? A threat? Retaliation? Is it possible that Tlixilians don't know the difference between Distlain and Chivial?"

"Very possible. The distance is enormous. It takes months to . . . They came in *Secondmoon?*"

"In bare feet in Secondmoon, some of them. We collected feather cloaks, labrets, gold, jade. Lynx, here, was almost massacred by one of your jaguar knights. We have his corpse—half man, half jaguar. Probably some of the eagle knights you mentioned were present also."

The Baron shook his head in amazement. "The Council must be seriously concerned."

"The Council is going out of its mind," Wolf said with relish. "Fortunately your father was available to take over. He did a wonderful job. It was he who identified the unknowns' gear as having come from the same place as your cat and the serpent head. Inquisitor, if you would be so kind as to open the bags? I want to show you some artifacts, my lord, and ask you to confirm his opinion. I am sure His Majesty will reward you well." That was a lie. "Lynx, show his lordship your pendant."

The doublet provided for Lynx was strained across his chest, so the neck laces were already loose. He reached into his shirt and brought out the mosaic plaque of the jaguar. He pulled it up for the Baron to see. The Baron held out a hand for it. Reluctantly Lynx took it off and passed it over.

Roland examined it with interest. "I've seen some of this mosaic work before. Definitely Tlixilian style. I won't swear it's from El Dorado itself, but somewhere very close by. Horrible thing, isn't it?"

Eventually he returned the image to Lynx, who put it on quickly, without looking at it. Hogwood was still working on the bags, so she hadn't seen it either, and apparently Wolf managed to control his face enough that the other men failed to notice his shock. The jaguar's eyes were now open.

3

*L*ater they sang songs while Lady Maud played on the virginals; they drank a nightcap with a toast to His Majesty, and they trooped upstairs to bed. Ivywalls was old, built to the antique plan of rooms laid out in sequence. Thus Hogwood's clothes, cleaned and dry, were tidily set on the dresser in the first, Wolf's in the second, Lynx's in the third, and the host and hostess continued on beyond that, since they would naturally use the most private chamber at the end. The others must just remember to draw their bed curtains.

There were no fires in the fireplaces, but in Wolf's room a pretty chambermaid was running a long-handled pan of hot coals back and forth under the covers. He gave her a farthing, thanked her, and bade her good night. She curtseyed as best she could without dropping the pan or meeting his eye.

She caught Lynx's though. "Could touch up your sheets again, sir? Was just about to."

He beamed. "Please do. I like my bed snug."

She hurried into his room. He followed. Wolf waited for her to leave. She didn't.

The door closed. Evidently she had agreed to warm the bed personally—either on the promise of a larger tip, or just because Blades were so cuddly.

Wolf marched in before things went too far. There was no sign of the girl, but the bed curtains were closed and the warming pan had been safely placed on the hearth. Lynx had his shirt off and was just about to blow out the candles. The thong was still around his neck, which must mean he wore the plaque both day and night.

He turned to scowl. Wolf scowled back, but less at him than at that hateful thing snarling amid his brown chest fuzz. His scars were as gruesome as ever.

"I want that pendant now, please."

"Tonight? Why tonight?" His refusal was worrisome but not surprising.

"I don't need it but you certainly don't. Have you noticed how it's changed?"

"What of it?"

Aware that the girl would be listening, Wolf said, "Lynx, that's a potent conjuration, the symbol of a jaguar knight. It's active. It's *alive*. Remember the thing that wore it? You want to change into one of those? Take it off *now!*" Wolf reached for it.

Lynx slapped his hand away. "No."

"Lynx! I'm your brother. And if you won't trust your brother, then I order you in the King's name."

"Right of conquest, remember?" He folded his arms. *Ratter* still hung on his belt and the move put his hand closer to her hilt.

"No. *He* conquered *you*. Please give it to me."

"No." Lynx grinned, little-boyish. "I'm a bound Blade, Wolfie, which means I'm as proof against conjuration as any man can be. Can't a lynx carry Mommy's picture next his heart?"

"It belongs to the King. Hand it over!"

"No! I have taken a fancy to my pussycat. I won't go to jail for it, but it means more to me than it does to Athelgar. So no. I will not hand it over. Want to fight me for it?"

"You are crazy!" Wolf left before they terrified the girl out of her wits. Back in the good old days, Lynx had done anything he said without a blink.

More trouble—the door to Hogwood's room stood open. She heard Wolf return and appeared in the opening, still in the jade silk dress.

She said quickly, "Don't panic. I didn't come to— What's wrong?"

Wolf removed his cloak and hurled it at a chair. It slid to the floor. "That plaque Lynx's wearing. Its eyes are open."

"No!"

"Yes. Set with amber and obsidian, I'd guess. But it's an active conjurement and he won't give it up."

She smiled sadly. "Poor Wolf! I do think Lynx's old enough to look after himself. Have the King take it off him tomorrow." She took a deep breath and went back to the prepared speech: "Don't panic. I didn't come to steal your virginity, just to deliver my report. Here." She held out some sheets of paper. They quivered slightly.

He stayed where he was. "What's it about—the raid or me?"

"Both." She spoke in a rush. "I said you carried out your mission flawlessly and I totally failed in mine. I agree with everything you've been saying about the raid. I gave you all the credit. They were from Tlixilia, they may have thought they were attacking Distlain, they may return, and Lady Celeste was taken as spoils of war, not for any personal reason. Baron Roland's talk of eagle and jaguar knights is ample confirmation of your theories. You want to hear what I wrote about you?"

"No."

"May I sit down?"

"No."

She stuck her tongue out at him. "I forgot to mention that your manners are terrible. I did say that you are a reluctant killer, that you would never kill for money, or even to win release from the Guard, no matter how much you despise the King. Grand Inquisitor will have to find another assassin. Read it!"

"I don't want to read it." He threw his sword on the bed, scabbard and all. "You couldn't make the King release me." He began unlacing his jerkin to see what Hogwood's reaction would be.

"Yes, we could."

"How?"

She smiled. "Suppose the King must choose between you and Sir Vicious? Which one would he keep?"

"Vicious. But how . . . ?"

"There is no rule that a Blade cannot marry. He does not need permission."

Wolf caught his breath. "That wouldn't . . ." Yes, it would. *Of course it would!* Vicious detested inquisitors with a passion. Rather than have one skulking around Blade married quarters, he would throw Wolf out of the Guard. In a flash. Release! His heart raced. "That raises prostitution to new heights. Or do I mean depths?" He flung his jerkin after the cloak. It slid off the chair, too. "You would sell your body just to please your superiors in the Dark Chamber?"

She had expected him to say something like that. "I told you the Chamber is the only family I have ever known. How many girls accept a husband their parents have chosen because the match is good for the family? I admit the thought frightened me when they told me you were a multiple killer and the ugliest man in the Guard, but they were just warning me. The choice was mine, they said, and now I know you, I like the idea. Truly I do."

He was tempted to tell her to prove that by undressing and getting into his bed. He didn't because he was certain she would do exactly that. This was her last chance to earn her promotion. Fortunately she had taught him how vulnerable he was. He knew that he would crumble like a puff ball at one touch of tenderness. He removed his doublet and this time scored a bull's-eye on the chair.

"You can't keep your eyes shut for the rest of your life."

"Wolf!" She straightened up and stamped her foot. "Forget your face! It's a fighter's face and it was probably a very handsome face once.

Scars don't worry me. You're not a slobbering lopsided village idiot who will breed deformed children. You've got a strong, attractive body and you're a strong, kind man. Women don't care what men look like on the outside, just what's inside."

He began unlacing his shirt, and there was nothing inside that but him. "Just how often will I be expected to kill?"

For a moment she thought he was serious and beamed. "Probably never. I don't know. You'd have to negotiate that with Grand Inquisitor. The Chamber doesn't slaughter men out of hand, Wolf, only for reasons of state. Just like the Blades."

About to deny the similarity, he saw that the argument would be fruitless and he might even lose it to her slippery inquisitor-talk. However tempting her offer, he kept remembering Inquisitor Schlutter. If the Dark Chamber wanted revenge, this would be a good way to trap him.

"I am not interested and you should not want to be friends with me. That would be much too dangerous! Keep your report and get some sleep. We've a hard day ahead tomorrow."

She sighed. "Yes, Sir Wolf. I was hoping for a hard night!"

The cruelest thing he could have said then was "How old are you really?" He didn't. "Good night, Inquisitor. Sorry about the promotion."

" 'Night, Wolf. I'll be here if you change your mind." She shut the door.

He finished undressing and climbed into a lonely bed. He had to plan his return to Court tomorrow, add the Baron's testimony to his report, prepare his expense account for audit. Yet his thoughts kept drifting to the salivating prospect Hogwood had dangled—the chance to wipe Athelgar off his boots forever. There was nothing he wanted more, but if he accepted her offer, which of them would be the whore?

4

*L*ynx was known to the Guard and tongues would flutter if he appeared in the palace without his ward, so Wolf left him at the Pine Tree Inn on Thistle Street with orders to await a summons. He still refused to surrender the jaguar plaque, promising only that he would give it to the King in person—which would be no problem if the King would send for him, thank him for his loyal service, and hand him a purse of gold. That would be regal, but did not sound like the Athelgar Wolf knew and loathed. The stupid cat face had so little real value that he might have convinced even his corrosive conscience to let Lynx keep it as consolation for all he had suffered, had he not given Grand Master a receipt for it. Even if it took them five years, Treasury's roach-chasers would notice its absence eventually, and Hogwood would surely babble.

Greymere Palace was huge. Willow and Sewald were on duty outside the doors of Chancery, and Wolf wondered what they'd done to deserve that—having to stay brass-button smart like brainless Household Yeomen, no dice, no lounging. From the appraising looks they gave him, he could tell that rumors about his mission were flying, but he nodded and walked on into the anteroom. There, it was said, the sorrows of the kingdom roosted. All the ills that government was prone to, all its errors and misjudgments, its cruelties and neglects, all eventually gathered there. As always, the room was packed with suppliants—wealthy burghers, widows and orphans, cripples, scabrous paupers—all come in desperation to the final court of appeal, the King's chief minister. Some might wait for weeks before being spared a few moments of some flunky's time, and only the most fortunate would ever catch so much as a glimpse of the Lord Chancellor himself.

In his case, Orders Had Been Given. The duty clerk almost knocked over his inkwell at the sight of him—the lowliest drudge in the palace knew the King's Killer.

"If you would wait in there, Sir ... er ... um ... Wolf, I will inform His Excellency."

The door he indicated opened into a library Wolf had never seen before. It contained no chairs, only bookshelves, a high reading desk, and two doors. A moment later the other one flew wide to admit Lord Chancellor Sparrow, all a-twitter.

Wolf bowed and rattled off the gist of his report in almost the exact words Hogwood had used the previous evening, stopping before he reached the marriage proposal. He proffered the written version, sealed and official, and his warrant with it.

His Excellency hissed out a very long sigh of relief. He beamed, rosy-cheeked. "Then there is no immediate danger of further attacks?"

"Not that I can see, but I do not know the reason for the first one. The conjuration potential is serious. They can undoubtedly seize any stronghold in Chivial as easily as they took Quondam. Since they know Quondam and how vulnerable it is, I recommend that either its garrison be substantially increased, or that it be abandoned altogether."

"I must notify His Majesty. He may want to hear your report in person."

"I have brought some evidence that he may wish to view."

The little man frowned, carefully opening the seal on the report. "Oh, I doubt that."

"For which I debited the royal treasury thirty thousand crowns."

It was not often one got to see a Lord Chancellor turn *that* color.

5

Having made himself respectable, Wolf arrived at the Council Chamber to find the baggage waiting under the limpid gaze of Inquisitor Hogwood, immaculate in crisp black robes. The two towering Household Yeomen who had been set to guard it seemed so desperately glad to see him that he guessed she had been flirting with them. She was a superlative tease, and he was still cursing his folly at not grabbing what she had so blatantly offered the previous evening. Lynx's companion must have enjoyed herself, for she had not left until dawn.

"You may wait outside now," he told the Yeomen.

The taller sneered. "Our orders are to stand guard in here, Sir Wolf."

"Now they are to wait outside." He no longer wielded the Crown's irresistible authority and the Yeomen usually found Blades extremely re-sistible, so he quickly added, "I must lay out certain secret materials for His Majesty to see. Will you keep him waiting?"

That scared them away and Hogwood went to de-ward the bags. By the time the privy councillors started drifting in, the long table was heaped with feathers and gold, jade labrets and glass-edged swords, a rainbow hodgepodge like wares in some bizarre bazaar. As he was tuck-ing the bags themselves out of sight behind a chair, she whispered in Wolf's ear, "There's one missing. A gold thumb ring with an eagle's head in jade."

Only an inquisitor could have performed such a feat of memory, but now she had told him, he could recall the item and confirm that it was not in sight. It would have been easily palmed—by Baron Roland the previous evening, even by the Lord Chamberlain, who was presently sniffing at the gold collection. Or Hogwood herself. Was this yet another ploy to trap him?

The first councillors to arrive had been the Lord Chamberlain and a couple of dukes. The Earl Marshal was wheeled in and set out of the way. Then came Lord Chancellor Sparrow, closely followed by Grand Inquisitor, who took their favorite place by the window. In swept Mother Superior of the White Sisters, a huge woman like a galleon on a calm day, all canvas set, with her steeple hat as main topgallant. She proceeded majestically over to the exhibit, displaying disapproval wor-thy of the minatory Sister Daybreak.

Commander Vicious entered and glanced around before stepping aside to admit the King. All knelt and were told to rise.

"Speak up, Sir Wolf," Athelgar said. "Tell us what you discovered."

Wolf did, while everyone listened intently and the King himself poked and scowled at the long table, concentrating on gold and ignor-ing art. He interrupted only once.

"How much?"

"Not quite, sire. Twenty-nine thousand, nine hundred eighty—"

The royal cheeks flushed. "But those men had no right to any of this! When enemies attack one of *my* castles, the booty belongs to *me!*"

"With respect, sire, if I had held to that principle, none of the gold you see would be here now. The men accepted Your Majesty's coinage at face value, so the hoard is worth more to your mint than you will pay for it."

A sensitive point! Athelgar grunted angrily. "And what is in this bundle?" He sniffed disapprovingly.

"A human forearm, sire, with a catlike paw in place of a hand." Wolf went to unwrap it. He had packed the grisly relic in salt, but it was definitely starting to rot.

"Never mind!" the King snapped, stepping back quickly. "Grand Wizard can examine it at leisure. Carry on with your report."

After he finished they all had to ask him questions. Then they started querying one another.

"He doesn't know if they were conjured to a ship waiting offshore," said the Lord High Admiral, who was not as stupid as he looked, "or all the way back to the Hence Lands. Grand Wizard, is such a transportation possible?"

"Not by any means known to me," the old conjurer said unhappily. "Our efforts to move people usually end in pâté."

"What do you know about Tlixilian enchantments?" asked a duke.

"No more than what Sir Wolf told us." Grand Wizard wrung bony hands. "I've heard the human sacrifice stories. Rubbish!"

"Well, Mother?" the Chancellor said. "Do you agree with Sister Daybreak's opinion? How many of these articles do you sense are conjured?"

Mother Superior turned at bay, like an ox mobbed by squirrels. "None of them, but I agree with Sister Daybreak that one cannot have a man-cat chimera without using conjuration. So, like her, I must assume that this trash may be tainted in a way I cannot detect." The galleon had run aground and didn't like it one bit.

Wolf said, "One article is . . ." No, *two* were missing. "In addition to these articles, sire, we brought back a mosaic pendant depicting the face of a Tlixilian pard, which Baron Roland called a *jaguara*. My brother, Sir Lynx, was carrying it and I failed to get it back from him this morning. That one I am certain is conjured, because it has changed its appearance since I first saw it."

The councillors demanded details and lost interest when they heard them.

"So your conclusion is that the attack was not intended specifically to abduct Baroness Dupend?" Athelgar was pleased.

"That is my personal belief, sire."

"This pin?" Mother Superior declaimed, holding up one of the palm-sized cloak fasteners. "Inlaid with turquoise, malachite, mother-of-pearl, and . . . is this pink shell?"

No one spoke.

"Wasn't Baroness Dupend once the Marquesa Celeste?" she demanded.

The King nodded with a brow of thunder.

Matron Majestic sailed on undeterred. "Hers had a cat's face. . . . Do you recall, sire, how some years ago you presented the Marquesa with a pin like this, displaying the visage of a pard?"

Athelgar shrugged. "Vaguely." He had given her everything imaginable.

"It came from the Hence Lands! Didn't it?" Her voice rumbled like surf.

"We do not recall!" When the King snapped like that, the subject was to be considered closed.

"I do," Grand Wizard mumbled in his fondly fuddy way. He might not recall what day this was, but he could remember when many notable mountains had been only molehills. "It was a gift from the King of Distlain to His Majesty's honored mother upon her accession. She made some remark about village craft trash . . . er, she did not care for it."

"Her judgment is usually sound," Athelgar said threateningly. This subject was *definitely* closed.

"She donated it to the crown jewels," Lord Chamberlain remarked.

Grand Wizard mused on, oblivious, "I was asked about it. The Marquesa wore it a few times at court functions. It was . . . er, outré as jewelry. Unique, really, but she had taken a fancy to it. She was deeply enamored of His Majesty—"

Flaunting a unique emblem of royal favor would have appealed to Celeste, no matter how ugly she thought it. Hogwood and Wolf exchanged looks. Now they knew the real reason for Lynx's fixation on the jaguar pendant—Celeste had worn one like it.

"I remember well!" Mother Superior boomed. "She wore it three times and every White Sister in the palace had nightmares of being stalked by giant cats. We begged Your Majesty to ask her not to wear it again! Not that we could find any conjuration on it," she concluded vaguely.

"It was delightful!" said the old conjurer. "Chips of stone glued on a silver plate. It was just after Your Grace appointed me . . ." That put the incident before Wolf arrived at Court, which explained why he had never heard of it.

"This is irrelevant!" the King roared.

"It's not!" Wolf said. "And I withdraw my conclusion that the raid on Quondam was not specifically directed at rescuing Celeste."

Even if one's sovereign was an idiot who gave crown jewels away to floozies, one never contradicted him. Alerted by the appalled silence that followed, the culprit babbled suicidally—

"Celeste wore that pin at Quondam, sire! My brother told me she wore all her jewelry all the time and that means she wore the Tlixilian jaguar, and if the new one has managed to conjure him in a few days, then what could the other have done to her in four years?"

More silence.

"Conjured your brother?" Athelgar said. "Sir Lynx?" His cheeks were as red as his goatee.

Wolf was underwater and sinking fast. "My brother is strangely fascinated by the pendant the jaguar monster wore. He joked that he'd earned it as a battle honor. He wore it on the journey back to Grandon. And I . . . I forgot to get it back—"

"The witness is lying," proclaimed the right-hand Grand Inquisitor.

"My brother insists he will deliver it only to Your Majesty."

"It conjured him?" the King asked again.

"Well, he is obsessed by it. And it did open its eyes!"

"Where is Sir Lynx now?"

Wolf explained.

"No, we do not want him seen at Court!" the King decreed. "But we do want that pendant. Now! Go and get it! And tell him he is to remain out of sight during our pleasure."

Wolf bowed and headed for the door. Vicious opened it for him, giving him a very nasty look.

6

$\mathcal{S}$corning to run, Wolf strolled out through the antechamber, scrutinized by a score of eyes, half of them Blades' and all of them curious, although no one was brash enough to ask him who had died this time. Then a voice shouted, "Wolf!" behind him, and Hogwood came swishing along in her robe. He waited for her out in the hallway.

"We'll take a coach," she said. "I'll meet you at—"

"We?"

She clutched his arm. "Wolf, it's not just the pendant! We must find him before he sells that ring! The King'll hang him for grand larceny."

"And you won't?"

"Of course not! Idiot!" She pushed him impatiently. "Go! I'll get my bag. Wait for me at the west door!"

He had been planning to take a horse, but coaches always stood ready at the west door, so that might be quicker. By the time the doorman had summoned a brougham for him, Hogwood arrived, clutching her black bag and puffing hard. The driver cracked his whip and they rumbled out under the arch.

The rain had stopped again while the clouds regrouped.

"Wolf?"

"Yes?"

"Can't you trust me just a little bit? I really do want to help Lynx."

Those eyes, those eyes! But if he trusted her even a little he was going to find himself trusting her absolutely, which smelled of rank insanity.

"You're not a typical inquisitor." He risked a smile, which he rarely did, since to describe his teeth as lupine would be flattery.

"You're not a typical Blade." She grinned impishly.

"In what way exactly?"

"You never bedded me."

"I was a fool."

She sighed. "Yes, unfortunately."

"I think that pendant has stolen Lynx's wits."

"His *binding* stole his wits. The pendant reminds him of his ward because she wore a pin like it, and his binding will give him no rest until he finds her."

"Yes. I mean no, it won't." The world was big, but a binding was implacable. "Why is the Dark Chamber involved? He has committed no crime." The plaque was no crime, so far, but the missing ring was likely to hang someone.

Hogwood made an exasperated noise. "It isn't! The Council went into secret session and dismissed me. So I'm free to help. I want to, Wolf! Honest! I should have seen Lynx pocket that ring. I swear I'm trying to help."

Wolf did not bother denying that Lynx must have taken the ring.

The Pine Tree was a clean, respectable tavern patronized by minor gentry visiting the capital. The Guard used it for business, as Wolf had by parking Lynx there, because the proprietor, Emil Montpurse, was notoriously discreet. He also favored Blades with favorable rates for private matters—so favorable that there were persistent rumors that the Pine Tree was owned by the Order itself, or perhaps Grand Master.

Rain was starting again, but Wolf sent the coach back to the palace rather than have it stand there and attract attention. Master Montpurse had seen him with Lynx earlier and raised no objection when he and Hogwood headed upstairs to visit him. Their knock went unanswered. The lock clicked open at Hogwood's touch. Lynx's baggage was there; he was not.

"He may have gone for a walk," Wolf suggested weakly.

"He's taken his brown pack. Open that big one! I need something you are certain is his."

Wolf's dagger severed the ropes. He pawed through contents until he found a shabby old jerkin he recognized. Hogwood wrapped her tracker in it and put it back.

"It needs an hour."

"Let's ask around downstairs."

She warded her bag and left it there, locking the door the same way she had opened it.

The taproom was almost deserted at that hour in the morning, smelling pleasantly of beer and new bread. A spotty boy was spreading fresh sawdust on the floor, Montpurse himself was wiping the tables. He was a trim man of middle years, whose flaxen hair was fading away altogether rather than turning white. His sky-blue eyes, which normally twinkled with professional bonhomie, were wary now as he insisted he had not seen Sir Lynx leave and had not spoken with him since he arrived.

An inquisitor and a royal guardsman together could demand and get very nearly anything they wanted, but Wolf had always preferred handshakes to arm wrestling. "I am his true brother, master."

"I am aware of that, Sir Wolf." It was the inquisitor that bothered him.

"We are on his side, I swear. The matter is extremely urgent. There has been a change of plan and we need to warn him."

Hogwood interrupted. "Summon the rest of your staff. He may have asked directions of someone."

"I'm sure he did not," Wolf said. "We'll call back in an hour or so, master. Ask him to wait if you see him, please." He chivvied Hogwood out to the spring drizzle. "Lynx is a Blade! His ward lived in Greymere so he knows the terrain here like he knows his ward's face. What did you think he might have asked for?"

"A pawn shop."

"A fence, you mean. He'd go straight to Greasy Tom's. Come on."

Tom's was three alleys east and a mile down the social scale. Women shorter than Hogwood would have to stoop to enter that dingy, gloomy basement, and neither she nor Wolf could straighten under its ancient beams. The agglomeration of junk down there had changed little in the five years since he had first seen it, and perhaps in the fifty or so since Tom acquired the store. A lack of buyers was hardly surprising, because the stock reeked of dirt and vermin and was barely visible. Greasy Tom had no desire to sell any of it, for then he would have had to go to the trouble of replacing it, and his real income came from fencing stolen goods. He was reputed to pay Blades top value for any trinkets their ladies gave them. There were bad apples in every barrel if you dug deep enough, and Tom probably made a handsome living off the Guard alone.

Their entry provoked spidery noises in back, until the nasty gnome came shuffling in from whatever horrors lay beyond the far door. He was a tiny, wizened scab of a man, smelly, corrupt, and old as the hills. He knew Wolf for a Blade at first glance, and bared a few dark stumps of teeth in a smile of welcome before he registered the inquisitor in the gloom. Then he shrank back like something slimy withdrawing into its shell.

"We have information," Hogwood said in tones grim enough to make any spine tingle, "that today you purchased a gold ring bearing a stone in the shape of an eagle's head."

Tom hunched even smaller, shaking his head but being careful not to speak. Wolf thought he looked as guilty as a dog with blood on its muzzle, but his opinions were not evidence.

Hogwood's were. "Did you? The article we are seeking belongs to His Majesty. Answer my questions. If you lie to me I shall call the Watch."

Tom moaned. "How was I to know it was stolen? I did not know! The man was a Blade. Aren't Blades always honest?"

"No!" Wolf said, for now he had a thief for a brother. "But always dangerous." He clicked *Diligence* up and down in her scabbard. "Hand it over."

"I'll fetch it, Sir Blade."

Hogwood nodded, so Wolf did not follow the spider as it withdrew into its web. It soon came crawling back to give her the ring, staying well away from the swordsman.

"How much did you give him?"

"Ten crowns, mistress."

Wolf had paid twice that for it.

"Do you want a receipt?" she asked. "Or shall we forget this happened?"

He gaped a toothless maw at her. "Forget what happened, mistress?"

"Let's go," Wolf said.

It was a relief to be back out in the street just to breathe, and in Grandon that was a damning comment indeed. They took shelter under an overhang and watched rain dance in the mud.

"Where now?" he asked bitterly. "The docks?" He was trying to recall exactly what the Baron had told him the previous evening—information Lynx had certainly taken to heart. Chivian trade with the Hence Lands was small, Roland had said, maybe six ships a year, and most of those left from western ports, not Grandon. None would set sail in Secondmoon, certainly, so Lynx's best strategy would be to cross the narrow seas to Thergy or Isilond, and either ship out from there directly or work his way south to Distlain, although officially Distlain still banned all foreigners from the new lands it claimed.

"Or livery stables," Hogwood said. "We'd do better to wait for the tracker than run around blind."

"Then let's eat," Wolf said. "That's an old campaigner's advice—fill your belly whenever you get the chance. We may have a long day ahead of us." The moment he reported back to the palace, his brother would be a thief on the run.

7

They went back to the Pine Tree to eat pork pie and cheese, both of which were good there. Wolf ordered small beer because his binding made anything stronger taste like bile after the first few mouthfuls. Hog-wood shocked him yet again by ordering porter.

Between taking manful swigs, she scorched him with her great in-nocent eyes. "You realize that this is goodbye, Wolf?"

"I'm sorry." It was true—no other lovely girl called him Wolf. "Why?"

"I failed in my mission. I'll be transferred elsewhere."

"No promotion?"

She frowned as she cut a tiny slice of pie. "I was still hoping for one grade. Now I doubt it. We missed Celeste's pin, so we got everything wrong."

"I'm sorry. And very sorry it's goodbye."

She smiled sadly. "I'll have to find another monster to fall in love with."

After a moment's chewing, he said, "That may be kindly meant, but it still hurts. Not the monster part. I know I'm a monster. But don't joke about love. You relayed an employment offer, I turned it down. Don't be hypocritical, blathering about love."

She reached across the table to him. "Wolf . . . truly, I am in love with you!"

He ignored her hand. "If you're feeling lusty it's my binding getting to you, that's all. I can't shut it off completely. Sorry."

"It isn't! I know what a Blade attack feels like. It's like being drowned in honey! Lynx's been trying to climb in my bed ever since Quondam. I am protected to some extent, but it was only being in love with you that let me hold out. One more night and—"

"Lynx wouldn't do that!"

"Wolf, Wolf! You're a child!"

No, she was the child, but he discovered he believed her and his anger veered. "I wish you'd told me. I'd have stunned him."

She shook her head, amused. "No, you wouldn't. You'd have snarled at him, but you love him too much to hurt him. And he loves you. He told me you'd always been father and mother to him."

"And why would he have told you that?" Wolf asked suspiciously.

She flashed the wicked little grin he had come to both fear and enjoy. "He asked me if we were bed partners. I said we weren't, because I knew what he had in mind. I hoped you'd see what he was up to and get jealous. And you didn't even notice!" She took a draft of porter. "Served me right—I surely had my hands full from then on!"

"Well you missed your chance. He's gone, I'm sure."

"If he caught the tide, he is."

"How do you know the state of the tide?"

"You can see the river from the palace." She grinned in childish triumph—one more point to her.

"He has ten crowns and some silver I gave him. Can he get to Tlixilia on that?"

"I think Lynx could get to Tlixilia on one copper groat as long as he had his sword and his binding was driving him."

"Likely." The problem was not Lynx, it was Athelgar. If that man truly appreciated his Blades and what they gave up in his service, he would recompense Lynx for four years' lost wages and give him every possible help to go in search of his ward. But a better man would never have bound Lynx to a strumpet in the first place.

"Dolly!" said a new voice. "Mother's looking for you."

The youth standing over them was slight of build, with whiskers too scanty to hide boyish rosy cheeks, but he was wiry enough to be dangerous. The dagger on his belt would almost qualify as a short sword. Young men who went armed with things like that were liable to be questioned by the Watch unless they were dressed like gentlemen, and this boy's fustian jerkin and cheap hose suggested a clerk or secretary.

Hogwood frowned at him. "Tomorrow."

"She needs help with the apples."

"Get Frank to help!"

The youth shrugged and then curled his lip at Wolf. That sort of open contempt usually heralded an insult inviting a fight. Royal guardsmen were forbidden to brawl with either fists or swords, but they had been known to treat chronic bad manners with minor surgery.

"Put it in writing, Flicker!" Hogwood snapped.

He shrugged and walked away.

"An inquisitor," Wolf said. "You were talking code."

She emptied her tankard and wiped her mouth on her sleeve. "*Mother* meant they want me for an important assignment right away. *Apples* means Flicker himself is probably going to lead it. I told him to eat rocks. Let's see how the tracker is doing."

They headed for the stair, and Hogwood walked as straight as Wolf did.

"You were showing off there, weren't you?" he said. "You're not tipsy in the slightest." Quaffing a pitcher of porter that fast would blur a blacksmith, let alone a sylph like her.

She laughed and squeezed his hand. "It's a Dark Chamber party trick."

"I'm not Lynx," he said, hurt.

"That wasn't what I intended!"

No? When she knew they must go back to the bedroom?

She allowed him a proper look at the tracker that time. It seemed to be an octagonal tile with the painting of a swallow on it, except that the image swiveled on the ceramic like a compass needle.

"A good strong trail," she announced when they reached the street. "You go in front."

The coming of noon and some sunshine was bringing out the crowds, but people made way for a man wearing a sword, so he led, turning corners as directed from behind. He was annoyed to discover that Lynx had known a shorter route to Greasy Tom's than he had. They did not go in; Hogwood picked up the trail returning, then veering off toward the river.

Big ports like Grandon were busy, smelly, noisy, and endlessly fascinating. The people, the ships, the goods, the birds . . . even otherwise nondescript buildings and wagons gained reflected luster on a waterfront. Wolf was not in a mood to admire scenery that day, though. He kept hoping they would find Lynx on a ship waiting for the next tide, or prowling the dockside taverns looking for a berth, but the spirits of chance withheld their support.

Wolf stopped with his toes on the edge of a pier and only rain-dimpled, garbage-speckled river below them. Hogwood ran into his back. Yellow-eyed gulls on the pilings stared curiously at them. He asked three men before finding one who could tell him that the last vessel to use that berth had been the *Lady Polly,* departed for Gevily on the morning tide.

They turned and retraced their steps.

"Gevily," Wolf said hopefully. "Wrong direction. I might be able to catch him in Gevily." Except that Wolf was still a bound Blade and could not desert his ward.

Hogwood took his arm. "He just needed to get out of Chivial. He'll jump ship when she puts in for water, in Isilond or Thergy. He's a grown man, Wolf. He's driven by his binding and there's no way you or anyone can stop him. What could you have done if we'd caught him?"

"I could have taken that accursed plate off him so he isn't leaving Chivial as a fugitive. I have some money I could have given him—not much, but some. I could maybe have persuaded him to wait until we organized some help for him, some proper finance perhaps. . . ."

He could have said goodbye! But Lynx was gone, and all for the sake of a shoddy trinket and a king who didn't know the meaning of gratitude. He could never dare return.

Wolf walked in silence most of the way back to Thistle Street, his hatred of Athelgar boiling like vomit. At the tavern door, Hogwood caught his arm again, and this time pulled him into a corner, away from the passersby. "Wolf, the assignment Flicker was telling me about is Tlixilia."

"You're joking! They'd send you into that fever-pit jungle? Pirates and cannibals and death?"

She nodded. "Think about it. We . . . the Dark Chamber . . . we had no warning of Quondam. It took us completely by surprise. It means Chivial has enemies we've never suspected. Thanks to you and Lord Roland, we now know *Who* killed all those people, but we still don't know *Why* and we do not have a clue about *How*! Of course we must send people to investigate! Of course one of them must be a conjurer, and I'm the best they've got who isn't senile. The Chamber will do anything it can to get its hands on that enchantment!"

Most of that made sense. Sending a child like Dolores did not.

"I just want you to know," she went on, her fingers still tight on his arm, "that if I run across any trace of Sir Lynx there, then I'll do what-ever I can to help him."

"Is this a final desperate effort to enlist me?"

"No." She smiled sadly. "It's a final miserable goodbye. Will you kiss me, Wolf? Just once?"

Trust her? Dare he trust her? He had worked with snoops before, more often than any Blade ever had, probably. He'd picked up a little of their code. "Put it in writing," she had told Flicker, and then she'd said it meant he was to go and eat rocks. But that was not what "Put it in writing" meant. It meant something like "The mission is proceeding as planned. Target will be met or exceeded."

So what if it was?

"Would they still send you if you were married?" he asked.

Oh, spirits! Could even an inquisitor fake that look of joy?

"No! They don't split up married couples. They'd send both of us!"

The combination was irresistible—marry Dolores, track down Lynx, and be rid of Athelgar, all in one roll of the dice.

Wolf cleared his throat, wondering if he were cutting it. "Then if the offer is still open . . . we could get married, I suppose."

She did not flinch. "Can you rephrase that with a couple of ro-mantic epithets and maybe an endearment?"

"No. I'm a killer, not a hypocrite. I'm not asking for a proper mar-riage. Spirits, I know what I look like! Finding that on the pillow every morning would be lifelong torture. You realize we have known each other barely more than a week? But you get me out of the Guard and I'll get you out of the Tlixilia mission, if that's what you want. If you really want to go, then I'll come with you and see if I can locate Lynx. But after that we can go our separate ways."

She regarded him quizzically. "It won't be legal until it's consum-mated."

"If you can stand it, that would be no problem for me." Her scent was tantalizing—mostly damp hair, but he found even that exciting.

"That was not the impression you gave me last night." She grinned.

He had been regretting that folly ever since. "Just once and you can keep your eyes closed. You'll get your promotion. Spirits know you'll have earned it." *The absurdity of her smiles was breaking his heart. This was only business for her, why could it not be business for him?* "You can't be thinking a real marriage! I can't *really* marry anyone. I can't support myself, let alone a wife. I have no money, no skills except killing, and my face makes children scream. No one would hire me."

"We snoops will."

He laughed. "Killing people? That's all I am, girl, a killer! You want my private *Litany*? Hengist, Hotspur, Reynard, Rodden, Jared, Arundel, Warren, and Quintus! Plus, of course, beloved Inspector Schlutter. The Dark Chamber may need a monster, but you don't. I'm *dangerous!*"

"No killing," she said firmly. "When I reported this morning that you didn't kill for pleasure, Grand Inquisitor said they knew that. They wanted you for something else. And I want you for this . . ." She kissed him.

She was a tall woman; he had no need to bend his head. She was surprisingly strong and she did know how to kiss. It was the sort of kiss that could lead to charges of public indecency. It was not the sort of kiss a man could ignore. It demanded cooperation and it lasted long enough to leave his scruples in ruins.

"Oh, Wolf!" she whispered into his collar. "Forget the Dark Chamber! Blades don't need permission to marry and neither do we. I want a real marriage! Bed and loving. And children, of course. I do want children because I want to be the sort of mother I never had, but I'd like to wait a few years yet, and spirits know we're young enough. A few years' adventure first, yes? Why not Tlixilia? We can be rich! Oh, Wolf! We're a good team!" She looked up, eyes full of stars. "That's what I want. You, and someday children by you, and a lot of love. I won't settle for less. Tenderness? Caring? That's not too much to ask. Adventure and wealth maybe. But no killing."

He could say only, "You're crazy!"

"Will that be a burden, a wife insane enough to be hopelessly in love with you? Decide! You must decide now, Wolf. Right now!"

"You really mean this?"

"Absolutely."

Life was a reflection in a soap bubble.

"Darling, I love you, will you marry me?" Was that the King's Killer talking?

"Oh, yes!"

"Now?"

"Instantly."

This time he began the kiss and by the time they could breathe again he had stopped caring what the Dark Chamber wanted of him. He would be an assassin if he must.

Two men in overalls came stumbling out the Pine Tree door. The taproom beyond was jammed full and raucous. Wolf led Hogwood in and almost fell over Emil, cleaning up broken pottery and spilled ale. He jumped up to move his pail out of their way.

"Master Montpurse, I am sorry to trouble you when you are so busy. Would you do me a quick favor?"

He wiped his hands on his apron. "If I can, Sir Wolf."

"I wish to marry this person. Will you and your wife consent to witness?"

The innkeeper waited a beat before saying, "I have done almost everything imaginable to oblige Blades, Sir Wolf, but I have never married one. Blades don't go in for marriage much."

"Sometimes it is a necessary, er, blessing. Isn't it, Dolores?" Belatedly, he put an arm around her and she snuggled against him. Tall, but slender. Now she felt dainty, vulnerable, precious.

"Yes, indeed," she said solemnly. "Necessary and urgent. I may give birth at any moment."

Montpurse allowed himself a small smile. "You wish me to call for silence and announce a wedding?"

"No!" Wolf said, having recognized a couple of Blades among the taproom throng. "We mustn't keep the King waiting any longer than we have to."

The minimum the law recognized was a man and a woman declaring before two witnesses that they were over the age of thirteen and were now married. Notaries and everything else were optional. The traditional six-question ceremony felt right and everyone knew it, but even that was not required.

They went into the kitchen. Montpurse asked Wolf the three ques-tions. An outraged Mistress Montpurse asked them of Hogwood. After six *I do*'s it was done. The bridegroom slid a heavy gold ring with a jade stone over two of the bride's fingers and told her to keep her hand closed.

"Thank you, master and mistress," he said. "If anyone asks, of course, you will confirm that this ceremony took place, but for the next hour or so, should anyone come looking for us, would you revert to more normal Blade treatment and tell lies for me?"

He lifted his wife into his arms and ostentatiously trotted up the stairs with her. It was time for some masculine assertiveness.

IV

On the eve of the hunt, the lord summons
his huntsmen, his trainers, his grooms . . .

1

"Viewed dispassionately, of course," Dolores said, "the act of love is gross animal behavior on a par with defecation or parturition."

Wolf said, "I had not realized you were viewing it dispassionately. In fact, I gathered a contrary impression."

They were walking hand in hand back to the Palace in a drumming, pitch-black downpour. Rain cast a golden glory over the link-boy splashing along ahead of them; it made his reeky torch hiss and smoke, its flames dance in every dimpled puddle. No one else was mad enough to be in the streets, which meant that even a starry-eyed sex-satiated Blade must keep an eye out for trouble.

"Sir, I have never been less dispassionate in my life. You are an expert."

Why did a man glow with stupid pride when a woman praised his skill in an act any billy goat could perform a dozen times better? She had known what to expect and her body had reacted in ways he was certain even an inquisitor could not fake, but she was not as experienced as she was claiming. He was secretly pleased at that—he was a prude, he knew, certainly by Blade standards.

"I already told you," he said. "You inspired me. You were stupendous. I love you beyond all reason. I am insanely happy. Am I telling the truth?"

She squeezed his hand.

"What does that mean?"

"It means 'Close enough.' It will do for now."

"I will do better the next time," he promised.

"Braggart!"

"I suppose . . ." Wolf wondered if the link-boy was listening to this salacious conversation. "You have been to see Cumberwell, I hope?"

She chuckled. "Isn't it a little late to think of that? No, I haven't. We provide our own conjurations."

Cumberwell was a fashionable conjurer, popular with the wealthy because he could guarantee a woman would not conceive. His fees were high and the cost of the antidote conjuration was considerably higher. But love spun its own enchantments. Wolf felt as if he and Dolores were now in some mysterious way a couple, a pairing set off from the rest of the world. He had been in love before, or had thought he was, which was much the same thing, but he had never known that sense of oneness envelope him so suddenly and so tightly. He had told her that, too.

"I'll turn in the ring," she said.

"Get a receipt for it."

"Of course. You think you married an idiot?"

"Yes. I'll report to Leader. I want to tell him in private, my love. I owe him that much. He may not be available tonight. Even if he is, the King may be partying. Are you quite certain this will work?"

Squeeze again. "If it doesn't then your inquisitor wife will have to hang around Blade quarters spying on everyone until it does. I must report in, too."

"To get a list of hits for me?"

"Will a dozen be enough to start with?"

"Make it fifty. Where can I find you? The Dark Chamber office?"

"No, that's just for show. Come to Thirteen."

"Amber Street?"

"Of course. That's the real rats' nest."

Under the palace lights, Wolf paid off the link-boy, over-tipping him. The lovers parted with a very damp kiss.

The number of flunkies lighting candles in the hallways and corridors told him that there was some royal function planned, but he dripped and dribbled his way to the guardroom unseen by anyone of consequence. He wondered if the Council was still in session, if it had wrestled all day with the Tlixilia problem while he had been wrestling his wife in bed. The current front office decorations were Bloodhand and Modred, comparing their date books.

Vicious was at his desk in the room beyond, working late and in full dress uniform. Next to inquisitors, he hated paperwork the worst. He looked up sourly as the newcomer loomed in his doorway.

"Lynx's gone, Leader. We traced him to the docks."

"Pity. Need full report. Quondam excellent job."

"Thank you, Leader."

"Five-crown bonus, cancelled because you blew your mouth off in Council this morning." That was a long speech for him.

"Did they decide anything?"

Vicious shrugged. "If I knew I couldn't tell you. They argued long enough." It was unusual for the Commander to be excluded from Privy Council meetings, but this affair broke all rules.

"Yes, Leader. One other—"

"Go get dry before you freeze." He bent to his toil again.

"Pardon, Leader. An application for married quarters . . ."

"See Lyon." Then Vicious looked up, surprised, even smiling. "Who?"

Wolf closed his door before telling him. His reaction was exactly what Dolores had predicted—incredulity, disgust, and finally anger. His swarthy face darkened until the great scar stood out like a jagged white rope.

"You've already *done* this?"

"Yes, Leader."

He slammed the desk with his fist and leaped up.

"Go and pack your kit. Wait in your quarters." With that he strode out.

Wolf's quarters were a poky cubicle with a squeaky floor and an absurdly narrow bed. Deputy always assigned that room to Wolf when Court was at Greymere, probably because he so rarely entertained visitors. He dried himself off, dressed in the only civilian clothes he owned, and threw everything else he wanted to keep in a bag, mainly books. His possessions were few, because the Guard led a peripatetic life, following the King around. Then he sat down to contemplate the incredible events of the day just ended and an even more incredible future.

Freedom! A wife. A journey to the ends of the world. Danger and action. A wife. Yes, he was besotted. He felt like a sex-drunk, harebrained adolescent again, like the spotty boy who had tumbled Amy Sprat in the heather so long ago. His new wife *was* an adolescent. She was brilliant and beautiful. He was years older and grotesquely disfigured. How long before she saw the ghastly mistake her ambition had led her into? He must learn to trust people. Yes, even love was not without its shadows. It brought both a driving desire to be worthy of the loved one and a terrifying certainty that one never could. Perhaps no one could ever be worthy of true love, but in the case of a gargoyle-faced multiple murderer, that conclusion seemed more than commonly evident.

Time passed.

Too much time. He began to worry.

Dreams curdled into nightmare.

If the King had been unavailable or had refused to perform the release ceremony right away, Leader should have sent word. No matter how angry he was, he would not leave a man sitting on the edge of his bed like this, not Vicious. Was it possible that Athelgar had balked, Vicious had resigned his commission in protest, and the Guard now had a new Leader? Who might that be? Not Lyon, surely! He lacked the necessary inner meanness.

If Wolf was *not* going to be puked out of the Guard, then he should get back into uniform. He fretted. He dithered. Just as he was about to start changing again, the door opened and Ivor stuck his head in.

"Leader wants—" His eyes widened as he saw the bag. "You leaving?"

"I hope so," Wolf said. *Oh, how I hope so!* As the two of them hurried off along the corridor, he asked, "What's been happening?"

"Don't know." No further comment. A portcullis had just dropped between them.

His Majesty was in his dressing room, being shaved by one valet while two others set out the royal finery. Florian and Neil were on duty, but Vicious was there also, glowering worse than ever, and so was Sir Damon. Certainly something had been happening, because Damon was wearing the Deputy Leader's baldric. The King stared frostily from behind a mask of shaving soap. Wolf sensed universal anger like boiling acid.

Vicious held out a hand for *Diligence* and in silence took it to the King. The valet backed away, razor in hand. Athelgar rose. Wolf knelt, busily unlacing jerkin, doublet, and shirt.

Typically, Athelgar went and spoiled his triumph. "Congratulations on your marriage, Sir Wolf."

"Thank you, sire." Wolf was surprised, but there was worse to come.

"The maiden we saw this morning?"

"Yes, sire."

"Breathtaking, even in widow's weeds. Clearly a perceptive woman, too. I wish you good chance together. I am going to miss you, Wolf! You have given sterling service these last five years and we must find other opportunities for you to serve your sovereign in days to come. Now we dub you knight . . ."

The sword that had bound him touched Wolf's bare shoulders.

How *dare* the Pirate's Son go and spoil it all by being gracious! Telling himself grumpily that Athelgar had just been taking a dig at the scowling Vicious in the background, Wolf withdrew to begin a new life, free as he had not been since arriving at Ironhall, ten years before.

When he had left the royal presence, Neil returned *Diligence* to him. He said only, "I'll see you out."

"What happened to Lyon?"

"Don't know."

That was certainly a lie, but a Blade who married an inquisitor was no longer one of the boys. Also, of course, the Guard would be happier without the King's Killer around, reminding everyone of unhappy times now gone.

But he was free at last.

2

With rain falling harder than ever, Wolf persuaded his overly tender conscience that Athelgar owed him one last coach ride, but he had the driver let him off in Ranulf Square, lugged his bag through a shortcut he knew to Amber Street, and trotted two doors along to the house he wanted. He was starting to think like an inquisitor already. Although he knew that some of these old mansions were more than they seemed, he had never been inside Thirteen. The door opened for him as he ran up the steps, and he stepped through into a scabby, cracked-plaster vestibule that had seen better centuries.

The alert lookout was the boy named Flicker, and his attitude had become no more respectful since lunchtime. He jerked his head and said, "That way."

Wolf stepped through to a fine, high hall sparkling with candles, polished paneling, shiny marble staircase. He dropped his bag, but Flicker did not take the hint. Anyone sporting a pig-sticker like that thing on his belt would not see himself as a porter.

"I am Sir Wolf."

"I know."

"And your name?" Meaning *real* name.

The youth smiled. "You are renowned, while I have yet to amaze the world. My congratulations on your marriage."

"Thank you. Is my wife here?"

"Possibly." He stepped close, too close. "Make her happy, Sir Killer."

He was trying to look Wolf straight in the eye but was not quite tall enough. Still, the threat was so blatant that Wolf's sword hand twitched.

"Or *what?*"

"Or you will regret it." He was still smiling, this weedy boy-child. He thought he could deliver on his bluster. Wolf sensed Dark Chamber trickery and was annoyed.

"You are her brother, perhaps?" He was about her age.

"We grew up together. We are all very fond of Dolores. Grand Inquisitor are waiting for you upstairs, Sir Wolf."

"I like to know the name of men who threaten me."

"I speak for many in this instance," the soft voice said. "Do not keep your masters waiting."

Furious, Wolf turned his back and advanced to the great staircase.

Once this mansion had been the home of rich and powerful persons. It seemed deserted and he knew it wasn't. He felt he was being watched by many eyes: *Welcome to the Dark Chamber.*

Upstairs the only light spilled from a doorway leading into a great ballroom. In contrast to the hall downstairs, this had been allowed to fall into decay, so that rich murals had peeled from the walls and the ceiling frescoes were crumbling. Only the central chandelier of a dozen or so was lit, spilling a puddle of light below it and leaving the rest shadowed, haunted by vague shapes of unwanted furniture shrouded in dust sheets and cobwebs. Like his old master, his new one was working late tonight. In the brightness a space had been cleared for a fine floral rug, and there sat a black-clad man at an ornate escritoire, flipping through papers amid baskets of books and documents awaiting his attention. It was half of Grand Inquisitor. Hearing feet crunching toward him over the gravel of crumbled plaster, he looked up and smiled.

"Sir Wolf! Good chance!" He came around the desk, hand outstretched. "Congratulations on winning a wonderful wife. And welcome to the sink of iniquity!" He laughed. He actually laughed! In candlelight and without his normal biretta, he seemed older and unexpectedly bald, gray-streaked hair fringing a shiny scalp, everyone's kindly grandfather. "Come and have some refreshment."

"Is my wife here?"

"She is." He ushered Wolf back into the shadows, to chairs clustered around a low table. "But you and I must have a quick chat, because time is short."

"Time for what?" Wolf perched on a spindly-legged chair.

"Time to find a replacement if you turn down our proposition. Let us drink to your future happiness. And congratulations on striking off your chains." He clinked crystal decanter against crystal goblet, poured ruby wine.

"Perhaps my wife should hear this also."

The smile did not waver, but there was annoyance in the way the old man's shoulders shifted. "She knows. Sir Wolf, I am not holding your wife hostage! She is making herself beautiful for your wedding night. Do you want to hear it from me or from her?"

"From you, Grand Inquisitor, please." Aware that he no longer had his binding to limit his indulgence, Wolf sampled the wine, which was strong and rich, with interesting aftertastes. Expensive, in other words. Had this whole palace been set up just to dazzle him? All those candles? Nice old Gramps?

Grand Inquisitor raised his glass in a toast. "To your happiness! We were greatly impressed by your performance on the Quondam mission, Sir Wolf. Very quick, very efficient work. Your identification of the raiders as Tlixilian was brilliant."

Grand Master had done that and he knew it.

"You knew all the time, of course."

The snoop chuckled. "We did not *know*. We suspected, because Grand Master's letter seemed to describe what the Distliards ran into— feathers, earrings and lip-plugs, attempts to stun or disable victims instead of kill them, et cetera. It was up to you to obtain the evidence. Which you did. Now we know *Who*, we still have no notion of *Why* and certainly none of *How*. The King agreed right away to let you investigate the incident. He can be quite competent at times."

Wolf passed on the invitation to badmouth Athelgar. "And when did you learn about Celeste's brooch?"

"Two days ago. Like you, we had concluded that her abduction was a random act of banditry and she was only a trophy. Then our ongoing inquiries into Hence Lands conjuration nudged an elderly White Sister into recalling the pin that caused nightmares five years ago. Like you—but perhaps not so quickly—we realized that this might be relevant. When you mentioned that the cat-man's similar badge displayed enchantment when worn and the Baroness had kept her finery on her person day and night at Quondam, then we arrived at the same place you did . . . although we did not blurt it out in front of a seriously upstaged monarch!" His mouth smiled; his eyes did not.

"What do you know now that I don't?" Wolf was starting to remember why he disliked snoops so much.

Grand Inquisitor shrugged. "Not much, all negative. No strange vessels have been sighted off the coast. To the best of our knowledge, nothing like Quondam has happened in Distlain, which ought to be the Tlixilians' main target for retaliation, but—as you again pointed out—they may not distinguish between the nations of Eurania. Or King Diego may be keeping his troubles secret. Lady Celeste still seems special."

"Why did you send Dolores along to snare me?"

"Why do you think?"

"Because you wanted an in-house assassin?"

"Sir Wolf!" He shook his head in mockery. "You don't believe that! Any inquisitor can kill people, and in much subtler ways than you can. We had to give Dolores some reason to pursue a notorious murderer. She soon saw through it." He sipped his wine, keeping his eyes on his guest. "Dolores is a genius and you have impressed us for years, Sir Wolf. Swordsmen are taught to improvise and react, but you can devise strategies and carry them out, a most unusual talent in a Blade."

"Are you hinting that the Quondam mission was an audition?"

"Call it a trial run, to see if you can work together. Which you can. You regret your marriage so soon?"

"No." Wolf would not thank him for playing matchmaker. "You got your dream team. The main event will be?"

"Go and find out *Why* the Tlixilians staged that raid and, most important, *How*. You may be able to learn Baroness Celeste's fate also, or even rescue her and your brother." This time his smile was more genuine. "Sir Lynx was a bonus we never expected!"

Wolf tossed back half his wine in a gulp. "Take my wife to the Hence Lands to be eaten?"

"With respect, I would give better odds on her survival than I would on yours."

No man liked to hear that he had been yanked around like a puppet on strings or tricked into marriage for cold-blooded business reasons. Nor that he was expected to lead his bride into a cannibal-infested jungle. Dolores would leap at this dazzling prospect of adventure. Spirits! How could he stop her?

"Pray be more specific, Grand Inquisitor. How do we do this?"

"That is up to you."

"Until yesterday about this time, I had never even heard of Tlixilia. Baron Roland was helpful, but I know nothing of the current political situation."

Chief Snoop shrugged impatiently. "The bats will brief you. In summary, the Distliards are actively arming the peripheral states for a combined assault on the Tlixilian Empire, but the Tlixilians know this and have learned the advantages of horses and steel weapons. Consequently, there is a huge trade in armaments. The Distliards are arming their allies: Yazotlans, Tephuamotzins, and others, mostly coastal states. Chivians, Isilondians, and various other Euranians are trading with the Tlixilians. Baels, as usual, are seizing any cargo they can get and selling it to anyone who wants it. The seas run with blood. Sigisa seethes with intrigue."

Also, according to Baron Roland, cannibals, snakes, and tropical fevers. "You believe we can achieve something worthwhile in such a snake pit?"

"Dolores will, if anyone can. Her grasp of conjuration theory is unmatched. Cherish her and keep her from swimming too near the sharks." Grand Inquisitor drained his goblet and set it down as a signal that the interview was over.

"It sounds like total insanity with very little hope of success," Wolf said brutally. "And for what? What wages do you offer?"

The snoop laughed. "That seems such a strange question! We reward success, Sir Wolf. You are aware of the Cumberwell conjurations, of course? Queen Malinda heard of those rituals, devised by a school of brilliant Fitanish conjurers, and decided Chivian women would benefit from them. We dispatched Inquisitor Cumberwell. He went to Fitain, obtained the formulae by devious means, and is now a baron with extensive landholdings. If he has prospered just by reducing the supply of unwanted babies, imagine what terms you could obtain from the kingdoms of Eurania if you had the ability to move armies halfway around the world."

Wolf became aware that he was gaping like a dead fish. The one thing no Blade ever expected was wealth, unless he could snare an heiress around Court. Perhaps Dolores was not quite so foolish, after all.

"If we discover the rituals you'll let us keep them?"

Grand Inquisitor smiled cynically. "Dolores would hardly be true to her training if she did not retain at least one copy."

"Fortune if we succeed and nothing if we fail?"

"Fortune if you succeed and most likely death if you fail. No one offers riches for nothing."

His words were harmless but his smile threatened. The prospect was El Dorado, but Inquisitor Schlutter's death still lurked in the shadows and always would. The Blade witnesses had lied brazenly to defend brother Wolf. Remembering Neil's cold dismissal as he returned *Diligence* that evening, Wolf realized that those days were over. Grand Inquisitor knew that, too. Wolf was vulnerable now. He did not ask if he had the option of refusing the mission.

And he was starting to feel excited. Adventure? Earn a great fortune?

Find Lynx!

"So my wife will be the brains of the investigation and I will be the brawn?"

Grand Inquisitor shrugged. "I hope you are man enough to endure that situation. We need a team whose members' skills complement each other. Men are physically stronger than women, but they are rarely more ruthless or as effective at gathering information."

"You say the Tlixilians are desperate for steel weapons, yet they took none from Quondam."

"That's another *Why* for you to answer." He moved as if to stand up.

"I wonder if their conjurations won't move iron?" Wolf mused. "We saw no weapons discarded down on the beach, but Sir Alden said a couple of pikes were found in the barbican, as if dropped during the withdrawal."

Instantly the inquisitor had his glassy-eyed mask on. "You did not mention that in your report."

"Like so much else, it seemed trivial at the time. I will discuss your offer with my wife and we shall have more questions in the morning. But explain to me, Grand Inquisitor, since I am only a stupid swordsman— why all the underhand dealing? Why not just ask the King to release me from the Guard and appoint me his agent in the Hence Lands?"

The old man stared at him without a blink. "The King is too erratic. He might refuse to spend the money or insist on appointing the wrong person. If he asks we answer. Otherwise we do what is required without adding to the royal burdens. Remember the stories of the Tlixilians' eagle knights and jaguar knights? The day hunter and the night hunter? Does that not remind you in some way of the Dark Chamber and the Blades? We supply the crown with information. The Blades defend it."

"Blades do what the King wants, not what they think he should want."

Grand Inquisitor sighed. "Let me tell you what happened tonight, after you broke the news of your marriage. Commander Vicious went straight to the King and demanded that you be dismissed from the Guard. The King refused. Vicious divested himself of his silver baldric and proffered it to His Majesty. The King refused to accept it. Vicious laid it at his feet and asked leave to withdraw. He was told to send in Sir Lyon, his deputy. Lyon, when he arrived, both declined promotion and resigned his commission also. Athelgar, faced with two baldrics on the rug, sent for Sir Martin."

Now Wolf understood. "Who also refused, of course? None of them would be seen taking my part against Vicious."

"Exactly. So the King was forced to reinstate Vicious and release you. He refused to take Lyon back, though, and appointed Damon in his stead. The distinction between Sir Vicious's mutiny and Sir Lyon's is subtle, but defensible. You see my point, Sir Wolf? The senior Blades of the Guard were not doing what His Majesty wanted at all. They were doing what they thought was best for him. Are our two orders so very unalike?"

"But . . . how do you know all this?" Did the snoops have spies behind the paneling in the King's quarters?

Grand Inquisitor smiled mockingly. "We know because it is our business to know, Sir Wolf. It is also our business to keep watch on the King's enemies, both here and abroad. The sack of Quondam revealed a foe who has struck at us from halfway around the world! Will he strike again? How big an army can he field at such a distance? What does he want of us and how can we defend ourselves? These are not trivial questions, Sir Wolf!"

"No, Grand Inquisitor."

"So, whatever your opinions of the current sovereign, I hope that you are truly loyal to your country, because the Dark Chamber is. Lead our new friend to the party, please, Flicker."

Crystal shattered, but even before the goblet hit the floor Wolf was on his feet and turned around. He could have been long dead. Dolores's surly young friend was standing behind his chair, calmly paring fingernails with his elephant-sized dagger. Wolf had not heard him come across that gritty floor and had no idea how long he had been there.

3

The party was informal, just a dozen people standing around while grinning youngsters circulated with trays of goblets and sweetmeats. The bride looked ravishing and half the age she thought she did in a gown of gold and cobalt brocade, which was obviously borrowed, because it was both too short and too large for her. Her cobalt velvet cap was trimmed with a coronet of what seemed to be genuine rosebuds, impossible though that was in Secondmoon.

The guests, about a score of them eventually, were friends of the bride. Most were her contemporaries, but they ranged up to a motherly woman of extreme antiquity—meaning about ten years older than Wolf. They were all snoops, and he was disturbed to recognize the Lord Chamberlain's latest mistress and one of the King's junior valets. That told him how Grand Inquisitor had learned of Vicious's attempted resignation.

Several senior black robes dropped in to pay their respects. All of them he had at least seen around the palace and a few he had worked with professionally, but they soon left so they would not spoil the fun. The arrival of the Gruesome Twosome stilled the hubbub as if they were the King himself. They were relaxed and pleasant, and their feat in kissing the bride in mirror-image simultaneity was obviously intended as humor. So, perhaps, was their joint speech:

Left began, "It is our great pleasure to—"

"—announce," Right continued without a break, "that Inquisitor Hogwood—"

"—has begun her professional career with a highly successful—"

"—independent investigation, whose details must unfortunately remain—"

"—confidential for the time being. But her success extended so far—"

"—beyond merely catching a notable husband that we are—"

"—happy to promote her two grades, to the rank of—"

Dolores uttered a squeal of joy. The others all cheered. Most seemed genuinely pleased, but Flicker and others of his age must be straining a little. A two-grade jump on top of a doctorate in conjury would be a coup in the battle for eventual Grand-Inquisitor-ship. The incumbents departed soon after, bidding everyone enjoy the evening.

The food and wine were superb, the merriment convincing, the cold dark firmly shut outside. Many of the guests had brought lutes or shawms and took turns providing music for minuets, gavottes, and pavanes. The bride seemed genuinely happy showing off her new husband, and her friends were too polite to ask if he was the best unemployed baboon she could find. Even so, Wolf felt very much a stranger and was glad when bride and groom could make their excuses and withdraw upstairs to resume what they had begun at the Pine Tree. Not all of Thirteen Amber Street was palatial. Even the so-called bridal suite was modest by palace standards, although it was better than the rainy streets for a homeless, unemployed swordsman.

The moment they had the door closed, the bride demanded, "What did Grand Inquisitor tell you?"

"I never discuss business on my wedding nights. Later."

Somewhat later, she asked drowsily, "So what did Grand Inquisitor say?"

"I'm asleep."

"You will waken in extreme agony if you don't tell me."

"He wants you to lead an expedition to the Hence Lands."

Her reaction was everything Wolf had feared. "Shush!" he said, pulling her back into his embrace. "You'll waken the whole city."

It was a tremendous compliment, she said when he let her speak again, a chance at a *huge* promotion, the opportunity of a lifetime. Wasn't it?

"It's exciting," he admitted. "The journey worries me. Months of danger and hardship and—"

"Stop it!" She pummeled his chest. "Don't *baby* me! I'm not a child."

"I do know that. But—"

"Tlixilia? To discover *Why* and *How* they sent an army to Quondam?"

"Right. We're a natural team, you see. You handle the conjuration and I do the human sacrifices."

She sniggered, which was quite an experience in such intimacy. "And you were worried about money? This could make us rich beyond dreams, Wolf! Like Cumberwell! If we can learn how to transport people by enchantment, we'll put every post house in the country out of business!"

Maybe, but she had married a lifelong cynic. Wolf knew that Athelgar's Parliaments had been quietly nibbling away at the "petticoat" laws Queen Malinda had forced through during her brief reign. He had heard much talk that Cumberwell and similar elementaries would soon be made illegal and shut down as contributing to public immorality. The Blades disapproved of many of the petticoat laws but were generally in favor of public immorality. Cumberwell had provided an enchantment that the Queen wanted made available. How would Athelgar feel about Isilond or Gevily teleporting armies onto his shores at will? What about thieves or assassins materializing inside the palace? Dolores would have serious marketing problems.

"And that's only a start," she said. "There may be *hundreds* of new things we could learn. Let the horrible Distliards have the gold from El Dorado, I'll take their spell books."

Marketing and production problems both. "Listen, my beloved. According to the Baron, the Tlixilians use beating human hearts in their conjury. Parliament may disapprove if you try to introduce this practice into Chivial."

"Oh, we wouldn't!" she said. "Sacrifices shouldn't be necessary. Grand Inquisitor saw that. The eight elements are universal. The Tlixilians are summoning the spirits in a different way, that's all. What we want to learn is how they control and direct the elementals after they're assembled. Tlixilians have glass swords, we have steel, but they're both swords."

"I'm relieved to hear it."

"And what did you mean," his bride said indignantly, "about *me* leading? *You* will lead!"

"You're a trained inquisitor, I'm not." Wolf knew he would lose this argument. She was much too proud of her brand-new husband to risk slighting him in her friends' eyes by taking away any of his manly authority. It would be easier for him to keep the title and then just do whatever she suggested.

Later still, when there seemed to be no chance of any sleep at all, he said, "Tell me about Flicker."

She shrugged in his arms. "One of the boys I grew up with. Why?"

"Why is he called Flicker?"

"He's so fast on his feet."

And quiet on them. "He has a doctorate in sprinting?"

"No! He's an incredible all-rounder. He was first in line for the Tlixilia mission. Even if I'm a grade or two ahead of him now, he's much more likely to become Grand Inquisitor one day than I am."

"Does he have chips on his shoulders?"

"One or two, maybe. Why?"

"I didn't like the way he was looking at you."

Dolores snickered all over. "Flicker? Don't worry about Flicker, beloved! We grew up together. There were six in our pod at Waltham—Bert, Spat, Kate, Quin, Flicker, and me. We shared a room until we were twelve. He's like a brother to me. Girls are not interested in their brothers!"

Wolf kissed her to change the subject. She might look on Flicker as a brother but Flicker did not look at her the way boys looked at sisters. At least one of his chips had a new name on it now. No matter! The newlyweds would soon be far away, seeking their fortune.

4

first let's discuss my wife's rank," Wolf said. "She was promised a promotion of three grades if she completed the Quondam mission successfully, so why did you only give her two?"

The Gruesome Twosome were four glassy eyes on the other side of a paper-littered table, and last night's camaraderie had gone with the morning dew. They occupied the only two seats in the room. Left-hand had just asked if Sir Wolf and Lady Attewell accepted the Sigisa posting.

"That offer was not explicit," said Right, "and she did not complete the mission successfully, because she did not question Sir Lynx's obsession with the jaguar plaque. Also, had she enlisted you as instructed, you would be more respectful now."

"Blades give respect where it is due," Wolf retorted. They also resented attempts at intimidation. "I will accept the mission provided Dolores is put in command. She is trained to the work. I am an outsider—helpers you call us, I understand. She must be in charge." They had argued this problem half the night, and Dolores had only grudgingly agreed that he could put the matter to Grand Inquisitor.

"When the two of you went to Ironhall," Left said, "you told her to pretend that she was in charge and you were her tame thug. When she asked why, you evaded the question. But His Majesty's Office of General Inquiry often appoints a nominal leader to distract the opposition and attend to time-wasting ceremonials so the real head can observe undisturbed from the sidelines. You learned this technique from us in the field, did you not?"

"I . . . well, yes."

"We did not expect," Right continued, "that we would have to stoop to spelling out that arrangement in this case, when the need for it is so obvious."

Lady Attewell emitted a small snigger.

"On that basis," Wolf said, "we are both happy to accept the posting to Tlixilia."

"Good. Dolores, you are promoted to third grade effective when you sail."

"Now go to Edgewyrd and the bats."

"And in future stop your helper from wasting our time."

Two heads bent in unison as they returned to their paperwork.

"Edgewyrd! *Edgewyrd!*"

Dolores bubbled with excitement as she led the way through the embrangled Dark Chamber warren. Like any Blade, Wolf hated not knowing where he was, and Number Thirteen had spread outward from the original building of that name, malignantly invading its neighbors. He was constantly being introduced to new people, all of whom hailed his wife with joy and felicitations on her marriage, making him feel like a new gown being shown off, but she was obviously well loved in this bizarre outsized family, and for that he was happy. He felt that only his grip on her hand kept her feet on the floor.

"Where is Edgewyrd?" he asked when they had a moment alone.

"Not *where,* love. *Who!* Edgewyrd is our chief strategist! A logistical genius! Only the very *biggest* missions merit Edgewyrd's attention." She peered at him and laughed. "You're not upset just because the old grumpies snapped at you, are you?"

"Of course not."

"They do that to everyone! It means you're accepted!"

"It's all right! I've been gnawed on by experts."

"Well, what's wrong, then? Aren't you excited about this marvelous honeymoon they're giving us?"

Cannibals? Jungle? Ships? "I'm suffering from lack of sleep. I haven't slept in five years and you didn't give me a moment's peace all night, you sex-crazed wanton."

"Me?" his bride squealed. *"You* call *me* wanton, you insatiable satyr, you lecherous glutton? You debauched . . . er . . ."

"Innocent?"

So they played. He was humoring her, not wanting to burst her bubble of happiness. She did not seem to realize that Baron Roland had painted the joys of ocean travel in all the wrong colors and a voyage to the Hence Lands would be a long and perilous torment. Wolf looked on the dark side of everything and she saw only the bright. Perhaps that made them a better team.

They arrived at a small room packed with papers and documents in baskets and boxes, overflowing shelves and tables, stacked on the floor. A staunch woman of around forty was hunting for something in this abundance. She straightened up with a guard dog's forbidding frown, changing it into yet another cry of joy and a motherly, all-enveloping hug for the bride. When that was over, Wolf was presented. Her name was Belinda Beresford.

"You are indeed a fortunate man, Sir Wolf."

He made his usual response about being aware of that.

Eventually she gestured to a door in the corner. "You are expected."

They had arrived at the celebrated Edgewyrd. Dolores's tribute had suggested something between a poison-fang monster spinning webs in a cellar and a mousy clerk with thick glasses. Yet now she led the way into a shabby little parlor, stuffy and poorly lit, where a tiny woman sat humped before a crackling fire—hairless, wrinkled, skeletal, swathed in a rug and a shawl. She looked likely to crumble into dust at any moment. Dolores dropped to her knees on the hearth rug and very gently clasped one of the spotted and knotted hands.

"Grandmother! They tell me you have not been well."

The other hand found hers. "I have not been well since before you were born, child." Her voice was softer than sea mist. "The man I smell must be your husband. Tell him to shut the door. I told them you were wasted on a killer."

The old crone nodded to the fireplace when Wolf was introduced, but did not offer fingers to be shaken or kissed. She was blind, although evidently not deaf enough to have missed his voice talking to Belinda.

"Be seated," she whispered. "We have much to do and little time." She carried on talking almost inaudibly even as he fetched two waiting chairs, putting them as close to the fire as he thought he could bear. "You will be writing to Grand Master to report your dismissal from the Guard, Sir Wolf."

"Well, no. Leader, that is, Commander Vicious, normally mentions—"

"You will write. You need twenty swords within three weeks."

Wolf opened and then closed his mouth, noting his wife grinning as if she understood, which he certainly did not.

"Without the jeweled pommel, of course," the ancient said. "Have them delivered to Cranton in Brimiarde. The gift of tongues—"

"Who? Wait! Why do I need twenty swords? And who is . . ."

Dolores pinched him hard, shaking her head. One must not interrupt the oracle.

"As samples," the crone whispered. "Enough to fill a chest and impress. You are a gentleman adventurer taking orders for arms. He is capable of that simple personation?"

"He'll make a very good gentleman adventurer," Dolores said loyally, grinning sideways at him.

"Ironhall swords are the world's best, are they not?"

"Yes they are, but . . ." Wolf began to explain that cat's-eye swords were limited to Blades, and even for them were merely a heriot, returnable at death. If the King himself could not give one away to a foreign monarch, how could Wolf persuade Grand Master to break the law in his case? Tell him he was on His Majesty's service but His Majesty mustn't know of it?

Ignoring him, Edgewyrd continued mumbling. ". . . many of the originals have not been translated from the Distlish. Is he a quick study?"

"Not by your standards, mistress." Wolf wished he had brought a slate to take notes. His wife would have to remember all this for him.

"He's smarter than the average Blade," Dolores said loyally, turning pink with the effort of not laughing aloud. She put a finger to her lips.

"I should hope so." The ghostly whisper continued relentlessly: "I need to hear drafts of your contract and commission by this time tomorrow. Oh, this isn't going to work, child! Time is so short and you have so much to do. Grand Inquisitor truly put him in charge? Not just as figurehead?"

"They did." Dolores winked at Wolf.

Edgewyrd grunted angrily. "Then direct him as much as you can. At least make him curb his lusts until the voyage. He's far too old to learn swift reading, truth-sounding, or eidetic recall, so choose a team with those skills. You are wonderfully talented, but you can't do it all yourself. See he's given the basics of brawl and applied conjuration, and of course talks to the bats, so he has some idea what you're supposed to be doing. Unless he's exceptionally stupid he may be able to pick up some of the minor adjuncts, like ciphering, narcotizing, sign talk, pocket picking, forging, even personation if he's deceitful enough. Remember you must all take a course in medicine, because there may be no octograms in Tlixilia. Pack an adequate supply of simples and potions. Make sure he understands the climate and travel hardships before he starts requisitioning gear. The sooner you open negotiations on finance with the bursar the better, but not until you've decided how long you will be gone, of course. The *Glorious* hopes to sail in the middle of Thirdmoon." She paused to catch her breath.

"Just a moment!" Wolf said. "How many people are we taking with us? How long are we going for? How are we going to travel? How—"

Dolores poked him hard in the ribs.

The dry-leaf voice rustled again. "Blade, I told you! I expect you to tell me all that tomorrow morning." She sighed. "You do not seriously expect this to work, my dear? I will try again to talk Grand Inquisitor into sending Louis instead. You'd really be much safer without this outsider blundering around, shouting orders about things he doesn't understand, upsetting people."

"I have watched Sir Wolf in action and am confident he will do a wonderful job." Dolores's tone was firm but her glances at Wolf were begging him not to take offense at the old woman's spite. He grinned back reassuringly.

When the ordeal ended and they emerged into cooler air and a now-deserted corridor, he pulled her into a corner for a reassuring hug. "So we write our own orders and submit them for approval?"

"Sometimes we bid for missions: several agents submit plans and Grand Inquisitor chooses one."

"Love, I probably know more about inquisitors than any other Blade does, but I never heard of that! What else have I got to learn?" It was still disconcerting to embrace a woman whose eyes were level with his.

She kissed the remains of his nose. "Lots! I used to discuss this with Sir Intrepid when he coached us in conjuration. Ironhall teaches cooperation, yes? Since you cannot be bound until everyone ahead of you is bound, you try to help the slower ones along, not do them down."

"That helps the team spirit. Besides, teaching is a good way of learning!"

"In fencing, perhaps. But we're encouraged from babyhood to compete, so we all become fiercely ambitious. When we're too young to have achieved anything, we brag about our skills instead. We're always trying to learn something new, even if it is part of the standard curriculum. Do boys at Ironhall ever boast that they've won medals for dancing? Or that they will be Leader one day?"

"Whatever for? Being Leader is just paperwork all night and too much King all day."

"Different rules, love. Come along, we have to meet with the bats."

He had already established that the bats were the Dark Chamber's political analysts, a coven of Masters of Protocol. It was their job to know where all the world's bones were buried.

As they walked hand-in-hand he said, "Where do I find these new rules?"

"They aren't written anywhere. We learn them in childhood, like walking. As a helper, you'll always have some leeway."

"How often are helpers put in charge of major missions?" Obviously that had been the root of Edgewyrd's complaint.

"Oh, helpers do all sorts of things."

"Including being put in charge of trained inquisitors?"

"I think 'in charge' is not quite the right expression." His wife's eyes twinkled in a way he was learning to distrust. "Inquisitors are rarely given outright orders. Let's see . . . I suppose Rule One is *Never get caught*. If you're exposed, we never heard of you. And Rule Two would be *Tell all*. You must report everything you learn up the chain of command as soon as possible. No keeping secrets!" She thought for a moment. "The one that will bother you most is *Be right*. You can ignore instructions if you think they're wrong and are willing to gamble on it, even flat-out disobey a direct order. A Blade who did that would be disciplined even if he was right, wouldn't he? An inquisitor would be promoted."

"What if he's wrong?"

"We use him as a model in assassination classes, of course."

"Reassure me that you're joking. You're warning me that I can never trust a subordinate?"

"Think of them as colleagues assisting you in your mission."

Wolf decided that his would be a very small expedition. "Eidetic recall?"

"Perfect visual memory. Flicker can quote you any book he's ever read since he was about nine, word perfect, starting at any page and line you ask, chapter after chapter. He can describe people he saw in a street a week ago."

"And I suppose personation is acting?"

"Oh, much more than that! It means taking on a new identity for months or even years. Living, sleeping, breathing another life, never stepping out of the role."

Perhaps the old woman he just met had been Flicker in drag? "And what's narcotizing?"

"Putting yourself to sleep. That's essential if you have to live on a knife-edge for weeks. Flicker can put himself into a two-day coma."

A ten-year coma underwater sounded like a better idea for that one.

5

By late afternoon—after another six meetings, each more bewildering than the last—Wolf had a vague idea of what was in store for the future unofficial Chivian ambassador to El Dorado. While climbing a long flight of stairs burdened with three weighty volumes written in Distlish, feeling like a hound who has tried to play catch with a wasps' nest, he turned to his irrepressibly cheerful wife and said, "Can we go back to bed now?"

She laughed and snuggled closer. "No, but that's enough work for one day. You've done very well, love! You impressed them all, yes, even Edgewyrd! Now it's playtime. I want you to give me fencing lessons."

"*That* I do know something about!"

"Yes, and I warn you, you'll be mobbed. They'll all want them."

"You'll defend me."

In a moment he heard the unmistakable echoing sounds of a gym in use. A few steps farther up he could smell it. It had once been the ballroom of one of those Amber Street mansions, but now it was stripped to bare plaster and a floor of scuffed boards, lit by late sunshine peering through high but very grubby windows, furnished with vaulting horses, bars, racks of foils, and full-length mirrors. It was large enough to look almost empty, although it currently held about thirty busy people, six of them adults. Five male adolescents were hopefully swinging dumbbells and others were being coached in fencing, but most of the noise and dust came from a dozen or so children enjoying a semi-controlled riot in a far corner. It was not unlike an Ironhall scene, except that the small fry were too young and almost half the people present were female.

By the time Wolf and Dolores had donned masks and plastrons—for he would take no chances with his bride and knew she would not pad up if he did not—everyone else had gathered around, eager to watch a Blade in action. She turned out to be a much better fencer than he had expected, and she used Ironhall style. He coached her, rapping out encouragement without having to lie at all. By the time the light grew too tricky and he called a halt, the audience had more than doubled.

"I am not the first Blade to teach here," he said.

"And won't be the last," Dolores agreed, puffing.

"I didn't believe you when you said you could handle anyone else but Blades, love, but I was wrong. I think you could take almost any other man."

"Not me," said a familiar voice.

Wolf turned to face the inevitable sneer. "You're the best, are you?"

Flicker said, "Yes. Want to try me?"

The kiddies buzzed approval like a fanfare of piccolos. Clearly he was the hero of the local immature.

Dolores made an angry noise and tossed him her foil, then her mask. He caught the first and batted the other away. Wolf threw his after it and stripped off his plastron. Then he said, "Guard!" and went for him.

It was soon obvious why the pest was known as Flicker, but he was not a Blade, and Wolf gave him a few bruises as reminders to watch his manners.

"Very good, though," he said at the end. "Certainly anyone but a Blade would have to be very lucky to take you, Inquisitor." He turned away to look for his wife.

"How are you at brawl?" Flicker asked.

The hall fell silent.

"I'm not familiar with the term," Wolf said cautiously. Anyone who would trust an inquisitor in that situation at that moment would have to be stark crazy.

Looking ominously content, Flicker tossed his foil to a girl nearby. "First, Sir Wolf, can you do this?"

He shot off across the gym like an arrow, slapped his hands down on a vaulting horse, spun up in a handstand, twisted in midair and then, instead of completing the loop to land on his feet, hit the floor spread-eagle, with a crash that made Wolf wince. He started to laugh and was silenced by wild cheers from the audience. Flicker sprang to his feet and came trotting back, grinning and acknowledging the applause. Clearly that had been an exceptional performance, even for him

"I rarely find a need for that skill," Wolf said, puzzled.

The smile grew wider, hungrier. "Then we'll go over to the polliwog corner and the mats. Bring your foil, Blade."

Having no choice now, Wolf followed him, with the spectators trailing behind or running ahead. He was not seriously worried. Fast or not, there was no way bare hands could beat a rapier. He wondered why Dolores seemed so concerned.

They stepped onto the mats and Flicker turned, dropping into a half crouch. "You have a blade, Blade," he said. "Kill me."

Wolf used Cockroach—a suckering feint at sixte and lunge at quarte. Flicker slapped the foil aside and kicked, tapping the top of Wolf's thigh with his foot to demonstrate what he could have done. In a real fight he would not have gotten inside *Diligence*'s guard like that and would have been disemboweled by Wolf's dagger if he had, but there was no denying he had won the make-believe bout and the smaller kids all screamed in joy.

"Try not to vomit all over the rug, Sir Wolf." Flicker himself was fizzing with excitement.

Wolf had seen bloodlust before and taken advantage of it. "I apologize for underestimating you. You knew that one, didn't you? Try another?"

"Kill me."

For a few moments Flicker circled around while Wolf held his ground, waiting for him to make a move. That was cheating a little, in that the man with the sword was supposed to attack; it would look like cowardice very shortly. Wolf was forced to keep shifting his feet, and Flicker chose his moment to leap within range. Wolf countered with a straight no-nonsense lunge that should have cracked his breastbone. It failed to connect, the foil was jerked forward, and Wolf went over Flicker's knee, impacting the mat hard enough to knock the air from his lungs. Flicker fell hard on top of him, sliding an arm under his to grasp the back of his neck. Wolf discovered he was helpless.

"You lost again, Sir Wolf," Flicker whispered.

"So I did."

Flicker chuckled and released him.

Wolf climbed to his feet and shook his head when offered his foil back. "What are the rules in brawl?"

The fuzz-faced pipsqueak was already back in his menacing stoop, hands waving slightly, as dangerous as a spanned crossbow. *"Rules?"*

"Don't injure your friends in practice matches is one!" Dolores's shout carried a strong implication that Flicker had a weakness that way.

"Don't injure *friends*," Flicker agreed, eyeing Wolf like his next meal.

Wolf was now mad—not about to froth at the mouth or charge in all directions like a mad bull, but too mad to pick up whatever shreds of dignity he had left and go while the going was good. He had been made a fool of in front of an audience that included his one-day bride and this was intolerable.

"And what decides the bout?" He spat on his hands.

"Results."

"Show me, then." Wolf raised his fists.

Both Flicker's feet hit him in the chest and down he went again, this time harder. Those meager mats might save a ten-year-old from bruising, but he weighed much more and lacked Flicker's superlative skill in falling. Flicker caught his foot and twisted it hard enough to hurt.

"Broken ankle, Blade. You're not doing very well, are you?"

In the next bout Wolf nearly landed a punch, except that Flicker threw him clean over his shoulder, to the worst landing yet. He tweaked Wolf's nose. "Gouged eye, Blade."

And the fourth time he pinned Wolf with *both* hands on the back of his neck.

"If I push just a little harder," said an odious whisper in his ear, "your spine will snap, Sir Wolf. They won't get you to the octogram in time, Sir Wolf."

Barely able to breathe for the pain, Wolf just grunted.

Flicker did not accept that as surrender. The junior members of the audience were making so much noise screaming with mirth that he could ignore their elders' disapproving shouts. "Then they'll send me to Tlixilia with Dolores after all."

"Try it and see," Wolf mumbled.

Flicker released him and he collapsed with a gasp of relief. In a moment he managed to sit up. Flicker was squatting just out of range, eyes burning.

"More, Sir Wolf?"

Only a fool failed to admit when he was beaten. "Not today. You really are the best, aren't you?"

Flicker nodded vigorously, still almost spitting venom.

Wolf was half again as old as he was and half again as heavy and yet Flicker could knot him like macramé whenever he wanted. He had lured Wolf onto his turf and rubbed his nose in it. Battered and bruised, Wolf could see only one way in the world to rescue anything at all from this humiliation.

"I'm a gentleman adventurer sailing to the Hence Lands with my lady wife. We have decided to take just two servants with us, no one else. You want to come along as my man?"

Flicker bared his teeth in anger. "Is that a serious offer?"

"Are you man enough to accept?"

He sprang to his feet. "Oh, master, let me help you up, sir! That was a nasty tumble you took there, master."

"Thank you, Flicker," Wolf said as he was raised, apparently effortlessly—Flicker was all whipcord muscle and knew how to apply his strength. "If you'll fetch the wheeled chair, my man, I believe I could just manage to sit upright in it." He was limping on both legs.

"Oh, please lean on me, master. You can depend on me always, Sir Wolf."

Dolores had probably not overheard their exchange, but she could guess what had been agreed just from seeing the transformation in Flicker, for now he was the perfect obsequious servant. She wore an expression of doubt and horror in roughly equal proportions.

"Congratulations, Flicker," she said. "I'm happy you're going to join us."

He touched his forelock to her. "It's very kind of you to say so, my lady. I will try to give satisfaction and justify Sir Wolf's faith in me. Oh, master, do let me carry those!"

She regarded her husband's condition angrily. "You should go downstairs and have your bruises healed."

"No need!" Wolf would not give Flicker that satisfaction.

He said nothing else of importance until they reached their room, because he had his faithful manservant in attendance, carrying his books. The moment he sank down on a chair, Flicker was kneeling at his feet, helping him off with his boots.

"With respect, master, these seem a little scuffed. May I take them and clean them now?"

Homage was certainly better than homicide. "Do that. Be quick, though."

"Of course, master. And have you some laundry I could attend to?"

Clothes were a problem. Now Wolf thought he might send his man out to buy some for him, but not yet. "Lady Attewell may have."

With a perfectly straight face, Dolores gave Flicker a bag of laundry and off he went.

"How long will he keep that up?" Wolf asked, chuckling.

"Until he returns from Sigisa. Night and day. He really will do that washing himself." Her voice rose. "Wolf, if you're doing this just because you want to lord it over him, you're making a bad mistake. You won't score points off him. He just sees it as more of a challenge to stay in character."

"That was not my intention," Wolf said gently. "I'm hurt that you would think it was."

"You're a fool to take him! Why didn't you ask me first?"

They must not have their first spat already, and over a pimple like Flicker. He stood up, wincing. "Partly out of wounded pride, I admit. Mostly because you told me he was the best and now I believe it. I have never seen a man move like that!" Not Wyvern, the current Blade champion, or even Quintus, the one Wolf had slain.

She stalked over to the window. "But he hates you!"

He followed. "If he hates me because he wanted to go on the Tlixilian mission, then I have given him his wish and will trust him to perform as best he can. If he hates me because he lusts after my wife, that's different. You told me he was like a brother to you and there was nothing between you. If that is not so, then of course I will withdraw the invitation."

"It's too late to do that. They'd all think I'd overruled you. No, Flicker won't pester me." She turned away when he reached for her. "A good servant wouldn't dare presume so and he will always be the perfect servant. But he will try to upstage you."

"A knife in my back?"

"No. When we make a final report, we are not allowed to mask our answers."

"Then let the best man win," Wolf said. "He can have all the credit as long as I get to keep the top prize." He turned her around to kiss her and they nuzzled as lovers do.

He broke free before he began running a fever. "Love, I must write the letter to Durendal and if it's to reach Ironhall before high summer, then it will have to go by Blade. I'll send Flicker round to the palace with it tonight."

"Won't they read it?"

"Not if it's addressed to Grand Master."

She shrugged, as if amazed at such naivete. "Then we must decide who else we take with us."

"That's up to you. Ladies choose their own lady's maids."

"Remember Megan, who was at the party last night?"

"Of course." Wolf recalled the older woman—motherly, loud-voiced, short and inclined to dumpy, and hair graying although she was probably only in her mid-thirties. She'd drunk two glasses of wine, told a risque story or two, and laughed a lot. "She seemed very pleasant, good company." Already he knew enough about Sigisa to know that Dolores would find no compatible female companionship there.

"Oh, she's a wonderful person. I love her. She was in charge of our pod, my foster mother, really. Until we were twelve, when she was reassigned and we began looking after ourselves, but we've never lost touch." His wife was pacing, avoiding his eye, and displaying symptoms of indecision. "Very competent, has an excellent record as an investigator. I'm sure she'd love to go on a wild romantic mission like this to wind up her active career."

"Are you suggesting, my beloved, that we take Flicker's *mother* along on his first mission to keep an eye on him?"

Dolores was wearing her inscrutable inquisitor face. "That was not my intention. I'm hurt that you would think it was."

Wolf hooted with laughter and embraced her. "But?" He knew that there was more to come. They were reading each other as if they had been married for years.

"But Megan was married to Ed Schlutter."

That ghost was going to haunt him as long as he associated with inquisitors. "You don't mean Schlutter was your foster father?"

"Oh, no. She met him later, on a mission to Gevily."

"Two knives in my back?"

"No. She was not sorry to be rid of him. But it will cause gossip."

"If you want her and trust her, my love, then you ask her. If she refuses, then nothing's lost. I trust you and trust your judgment."

So Wolf sat down to write an impossible letter while his wife went off to invite her foster mother to join the mission. His quest was turning out as unorthodox as his marriage.

6

Wolf led the way into Edgewyrd's stale, oppressive den. She looked as if she had not moved since the previous day, but Dolores had warned him that nothing happened in Thirteen without her hearing of it.

"Good chance, Inquisitor," he said. "I have brought my team and a first draft—"

"You met your match yesterday, I hear. Louis?"

Flicker was arranging the visitors' chairs. "My lady?"

The old beldam uttered a squeal that was apparently an attempt to shout, for she went into a paroxysm of tiny coughs. When she could speak, she whispered angrily. "Wolf! Stop this nonsense!"

Dolores bit her lip. "You have to declare this a conference, darling, so he can drop his personation." She was unhappy, because she knew the plan Wolf was about to present was not going to be popular.

"I see. Megan, Flicker, this is a conference."

"About time!" Flicker said. "Yes, I'm here, grandmother."

Sir Wolf and Lady Attewell sat down, Flicker and Megan stood behind them.

Edgewyrd was showing her gums in a smile. "I'm glad you're going, Louis, because you can stop this murdering swordsman from messing everything up."

"I'll do my best."

"Don't take any nonsense from him! You'll have to do all the work, because he doesn't know anything. And you, Megan Schlutter! What are you dreaming of? Supporting the monster who murdered your husband?"

Megan hid her fangs behind a motherly smile. "I have heard Sir Wolf's version of events and I am satisfied that he had considerable justification for his dilatory response. I am honored to have been invited to assist him."

The crone ignored that. "Well, Blade? What are you waiting for? Report!"

"First problem," Wolf said, "is obvious—there is a war on. We want to collect information about Tlixilia, but the Empire does not extend to the coast. It has been driven back, and that area is now held by the Distliards and their allies—Tephuamotzins, Yazotlans, and others. El Dorado itself lies many days' travel inland. Distlain more or less rules the seas, and tries to keep all foreigners out of the Hence Lands completely.

"Secondly, while Dolores and I cannot suggest a better cover story, the arms-peddling masquerade you proposed is a very wobbly boat. It makes enemies at the same time as it makes friends. It is even illegal under the laws of Chivial. According to the bats, His Majesty is strongly opposed to the prospect of King Diego getting his greasy hands on the fabled gold of El Dorado, which would make him the richest monarch in Eurania and upset the balance of power. Until we provide evidence that El Dorado deliberately attacked Quondam, Chivial favors the Tlixilian side in the war."

"Why is that a problem?" the old woman croaked.

"Because two years ago the Privy Council forbade any shipment of weapons, armor, or horses to the Hence Lands, in the belief that they would certainly end up in Distlish hands, no matter whose name was on the boxes."

"So?"

The Dark Chamber did what it thought the King needed, not what he ordered.

Wolf said, "If the Council hears of illegal shipments of—"

"It will order Grand Inquisitor to investigate." Flicker waited a beat before muttering, *"Stupid!"* so it became an aside and not a direct insult.

"I was just making a point," Wolf said calmly.

"Get to the plan!" Edgewyrd croaked. "You think I have nothing better to do than listen to you drone all day?"

"Very well. We will ship out in *Glorious* and proceed to Sigisa, which is the main port for the whole of Tlixilia." Lynx would almost certainly have to pass through Sigisa, too. "There we will set up house and gather whatever intelligence we can. We will send word to El Dorado that we have arms for sale. If we fail to make significant contact in half a year or so, then we shall give up and come home."

Edgewyrd opened her mouth but Flicker was quicker. "That's ridiculous! Go all that way and stay only six months? Sit around an offshore trading post handing out glass beads and trinkets in return for saloon gossip? That's not what you're supposed to do!"

"We'd also pay gold." The meeting was going much as Wolf had expected. "Beads for *naturales,* gold for Distliards."

"Oh, *stink!*" Flicker said. "Dolly, you don't approve of this rat shit, do you?"

Since her own first reaction had been similar, Dolores was ready with the arguments Wolf had used to convince her. "It makes a lot more sense to me than plunging off into a land the size of Eurania, all full of mountains and jungle, when we have no maps and no local support. The rebel kingdoms would never let us through and if we did get past them, the Empire would take us for Distlish spies. We can always change our plans once we know the current situation."

"Send word to El Dorado?" Flicker growled. "How? Smoke signals? Mail them a letter? And suppose you do make contact with the Emperor? Even if he is willing to trade his spell books for swords, how do you get the weapons to him? It would take a year to send an order back here to Chivial, fill that order, and deliver the goods. Maybe even two years. Nobody cares what happens so far ahead when there is a war on *now!*"

"Details," Wolf said airily. It was fun to needle Flicker and he wanted to see if Edgewyrd could live up to her reputation.

She was nodding. "That's all?"

"That's all," Wolf said.

"Very good plan! Simple and flexible! Dolores, you did this, didn't you?"

Wolf nodded vigorously.

Dolores grinned and said, "Yes, it was really my plan, grandmother."

Edgewyrd could still truth-sound, apparently, because she scowled horribly. So could Flicker, for his face went blank.

"The roads are frightful," Wolf said. "To be sure of catching *Glorious,* we must leave here no more than four days from now."

"I see no problem," Flicker sneered.

"You will. How long can you get by with no sleep at all?"

"Five days. How about you?"

"Five years at last count. Conference is ended. Put the chairs back where you got them, Flicker."

"At once, master."

7

In the mad scramble to equip the expedition, the conjurations were the worst. Wolf's sensitivity to spirituality, a minor nuisance until then, suddenly became torture. He had to undergo many more enchantments than the others, because real snoops were routinely provided with defenses against bad food, seasickness, travelers' vermin, and even mosquitoes. Every member of the team was given the ability to pick up foreign tongues so fast that within an hour Wolf was starting to make sense of those weighty Distlish log books he had to study, but every visit to the octogram meant hours of pounding headache for him.

In the odd moments when he was not bleary from pain, Dolores gave him lessons in *applied* conjuration, which meant practicing with the cute little gadgets inquisitors carried: golden keys, coding sticks, warding cord, and others he had never even heard of before.

Why the rush, when it would take months to travel to the Hence Lands? Obviously because the snoops had failed to foresee the attack on Quondam, and even an idiot like Athelgar might start asking questions about the safety of the realm. If that happened, they could now report that they had snatched up His Majesty's favorite killer, Sir Wolf, the moment His Majesty had released him from the Guard and Sir Wolf was already on his way to the Hence Lands to investigate. When he returned—if he ever did—odds were that the King would have forgotten the whole affair. Wolf was a cynic, especially where Athelgar was concerned.

As a stickler for detail, Edgewyrd put even him to shame. She had been organizing spy missions for a hundred years or so, interviewing the survivors and forgetting nothing. She suggested scores of items that were always to hand in Chivial but might not be available in the Hence Lands—needles, scissors, salt to clean teeth, oil and whetstones, spare buttons and buckles because they got stolen, tinder, and so on.

Megan was practical, soothing, and capable of teasing anything out of anyone. She supervised and catalogued the steadily mushrooming heaps of gear in the stock room, oiling the squeaks between Flicker and Wolf without annoying either of them. One day Wolf found her weighing bags of gold coins bearing a face he did not recognize.

"King Diego's ugly jar," she explained. "They're Distlish pesos."

Wolf bit one and decided it was even worse currency than Athelgar's, containing little gold. According to the bats, the Hence Lands war was bleeding Diego into bankruptcy. "Is it real?"

"It's better than real," Megan assured him solemnly. "But don't offer it to any White Sisters."

Flicker was so determined to prove himself the better man that he seemed hellbent to work himself to death. Fortunately, Wolf could exploit his vanity. On the third morning, when he reeled into the stock room like a walking corpse, Wolf ordered him to lie down and sleep until the palace clock struck noon. Flicker could not refuse a direct order without breaking out of his servant role, but he had not actually been told to go to bed, so he accepted this as a challenge and crawled under the table to stretch out on the flagstones. Soon afterwards a porter tipped out a barrow-load of cuirasses and vambraces not a yard from his head and he did not even twitch. He opened his eyes about a minute before the chimes began. He thought he had won, but Wolf had a useful helper again.

There was no mail service from the Hence Lands to Chivial. At Dolores's suggestion, they added a fifth member to the team. Quin Barnhart was another of her foster-brothers, but as unlike Flicker as could be imagined. He was solid, even pudgy for his age, but quiet and perpetually cheerful, a good-natured plodder who would do his duty as best he could and leave the thinking to others. He accepted the invitation with a grin and a fast "Yesr!" His duties would be to turn around and sail all the way back again to report to the Chamber that the expedition had reached Sigisa. Wolf appointed him his personal secretary, which meant manservant Flicker had another pair of boots to clean.

They decided to take supplies for a one-year stay and two years' travel. But what gifts should they take to bribe both haughty Distlish officials and cannibal chieftains dressed in feathers? How best could they conceal all the gold they might require? How long did boots last in a tropical jungle?

Swords? In the end Wolf's letter to Grand Master had merely told him of his marriage and release, Lynx's departure in search of his ward, and Wolf's intention to go abroad for a while. Better than anyone in the kingdom, Roland could put two and two together and get the whole dozen. Wolf did not ask him for any spare cat's-eye swords he had lying around, mostly because he would not ask Grand Master to break the law, but also because he could not believe Tlixilians would appreciate such quality if they saw it. After chips of glass, any edged steel must look good. He bought what he needed in Grandon.

Amazingly, it was all ready on time. By dawn on the fourth day, the wagon was loaded, the team harnessed, and they were ready to go. Nobody came to see them off, but they all went to say farewell to Edgewyrd. She wept and told them to come back safely.

They reached Brimiarde two days before the ship was due to sail, and the spirits of air and water smiled on them. Westerlies that had been howling up the Straits for weeks suddenly backed to mild northerly breezes. On the appointed morning Wolf stood on the aft castle with his arm around Dolores and watched the green hills of Chivial sink below the skyline.

"You realize, love," she murmured, "that today is exactly a month since the attack on Quondam?"

Chivial was making a fast response to that aggression, but not a very convincing one. "For every tail there is a head. In that month I have gained my freedom, a wife, and a chance to win untold wealth!"

She chuckled. "I won't ask you to put those in order. You also lost a brother."

"Gained him and lost him again."

"Don't worry," Dolores said, pecking his cheek. "We're going nonstop. Lynx has to hop from port to port and ship to ship. We'll get to Sigisa long before he does."

If he ever did. Poor Lynx! Wolf worried about him all the time.

V

Hearing the horns' call and the baying of hounds, the stag taketh flight

1

*L*ife was mud. Rolling like a drunk, *Lady Polly* was standing in to Mauxville, which was a port in Isilond and obviously not much of one. Running before a rising gale, she had made a fast crossing, but the next few minutes would be critical. Frozen and drenched by the rain, Lynx leaned against the ship's side and waited to see if she would cross the bar safely. If she did, life would continue to be mud; otherwise it would be over. He didn't much care either way.

As far as the crew was concerned, he was a thief on the run, which he was, of course, but not for stealing a cat's-eye sword, as the sailors suspected. He was entitled to wear *Ratter* and he looked the part well enough that no one had tried to cut his throat for her, so far. Since he had not slept, they had had no chance to go through his pockets and had thereby been saved a severe disappointment. Lynx was no trader, and in his desperation to get out of Chivial he had paid out almost all his ill-gotten cash just for the fare.

Night falling, wind rising. The only wisp of light in his personal dark swamp was that he was currently facing southwest and could feel the jaguar plaque burning hot over his heart. That was his compass, pointing the way to his ward. But even that was stolen.

Thief!

He kept thinking of Wolf, and Grand Master, and the four centuries of Blades he was shaming. Not just by theft, either. He was the only Blade in the history of the Order to let his ward be kidnapped! Of course a Blade would do anything at all to ensure his ward's safety, so an absentee Blade could justify any crime that helped him return to his proper place beside his ward. Lynx just wished he hadn't had to steal from his brother, which is what he had done, in effect, since Wolfie had been custodian of the ring and the plaque. Wolfie would howl with shame. And Lynx's life of crime had barely started. He spoke no Isilon-dian, knew no honest trade, had virtually no money. He would know no rest until he found his way back to Celeste, yet his most immediate problem ashore would be finding food to stay alive. Assuming he did not drown in the next few minutes, he would die of starvation crawling on hands and knees along the road to Distlain.

Every time *Lady Polly* crested a wave, the bar was visible as a line of surf glowing in the gloom. The gap ahead looked impossibly narrow and the tub was drifting sideways, too.

"Tide's out," Cook muttered. Cook was the cook, and seemed to have no other name. He was young, blubber-fat, had a wooden leg. He hung on the rail beside Lynx, the two useless men aboard, while every-one else stood poised to leap into action if needed. If Cook thought it safer to be on deck in this weather, so did the passenger.

"She won't make it?" Lynx asked.

Cook chewed his lip. "It'll be close."

Lady Polly was turning, so Lynx turned to compensate, keeping the plaque facing the southwest, burning hot. It was not hot to his hands, just on his chest over his heart, and only when it was facing toward the other jaguar image, Celeste's brooch.

He had first seen that brooch on the night he was bound. Celeste had brought it with her when she came to Ironhall, probably choosing it because she was forbidden to wear it at Court and would not care much if it were lost or stolen. The gown she donned that night made her Guard escort gibber. It might pass at Court, Lyon insisted, but never at Ironhall. Elderly knights would die of apoplexy and candidates drown in their own drool. He refused to allow her out of the royal suite until she draped a shawl over the abyss and fastened it securely. For that she used her jaguar brooch.

So there was the young Alf Attewell sitting on the anvil with his own chest bare, certain he was about to die at the hands of a royal trollop who had never held a sword before. He locked his eyes on that brooch, concentrating furiously on what he imagined lay below it, and those lustful thoughts distracted him enough that he managed not to disgrace himself. But when the Marquesa pleaded exhaustion and retired right after the ritual—spurning the traditional banquet—she left Fell and Mandeville on guard in the antechamber and invited the new Sir Lynx into her bedroom "to help her unfasten this pin." Hands trembling, Lynx reverently lifted away the shawl to reveal the glory beneath. His imagination had fallen short of reality, but he was later assured by an expert witness that he acquitted himself well thereafter.

At Quondam, of course, he saw the accursed brooch every day and night, and never without remembering the first time and knowing he could relive the rest of that experience whenever he wanted. Celeste would not merely welcome his presence in her bed, she repeatedly demanded it, yet none of her Blades dared gratify her. Old Dupend would have them all in divorce court in no time, testifying before inquisitors.

The ship shuddered, staggered, and then seemed to settle. Sailors cheered. She was over the bar! Lynx peered through the rain at the huddle of low, slate-gray houses ahead, then he looked at Cook, whose globular face now wore a stupid grin of relief.

Lynx had bought passage to the first port they reached in Isilond or Thergy, so he was stuck now with Mauxville, and it seemed fishing boats were about Mauxville's limit. "Tell me about this place."

Cook spat over the side. "What'cha want to know?"

"Not much of a place?"

"Any port in this weather."

"Yes, but what about other ships? I need to go south."

"Nothing sails in Secondmoon."

Cook did not explain why *Lady Polly* did, although Lynx suspected she was smuggling something. Did excise officers fly south with the storks for the winter? With the present storm showing signs of getting worse, nothing would leave the harbor for days.

"How many people in Mauxville understand Chivian?"

The fat boy looked at him contemptuously. "None."

So Lynx had better find some answers before he went ashore, and this youth was the only man aboard not busy.

"I need work until I can find a ship heading south. Who might hire a good swordsman?"

Cook wiped rain off his stubbled face, but not quickly enough to hide a sudden craftiness. "You really a Blade?"

"Got the scars to prove it."

"Know a madam who might hire a bouncer. She's Chivian."

A woman, of course! Lynx should have seen that. Men didn't trust Blades, especially Blades with no ward in sight; Blades were dangerous. Women were intrigued by their reputation. He should have seen that the alternative to theft would be sponging off women, living by what the Guard called "that other swordplay."

"Sounds promising," he said. It was almost certainly the best offer he would get in the squalid little settlement coming up ahead. Of course he might have to take his wages in trade, but even that he wouldn't mind if food was included. Flames, he didn't need a bed, just a roof and his bread! "What's her name? How do I find her?"

"What's it worth?"

Worth not running a sword through you, sonny. "You never been down on your luck?"

Cook pulled a face. "Her name's Hermione. She runs the only house in town. I'll take you there."

"Good man."

Life was still mud, though. Lynx turned until he was facing the sea, so he restored the glow in his plaque, the other jaguar face, the cat-man's toy. Maybe he'd have to swim to this Tlixilia place.

For a few days after the fight at Quondam he had been too close to death to appreciate his torment, but Intrepid and his gang kept working on him and the pain kept getting worse. The first Blade in history to lose his ward! When Rituals told him he would die if he tried to ride back to Quondam, that made it certain Lynx would try. His binding would not let him kill himself directly, but he desperately wanted release from the agony.

At Quondam, Wolf flashed that larger version of the jaguar at him. When Lynx touched it, a tingle ran up his fingers. At first he thought of it as just a memento of Celeste, but from the moment he put it on, he was conscious of it all the time. If a man noticed his shoes or clothes like that, they would drive him crazy, but the plaque never let him forget its presence over his heart. It seduced him. It tantalized him. It whispered constantly in a language unknown. He soon discovered it felt warmest when he faced roughly southwest. That was a clue, and the very next day he saw its eyes had opened. After that, Wolfie couldn't have pried it off him with an ax.

The plaque was not alone. Cat's-eye swords had spirituality too. The plaque and his sword were working together to lead him back to his ward. They were in cahoots. He was convinced of that. He dared not tell even Wolf, though. Lynx lost his last doubts when Baron Roland said that Tlixilia, which Lynx had never heard of before, lay far to the southwest. Right! Tlixilia it must be! Knowing he would need money, he palmed one of the baubles being passed around. That would break poor Wolfie's heart.

The ship drifted toward a jetty. Sailors were preparing to throw ropes.

"How far is it to this house?" Lynx asked. His feet hurt.

"Nowhere's far in Mauxville," Cook said.

Lynx could certainly keep up with the fat boy's wooden leg, no matter how sore his feet were. Food and shelter and a nice fire . . . he blew on his hands. They hurt with the cold. Well, his fingertips did . . . why were his fingernails so dark?

And why did his feet hurt, anyway? They were not cold. He'd owned these boots for years, ever since Celeste had lived in Grandon, and they had never pinched his feet like this. Both feet. Curious. Bothersome.

One more thing to worry about.

2

The Widow Hermione had no need to hire a bouncer. "Who do you think my girls are, anyway?" she asked Lynx. "In a town this size? They're daughters, sisters, and wives, making a little extra when a ship comes in. Anyone starts trouble, I just whistle for the local men."

Lynx turned on his most winsome smile. "You're from Grandon, aren't you? Somewhere near the Elmbrook? I know your accent."

The Widow Hermione thawed slightly. "After all these years?"

He said, "Oh, it *can't* have been *very* many years . . ."

It had been very many, but not too many, and she did get lonely sometimes, among all the foreigners. She let Lynx dry himself at her fire. He sort-of-accidentally let her glimpse his scars. She was appalled, so he had to explain how he had lost his ward and must go in search of her, even if it took him the rest of his life. He had always been good at getting along with people, and when Hermione turned out the last of *Lady Polly's* crew at dawn and sent the girls home, she offered him a place to sleep.

She was intrigued to discover that bound Blades did not sleep.

When the wind dropped, a few days later, and *Lady Polly* sailed away northward, Lynx remained, making himself useful, by day and by night. His toes, fingers, and teeth ached. His nails seemed darker and thicker. His hair and beard began falling out, making way for fur. Wolf had been right, telling him he must not wear the plaque, but he could not take it off now. Even when he romped with Hermione, he just turned the thong around and wore the pendant on his back. He could not bring himself to remove it, no matter what it was doing to him. It would be like cutting his heart out. Besides, he needed it to lead him to Celeste.

By the end of the first week he was having trouble forcing his feet into his boots. *Death and fire!*

He genuinely enjoyed Hermione. What she lacked in agility she made up for in experience, and she was still more voluptuous than blowsy. She enjoyed him too, for company and sex—neither of them called it making love. She was discreet as only a village madam could be, but she was also smart enough to notice the changes in him. They frightened her, naturally. He promised he would go away the moment she asked him to. Fortunately, Hermione was very fond of cats. Unfortunately, every cat she owned disappeared rather than share the house with an apprentice jaguar.

How long until *people* noticed that his hands were turning into paws?

Chance smiled on him. Another southwester brought another ship into Mauxville. *Papillon* was bound for the Sauelas, which were halfway to the Hence Lands. The master was worried about Baelish pirates and Distlish coastguards, the bosun spoke some Chivian, and a healthy deckhand with a Blade's famed skills was a good buy for them. Hermione spoke up for him, so Lynx was hired and *Papillon* sailed two days later. By then people were staring at his ears.

The weather turned sour again. He discovered he was proof against seasickness, even when lifelong salts were draped on the rail like laundry, but the changes in him were becoming obvious. His thumbs were shrinking and the fur replacing his beard was spreading ever closer to his eyes. He especially had to remember to keep his mouth closed. The pains were growing worse, too. As soon as the storm ended and the crew viewed their swordsman in sunlight again, they would certainly throw him overboard to see if he could grow gills as well. Sailors were a superstitious lot.

He was likely to drown anyway. The storm grew terrible. It ripped the tiny rag of a sail they were carrying, so they had to throw out a sea anchor. *Papillon* was somewhere off a lee shore, but nobody knew how far. She rolled and pitched, starting to leak as her seams were sprung. When they were not fighting for their lives on deck, the men crouched belowdecks in darkness in a stinking, rolling, pitching coffin, working the pumps or just listening to her ribs creak and wondering how long she could stay afloat, wondering if every roll would be her last. The oldest man aboard had never known such weather in those parts.

On what Lynx was convinced must be his last night on earth, something hit the deck right above his head. It could have been the start of *Papillon* breaking up. It could never be boarders in those seas, but the plaque seemed extra hot over his heart, so he buckled on his sword and went up to investigate.

The night was as dark as a cellar. He knew he was on deck only because the wind was howling past him, more salt water than air. He had not known waves could stand so high, looming black walls of water, while the spume blown from their tops enclosed the ship in a fog. Every rope and board groaned. The master and bosun were bent over Marcel, who had been one of the best hands and was now a heap on the deck, very dead, a pile of oilskins leaking dark fluid into the scuppers.

"What happened?" Lynx yelled.

"Screamed," the bosun said. "Yelling? Then fell."

Lynx looked up. It was a night as wild as they come, but Marcel must have been aloft a million or two times in his life. Why had he been screaming? What could he have seen in this murk?

"You," said the bosun, "go up to see!"

Lynx hesitated. Even Blade eyes would be useless in that murk, and if he saw breakers directly downwind, *Papillon* could do nothing about it. Then something screamed overhead, up there in the darkness, a harsh, inhuman sound whipped away by the gale. There was no one up there. The plaque throbbed like flames.

"Belay!" The bosun changed his mind, grabbing Lynx's arm. "No!"

Yes. That inexplicable cry was just one more of the bizarre things that had started when the raiders came to Quondam. It was his business, no one else's. Lynx pulled free, fought his way through the storm to the shrouds, and began to climb. He had forgotten he was wearing *Ratter* until she tried to tangle herself in the ratlines.

The storm grew ever more savage, doing its damnedest to tear him off. His cape billowed and beat at him. He imagined his feet slipping and him helpless, streaming out like a flag until it tore away his hands as well. *Papillon*'s roll was incredible, sweeping him across the sky so he overhung the ocean, first to port, then to starboard. For heart-stopping moments she would just hang there, almost on her beam ends, before she began to right herself. He wondered how Marcel had ever found the deck when he fell. Or was pushed. Frozen and battered, Lynx dragged himself up to the top. The trap was open, so he heaved myself inside, and paused to catch his breath.

The top—landlubbers would call it the crow's nest—was basically a barrel with a hatch in the bottom of it for access. It provided shelter, but he was bulky in his leathers and had to share the space with *Ratter* and the topmast, so it seemed cramped. Marcel could have fallen out of the barrel only when the ship was listed well over, and then he would have dropped in the sea. The trap had been open; he must have abandoned his post and slipped on his way down. Why had he? Why had he screamed? Had he screamed?

The strident noise Lynx had heard on deck was repeated, much louder, very close.

He shut the hatch for safety, then struggled to his feet. The wind tried to tear his head off. The sea anchor hung over the bow, so *Papillon* was drifting stern first, but he could see absolutely nothing astern, just more mountains of water. Nor could he see anything forward. The top rested on the crosstrees, which were short spars extending out to either side, and on the far end of the starboard crosstree was something that should not be.

It was larger than he, a bulky shape ruffling in the wind like a stack of feathers, writhing so much that he could make out no details in the dark. To eyes full of tears and spray, it was just a huge and evil *thing,* no more. If it was a bird, it was clinging to that impossible perch with its feet, but the only bird Lynx had ever heard of that could be that big was whatever had left the tracks Wolfie had seen at Quondam. A human being could be holding on to the shroud, but only a madman would stand there at all. What was it and why was it there . . . ?

When Lynx first saw it, they were about level. Gradually it rose as *Papillon* heeled over to port, until it was well above him. It had seen him arrive, likely had watched him climbing. It screeched at him repeatedly, as if it were trying to talk.

"Who are you?" Lynx yelled. "What do you want?"

More hoarse cries. He recognized the language he had heard that night in Quondam, when he and Fell slew the jaguar knight.

This monster might have come to revenge that other monster. Or it might be asking for the plaque back, please. But Celeste had been whipped away from Quondam by conjuration, so perhaps this thing had come to take him to her. That idea seemed like rank madness even at the time, but Lynx's world was a nightmare in many ways right then, not the least of which was that the ship might be going to sink under him. Even if it didn't, he would soon look so inhuman that he would be fed to the fish anyway. Or he would go mad with pain. No, this insane longshot was his best, his only, chance of ever finding his ward.

As *Papillon* continued heeling over to starboard, he struggled to climb out of the top. By the time he was straddling the rim of the barrel, he was looking almost straight down at the giant bird and the ocean below it.

His foot slipped, his hands were yanked loose, and he fell.

3

The world exploded in brilliance. It spun like a churn. Lynx cried out and covered his eyes. He became aware of heat, of unfamiliar scents, and of a strange lethargy. He was facedown on a woven rug in glaring sunlight and a summery warmth. The tumult of the storm had changed to a jabber of excited voices all around him, so obviously he was no longer on *Papillon,* and yet he had no sense of motion or time passing, no mysterious nothingness. He just was. It was very pleasant, very restful.

The spinning was almost fun, but something very odd had happened and he probably ought to be terrified out of his wits. He sniffed, identifying odors of dust, vegetation, and cooking, hot in his nostrils. The voices were all male, a discordant yowl that reminded him of the terrible thing on the ship, plus a harsh screeching like the noise the catman had made at Quondam. Rubbing his eyes to dry them, he peered around, squinting at the glare.

There were two bird's feet—*enormous* bird's feet—right by his nose.

Dismissing them as illusion, he looked the other way, raised his head. The world wobbled, steadied. Above a low wall towered a mountain and a clear sky with a sunset. It had to be a sunset; dawns were yellower. He rolled over. Above him, staring down, stood an eagle knight, his green plumage still bedraggled by rain and sea spray—fierce golden raptor eyes and a beak fit to behead horses.

Lynx had never moved faster in his life. He was on his feet and running . . . running downhill, then up . . . crashing into a waist-high wall, spinning around and drawing *Ratter* . . . again the world reeled, took a moment to steady.

There was no uphill-downhill. He was on a roof, wide and flat and white-stuccoed, splotched with fine bright rugs and long shadows cast by wicker gazebos. Ornate pots held flowered and fragrant shrubs. The eagle knight stood near the center—something between a gigantic green owl and a big man bundled in a feather bed so that only his head and feet were visible, although those were not human.

Nearest to him was a jaguar knight like the Quondam monster, with pard head and paws on a male human body wearing a two-flap loincloth, golden bracelets and necklaces, a jeweled belt whose buckle bore the mosaic jaguar emblem. Lynx vaguely recalled it . . . him . . . showing feline teeth and snarling as Lynx hurtled past him, but that reaction had probably been laughter, because if it was anything like the Quondam onc, it could have slashed him down with a single stroke of its paw. So the Quondam monster had not died halfway through a shape change, it had always looked that way, and somehow the eagle was easier to believe, because that had no human flesh visible.

About two dozen other men stood around in attendance on their lords. Most of the young ones wore only loincloths, others had various mantles, ornate cloaks, superb feathered headdresses, and a couple in the background were robed in black. Body paint, labrets, nose plugs, rings of all types, plus swords, spears, shields—these and the brown, beardless faces were all horribly familiar from last month's attack on Quondam.

How could it be only last month when this was summer? Where was he? He began to take stock, trying to be methodical. He was in a far corner of a flat roof, pressed back against the walls with his sword out, muffled to the eyes in leather and oiled cloth, with layers of wet wool underneath, dribbling seawater and due to boil in a few minutes. No doubt he had reacted very foolishly in front of these savages, but he knew he was not capable of thinking clearly yet and the world lurched every time he moved his head.

Beyond the roof? He had enough wit to realize he must be in the legendary city Baron Roland had described, El Dorado. The world could not contain two such marvels. It was vast, far larger than Grandon, a stunning vista of white, flat-topped buildings, mostly one-story, although some had two. Its streets were wide, its canals innumerable. He gaped at wooded parks and gardens and great market plazas galore. Within this jewel box, like trees in a meadow, stood many of the towers of sacrifice the Baron had described, tapering in four or five great steps from a broad base to a small flat summit. They cast long evening shadows, and the greatest among them must stand twice as high as Grandon Bastion. They, too, were of white stone, although each seemed to have a steep staircase on one side, and the staircases were black.

No Euranian had seen the floating city and returned alive, the Baron had said. All around it lay shiny blue waters, the lake that made it impregnable, and around that stretched a very wide, but fair and fertile valley, enclosed by distant mountains like battlements. As the chatter of the spectators stilled, Lynx heard a distant clamor of drums and some sort of horns or trumpets. Nothing else—no horses, no carriages.

Meanwhile he had been kidnapped and was about to be thrown in a cookpot. The spectators had found him stupendously funny. Picking up the jaguar knight's cue, they roared with laughter at his antics and obvious terror. The cat-giant silenced them by turning to the eagle-giant and saluting him—he crouched down, touched the floor with one paw, which he then raised to his lips. That was an obvious reverence and everyone else did the same. Even a terminally confused swordsman could guess that they were honoring the big bird for a magnificent feat of conjuration in finding and bringing back the man who dared to wear a certain plaque.

The Eagle croaked his thanks for the compliment, shook himself, and was instantly dry, glorious green plumage all shiny-bright.

The cat-man spoke a word and waved a paw. One of the youngsters sprinted across to a hatchway and disappeared. A slightly older man laid down his spear and shield, untied his glittering embroidered cloak, and brought it across to Lynx, who brandished *Ratter* at him. He stopped and held out the cloak, but Lynx just threatened him again, being unable to think past cookpots. The roof was too high for him to jump off, and where would he run to?

The jaguar knight stepped closer and spoke again, impatiently.

Desperately Lynx said, "Celeste?"

The monster flashed his fangs and nodded his great cat head. "Celeste!" The word was distorted, but comprehensible. He pointed north. Lynx wondered if he was being ordered to the kitchen.

Out of patience, the jaguar knight snarled. *Ratter's* belt and scabbard dropped around Lynx's feet. His weighty leather cloak fell apart at the seams and followed. The same thing happened to the blanket coat he wore under it. He howled in alarm, setting the audience to laughing again. The knight wanted him to shed all his sodden and unnecessary garments, but Lynx did not want to reveal the jaguar plaque. Despite his wails and protest noises, his clothing disintegrated, layer by layer, until he was completely exposed, wearing only the pendant. He realized that to the onlookers he must seem obscenely hairy and sickly pale, like something growing in a damp cellar.

The laughter changed to shouts and cries of wonder. The audience milled forward to see, making Lynx realize how stupid he must look defying such a company. He lowered his sword. Evidently it was his scars causing the sensation, because the jaguar knight himself strode over and reached out to match his talons to the red traceries on Lynx's belly.

Then, balancing perfectly on one foot, he raised the other to try that for size. Mostly there were too many overlapping slashes to tell apart, but in a couple of places the start of a stroke was visible, the four talon marks of a single paw. The audience gasped at the obvious fit, clamoring at the wonder of a man surviving such injuries. The fang marks on his shoulder were another sensation. Someone noticed his old binding scar, which was more visible than most, thanks to Celeste's ineptness, and they gestured for him to turn around and display its mate on his back.

Continuing the dumbshow, the jaguar knight pointed a claw at *Ratter,* the plaque, and then to his own heart. Lynx took this to be a query whether he had slain the original wearer, so he nodded. The cat-man made a speech that brought cheers from the spectators.

Now the eagle knight came stalking over also, moving with an awkward chicken gait, folding up toes as he lifted each foot, spreading them again as he lowered it. Golden eyes glaring, he made a speech, too, a longer one. The Jaguar responded, and then all the spectators crouched to offer Lynx their kiss-hand obeisance. He had slain a cat-monster and survived; he was an honored hero. Even in his muddled state, he began to hope that he might enjoy his next meal *at* a table and not *on* one.

The boy who had run downstairs returned with a bundle and gingerly approached Lynx. Feeling more confident now, Lynx raised his arms as a sign that he was willing to be dressed. The boy tied a two-flap loincloth around him, covered it with a triangular cloth knotted at one side, then retrieved and restored the scabbard and sword belt from the heap of rags at Lynx's feet. Lynx shamefacedly sheathed *Ratter.* The man still holding the fine embroidered cloak stepped forward, draped it over Lynx's left shoulder, and fastened it with a silver pin on the right.

Finally the Jaguar held out a paw to an attendant, who unfolded a gold bracelet from his lord's wrist and bent it around the visitor's, probably a great honor. Lynx was now fully dressed, feeling much better. No one offered him shoes and he was content to go barefoot, walking on his toes.

Meanwhile the Jaguar himself had been robed in a splendid cloak of feathers and gold embroidery, topped off with a high plumed headdress. He took his leave of the eagle knight with an embrace and many mutual flowery compliments. Beckoning for Lynx to accompany him, he glided over to the stair with feline grace, and his entourage closed in behind them.

4

The jaguar knight did not deign to walk the streets like mere people. He sank onto plump cushions in a magnificent palanquin, ornamented with gold sequins, jade plaques, and a canopy of tall green feathers. Sprawled at his ease, he gestured for Lynx to join him. Then eight brawny men raised the litter shoulder high and set off at a fast walk. The bearers were not slaves, but some of the most adorned and bejeweled of his attendants, so this chore must be an honor. Lesser warriors stalked along before and aft as guards, while servants alongside whisked away flies. Harbingers blew on conches, warning spectators to touch their faces to the ground until the procession had passed.

Confident that he was being paid a great honor, Lynx reclined facing the rear. His host faced forward, leaving little room to spare, for he was at least as large as the Jaguar who had died at Quondam. His feet smelled faintly of cat, but Lynx must stink obscenely after a week aboard *Papillon*. He had great trouble believing any of the scenery was real, except that the city was too incredible to be a dream. In the dusk people were heading homeward. Canoes streamed like ants along the canals and the wide avenues were crowded, but to him they seemed to be paved with stationary human backs, mostly bare male backs, with some robed women among them. He saw no wheeled vehicles and no horses.

The warmth of the air amazed him. Was this summer, so his journey had lasted months, or just normal Thirdmoon weather in the Hence Lands? And how had he gotten from night to sunset—had he been unconscious for many hours, or had he moved fast enough to overtake the sun?

Guards saluted as the bearers passed in through the gates to a place of flowers and trees, an enclosure containing several buildings. Servants made obeisance to their returning lord—a man who wore gold could not be expected to live in a tenement. Dismounting, he led his guest to a pleasant hall with one side open to a flowered garden, and a strange absence of furniture, other than some works of art and a small mat, but the Jaguar ordered another mat brought for his guest and remained standing until it arrived. Knowing the difficulty of injuring a Jaguar, Lynx decided that the stripling warriors guarding the doors were merely ornamental. The hazel-colored maidens who brought water to wash his feet and hands were much more so. They offered sweet drinks cooled in bowls of snow, and golden platters laden with honeyed treats and fruits. Somewhat hysterically, he decided he preferred this life to being thrown about in *Papillon*'s stinking hold. A jaguar knight lived better than King Athelgar.

A jaguar knight did not even feed himself. A winsome girl did that, popping morsels in his mouth, and holding a reed for him when he drank. She was obviously special, although even she did not look him in the eye. He purred at her sometimes, and stroked her cheek with the back of his paw, making her blush. Evidently his tastes did not run to she-jaguars.

Then a youth hurried in, flushed and sweating as if he had been summoned from a distance, and prostrated himself before his lord. He had the coloring of a *naturale,* but dark stubble on his chin and upper lip, as if he were of mixed race. The Distliards had been in the Hence Lands for forty years, after all.

The knight spoke. The newcomer passed on his words to Lynx's knees in a language he had heard aboard *Papillon* and sometimes from Celeste when she was feeling bitchy.

"Distlish?" he said. "Don't understand. *No entiendo.*"

The interpreter looked worried. *"Isilondo?"*

"Chivian."

"Ah!" Beaming with relief, the boy explained to the knight that Lynx was *Chiviano* and what that involved. Celeste's name was mentioned.

"Celeste?" Lynx repeated.

Nods and sign language informed him that she had been summoned. At that news some of his mental fog seemed to lift and he half-melted with relief. He had done the impossible. In a mere month he had traveled halfway around the world and found his ward. Never underestimate the power of an Ironhall binding!

Celeste swept in, cool and poised in a simple wrap of white cotton.

She wore no jewels, but her magnificent braids shone like copper and somehow she had managed to keep her milky skin from turning brown or exploding in freckles. Four young girls followed her in and knelt at the door to wait. She looked vastly better than she had a month before, much more her old confident self.

She kept her eyes lowered as she approached, but Lynx could not restrain himself. He sprang up to salute his ward. Celeste spared him the briefest of glances and continued on her way without missing a step. She had her faults, Amy Sprat, but she was as tough as a veteran warhorse.

She prostrated herself before the jaguar knight. He spoke. The half-breed interpreted.

Celeste rose to her knees and spoke to her Blade's knees. "Lord Lizard-drumming welcomes you, Sir Lynx. I have been expecting you. Be very careful. He is dangerous."

Lynx had already decided that. But so was Celeste. She could recognize power at a glance and was firmly of the opinion that the more of it a man possessed, the more he needed her in his bed. The cat-man would have had to be a lot less human than he looked for Celeste not to have taken him by then. If Lynx let himself be seen as a rival for her favors, he might glimpse a last, brief view of the city from the top of a pyramid.

The four of them held an awkward and protracted conversation, with questions going from Lord Lizard-drumming to the interpreter— whom Celeste addressed as Manuel—in Tlixilian, from Manuel to Celeste in Distlish, Celeste to Lynx in Chivian. Answers had to retrace that path and the opportunities for misunderstandings were legion. But Celeste was not merely tougher than boiled leather, she was sharp as a fresh obsidian flake. Lynx had no doubt she was amending his answers as required and she salted the questions with cues, keeping them brief so the jaguar would not suspect she was prompting him.

"Oh, *mighty conjurer,* the lord hopes you were not distressed by your ride on the Spirit Wind."

"Only briefly. All better now. Er, tell him he has a nice place here." Translations . . .

"He hopes the floating tree you were riding will not suffer by your absence. I don't think he can truth-sound but he can probably stop you lying to him."

"The floating tree is of no importance," Lynx declared. "Um . . . Looking upon his glory is reward enough. Do you swive him?"

Celeste ignored that question. "The noble lord apologizes for killing your warriors and stealing your concubine, great conjurer. He was really after the brooch I was wearing, which was his father's."

"Um. He could have just asked nicely." But if recovering Celeste's pin had been worth scores of lives, how much was the one on Lynx's chest worth? "I expect compensation. And we want to be sent home."

Translation. "He gladly returns me to you, together with all the rest of your jewels and with many rich presents besides, begging you to forgive his error. He assures you that he has avoided quickening my womb so he could continue to enjoy me."

This was the strangest day of Lynx's life to date and growing stranger by the minute. "Bet you're glad to hear that bit," he said. "You might end up with quite a litter. Answer however you think best, but I'd suggest accepting his offer. Tell him it is urgent that I lie with you as soon as possible."

"Keep hoping, Muscles." She turned to the humble Manuel and reported whatever she thought the reply should be.

No expression showed on Lizard-drumming's muzzle, of course, and Celeste frowned at the response. "He asks if you support the Hairy Ones who perform such terrible acts against his Emperor. I think Emperor is what they mean."

Whatever the truth, there could be only one reply. "Say that the King of Chivial is very much against the Distliards and strongly supports the noble Emperor and people of wherever this is. When he sends us home we will tell our King the true story."

"Don't look so scrutable, Lynx! Be mighty. Kitty-cat is honored to have you as his guest. He's hedging on sending us home."

Lynx sensed that Celeste was hedging too, suddenly. Was her Blade a better bet than her present owner or wasn't he?

"Tell him the first time you throw one of your tantrums he'll get you straight back and welcome."

She told Manuel something suitable. Lizard-drumming replied. Celeste queried the answer.

Eventually she said, "The great lord offers you rest and security for tonight. Tomorrow he will send word to the great family of Plumed-pillar, telling them that you have brought back his regalia. He thinks Plumed-pillar's heir will load you with rich gifts in return. He's fishing for something, but I don't understand what!"

"He may be threatening—I admitted to killing one of his buddies. Just tell him his generosity outshines the sun and the stars and can we go to bed now, please?" Lechery was not Lynx's only aim, or even his main one, for fatigue sat on him like a cartload of rocks.

Celeste spoke to Manuel. Whatever she said worked. Their host gave them leave to retire. He saluted his guest by touching the floor before him and then kissing his paw. Lynx responded in kind, and then demonstrated a courtly bow. Lizard-drumming purred in amusement and gave him one, graceful as a cat for all his size. Everything was very genteel and elegant, and a dozen torchbearers lighted the guests' way through the grounds. Lynx walked on his toes.

They arrived at a small guest house, containing a single sumptuous bedchamber, decorated with multicolored murals, but furnished sparsely, with mats and some baskets. Attendants were already laying out food. Celeste chased them all away, demonstrating that she had already learned a little Tlixilian. They closed the door behind them and Lynx flopped down on a mat, deathly tired. That Spirit Wind traveling really took it out of a man! He did not even want to eat.

She said, "Where is this?" just as he said, "What in flames is going on?"

He reached a hand for her. She stepped away.

"Talk first!"

And love later, he hoped. Once in Ironhall, long ago. Never at Court. Since then, five years of close-quarter longing. Celeste dulled the appetite for all other women, as Athelgar had been heard to admit more than once. He got over her eventually, but Lynx was forever bound and never would.

"This is El Dorado." He explained what little he knew of the geography.

Unimpressed, she tossed her head. "Why was I brought here?"

He explained about her brooch. She pouted when she heard how her other Blades had died in her defense, but did not give way to emotion. Celeste never did. Even her tantrums were staged.

"That's ridiculous! Now tell me how you're going to get me out of here."

"No, you tell me what that overgrown mouser thinks is going on."

The result was a roaring row, but no ward had ever quarreled with her Blades as often or as fiercely as Celeste did, and she had always picked on Lynx more than on the other two. They had fought every day at Quondam. He was too weary to go stamping around the room as she did, but he could yell louder. If Lizard-drumming had posted guards outside, they would surely be amazed to hear a handmaiden shouting at her mighty conjurer lord.

Celeste could be utterly unreasonable. "Of course you will get me out of here! You're my Blade. That's what you're for. I have been waiting a whole month for you to turn up and rescue me!"

"Then show me a map. Bring me some horses. Tell me which way the sea is and how we get over those mountains— Food? Port? Ships?" They could not even speak the language.

She howled that he was useless, Blades were useless. He repeated that two had died for her. She would not listen. She would not look at his scars or hear how he had crossed half the world to reach her.

"What's wrong with your ears?" she demanded.

He told her what his plaque had been up to.

"Take it off! Now! This instant! I will not have you turning into another monster. Can you imagine what I've been through? He has a tongue like a wood rasp and those claws . . . ! I've seen him rip a bed apart with his feet when he's worked up. And the teeth . . . !"

"I can't take it off. It's like *Ratter* now, part of me. And you're just mad because you made a mistake. You backed the wrong horse tonight."

A hit! Celeste screamed even louder, because she would never admit a mistake. She should have spurned the penniless castaway and stayed with the power-wielder, Lizard-drumming. Believing Lynx had come to rescue her, she had chosen the wrong man for the first time in her life.

Lynx was too tired for more argument, and he had a bad toothache. He shed his cloak and loincloth, rolled himself in a blanket, and pretended to go to sleep. He knew Celeste, though. He was not surprised when she jabbed him in the ribs a few moments later.

"You're not fooling me, Muscles," she said. "Say please."

5

Forget the Emperor. He was ruled by the Great Council and the Great Council could do nothing without the knights. The Eagles and Jaguars were the real power in the Empire, the cream of the nobility, owners of great estates, and their personal troops were the Empire's army. Every knight was a superlative warrior himself, trained from childhood, proven in battle. Only knights possessed spiritual power. They gained that virtue by sacrificing prisoners and used it to bless their warrior followers with special abilities, keeping them loyal and making them better fighters. Better fighters took more prisoners, which they turned over to their lords for sacrifice. It was a delicious circle, and no one understood it better than the third most senior Jaguar, old Basket-fox.

All his life he had excelled at the scheming and infighting that kept the knights amused when they were not engaged in a real war. Now the Empire was fighting for its life, the Eagles and Jaguars were at loggerheads and divided among themselves. The winners of the current struggle would determine the strategy that would decide who won the war—El Dorado or the Hairy Ones. Now, suddenly, just tonight, Basket-fox had seen an opening. It would be expensive for him, but if his idea worked he could confound the opposition within his own order, so his views would prevail. United, the Jaguars could persuade the Eagles, so the Empire would crush the rebel states and drive the Hairy Ones into the sea. These were worthy stakes.

A Jaguar could expect to be spied on, and there was nothing much to be done about it if the spies were Eagles, who could see anything anywhere anytime. But Eagles were outnumbered by Jaguars in the service of the Emperor and they had many duties more important than just snooping on their rivals, even wily old Basket-fox. Besides, eagles usually slept at night, when jaguars were at their best.

Against his rivals within the Jaguar order he should take precautions, though, which explained why Basket-fox was not visible as he paced the grounds of his own palace in the floating city, known to the Hairy Ones as El Dorado. Another knight could have seen him, if he tried hard enough, but his own guards could not. Monkey-blue, the boy he had been talking with earlier, had not yet been blessed with true sight and could not even see the guards standing over him. He knelt there in the moonlight, completely unaware of the four spears poised ready to strike him the moment their lord gave the order—which Basket-fox never would, because that would be a wasteful way to dispose of a man, even if he turned out to be a traitor. Another fifty or so warriors patrolled the grounds and palace, equally unseen.

Basket-fox was almost as rich as the Emperor. His palace was one of the greatest and his pyramid the second highest in the city, shining in the moonlight. Even home alone, as now, he wore the finest feather-crafted cloak, and was bedecked in gold and jade and seashell. Bats flitting overhead made more noise than his paws on the gravel paths.

Monkey-blue was a spy—a very fortunate spy, because he had been present that evening when that spotted idiot, Lizard-drumming, had spoken with a very unusual Hairy One. Also a very clever young spy, because he had seen that the talk he overheard justified his climbing the wall and running to report to his true lord, Basket-fox. Since he could never dare go back to spying on Lizard-drumming, he had risked the wrath of his lord for wasting two years' work, but his lord was not wrathful at all.

Pacing, pondering, Basket-fox came to the marble edge of a fish pool and paused to peer down, past his furry toes. He saw only the moon like a great silver bubble, a few stars struggling against its glare. Idly he thinned his virtual cloak until his reflection began to appear— old and scraggy, ugly and grizzled, with one ear gone altogether and the other tattered. Soon he must go to the altar stone. But not yet! Chuckling, he faded out of sight again.

El Dorado had been at war for generations. It was always finding excuses for war—extending the limits of the Empire or bringing subject cities back into line when they fell behind in their tribute, which they did all the time because they were run by the same system. Their Jaguars and Eagles needed prisoners also. The dry season was wartime, every year. The cities ran real wars or pretend wars, and the losers were the peasant boys conscripted to fight them. It was they who fed the altars. Senior warriors were usually safe enough and the knights almost invincible. In a pinch, an Eagle could simply transport himself and his favored followers right off the battlefield. Jaguars and their warriors just vanished.

Knights did die eventually. They lived a long time, preserved from decay by their spiritual power, but when an old campaigner began to slip, he issued a challenge to an aging counterpart in an opposing force, and the loser went to the altar. That was the honorable way to die. Basket-fox had been challenged three times so far and had not lost yet.

The Distliards, the accursed Hairy Ones, had changed everything. They had little use for prisoners and observed none of the proper rites of battle. They cared only for victory, had no respect for rank. No atrocity was too shameful for them, even using trained dogs to track invisible Jaguars.

Thus poor Quetzal-star—longtime friend of Basket-fox and one of the most respected jaguar knights of El Dorado—had gotten himself slain in one of the first battles, one that Basket-fox remembered well. Tlixilians had not even known what a crossbow was in those days and Quetzal-star had not expected any rank-and-file archer to be so uncouth as to shoot at a great lord like him. So he finished up dead on the battlefield and his regalia went to the Hairy Ones. That had been a national tragedy.

Ah! Basket-fox sniffed the air. A moment later a ragged black-clad figure came hurrying through the grounds, hugging himself against the chill. When he reached a small lawn, he stopped and knelt down to wait, confident that his lord would know he had arrived. Even a commoner could have smelled him before seeing him, for acolytes never washed. They were black all over from dried blood and wore their clothes until they rotted away under newer layers.

Basket-fox padded around to approach from upwind. When he was about two spear-lengths away, he revealed himself. The acolyte doubled over in obeisance.

"Speak," the knight said. If acolytes had names, those were known only to other acolytes. "Speak of the death of Plumed-pillar."

"A most noble knight of your great order, lord," the acolyte told the grass. "Slain by demons in the battle of the Feast of Conches." He paused and took silence as an order to continue. "His cousin, the noble Lizard-drumming, having heard the soul of his dead father, the great Quetzal-star, lamenting from afar, asked the valorous Plumed-pillar to aid him, and together they besought mighty Eagles, Bone-peak-runner and Amaranth-talon, to bear them to this place of torment. Alas, the demon defenders slew many fine warriors and the deadly Plumed-pillar also."

Lizard-drumming was a fool. He had done so well in several recent battles that he had ended up with more captives than his slave pens could hold. Instead of using the excess to buy friends and alliances, he had squandered them on a mission of utter folly. Why would he want his dead father around anyway—to claim back his inheritance after all these years? Honor should not be carried to such extremes. Worse, anyone knew that riding the Spirit Wind a great distance jangled wits. From what Basket-fox had heard, the young idiots had led their troops straight into battle, without giving them time to recover.

"Did they really find the soul of Quetzal-star?"

"Lord!" the acolyte quavered. "We do not know! They brought back a *woman*. She had been wearing . . . Lord, a knight's regalia is burned with him, always! We do not know what happens if it is not."

The thought that some part of a knight's soul might be left trapped in his regalia after his death was extremely disconcerting.

"You're saying that there was enough virtue still in the emblem to bless a commoner who wore it, even a *woman*?"

"It may be as my lord says."

Or not. "And then the soul of *Plumed-pillar* was heard weeping?"

"As my lord says. But much, much louder, stronger."

The regalia had been fresher, the death more recent. But Lizard-drumming had been in terrible straits, a laughingstock, having suffered humiliating losses with nothing to show in return except a female captive and some exotic, unfamiliar jewels. He was out of favor with everybody—the knightly orders, Plumed-pillar's family, the survivors of Plumed-pillar's retinue, even the Grand Council. Nobody needed more enemies than that. Basket-fox neither knew nor cared which of them had forced Lizard-drumming to try to make amends.

"I hear now that he tried . . ." When a knight made a statement a mere acolyte would not contradict him. "Tell me what you have heard about him lately."

"Lord, it is said that he persuaded the great lord, Whirlwind, to aid him but the noble Eagle agreed only to go and see."

"Just to look? You don't happen to know what he paid Whirlwind, do you?" Whirlwind was a very new Eagle with a great need to acquire captives; borrowing them from some greater lord might require him to mortgage the rest of his career.

"Alas, I fail my lord. I am ignorant and worthless."

"No matter. Continue."

"I did hear a rumor tonight that the Eagle Whirlwind brought back a warrior of the Hairy Ones wearing the emblem of Plumed-pillar, but this is mere gossip, lord."

Yet it was the confirmation Basket-fox needed. If an emblem could respond to a woman, it would certainly react to a warrior.

"I heard the same. And I heard that the warrior has started the Flowering. Could the regalia alone do that? Without ritual, without sacrifice?"

"It may be as my lord says." Pause. "But it cannot last long, lord."

"He will die?"

"He will die of pain."

As every knight knew, the Flowering was ordeal enough even when correctly performed.

"Could he be blessed just to let the change continue, or does it require the full ritual?"

What Basket-fox was planning was very close to sacrilege. Even to suggest giving a foreigner slave a full initiation would land the pair of them on the altar stone in a twinkling, and his acolytes would never obey such orders. But something less might be possible.

"I am worthless to my lord."

"You mean you don't know?"

"The words of the ancestors do not speak of it."

"Then it may be interesting to try. You may go. Do not speak of this." Mind made up, Basket-fox stalked off to where Monkey-blue knelt, shivering in the chill night air.

Spying on brother knights was so close to dishonorable that it was governed by very strict rules. To turn a colleague's own followers from their loyalty was unthinkable. It was permissible only to choose a promising lad of one's own clan and bless him with a disguise so he could enlist in the other's retinue undetected. He faced vivisection on an altar if he was discovered, but he was serving his own true lord; his first oath took precedence. Monkey-blue had survived in Lizard-drumming's retinue for over two years. That took real courage. And tonight he had displayed good sense.

His lord appeared in front of him. He buried his face in the grass.

"Tell me again," Basket-fox said, "what Lizard-drumming told the Hairy One he was going to do with him?"

"Lord, the knight said he would return his woman to him and his jewels and give him rich presents." Pause. "Er . . ."

"Continue."

"But later he told his steward that he would sell the man to the mighty Jaguar Flintknife, lord."

Of course. Flintknife was Plumed-pillar's brother and heir.

"Did great Lizard-drumming address the Hairy Warrior as Plumed-pillar?"

There was a pause, while Monkey-blue stared at the ground in front of his nose. Good man, taking time to think. "Not that I heard, lord." He sounded puzzled, so he had not seen the real game either. But that would be asking a lot of one so young.

"On your feet!"

Monkey-blue scrambled to his feet, keeping his eyes lowered, rigid with worry at standing in his lord's presence. A sturdy, promising lad. Not by any means a close relative, but of a branch that had thrown up some excellent warriors in the last generation.

"You have done me great service," Basket-fox declared solemnly, "and displayed great courage. Long ago I served as a spy and I know how hard it is. If I send you back now you will be uncovered, and that would be a waste of a fine young warrior. What was your original company?"

"The Flesh Eaters, lord!" Monkey-blue's voice was suddenly hoarse with excitement.

"You will return to training with the Eaters, then. You are promoted to taker of two captives. Take time to visit your family if you wish. When you return you will be assigned quarters and may choose two concubines from the pens. I will find you a wife of good rank." Widows he had aplenty, alas.

"Praise to my lord!" The boy crouched to salute. "I weep before my lord's benevolence."

"And I rejoice at gaining a proved servant." Power had its enjoyable moments. "One last thing. Do you know how many captives Lizard-drumming has left in his pens?"

"I heard none, lord," Monkey-blue said hoarsely, "but I do not—"

"Oh, I believe you. You may go, Taker of Two Captives."

One of the invisible guards stepped aside as the running youth almost cannoned into him.

So the third Eagle had cleaned Lizard-drumming out completely, had he? How much did the idiot think Plumed-pillar's heir would pay just to recover his brother's regalia? The man would be worth *much* more to Basket-fox.

The old Jaguar squatted down in a patch of shadow to think. Should he start low, offering perhaps ten captives under the pretense, say, of wanting to torture information out of the prisoner? Or should he try to overwhelm Lizard-drumming with a fortune, say ten twenties, and hope to win agreement before the dolt had time to think? Unfortunately, Lizard-drumming was probably not stupid enough to overlook the possibility of asking Flintknife for a counterbid. Plumed-pillar's heir had far less virtue and influence than Basket-fox did and had far fewer prisoners in his pens. He would need most of those for his own Flowering, which he had just begun. Nevertheless, an auction could really hurt. Ten twenties might not be nearly enough. No, Basket-fox had better start even higher, to show he meant business—offer *twenty* twenties and hope young Flintknife would be frightened to bid higher in case Basket-fox was setting a trap for him and did not really want this mysterious Hairy One after all.

6

By dawn, Lynx knew he was in mortal trouble. His long-longed-for reunion with Celeste had been a disaster, to her disgust and his horror. No Blade had ever suffered from lack of virility before—at least none had ever reported such a problem. He had no strength for anything else, either. Even sitting up was an effort, and he was repeatedly racked by jabs of pain: in his teeth, feet, hands, even his skull. When he wasn't suffering he was waiting for the next torment to start, which was almost worse. The plaque was obviously to blame, and yet he could no more remove it than he could have bathed in boiling water. When he allowed Celeste to take it off him, he went into convulsions and she had to put it back.

Her four attendants arrived with fresh food and clothing. Then Manuel appeared to start language lessons. Lynx sat outdoors on a mat and tried to concentrate on how to greet knights and warriors of a dozen different grades. Celeste already knew many such flowery phrases, but those were for women and men's were not only different, they also varied depending on the speaker's rank. Manuel had no more idea of Lynx's status than Lynx himself did and played safe by trying to teach him all of them. Celeste had to interpret, of course. The instruction proceeded very slowly.

Then a troop of spear-carrying warriors arrived at the double, a score of them. Without explanation, they ordered Manuel and the girls away and took up position around the prisoners. Their eyes were chips of obsidian.

"Gorgeous, aren't they?" Lynx muttered through a mouthful of hot coals. Feathers and paint, bangles and lip-plugs.

"Half of them are wearing heraldry I haven't seen before. I think those are not Lizard-drumming's men." Why was she bothering to whisper?

Lynx was past caring. He sat with his back against a tree and stared vaguely at a ceremony in progress on the summit of a nearby pyramid. He could make out no details, but the eerie music from drums and conches was unsettling. Celeste went indoors and left him alone. He sat and suffered and sweated and wondered how soon he could die.

Later another dozen warriors appeared, accompanied by a slave carrying a basket that contained Celeste's missing jewelry. She came running out to welcome it with cries of joy, which turned to screams of rage when she was not allowed to touch it. Instead Lynx was ordered to stand up. Unwilling to argue with an obsidian-tipped spear, he struggled to his feet. Then he stood on his toes and tried not to twitch at the jolts of pain running through his jaw, while two of the youngest, least decorated warriors proceeded to adorn him. They were puzzled that he had no openings to take earrings or a lip-plug. The rings that would not fit on his pinkies they strung on a cord to hang around his neck beside the real necklaces, but in the end they seemed satisfied with their handiwork. He was confident that the infamous emerald tiara which had caused such a scandal in Athelgar's Court five years ago must look very good on him.

By that time half the original guards had departed and there was no one else in sight, which seemed ominous. The escort formed up around the two prisoners, the leader beckoned, and off they all went.

"I think," Lynx remarked, "that we have just changed owners. Don't—*Eyaaa!*" Flames of agony in his right wrist made him bite his lip until it bled. By the time the spasm ended, they had been herded through a gate in the perimeter wall and out to a quay where three dugout canoes were waiting, complete with brown-skinned paddlers and more armed warriors.

From there they proceeded along successive canals. Neither the warriors nor the slaves spoke at all, and the many other canoes they passed were equally quiet. So were pedestrians on the bridges. Did no one in this city ever laugh, or even smile? Apart from sounds of pyramid rituals farther away, it was eerily silent. Reflections swam on silver ripples in a dreamlike repetition of blue water, white buildings, blue sky, white peaks. He wondered if the first Blade ever to visit the Hence Lands would merit mention in the chronicles at Ironhall, and who would take the word there.

Lizard-drumming's mansion had been impressive. The one they were taken to overwhelmed. Its pyramid was three times as high, its grounds enormous, even its polychrome sculptures were breathtaking, despite their bizarre, convoluted style. Lynx noted Celeste smiling again, confident she was moving up the social scale. If this was not the home of the Emperor himself, it must surely belong to a lord chancellor or someone equivalent.

The prisoners were escorted to a small, secluded terrace, flanked by a colonnade on two sides and unfamiliar trees on the others, furnished with a pond and flowering bushes. There another Jaguar waited in the blossom-scented shade, lying half curled up on a richly colored mat, with his head in the lap of a scantily clad, eye-catching brown maiden. She was fanning him gently, keeping flies away. This knight's muzzle was grizzled and his human skin lacked the tone of youth, so by human standards he would be at least sixty.

Behind him stood a scrawny, balding man leaning on a crutch, wearing the invariable two-flap loincloth and nothing more. He was a stubble-faced, hairy-chested Euranian of perhaps forty, although deeply tanned by the tropical sun, and likely a war captive, for he had lost his left leg just above the knee. The wasting of his thigh showed that the injury was not recent. He raised a finger to his lips to urge silence.

Having no sane alternative, Lynx stood where he was, waiting for his host to finish his catnap. There were swordsmen in the bushes and more in the shadowed interior beyond the arches. Sensing Celeste standing very close to him, he gently took her hand, and she squeezed his fingers. Unexpectedly, the move sent a spasm of pain shooting through his wrist. He did not cry out, but he did take a very deep breath.

The cat's eyes opened. The Jaguar sat up.

About to salute, Lynx thought better of putting his hand near his sword and bowed instead. Celeste knelt most humbly.

The old jaguar knight stretched and yawned, displaying a fine set of fangs and a long, pink tongue. Then he flowed effortlessly to his feet. He wore a loincloth and a jeweled belt with a jaguar-emblem buckle, but as he paced over to Lynx with his front paws behind his back, he resembled nothing so much as an aging alley cat, all scars and one ragged ear, full of sin and ancient evil. His feline eyes were inscrutable and blood-curdling.

He looked Lynx over, from his tiara down to his toes.

Then he did much the same with Celeste.

With a needle-sharp black claw, he lifted the front of Lynx's cloak so he could inspect his scars. Then he sauntered back to his mat. He bared his fangs in what might have been a jaguar leer, and spoke some gibberish.

Lynx shrugged.

The old knight said, "Jorge!"

The man on the crutch spoke. Celeste replied.

Jorge spoke again, and it was clear that he was a much better interpreter than Lizard-drumming's Manuel. Celeste translated his Distlish into Chivian, phrase by phrase.

"Basket-fox, lord of the dark . . . welcomes his unfortunate and dearly loved kinsman . . . jungle terror Plumed-pillar . . . to his humble house . . . and extends sympathy to him . . . in his misfortune."

Celeste's expression told Lynx that she understood no more of this than he did.

"Er . . ."

Jorge had not finished. He frowned a warning and continued what could only be a prepared speech. "He feels a mountain of sorrow . . . that the noble lord's heir and brother . . . the midden cur Flintknife . . .

has wrongly claimed his inheritance ... has seized the dread killer's estates, followers, captives, concubines, and slaves. The jungle slug Flintknife ... refuses to admit ... that his brother has returned from ... the place of demons ... in a borrowed body and will ... require some brief time ... to recover his memories ... and be restored to his former self."

Celeste finished the translations with her eyes as big as water jars.

Could he settle for a half dozen concubines back, Lynx wondered, teetering on the brink of hysteria. "There may be some mistake——"

Jorge read his face and did not wait for Celeste to begin translating. "I mention that the dread hunter Basket-fox paid thirty twenties of captives to rescue his kinsman from the avaricious Lizard-drumming this morning. If he was in error, then the consequences will be dire indeed."

Translating, Celeste added, "Bargain, you idiot, bargain!"

Before Lynx could speak, he felt a spasm of agony coming on, as if his skull was being crushed in a vice. He sweated and gasped, unable to hide his agony. It was terrible—and then it stopped. Instead of dying away as usual, the pain was shut off instantly. The world unfolded like a flower. He opened his eyes and found Lord Basket-fox standing in front of him with one black talon touching Lynx's jaguar plaque. He snarled something to Jorge. Jorge spoke to Celeste.

Celeste said, "Kitty-cat says he apologizes for not noting your distress. Like spit he didn't, darling! But he says he has blessed you now and you should be all right for a day or two."

Basket-fox walked over to the pond, stepped in with both feet and sat down on the marble edge, resting his top paws on his human knees. He showed his fangs in what Lynx hoped was a smile.

Lynx was certainly cured for the moment—pain gone, horrible lethargy gone. Tonight he would triumph on the sleeping mat. "I thank him from the bottom of ... my heart." *Whose heart?* By the time those words emerged from Jorge, they had multiplied into a speech. "And tell him," Lynx added, for his thinking was clearer now, "that I shall be guided by him in all things until my memories return. I am his devoted, lifelong servant."

Jorge was still translating this when half the pond seemed to explode in Lynx's direction, a storm breaker of bright droplets. Blade reflexes flashed; his hand streaked out to snatch a silvery fish out of the air. Only then did Celeste utter a squeak of alarm.

Lynx solemnly stepped forward and replaced the bewildered fish in the water, where it darted away to safety under a rock. He nodded to Basket-fox and returned to his previous place. The Jaguar regarded him with a piercing feline stare, idly shaking water off his paw.

Basket-fox to Jorge to Celeste: "He says you are very fast."

Lynx to Celeste to Jorge: "Tell him he is faster."

Right answer. The Jaguar uttered a rumble of amusement and stepped out of the water. He went back to his mat. Another mat was brought for the honored guest. So they were all friends together now? Spear carriers still lurked in the shrubbery.

Refreshments appeared. The knight's lithesome handmaiden fed him tidbits and held a reed when he wished to drink—*pulque,* Celeste said, fermented cactus sap. Perhaps she was expected to serve Lynx in the same way, but he could still use his fingers. *For how long?*

Basket-fox had become charming, making small talk and purring. It made him seem very cuddlesome. *Play safe and pet a pit viper?* Describe the floating tree. Do all women in your city have hair that color? Were the eyes you are now using that brown color from birth or has the Flowering changed them already? But then—

"You may not remember yet the battles in which we fought together."

"The truth is as my lord says."

"And language takes time."

"My lord is all-wise."

"The noble Flintknife is a warrior of irreproachable honor."

"As my lord says."

"But not all his supporters may be of equal scruple. The stakes are high. The time of the Flowering is one of great vulnerability."

"Who knows these things better than my lord?"

"The knights have not yet reached a judgment in your case, kinsman. The matter is so unusual that I am sure they will decide to suspend judgment for a while. Long enough for you to complete your second Flowering and calm their unworthy doubts."

"This is most reassuring." The mud was beginning to settle, and the water had snakes in it.

"Until then, my house is at your disposal, son of Trumpet-pillar."

That was Lynx's father's name, was it? "My lord's kindness passes all measure."

Basket-fox's warriors were as the sands of the plain and would defend the gallant Plumed-pillar, skillful acolytes could aid him through the Flowering, allies and friends would rally to his cause. . . . Lynx was not inclined to argue. A dead Blade could not serve his ward.

Later he was installed with his supposed handmaiden in sumptuous quarters, plied with servants and hospitality. His whims were commands.

Soon after dawn the next day he began serious language lessons.

7

The Hall of the Jaguars was vast and grand, an adjunct of the Imperial Palace itself. In Tlixilian style its walls and columns were carved into intricate pictures, brilliantly colored. One side was pillared, open to a courtyard to admit air, sunlight, and even birds, but temperature was rarely a problem in El Dorado. Lynx estimated it could have held half a thousand people, but that day about sixty men were standing around arguing. One woman stood discreetly outside, behind a pillar—Celeste, who was needed as an interpreter. She had been marched across the city on foot, which had done nothing to improve her disposition.

Lynx had been carried there in Basket-fox's personal palanquin, with an escort of eighty warriors. Having thrown the noble Jaguar order into chaos with his outrageous claim that a disgusting Hairy One was in fact Plumed-pillar Redux, the sly old rascal had stopped just short of giving him a knight's drums, trumpets, and harbingers. The meeting had been called to examine the evidence, namely Lynx.

Neither Basket-fox himself nor Flintknife, Plumed-pillar's brother and authentic heir, was in evidence. No knight was, because none of them would ever bother to attend anything as tedious as a committee—not so anyone would notice. There might be some lurking unseen in the shadows, Jorge had warned. They were a curious lot, Jaguars. Officially, each knight had sent one of his senior warriors to represent him.

The agenda was Lynx and whether or not to kill him out of hand. There were no precedents and no formal procedures. Two or three of the more respected older men tried to keep some sort of order, but it took a long time to examine the evidence and agree that he did show signs of beginning the Flowering. Lynx had always had a rare ability to wiggle his ears and he was a lot better at it now. His eyes were close to yellow already and his teeth were taking on new shapes.

The plaque was accepted as undoubtedly Plumed-pillar's regalia. Lynx's scars confirmed that he had survived a mighty battle. The warriors peered at his fingers and eyes and teeth, scowled at the hair on his chest, and nodded approvingly at the fur sprouting on his hands, face, and feet. They enthused over his jewelry like a pack of greedy dowagers. And they asked innumerable questions, which Jorge passed out to Celeste, who passed them back in to Lynx, and so on.

Jorge had assured him that Tlixilian conjuration did not include truth-sounding. Eagle knights could compel people to speak the truth, but that was a form of aggression, and the Jaguars would never call on the Eagles for help in an internal matter such as this—although Eagles would certainly be monitoring the proceedings. Free to bend the truth, therefore, Lynx and his mentor had devised a pleasing shape for it. Lynx was, after all, a knight back in his own land. He explained that *Ratter*, with her mysterious cat's-eye pommel, was a Chivian knight's regalia, empowered with his own heart's blood. He showed his binding scars as proof of this. They understood that and assumed that he must be a mighty conjurer, as Tlixilian knights were. He *must* be mighty just to have survived the first stroke in the duel with Plumed-pillar—described by Lynx in a dramatic narrative sorely lacking in modesty.

At the end, he explained, it was Plumed-pillar's soul that had survived in Lynx's body, so he had made the best of it and set off to return to the floating city. Since he was not dead, his usurping brother could not have inherited his rank and wealth, and should not be allowed to continue the Flowering. Then he would die, of course. Pity. Lynx salved his conscience by reasoning that he was not really telling lies, because no one was going to believe a word of that balderdash.

As Jorge had explained, all Basket-fox's clients and allies would pretend to believe. Some of Flintknife's weaker supporters might waver in their loyalty. Many, perhaps a majority, of the knights would wait to see who was going to offer what for their votes. No doubt Basket-fox was merely establishing Lynx as a valuable property that he could trade off at some future date in return for whatever it was that he really wanted, which would be something completely different. Think of cats, and mice.

Eventually the warriors ran out of questions and sent Lynx away. He had no real hope that he would ever be accepted as Plumed-pillar Redux, but he would live at least until the knights reached a verdict, which would probably be appealed to the Emperor and Great Council. From a pawn's point of view, this was better than the alternative, which was a one-way trip up a pyramid, and until that day came, as it must, he could live in a palace and guard his ward as closely as physically possible.

A few days after the meeting in the Hall of Jaguars, Lynx had his fourth interview with his mentor. He had asked for it, indeed begged for it, because his feet and hands burned as if every bone in them had been hammered to slivers. They would continue to do so until Basket-fox instilled more virtue into the plaque in the process the Tlixilians called "blessing." Even that might not completely cure the problem.

Jaguar Flowering took a lot longer than an Ironhall binding—a year was standard. It involved rituals whose details Lynx preferred not to know, and long study to master the powers the knights wielded after their apotheoses. What Plumed-pillar's plaque was doing to him—helped along by Basket-fox's infusions of power, although no one admitted that, and perhaps by his Ironhall binding also—could produce nothing more than a change in his physical appearance. No one had ever heard of such a thing happening before, or could guarantee that this partial transformation would not kill him or drive him crazy.

The sun had just set, painting the eastern volcanoes orange under a cobalt sky speckled with a few early-bird stars. The air was still, heavy with flowery, leafy scents. Lynx sat with Celeste outside their cabin, chatting endlessly with the interpreter, Jorge, and hoping fervently that he would soon be summoned to the Jaguar's presence.

"The . . . weather? What's the word for weather?" Celeste asked Jorge. This was what they did all day—talk. They were making progress.

"The weather is very fine," Lynx said miserably. A life of pain would not be worth living.

"The weather is pleasing," Celeste agreed.

"The weather is rarely mentioned," Jorge said, "because it is always pleasant. Even in the rainy season, this is not a stewpot like the coast."

Celeste asked him to explain a couple of words he had used, and he did.

"You are happy here?" Lynx said.

"Happy? I have accepted my fate. There are worse lives. I am a cripple, so I will never be sacrificed on the altar stone. There is no finer city in the world than El Dorado." Jorge was an educated man and had traveled widely in Eurania before coming to the Hence Lands. He had been a captive and slave for five years. "The worst part of my duties is helping to question my countrymen when they are made prisoner. That part I do not like."

"Torture?" Lynx wondered what torture could be worse than what he was enduring.

"No torture. Eagles use the Serpent's Eye on them, so they cannot lie, but I translate. And when they ask me, I must tell them that they will die."

Celeste started to ask a question in Tlixilian.

Lynx was distracted. His pain faded away, icy water quenching the fires. All his knotted muscles relaxed.

"He is here." He peered around the shadowy patio.

There was no one in sight . . . except Basket-fox, where he had not been an instant before. As his prisoners genuflected to him, he made a sound somewhere between a chuckle and a purr. "That feels better, noble Plumed-pillar, slayer of hundreds?"

"Wonderfully better, mighty hunter of the night." Lynx managed that speech all by himself. "Except . . ." He frowned and flexed his right hand. "Still a little . . ." He pointed, and Jorge supplied the word for wrist. "In my wrist."

The knight sank to the ground, graceful as a cat. He rested his front paws on his very human knees. He was unusually grandly dressed, glittering with jewels and bright feather work.

"You will have to endure some discomfort. Even the normal Flowering is not for the faint of heart."

That sounded ominous. "I endured it once, I can do so again."

"Of course. I hear the carrier-of-nightsoil Flintknife is racing through the Flowering as fast as he can stand it, recklessly squandering captives."

"His crimes will catch up with him."

"Of course. And your fair concubine?"

Celeste sighed. "The renowned silent slayer honors my life by asking. His kindness rules the night as the sun brightens the day."

She must have rehearsed that! She missed no chance to flirt with the old scoundrel. "Nothing personal, darling," she had said the last time Lynx complained of her behavior. "You are a wonderfully strong lover, while that old tabby will be a wearisome chore, but my safety is your duty, is it not? Will I not be more secure as handmaid to such a great lord than I am shut up with a penniless imposter?"

Her logic was impeccable, and she was being especially nice to him these days to console him.

Basket-fox licked his fangs with a tongue like an insole. "We must think to your estate, kinsman." He kept his great cat head toward Celeste, but his words were directed to Lynx, or rather to the fictitious Plumed-pillar.

"I am already overwhelmed by my lord's generosity."

Waiting for the interpretation, the Jaguar stretched, making his finery clink and sparkle. "But a knight of your eminence needs warrior attendants."

Lynx was suddenly permitted to notice a stripling warrior standing in the background clutching spear and shield, his face carefully impassive. He had not been visible a few seconds ago.

The knight waved a paw. "This staunch young man is my great-grandnephew, so he is related to you also." Any two knights in all Tlixilia were related to each other in some convoluted way. "Night-fisher is his name. He would be honored to wait on you."

Lynx glanced at Celeste and saw triumph. Strangely, Lynx sensed that his binding would not resist the change. Basket-fox would be a much more effective protector for Celeste than he would be, and to resist him would be dangerous for both ward and Blade. There was nothing to be done, and he appreciated that the Jaguar had eased his pain before stating the price, which was the gentlemanly way to do it.

Sigh! "Nothing can ever match your generosity, shadow of the dark, not even close. All the world knows that your wealth is as boundless as the stars, but if there is any trifle left to me in my present downcast condition that might amuse you, I would be overjoyed to cast it at your feet."

The cat-man departed soon after that, with an arm around his exotic new playmate. Lynx remained, and so did his new aide-de-camp. Doubtless this Night-fisher would be deft at cleaning teeth and brushing fur, but he would never replace Celeste.

VI

Send not valued dogs against the wild boar in his wallow . . .

1

The incredibly misnamed *Glorious* was a two-masted carrick, high front and back and low in the waist, a scruffy tub the size of two hay wains, carrying a crew of fifty. Dolores and Megan shared a closet-sized cabin in the aft castle. Quin, Flicker, and Wolf slept with the hands, which meant on deck whenever possible. In bad weather, they were battened down in the hold like apples in a cider press, a solid carpet of seasick men in windowless quarters barely chest-high, dimly lit by a few wildly gyrating oil lamps, reeking of bodies, bilge, vomit, feces, and rotted food. Only fools stood downwind of sailors.

Like his ship, Captain Clonard was nigh as broad as he was long. He wore a fringe of curly brown beard, a kerchief around his head, and a large silver earring that was almost certainly a talisman. He claimed to be a trader, but probably dabbled in piracy, smuggling, and slaving whenever the wind was fair. His officers were as scabrous a gang of villains as could be found anywhere, while the hands were a mixture of similar rogues and baby-faced innocents fresh off the farm. He would not discuss his relationship with the Dark Chamber—wiser not to know that, Dolores said—but he dealt honestly enough with his passengers, to Wolf's continuing surprise.

The menu varied as the voyage proceeded, but beans, bacon or pickled pork, salt fish, and hard, salted biscuit were the staples. Fresh pork, onions, garlic, cheese, bacon, and chickpeas appeared briefly after each landfall, even fruit for the first few days. They drank foul water or beer, and later wine, but never enough, because the diet was so salty. Washing was a fond memory, yet no one was ever dry. Sea water corroded the skin.

Any unattached single woman among so many men would have been pestered, and Megan was winsome enough. With an experienced eye, she quickly selected Duff, the ship's carpenter, to be her favored friend. He was a solid, soft-spoken man of around forty, seemingly easygoing, but when his good fortune was challenged, as it inevitably was, the battle was both bloody and decisive. Thereafter he was left to enjoy his victory.

Not only were the passengers expected to help defend *Glorious* against Baelish pirates—which would certainly have been the wise thing to do had any appeared—the contract also required them to train the crew in the finer points of sticking sharp metal in people. Fencing helped pass the time, but until Wolf tried teaching swordsmanship to a squinty-eyed buccaneer on a wildly rocking deck with barely room to move between the mast and the rigging, with spray in his face and clothes drenched, while at any minute a foam-topped green wave might roll over the side and wash him into the scuppers, he had never realized how much Ironhall had spoiled him.

Ships were the worst torture chambers ever invented, places of constant torment with death one plank away. At first the travelers were bounced and frozen, later bounced and boiled, and near the end they almost died of thirst, becalmed for three weeks with the sun balanced atop the masthead. *Glorious* first cut south from Chivial to Isilond, then bypassed Distlain itself to make landfalls in Granaira and the Llaville Isles, which Distlain owned, plus the Sauelas, which it did not. In

Granaira the inquisitors picked up Distlish with a despicable accent. From the Sauelas they made the long sweep west and south to the Hence Lands, but the wind failed them a few days from their expected landfall. Just in time a stray breeze came by and wafted *Glorious* to one of the smaller islands, but one where there was water.

"Nine months since Quondam was attacked," Wolf said. "Maybe at last we may be able to do something about it."

"And make our fortunes, too," Dolores insisted.

Although it was the capital of Condridad, largest of the islands, the town of Mondon was only a splatter of timber or mud shacks, with no stone or brick buildings. It was also at its worst just then, near the end of the rainy season, with air like steam and a downpour every afternoon turning the streets to red quagmires. Thousands of gaudy birds swooped and screeched, the roaches were bigger than mice, and vegetation erupted in every corner, as if the entire settlement would revert to jungle the moment the people turned their backs. Mondon Bay was a magnificent natural harbor, though, and a busy one. Officially only Distlish vessels were allowed to drop anchor, but all eyes winked at that law. *Glorious* needed a refit, which would take a week or two.

The inquisitors' program there had been decided early and confirmed by months of wistful longing: first comfort, then society, then language. Their long ordeal afloat had left the team filthy and haggard, with every bone showing. By rights they needed several weeks' rest to recuperate, but time did not permit this. So Don Lope Attewell moved his household into the town's best hostelry in search of landlubber luxuries like soap and hot water. As soon as everyone felt human again, Flicker went off in carefully preserved livery to deliver a carefully forged letter of introduction to the Distlish governor.

Wolf himself went hunting through the saloons until he found a penniless, highborn, insufferably arrogant Distlish don drinking himself to death, then lured him back to the hostel to sample some excellent Granairan red. By midnight, when the boys laid the lush out to dry on the boardwalk, Dolores and Wolf had acquired accents matching those of the bluest of azure-blooded Distliard aristocrats, albeit slightly slurred.

Predictably, His Excellency was diplomatically indisposed and unable to receive the foreigner, but his wife and the other permanently bored upper-crust ladies of Mondon were snobs. They swallowed the bait and invitations began arriving the next day. Having no training in personation, Sir Wolf remained Sir Wolf. Lady Attewell, wife of a mere knight, became Lady Dolores, a noblewoman who had retained her title after marrying a commoner. Society ladies in the colonies would understand such matters. Indeed they would soon discover—from her servants, say—that Lady Dolores was a daughter of the Duke of Twobridge, no less. The tragic love story, the unwanted baby, the expulsion from Court and even from Chivial itself, could all be deduced from that, while especially sensitive noses would detect the fragrance of money available to make sure the reprobates stayed away. Why else would they be here, at the wrong end of the earth?

The governor and his wife attended several of the dinners that followed. In fact the same faces appeared every night, and only the houses changed. Dona Dolores played her role so magnificently that she awoke some mornings weeping over the poor dead baby.

For that first evening in society, Megan miraculously transformed milady from storm-battered waif back to ravishing beauty. Quin having hired a carriage and driver, Don Lope and Dona Dolores whirled off in state, with two footmen clinging on the back. Since they could find no excuse to take a lady's maid to a dinner party, Megan went to bed, swearing she would sleep the clock around yet again.

The tropic sun set early and a languorous night descended, the sky all stars, like silvery lace draped just above the treetops, and the steamy air scented with flowers and vegetation. With Distlish men greatly outnumbering Distlish women on the island and native wives banned from society, an admiring crowd soon gathered around Dolores. The men mobbed Wolf, most of them trying to sell him their plantations so that they could retire home to Distlain or head west to join in the war. Quin and Flicker scoured the kitchens for crusts of information. In short, all four inquisitors spied their heads off.

Although they were staggering with weariness when they returned to the hostel at midnight, Dolores insisted on holding a conference, for that was standard Dark Chamber procedure, and Megan was wakened to listen. Shunning the stifling bedrooms, the team assembled on a balcony overlooking the harbor, dropped the role-playing, and conversed softly in Chivian. A gibbous moon shone peacefully over the bay, but the night was alive with frog songs, saloon quarrels, lute playing, and the constant whine of insects.

The rules said they must start with the most junior, so he could show his stuff, if any.

"Didn't learn much," Quin said complacently, leaning back against the rail. "Politics hasn't changed from what the bats told us. The rainy season's almost over, so the war's about to start up again. This new *Caudillo* that King Diego sent out, Severo de la Cuenca—everyone has great hopes for him, but the Tlixilians are still holding their own. Last spring they sacked two towns and stamped out a major invasion, losses heavy on both sides. Dead, wounded, and missing in action are all equally dead in this war, of course. There's talk of the El Dorado forces using metal weapons, so some of the smuggling is getting through."

He glanced sideways at Flicker, who had not said a word yet, but was quivering like a hound on a leash. Quin grinned and let him loose. "That's about all that I—"

The greyhound shot off. "You can't be sure about the smuggling—they must have captured lots of weapons by now . . . but it's likely. Even the locals hereabouts want to stretch the war out as long as—"

Wolf started to ask why and Flicker leered triumphantly.

"Because for thirty years the Distliards have been setting themselves up with wide estates . . . here and on Mazal . . . plantations growing cotton, sugar cane, beans, ranching on higher ground for horses, salt beef, and leather. . . . They're all in over their scalps in debt and the only cash market they've got is the army on the mainland. It's a great pyramid built on war and slavery. . . . Slavery's absurdly inefficient, because the initial investment and the capital tied up in security and housing is much more than the wages you'd have to pay free folk to work far harder, so the moment the war is settled the *haciendas* are all bankrupt."

He drew a breath about then. "I also heard that there's not much wrong with glass swords."

Wolf made disbelieving noises.

"So they say!" Flicker snapped. " 'Long as you don't parry with them. Use a shield for parrying and they're *more* deadly. A glass sword can cut off a horse's head with one stroke! The great advantages the Distliards had at first weren't swords, they were horses and war dogs, which the Tlixilians had never seen before, so those are what we ought to be offering, not swords. Steel armor might sell, but cotton's cooler. Horses . . . Tlixilians have captured a few and learned to ride them."

Dolores was nodding that she'd heard that too.

"The ones who are really making money here," Flicker said, "and will make a lot more, are the harbor merchants and shipwrights. If the Distliards can take El Dorado, then the trade through Mondon will be enormous!" Another breath. "If they can't, then Eurania will start treating Tlixilia as a sovereign state and trade will bloom anyway!"

He was an ingenious little slug and might even be likeable if he did not keep making eyes at Dolores. He had learned more in the kitchen than Wolf had in the dining hall.

"Interesting but not immediately relevant. Thank you, Flicker. Good work. You, love?"

"I collected the names of some grandees in Sigisa," Dolores said. "It seems there's only one counts for much at all."

"Severo de la Cuenca?"

"Ruiz de Rojas."

"But Cuenca is the *Caudillo,* the Governor, *El Supremo.*"

Dolores fought back a yawn. "But Cuenca is away inland, fighting the war. Don Rojas runs Sigisa, which is the gateway to all Tlixilia. We're going to have to deal with Rojas. How about you, love? Did you hear anything we haven't mentioned?"

Fortunately Wolf did have one scrap to add to the heap. "Just a man they call *El Chiviano.* Seems he has a ranch hereabouts, in the hills north of town, a big one."

"I thought only Distliards could own land?" Flicker said suspiciously.

"He's a friend of the governor. They say he's the largest supplier of horses to the Distlish army, so he's doing well. He may have good sources of information. I'll see if I can arrange a meeting. Well done, all. Good start! Now let's get some sleep. We have work to do tomorrow."

2

*M*ondon was the center of the slave trade in the Hence Lands. Ships bringing prisoners from the mainland unloaded at dawn; ranchers and planters bargained; and by noon, when the sun became murderous, it was all over. Horrible as Wolf found the business, he and Dolores were there every morning to watch the chain gangs shuffling into the plaza—a few dozen men, women, and children, naked or close to it, fastened by the neck, and wrapped in ultimate despair. Young women sold first.

That was the best place to study the languages of the *naturales.* The slavers shouted commands to their wares, sometimes even translating questions and answers back and forth between the merchandise and prospective buyers. It soon became clear that there were many dialects, but only two languages, one from the islands and the other from the mainland. That was the one that interested the Chivians, of course. They stood in the shade with the buyers, declining offers to bid, but watching, listening, and applying their conjured gift of tongues. Within a week they knew enough Tlixilian to try whispering it to each other in bed, although slave market talk included more curses and insults than endearments.

Wolf was amused to discover how quickly he adjusted to the brown faces and coal-black hair of the *naturales,* men's lack of beards. He soon stopped seeing them as irredeemably ugly, as he had when viewing corpses at Quondam; the younger women were gorgeous. Most of the slaves seemed lost in bewildered despair, but he saw some who still held their heads high. In contrast, the worst gutter dregs from the slums of

Distlain had found their way out to the Hence Lands, where they could strut around like kings and buy slaves to gratify their whims.

On the tenth morning, Dolores said, "Buy that one."

"Which one?"

"The big one. I love the way his muscles ripple. He gives me goose bumps."

Wolf said, "He gives me goose bumps too." The object of her interest was a fearsome giant, his powerful brown body still bearing traces of war paint. The iron collar had abraded his neck and his chest showed marks of the lash. Alone in that tragic parade he wore manacles and leg irons, yet he held his head high and glared back at the world that maltreated him so. That mattered, but more important were the crusted wounds on his ears and lower lip, where ornaments had been ripped out. He was a Tlixilian of high rank.

"He won't fetch much," Dolores said. "We could try later when prices are lower."

"Not too much later. There are ways of taming stallions."

"Wolf! No! They'd really do that to a man?"

"He's not a man, he's a chattel." Appalled at the thought, Wolf said, "Spirits take the money! Let's buy him now."

As soon as they moved out in the sunlight, a greasy trader attached himself to them, fawning and querying their needs: "A fine kitchen maid for the lady? A child or two to teach. The little ones eat so much less. . . ."

Dearly wanting to cut out the brute's tongue, Wolf did not answer, but escorted Dolores directly over to her choice, knowing that this would drive up his price even more. As they drew near, the giant glared at them, and especially at Dolores, a woman viewing him in his shame. His chains rattled.

"Ah, this is Dominique! Very strong. Feel those arms! The *señor* will buy the strength of three ordinary men."

Dominique turned his back on the customers, ignoring what the rough iron collar did to the sores on his neck. He undoubtedly meant to demonstrate contempt, but he also revealed the amount of flogging he had endured. Wolf shivered at the sight of so much raw flesh, welts weeks old repeatedly overlain by newer, all suppurating and crawling with flies. The man might be terminally stupid, but he certainly had courage.

The slaver snarled and raised his whip.

"Leave him! You'll never tame him that way."

The greasy man smirked and gestured with his fingers. "As the *señor* says—snip! In a week he is docile, yes?"

"No, I fancy him for breeding stock. Ten pesos."

"The *señor* is joking! Seventy pesos and cheap at the price."

Wolf let Dolores take over the bargaining—inquisitors were very good at it. The dealer settled for nineteen pesos and two hundred maravedís.

Wolf paid up. Not wanting the slavers to know he spoke the language, he said, "Tell him to turn around and look me in the eye as a man should." Dominique, who must have been steeling himself for the whip throughout the proceedings, obeyed the order, except he was looking over Wolf's head and Wolf's eyes were level with his collarbones. "Tell him he is a warrior, and I also am a warrior." Wolf tapped his sword and the dark eyes glanced down at it. "Tell him he is my prisoner and I will treat him with honor."

The slaver obeyed, then chuckled. "The *señor* should play safe and buy those leg irons from us."

"I will buy a cloth from you," Wolf said, and had to pay an outrageous eighty maravedís for a dirty rag. As soon as his slave's shackles were unlocked, Wolf handed it to him to hide his nudity, then beckoned for him to follow, and the three of them walked together from that hellish, verminous place. The moment they were around the corner, Wolf stopped and looked up at the face of hatred, wondering if this warrior might prefer death to dishonor and choose to take one last bearded enemy with him.

"You are a warrior from Tlixilia?" he asked in Tlixilian.

The man's eyes jerked wide but he did not speak.

"Tell me your real name, warrior, not what those nightsoil carriers called you."

Suspiciously the giant said, "I am Heron-jade, taker of four captives among the sons of Sky-cactus."

"And I am—" It came out as *Wild-dog-by-the-spring*. "You fight in the armies of the floating city?"

Looking very puzzled, the big man said, "I did. Now I am meat."

"If you could return to Sky-cactus, you would be a warrior again?"

The dark, tortured eyes flickered to Dolores and back to Wolf. The world was making no sense for him—despair numbed, hope hurt. "In time it might be granted."

"If you do more noble deeds?"

He nodded.

"In a few days we sail west. I will return you to the great land, warrior Heron-jade. I will send you with a message to the Emperor. This I promise by my honor, as warrior to warrior. That will be a noble deed, for you must cross the land of the traitor rebels. Take my words to the floating city and live to fight again."

The chattel sneered in disbelief, refusing to be seduced by hope.

"Now we take you to the place of spirits to heal your wounds."

His chin jerked higher. "I will give my precious jewel."

"Wolf!" Dolores squealed. "He thinks you're going to tear his heart out."

Wolf explained as best he could, but Heron-jade was still perplexed and apprehensive when he arrived at the elementary. He grimaced at the robed conjurers lurking in the shadows, but went and stood in the center of the octogram as Wolf ordered. The chanting had scarcely begun when he gasped and raised a hand to his torn lip.

Healing was the only conjuration that did not give Wolf a headache—or if it did, it cured it immediately.

When the ritual was over, he said, "Now you feel better? Now you see we mean you well?"

Heron-jade strode across to him, dropped to his knees, and laid his head on Wolf's boots. "I am my lord's meat."

That might mean no more than a polite "Good chance!" or it might mean what it said. Wolf told him to rise, and took him out to the ship, leaving Dolores to inspect the traders' stalls.

As he was being rowed over the silvery bay, the slave kept his eyes fixed on his master's face, but Wolf could not tell whether he was being respectful or plotting murder. Their worlds were too far apart. Captain Clonard had grumbled hugely when told of Wolf's intention to buy slaves, but he had lost five men on the voyage to sickness and mishap, so he could not deny that he had room. Now, when he saw the ogre who climbed on board, he insisted that Heron-jade be put in irons, and Wolf reluctantly agreed.

Two days later he bought Serpent-night, who was a more manageable size and younger, a taker of one captive, but just as stubborn, for his back had been flogged to strips. With two prisoners, the Chivians could eavesdrop and polish their grasp of the Tlixilian language. The slavers began saving their intractable livestock for the madman, and on his last day in Mondon he acquired Pulse-obsidian and Blood-mirror-walks. He had to be content with four, although he wished he could buy and release them all.

He was much relieved when *Glorious* completed her refitting and prepared to sail. Having never been much of a partygoer, even before becoming the King's Killer, he had quickly wearied of Mondon's social life—humorless, cheerless guests sitting around soggy courtyards by the light of torches, drinking rum, being served hand and foot by sullen brown people whose world they had stolen. They ate meat, meat, and meat. They had nothing to discuss except the bad counsel King Diego was receiving and the incompetence of his army. They feared that El Dorado might yet reconquer its rebellious colonies and hurl the Distlish into the sea. Wolf's associates were more skilled at extracting useful information than he was, and the parasite lords of Condridad had little more knowledge to be extracted. To learn more, the team must move on to the notorious Sigisa, island of vice.

But Sigisa was run by the self-appointed *alcalde,* Ruiz de Rojas. The more they heard about him, the clearer it became that he was going to be a problem.

Wolf had expressed a passionate desire to meet *El Chiviano*

Alas, señor, the rainy season! You cannot possibly.

But anything was possible if the spirits of chance willed it. On his last night, the hostess, beaming with pride, announced that *El Chiviano* was here! In town! In this very house! To meet Don Lope! And she swept Wolf across the courtyard to make the introduction.

He was standing with three ranchers Wolf already knew, listening rather than talking. He was slim, average height, a weathered forty or well-preserved fifty. He wore the same knee-length pleated tunic as his companions did, with the same greatly puffed sleeves, the same silk hose below and pancake hat above, plus the inevitable sword, which was more necessary in Mondon than in Grandon. He greeted the newcomers' arrival with an expectant smile. As the hostess uttered Wolf's name, he offered a hand—and then dropped it. His eyes slitted. The threat was as blatant as a slap. The *señora* gasped and fell silent. The onlookers instinctively pulled back a pace.

"Wolf?" he said. "You Blades do choose silly names, don't you?"

Wolf raised his eyebrows. "You have the advantage of me . . . brother?"

Although the man's sword bore no cat's-eye, he might as well have had *Made on Starkmoor* written on his forehead. Blades aged well, but this one was too old to be a threat to Wolf.

"No brother of yours. My name would mean nothing to you. I hear the stupid bitch is actually queen now." Fortunately he was speaking Chivian.

Wolf ignored the sneer. "If you mean Queen Malinda, she kept the throne warm until her son came of age. Then she abdicated and sailed home to rejoin her husband."

"I wonder what even a Bael could do to deserve that one."

"She ruled well, *Chiviano*. Another twenty years would have been even better."

The expatriate shrugged. "If King Whatsis is worse, then Chivial must truly be in a mess."

"Chivial is in excellent shape for a country ruled by a homicidal halfwit." Wolf was enjoying himself. Wonderful party!

And *El Chiviano* was puzzled. "He sent you here to spy, of course."

"I swear by my soul, my sword, and my wife's virtue, *señor*, that King Athelgar did not send me here, and I would rather starve to death in a chain gang than ever lift a hand to help that man. Do I convince?"

"Nevertheless, perhaps I should inform His Excellency exactly what Blades are and what sort of dirty work they do."

The governor's friend was threatening to have Wolf hanged as a spy. Fortunately he was still speaking Chivian.

"Of course, *señor*. Tell him how they keep slaves now."

El Chiviano did not like that. "Sonny, if I put slaves to herding horses, I would own no slaves and no horses. Understand?"

"I do. Do your friends?"

The exile almost smiled. "Some of them are still lost in the trees." He started to turn away. Then he said, "Who is Grand Master now?"

"Durendal."

He nodded, as if that was to be expected. "He aided me once, at great risk to himself, I think. If you ever see him again, tell him Eagle is grateful."

"Any friend of Lord Roland's is a friend of mine."

"But none of mine." He strode away.

"*Señora*," Wolf told his hostess, "*El Chiviano* has insulted my King. I have no choice but to withdraw." Oh, horrors! He was defending Athelgar's honor! He collected his wife and servants and departed, huffing ferociously in case he burst out laughing. They sailed unhindered the next morning, so Eagle had not betrayed him.

No doubt the story was buried somewhere in the archives at Ironhall. Certainly the *Litany of Heroes* mentioned a Sir Eagle dying with glory two centuries ago, but the name was no longer on the permitted list. Wolf knew that because he had wanted it and been refused.

3

The final leg of the journey was the most dangerous, for they had left the last traces of the rule of law behind in Mondon. Baelish pirates or Distlish warships might challenge them, or Captain Clonard might spot a likely prize and throw off his cloak of respectability to give chase.

Even assuming the passengers reached Sigisa safely, they would need help to survive in that cauldron, so they had already begun subverting the best men among the crew with offers of good wages ashore. Clonard knew of this and liked it no better than he liked the four killer slaves in the hold.

At noon the first day, as *Glorious* wallowed with all canvas spread, Wolf unshackled Heron-jade and took him up on deck to exercise. He pointed at the sun. "See, we sail west, to the great land."

"The lord spoke as a true warrior."

"You exercise now. Grow strong again."

The big man threw his head back and began to clap. Once he had the beat, he went to stamping, then a dance, and eventually wild gymnastics, as best he could in that cramped space. Crew and passengers watched openmouthed. Sailors danced for exercise too, but they did not go on to balance on one hand on a rolling deck or perform twelve consecutive back flips. When he finished, gasping and running sweat, the audience applauded. He frowned until Wolf explained, then shrugged. Dolores gave him water and led him forward to the forecastle.

Being the smellier end of a ship, the bow was the least frequented. Flicker and Quin arrived. Heron-jade had met them earlier, but servants were beneath his notice. He tried to ignore Dolores, also, but that was much harder. Megan was not present, probably reuniting with Duff.

Very warily Wolf began asking questions. He knew from early conversations and eavesdropping that the giant was an eagle warrior, vassal of an eagle knight, Sky-cactus. The other three warriors were followers of jaguar knights, and there seemed to be a coolness between the two orders, even there in the enemy's clutches. There were more complexities. Heron-jade and Blood-mirror-walks were warriors of El Dorado itself, the floating city, while the other two were from lesser towns within its empire, and therefore had lower status. This pattern matched Euranian society, but Wolf dearly wanted to know how the two orders of knighthood differed. The corpse at Quondam had sported jaguar claws. Did an eagle knight have wings as well as the taloned feet whose tracks they had seen? He left that point for later.

"There are towns that make war on the floating city," he said. "Zolica, Yazotlan, Tephuamotzin."

Heron-jade's eyes flashed. "Offal! Turncoats! Slaves of the Hairy Ones." He thudded a huge fist on the rail. "They will be meat!"

"Our town is not the town of the Hairy Ones you fight. Our king is not their king."

Heron-jade considered that information. "So?" He was neither stupid nor especially quick-witted, but his mind walked unfamiliar paths and speech was beset with traps.

"Our king does not want the Hairy Ones and their slaves to burn the floating city."

"Your king will send his knights to fight with us?"

"First he sends me to ask a thing. Nine moons ago, knights of the floating city came across the ocean to the lands of my king, invaded his stronghold, slaughtered his men, abducted—"

As much as this terrible giant could display fear, he did so then. He shrank away, his brown face pale below its tattoos, white showing all around his coal-black irises.

Wolf said, "You are troubled and I know not why, Heron-jade."

He looked wildly around, at the birds floating by, the great swoops of sail overhead. Wolf began to fear he might leap into the sea.

"What makes a warrior so afraid?"

Even for his size, Heron-jade had enormous hands. One of them shot out and grasped Wolf by the throat. Wolf grabbed his dagger, realized he could be dead already, and quietly sheathed it again, while glimpsing Dolores tucking a knife back in her sleeve. He was released.

"You have a precious jewel," the eagle warrior said. "It beats."

"Why did you think I might not?"

"It is a sad song."

"Songs may speak true. Sing me the song."

Heron-jade nodded, thought for a moment, lips moving. Then he began to chant, hoarsely at first, gathering confidence as he went.

Words rarely translated exactly, so that even in ordinary speech Wolf had trouble seeing the world his slaves described. Heron-jade would refer to Sky-cactus as his father and himself as Sky-cactus's fledgling, yet he would also tell of his father having been a taker of three captives who had given his precious jewel to a jaguar knight of another town many years past—which meant he had been sacrificed in the ghastly conjuring ritual, of course. When it came to song, meaning was as intangible as mist.

Great the gifts—myriad the precious jewels
Lizard-drumming of perfect valor—spotted slayer
brings to the halls of Amaranth-talon—unconquerable soaring one

Hear words of my father—Quetzal-star blood spiller
after many years whispering on night winds

Terrible the battle—more terrible the Hairy Ones I slew
most terrible—the house of demons that holds me

Thus speaks Quetzal-star—prowler of darkness
crying out for aid

Far-seeing one take these cloaks, these rings, these riches
the myriad precious jewels—bear me thence

Send with me—Plumed-pillar
my brother—silent slayer

Amaranth-talon—hears the clawed one
the cloud chaser rises—wings spreading
calls his brother—Bone-peak-runner

Swift and terrible—the sky darkener
comes storm-riding

They spill the precious jewels—knives drink
A wind they raise—blowing into the cold, the dark
the hell—where demons torment Quetzal-star

Wind-borne they go—dread slayers of demons
Lizard-drumming—Plumed-pillar

Great the slaughter—demons bleeding
the soul of Quetzal-star—is brought forth

Alas

Demons rally—falls Plumed-pillar
ax strikes—mighty cedar falling falling

Out from the cold, the dark, the hell
Bone-peak-runner—Amaranth-talon
Lizard-drumming—heroes triumph

But weep weep for the new lost—Plumed-pillar
Wasted—mighty jewel wasted

The Chivians exchanged smiles of triumph. Even Flicker looked pleased.

"Lizard-drumming was the true-born son of Quetzal-star?" Wolf asked.

"And mightier," Heron-jade said solemnly. "Uncounted precious jewels wept for him."

"Questions?" Wolf asked in Chivian. "Pass them through me."

Flicker jumped in before Dolores could speak. "What can the witness tell us about the warriors who accompanied the four knights?"

"Just their regular war bands, I expect." Wolf translated the question.

Heron-jade's eyes seemed to turn even darker than usual. "Many great warriors. Men of great courage. Mighty lords."

"Well done, Flicker! Of course an expedition into demon hell would call forth the show-offs. Volunteers, likely."

Flicker looked smug. "It explains all the finery you collected."

Boy Genius had seen what Wolf had not, that regular troops would not have worn so much gold, every amulet and talisman available.

"Any more questions?"

"How did they work the conjuration?" Dolores asked.

"I suggest we leave that for another session, love. I don't want to push too hard. We have several days before we reach Sigisa. Quin, my lad, you will repeat this testimony to Grand Inquisitor, but how will you interpret it for them?"

Quin's face went blank for a moment as he pondered. That plain, honest, workaday face was a good inquisitor face, dangerously easy to underestimate.

"Interpretation," he said. "The attack on Quondam Castle was a unique event, not the opening of a general offensive. The Baroness's jaguar pin had been regalia of a jaguar knight named Quetzal-star, who fell early in the Distlish invasion. Its new owner sent it home to Distlain and King Diego, who passed it on to Queen Malinda, who left it behind when she departed, and His Majesty gave it away to Marquesa Celeste. The implication is that nobody wanted to own it, and the effect it had on the White Sisters when it was worn is further evidence of its residual spirituality. At Quondam the Baroness wore it constantly and thus stimulated this remnant power to action. Lizard-drumming, Quetzal-star's son and successor, sensed it in use and interpreted the call as his father's spirit requiring rescue, so he and another jaguar knight purchased the aid of two eagle knights to go in search of it. Implication is that the eagle knights provided the transportation and the jaguars did the fighting. The jaguar knight killed by Sir Lynx was Plumed-pillar."

"Very concise analysis, Quin. Any comments, anyone?" Wolf turned to Heron-jade. "Your words move us, Taker of Four Captives, but it is only a song. That was our land the great warriors saw. It is not always cold, not always dark. It bears flowers in abundance, in season. Nor was Plumed-pillar the only corpse they left behind. Many of our warriors and your warriors died. The person they took back to your land with them—what of her?"

"Her?"

"It was a woman they brought back."

The giant howled, startling the entire ship. "The demons did this? Weep, weep for Quetzal-star!" He beat on his head with his fists.

Dolores's face turned bleak, as if Heron-jade had just made his muscles seem less sexy. Quin and Wolf exchanged manly grins.

When the warrior stopped wailing, Wolf asked, "What happened to Quetzal-star after the rescue?"

He did not know. Lizard-drumming was not his lord. But if Celeste had since been murdered—to release Quetzal-star's soul?—then Lynx would have sensed it, wherever he was. Had that most unfortunate of Blades gone mad in some foreign port?

Wolf told Flicker to escort Heron-jade back to the hold and bring up Pulse-obsidian and Serpent-night so they could have their turns on deck. They did not dance or sing; they just went straight into calisthenics. Despite the cramped conditions and although they could never have practiced together before, they put on an incredible acrobatic double act of warrior gymnastics.

Later they were questioned about their youth and training, none of which turned out to be of interest. They did confirm that Tlixilian politics were as complex as Euranian. El Dorado was ruled by an aristocratic warrior-caste, with the Emperor only chairman of the council. He would be succeeded by a close male relative, not necessarily a son. The greatest lords were the warrior-conjurer knights, but birth alone would not admit a man to the great orders; he must also be a great fighter. Pulse-obsidian let slip that Blood-mirror-walks stood highest among the four ex-slaves, being of very high birth, related to the imperial family. That and his growing battlefield prowess had destined him for eventual knighthood until he was wounded and captured by the Distlish.

Those two were sent back to their chains and up came Blood-mirror-walks himself. He was probably the youngest and certainly the shortest of the four, although almost as wide across the shoulders as Heron-jade. He might also be the smartest. He had limped when Wolf first bought him, but the healing had cured that. Seeing him looking curiously at *Diligence,* Wolf drew her and passed her over to him to study. Dolores glared at him for this foolhardiness.

"We Hairy Ones have better weapons than you do," Wolf said.

The young warrior fingered the edge and tried the balance. "Sky metal. And you ride on deer. This is the regalia of a knight?" He pointed to the cat's-eye.

"It is . . . How did you know that?"

"I was told so by someone." Blood-mirror-walks returned the sword, hilt first. "But not all flowers bring fruit."

"Why do you not acquire weapons like ours? We will trade them."

The dark eyes were expressionless. "That is for the lords to say."

"But when the knights went to the cold hell to rescue the soul of Quetzal-star, there were many weapons of sky metal there and they took none. Why?"

"I do not know."

He did know. He just wasn't going to tell. He had already learned from Heron-jade that the soul of Quetzal-star had been imprisoned in the body of a woman, and was equally appalled. This, in his opinion, was what came of fighting Hairy Ones. "A warrior must give his precious jewel to an honorable conqueror," he explained.

"It is best to win, surely?"

He sneered. "And die of old age?"

"Had it been the rebels who captured you, instead of the Hairy Ones, would they have taken your precious jewel?"

"Of course."

"And you would have submitted?"

"Proudly."

His smile was chilling. To a Tlixilian, ritual vivisection was the finest death.

"Why did the jaguar knights ask the eagle knights to raise the wind? Do jaguar knights have lesser power?"

"Our knights have other powers."

That was the last information Wolf got out of Blood-mirror-walks that evening, and next day the others were much less communicative than before. Quin overheard some of the harangue. They had been tricked, Blood-mirror-walks argued. It was better to die a slave than be indebted to a Hairy One of any sort in any way, and if the new kind imprisoned knights' souls in female bodies, then they were even worse than the Distliards. He ordered his companions not to cooperate with their captors and they swore to obey.

4

"This is romantic!" Dolores said.

Which merely demonstrated, in Wolf's cynical view, that one could get accustomed to anything, even shipboard life. They were up on the forecastle, sitting close, hugging tight while *Glorious* ploughed onward through a moonless night. Her sails were plumped by the warm trade wind, the sky was a glory of unfamiliar stars, and even the waves had a spooky glow. The rhythmic swish of waves against the bow and the creak of cables added a sort of lullaby. But this was the downwind end of the ship and somewhere ahead was a continent full of cannibals.

"Anywhere is romantic when you're there, my love."

"You're learning." She kissed his ear, the larger one. "Anyone but an inquisitor would be utterly deceived and swept off her feet."

"I don't have to sweep you off your feet. You are putty in my hands."

She chuckled happily. "True."

He was about to try a serious kiss when he heard voices and the rest of the team came trotting up the ladder to join them. A fiddle struck up amidships, a sailor began singing a lament, and others joined in.

Wolf began with a lament, also, stressing the problems that lay ahead. "Conference. We were sent to discover the *How* and *Why* of the attack on Quondam. Heron-jade has answered the *Why* question for us, so you get to go home and report, Quin, you lucky fellow. *Why* was easy, *How* will be hard. We were told in Mondon that in all their years here, the Distliards have learned nothing about Tlixilian conjuration. If even their allies guard the secrets so closely, would we do better if we were free to walk the streets of El Dorado? Who feels that we should declare our mission impossible and all go home with Quin?"

He was appealing to Dolores, although he knew she would be the last to quit. Tlixilian conjuration was to be her life's work or the death of her.

Flicker said, "No one."

"Let's talk about it," Megan said. "We did confirm that the *How* is human sacrifice. Chivial would never tolerate that. Do we even *want* to know any more about how they do it?"

"Yes!" Dolores never wavered in her enthusiasm. "I've told you! Conjuration requires both summoning and commanding. We summon the spirits inside an octogram and it's almost impossible to apply their power outside it. Things or people can be enchanted and then taken out of the octogram, the way we were enchanted against fevers. The eagle and jaguar knights don't cut out hearts on the battlefield, but they certainly do apply power there. It sounds as if they can enslave the actual spirits and take them away to use at another time and place. That's the *How* we need to know! They just use sacrifices to summon the spirits, but we can do that in other ways."

She was the expert. The sailors' chant ended and for a moment only the ship and the waves spoke.

Wolf sighed. "Forsooth, then we press on, my hearties. We have our four messengers. We send them off to El Dorado, and stay put in Sigisa, drinking rum and dancing till dawn. Tell me what we do about de Rojas."

Their sources in Mondon had known little of affairs in the interior, where *Caudillo* Cuenca battled the Tlixilian Emperor, but they had been well-informed about the scandalous, depraved island of Sigisa. King Diego's writ did not run there. The government comprised an *Alcalde,* Ruiz de Rojas, and a city council. The council elected him and he appointed the council—a very tidy arrangement that kept all the crime under one management. Every saloon, dice game, and brothel paid its toll to Rojas. Not a bean was sold or a water cask filled without his sanction.

Rojas was said to be discreet in what he skimmed off the army's supplies, though, and the *Caudillo* was currently too engrossed in the war to pay much attention to the racketeer at his back. That situation could not last very long. Even if Rojas was tolerated as a welcome control over inevitable corruption that might grow even worse without him, sooner or later King Diego and his general would move to establish the rule of law. Or the Tlixilians would win and no Distliard would be left breathing in Sigisa. Rojas must be amassing loot as fast as he could by any means he could. To the Chivians he was a monstrous looming threat. Why should he cut them in on the smuggling?

"Quin?"

Again Quin smiled and shrugged. "I won't be staying, Sir Wolf. Doesn't feel right for me to speak."

"We can use anybody's good ideas. Flicker?"

Flicker's teeth shone in the starlight. "Why waste our prisoners just as messengers? Use them as guides. Ignore Rojas. Slip by him before he notices and head inland. Go straight to El Dorado."

Wolf had expected this. "You are proposing a major change of plan."

"The situation has changed. The bats didn't know about the *Alcalde*. He's more dangerous than the mainland would be. Can't you see that?"

"It's possible, but you can't prove it yet and the only place to find out is Sigisa itself. Secondly, you're assuming we *can* slip by Rojas. Efficient robber barons keep a very close watch on the road—or harbor, in this case. I'm sure his goons will go through the ship like a business of ferrets, and they'll want to look in our baggage. Thirdly, eventually we hope to come back out. I don't want to burn our bridges. Or boats. Let's hear the others. Megan?"

Megan was just as predictable. "Stay away from him as much as we can. We have ways of being unobtrusive."

Dolores said, "I agree we must try and avoid trouble, but I'd rather tell him what we're planning than have him torture it out of us. His price will go up, but we have lots of gold."

Flicker made a snorting noise. "Offer him a thousand pesos and he demands ten thousand? Give him ten and he demands a hundred? Give—"

"Point made," Wolf said. "You want to bypass him, Megan wants to hide from him, and Dolores wants to cut him in. I have another idea."

For several nights he had been dreaming of his stepfathers, especially the last one. Normally he paid little heed to dreams, but sometimes they offered warnings, and one should at least try to understand their advice. "You're snoops. I'm a bully boy. I don't think the way you do. I agree with Dolores that we'll have to cut Rojas a slice of our imaginary goose. I'd like to have him as an ally, but I prefer to negotiate on my feet, not on my knees."

"Meaning what?" Flicker sneered.

"Meaning I'd start by kicking his shins."

They talked amicably. Megan stuck to her original position. In the end Dolores supported Wolf out of loyalty. Surprisingly, so did Flicker, either because he just enjoyed brawling or because he hoped to watch Wolf botch up the mission.

Quin had the last word. "Keep me out of it, Sir Wolf, so I can report on your funerals." Another six months at sea might not be such a terrible prospect after all.

Captain Clonard had refused to hire a pilot in Mondon. Finding Sigisa, he had explained, was a feat of navigation within the abilities of the average spaniel. All you did was sail due west until you made landfall and then go north, keeping an eye out for Smoking-woman, one of the great volcanic peaks of Tlixilia. When you had passed that and were almost halfway to an even bigger one, Sky-is-frowning, you made a left turn and entered the river mouth.

Fortunately he was right, and one sunny morning *Glorious* was towed into the harbor. Wolf leaned on the rail beside a wildly excited Dolores, admiring the gateway to the mainland, of which they had heard so much. Baron Roland had described Sigisa as two miles of brothels and dens, but since his day it had grown longer and wickeder, until now it was a dull night when no bodies departed on the morning tide. Into this pestilential pit had poured Distlish soldiers, sailors, and adventurers by the thousand, plus all the human parasites that fed on them. Having seen how big the world was, Wolf had almost given up hope that Lynx would ever reach the Hence Lands, but if he did, his quest to find his ward must lead him through Sigisa. The brothers would meet again here or nowhere.

Languid and greasy, the river drifted northward along the coast, held captive on the east by Sigisa, which was a sand spit, not a true island. In the dry season the river shrank and the wells turned brackish, but at that time of year, with the rainy season just ended, the river was a safe harbor, and a dozen ships were anchored there, most of them surrounded by dugout canoes, loading or unloading cargo. The western bank was jungle and swamp, reputed to be full of poisonous snakes, spiders, insects, and even frogs, little scarlet blobs no bigger than a thumbnail whose touch burned a man's skin.

"I don't like the look of that side." Dolores was pouting at the impenetrable green tangle. "Let's not stay there."

They turned to study the equally dense tangle of shacks and tents on the sandbar. Wolf said, "Do you think the town looks any better? I think I'll sleep in plate mail."

"Not in my bed you won't."

Their first requirement must be to find somewhere secure to live and store their valuable baggage. Real estate was reportedly volatile in Sigisa, with houses changing hands all the time on the roll of a die or twist of a knife. Anyone wishing to breathe the air there was expected to pay off the goons, from the mayor down to the junior assistant deputy harbormaster who would be the first aboard when *Glorious* dropped anchor. There were limits, though. If Rojas shaved his victims too close to the bone, ships would find another port. Estimating what could be plucked off *Glorious* would take hours of negotiation in that murderous heat, but that was Clonard's business. Wolf planned to go right to the top.

Although Sigisa was the main port for the slave trade, he had been told in Mondon that there were no slaves in Sigisa itself, because they would escape too easily. As evidence that one should not believe all one heard, the dozen sweating brown rowers in the lighter that was towing *Glorious* to her anchorage were very obviously chained, and the man standing over them held a whip. Just as *Glorious* was moving slowly past a ship loading a fresh cargo of prisoners, Flicker and Quin emerged on deck with the four Tlixilians, who recognized the place at once and glared around as if they would much enjoy burning it to the ground with all its inhabitants.

Wolf addressed the one who mattered, the youngest, a great-great-grandson of a former emperor. "I have kept my promise."

Blood-mirror-walks studied him distrustfully, eyes black as coal. "And what must we do now, Wild-dog-by-the-spring?"

"*Must?* I do not use that word to warriors. That way lies home." Wolf pointed to the jungle and the snowy cone of Sky-is-frowning peering over it. "Swim now if you wish. Or wait for dark, and I will have you rowed across. I will give whatever you need for your journey—food, canoe, gourds, blankets." Blankets seemed absurd in that tropical sweat house, but El Dorado lay beyond high ranges. "I ask only that you take word to the floating city that we will help its struggle if we can. I showed you the weapons we offer in trade. You are free to go at any time."

The chunky jaguar warrior was still suspicious, sniffing the air for a hint of treachery. "And you remain here?"

"I hope to. You could help me in that, if you wished."

Blood-mirror-walks curled his lip in an *I-knew-it* sneer. Here came the bargaining he had been expecting. "Help how?"

"It is possible that there will be some Distliards in need of dying."

Heron-jade made a blood-curdling noise in his throat. "Is that a promise?"

Wolf laughed. "No, but I will arrange it if I can. Today I must challenge the lord of this town and he may send his warriors against me. I will fight, but I need friends. I freed you, I healed your wounds, and you have eaten my salt. Are not the best friendships sealed in battle? Within three days I will win a home here, or I will be dead. But the choice is entirely yours. Go now, or tarry three days and help me against the Distliards."

The others just watched Blood-mirror-walks, and he did not consult them. He was young and assertive. To refuse a fight against the Hairy Ones was unthinkable. "We have eaten your salt," he agreed. "We will stay and fight at your side, Wild-dog-by-the-spring."

5

The anchor had barely splashed down before a gang of harbor officials came swarming over the side, looking at least as villainous as Wolf had expected. They closed in on Captain Clonard, who had an unlimited supply of impressive fake documents to flaunt on such occasions.

They were intercepted by a gentleman resplendent in fine linen tunic and silk hose, the garb of a wealthy planter or rancher in Mondon, topped off with a couple of glittering decorations. Dolores, on his arm, was even more impressive in bright brocade, twirling a silk parasol. Wolf announced in his haughtiest aristocratic Distlish that he had urgent business with the *Alcalde*.

The chief ruffian said, "No one goes ashore until I am satisfied."

Staring at him in disbelief, Wolf pointed to the ship's standard, which was undoubtedly large and multicolored, but hung so limp that its heraldry was unreadable. Then he unwrapped a package to reveal a scroll bearing much scarlet wax and ribbon. "You would argue with the King's seal?"

No, even a senior de Rojas minion would not do that. A lighter was brought alongside; Dolores was lowered into it in a sling. There was— *much apologies, señor!* no such thing as a lady's carriage in town, but the distinguished visitors were assured that the walk to the *municipalidad* was not far. Leaving the rest of the team to guard the precious baggage, Don Lope and Dona Dolores set off to call upon the ill-famed de Rojas.

It was a very educational stroll. Baron Roland had explained that the business district lined the riverbank, the center of the spit was occupied by a residential squalor of tents and wattle shacks, while an avenue of large villas stood shoulder-to-shoulder along the seafront to divide the riffraff from the fresh air. He had not mentioned that there was almost no room left to move.

Every gap was packed with people. Most of the men were Distliards, almost all the women *naturales,* but there were exceptions—haughty Euranian ladies with trains of servants, even haughtier warriors in feath-

ered cloaks and body paint; child pimps, child hookers, child pickpock-
ets. Unlike drab old Chivial, Sigisa shimmered with color: rainbow loincloths and fine gowns; gaudy half-naked prostitutes soliciting; hucksters
thrusting fabrics, beads, or pottery at passersby; blinding sunlight and
inky shade; foliage against the cloudless sky; flowered creepers; parrots,
macaws, and toucans. The air was a potpourri of exotic scents of spices,
flowers, and people. No one was hurrying, everyone going somewhere.
Blank-faced servants, swaggering pirates, armor-plated men-at-arms
blazing in the sunlight and close to heat stroke, enormous war dogs and
their handlers . . . carts and wagons and horse-drawn drays.

The slim hand on Wolf's arm was steady, but he knew Dolores well
enough now to know that she was nervous. She would be crazy if she
were not. The shore was lined with shipyards, marine chandlers, livestock pens, distilleries, lumber yards, and a dozen other enterprises. Behind them lurked lath-and-wattle shacks, houses mixed with
grog-shops, stalls displaying fruits and fly-infested meat, leather workers'
shops, potteries, and certainly brothels. Every breath brought a new
scent, every moment new peddlers shouting their wares. Dull it was not.

The visitors had leisure to admire the bustle, for their guide naturally took them by a roundabout route, so one of his boys could sprint
more directly to their destination and warn of their coming. At last they
came to the Rojas palace, a complex of fine wooden buildings on the
seaward side of the town, enclosed by an impressive palisade and
guarded by troops in shiny cuirasses and helmets. If there were many of
those beauties around, Wolf decided, this hacienda would be a very
tough nut to bite on. He was even more impressed by the interior,
which had the same air of wealth and taste as Baron Roland's Ivywalls,
meaning it did not look as if it had been designed by King Athelgar.
Some of the furniture might have been imported all the way from
Distlain; the pottery and wall hangings were Tlixilian.

One side of the reception room looked out on a garden, and another was open to the spangling blue sea and its cooling breeze. The visitors were granted a few moments to admire it before the *Alcalde* strolled
in, displaying remarkable grace for a man who must be puzzled to the
marrow. An emissary sent by King Diego ought to arrive with a squad

of men-at-arms and a warrant for his arrest, not just a skinny girl dressed as a grand lady. Gang boss, vice lord, murderer, local tyrant, Ruiz de Rojas had been born on Mazal, his father one of the first settlers, his mother a *naturale*. Wolf had expected someone of villainous appearance like Captain Clonard, but Rojas was thirtyish, handsome, superbly dressed, and instantly charming. His mixed blood showed in his features. He wore his heritage proudly, letting it add to his hauteur: *You may claim conquest or inheritance, I have both. I rule here by right.*

He was respectful to an envoy bearing a royal edict, but he did not fawn or grovel. Informed that the señor's companion was in fact his wife, he bowed gracefully and kissed her bejeweled fingers in proper Distlish style. Then he turned to a waiting servant and nodded.

The man vanished and a moment later ushered in a striking young woman—almost as tall as Dolores, svelte, and the color of ripe chestnuts, as Lynx would have said. She wore a shimmering white silk gown, and her jet-black hair was wound in coils held by silver combs. She moved like gossamer on a summer dawn.

"Don Lope, Dona Dolores, may I have the honor of presenting my dear wife, Fortunata?" Rojas had arranged for her to be on hand, of course—a very quick reaction to the news of the important arrivals. Wolf found it doubly remarkable because the grandees in Mondon kept their native or part-native wives and concubines out of sight of Euranian visitors.

According to the gossips of Mondon, Fortunata had been born into the highest level of Eldoradoan nobility. While still a child she had been dispatched to one of the minor cities to become a royal wife, and her caravan had been captured by a Distlish raiding party. After passing through various hands, she had become the gangster's wife in settlement of a gambling debt. She spoke Distlish hesitantly, so Wolf and Dolores responded in Tlixilian.

Her eyes widened. "I thought no Distliard spoke the pure tongue, señor!" She meant they spoke the El Dorado dialect—courtesy of Heron-jade and Blood-mirror-walks, of course.

Now the *Alcalde* was even more puzzled, but he bade his guests be seated. They babbled flowery trivia about the voyage out from Distlain and the news from Mondon. Considering that most of the social life in Sigisa was at the saloon-and-brothel level, Fortunata was amazingly poised. After his servants had brought refreshments and withdrawn, Rojas's curiosity won out.

"Your visit to Sigisa is more than social, Don Lope?"

Wolf smiled. "Personal business."

The major glanced inquiringly at the package bearing the royal seal.

"This?" Wolf said. "It's a forgery, but quite a good one. Care to see?" He handed over the package, which was not in fact sealed by the seal dangling on the ribbon. The inside was blank. Wolf kept his smile firmly in place, for this was the point at which the mayor might send for thugs and thumbscrews, and then the visitors would leave with the flotsam on the morning tide.

Rojas studied the wax and the vellum carefully. "And its purpose?"

"Merely to get your attention, Excellency. I never *said* it was the King's seal."

Rojas laughed with every indication of real amusement. "Just to own this would get you hanged back in Ciudad Del Rey, *señor!*"

"But this is not Ciudad Del Rey."

"True. So what can I do for you?" Smiling, he offered Wolf back the forgery.

"No, please keep that as a souvenir of a brash intruder, Excellency." A little penmanship and a hot knife could make that document extremely valuable for anyone with a low scruple count. "I am considering tarrying awhile in your fair city to pursue . . . certain interests . . ."

The inquisitors had rehearsed him half the night. Distlish grandees did not sully their hands with trade, so ostensibly he was talking about land, but no one could acquire clear title to land here, for all of it was claimed by at least two monarchs. So there was meat under the pastry, and Rojas set to work to find out what it was. Wolf declined to be pinned down. In practice they talked about how the war was going, how a stranger might go about buying or renting a villa, and how one might meet interesting people in Sigisa. Money would be no problem.

Rojas was witty, subtle, and as cynical as only a vice lord could be. The war was nothing to him. Neither King nor Emperor claimed his loyalty. "The Distliards are fools to pursue such a bloody struggle," he said, "when they could gain so much by peaceful trade. And the Emperor is paying the price of arrogance. Had he been less greedy when he was overlord of the coastal cities, they would not have rebelled when the strangers came."

"What of them?" Wolf asked. "Zolica, Yazotlan, Tephuamotzin?"

"Fools! We see their emissaries around town sometimes. You can know them by their high manner and low intelligence. They are so keen to settle scores with an ancient foe that they cannot see how much more dangerous Distlain is. They buy a jaguar to silence a noisy dog."

"What will happen to them when El Dorado falls, señor?" Dolores asked. Wolf had been careful to keep the women involved in the conversation, so she could rescue him if he blundered into trouble.

Don Ruiz shrugged with both hands. "Then they will follow right after. That is if El Dorado falls."

"Can it be that it will not?"

He smiled. "They are learning. You know the ways of the bullring, señor. If you do not kill the bull inside of twenty minutes, he will kill you."

6

"That," Wolf said as they left the Rojas mansion, "was without doubt the hardest conversation of my life. I never met any man so incredibly winsome. I hated lying to him! I am never any good at lying, anyway."

The nightlife of Sigisa was beginning to waken—bands, drunks, drummers, lutenists, and singers, backed by massed choirs of frogs and monkeys in the jungle.

"That's what I love about you, your naivete."

"A simple 'no' would have sufficed. He saw through us, didn't he?"

Rojas's questions had been inoffensive, but he had kept pick-pick-picking at Don Lope's fraudulent life story until he had unraveled it and could see that Wolf had never set foot in Distlain any more than he had. So the visitors were spies. He had been too polite to say that, but knew. He was supposed to know, of course.

Terms had been settled over an excellent supper. His Worship the *Alcalde* knew of just the respectable villa the august Don Lope needed, and the owners—who had gone Home on some important business— would accept a very reasonable rent. If the spirits were kind, Fortunata could find the charming Dona Dolores some excellent servants by to- morrow. Don Lope and his lady were more than welcome to spend tonight here, at his hacienda. The spies had declined with thanks.

Wolf said, "I think he swallowed the bait, don't you?"

"I don't know." Dolores was unusually subdued, holding tight to his arm and keeping her head down. "His wife loves him."

"Does that matter?"

"It's puzzling."

"Did he ever tell us the truth?"

"I don't know! In a way he never told us any lies at all."

"What?"

Wolf felt her shiver. "Our teachers warned us that some people have no sense of wrong. They do not understand evil, so truth-sounding will not work on them. Ruiz must be one of those." She laughed nervously. "He's very good company, isn't he?"

"Very. We can still take Flicker's advice and strike inland."

But she was not willing to consider that yet, and when they reached the ship and held a whispered consultation with the others, neither were they. Even Flicker wanted to press on with the dangerous challenge Wolf proposed.

Quin had already shipped out as a deckhand on a Distlish vessel, homeward bound.

Next morning the mysterious Don Lope and his charming lady arrived at their new home—just the two of them plus one female servant and four great sea chests. *Glorious* had already raised anchor and caught the tide. The villa was luxurious, at least by local standards, but one month's

rent would have sufficed to build it in Chivial. Wages for the three servants waiting there came to almost as much, and the cost of the food
they had already bought could have provisioned Greymere Palace for a
week. This was Sigisa, the crumbling cliff-edge of civilization.

Rojas had been a little obvious with the servants, because they were
all Distliards and any Distliard in the Hence Lands would rather starve
than touch menial work. Perhaps Wolf was not supposed to know that.
Or perhaps he was. None of the three impressed him, although Estavan,
the gardener, could have uprooted palm trees with his bare hands, having being cast in the same giant mold as Heron-jade. Gustavo of the
black fingernails was chef, and the smiling Che said he was to be ma-
jordomo, although he had no evident qualifications except a sensational
profile.

Still, the hacienda was a mansion, a thatched, single-story wooden
structure with several outbuildings, all reasonably furnished, all set in
spacious grounds surrounded by a high stockade. The front entrance
boasted a reasonable garden of trees and flowered shrubs. There was a
gate on the ocean side, too, just above high-water mark, but currents off
Sigisa were too treacherous for swimming—so Don Ruiz had said. Wolf
ordered chairs set out on the lawn, where he and Dolores could relax in
the shade of palm trees to enjoy a snack and the noble lifestyle they so
richly deserved. The lawn itself was a scabby mess, only to be expected
in the tropics and so near the sea, but the ground sloped down toward
the ocean, giving them a fair view over the palisade. They debated
whether the sail just dipping below the horizon might be *Glorious* de-
parting.

Young Che brought out the food. "With your permission, *señor,* I
will go out this afternoon to hire more workers, yes?" He flashed teeth
like the breakers, white and dangerous.

"No," Wolf said. "Until we discover on what scale we shall be entertaining I cannot determine what staff we need."

"But, *señor!* A porter? Women to clean, surely?"

"Not yet! Meanwhile . . . tell Estavan I want those cactuses dug out.
You can read and write?"

Che said, "Of course, *señor.*"

No need for truth-sounding to know he was lying. "Then prepare for me a detailed list of everything on the property from the beds down to the smallest spoon."

That ought to keep him busy. Wolf cut his food with a special Dark Chamber belt knife and so did Dolores. Neither blade changed color.

"The quarry is running true so far," he said. It was too soon for poison.

She nodded, not as cheerful as usual.

"And Megan is willing to sing her solo?"

"She says she can handle all three of them at once if necessary."

They did not expect the violence to begin yet, or they would not leave Megan alone, although even Flicker admitted Megan was no mean brawler. She bragged that she had taught him all he knew.

When they had eaten as much as they could of Gustavo's vile cooking, Don Lope and Dona Dolores announced that they were going out to explore the town. They began by strolling along to the *Alcalde's* residence, where Dona Dolores called on Dona Fortunata to present her with a spectacular pearl necklace in gratitude for all her kindness. Curiously, Fortunata was as beautifully clad and groomed as she had been the previous day—apparently he kept her like that all the time. She wept over the pearls, and they certainly looked genuine. Rojas himself was not at home, to Wolf's relief.

They did explore the town a little, but not enough to lose their supposedly unseen followers. When they returned to the hacienda, they were admitted by Che, who seemed not quite his former joyous self.

"Something wrong?" Dolores asked innocently.

Alas, Estavan had been bitten by a tarantula and had gone in search of a herbalist.

"It is not to be tolerated!" Wolf said. "A gardener so careless? Do not admit him if he returns."

"I was hoping it would be Gustavo," Dolores said as they went in search of Megan. "The shock might have shaken the dirt out of his nails."

"How long until the conjuration wears off?"

"Three days. Maybe four for a man that size."

They found Megan where they had left her, sorting Dolores's clothes. She seemed a little flustered, but no worse off than that.

Dolores gave her a hug. "You all right?"

"I am very well, thank you, mistress."

"And Che?"

Megan rolled her eyes. "A hard-fought battle. He was using some sort of charm, not just eyelashes, and I swear he has more hands than the King's stables. I had just decided I was fighting on the wrong side when we were interrupted by Estavan's screams." She sighed regretfully.

Dolores grinned. "And where was Estavan?"

"In the master's dressing room."

A strange place to dig cactus! Che had been distracting Megan while Estavan tried to open a warded chest. Estavan's arms were now useless.

"It is hard to find good help," Wolf said.

They had raised the stakes and it was Rojas's turn to roll again.

7

Just after sunset that evening, Che served dinner on the patio. Nights were darker and stars closer in the Hence Lands than they were in Chivial and Wolf found the tropical air as soporific as sweet wine. There was something sublimely relaxing about the ageless rumble of the sea.

"This does beat ship life," he remarked, unobtrusively stirring his wine with his belt knife. He peered at it. No danger.

"Except possibly for the food." Dolores was inspecting her plate of hors d'oeuvres. "The mushrooms."

"Odd-looking mushrooms!" Wolf cut one and held his blade near the candles. "Remind me what blue means?"

"Probably not fatal, but certainly not wholesome."

"Right." He scooped up all the mushrooms and put them in his pocket. "We go with Plan One. You get Megan."

Feeling the joyous tingle that came before a fight, he strode around the house to the kitchen, which was an open-fronted shed, set apart from the main building as a fire precaution. Gustavo was stirring a pot on the stove, virtually outdoors, but Wolf's approach from seaward cut off his best line of escape. Megan had been backed into a corner beside the larder by the glamorous Che, although she did not seem very troubled by this situation. Wolf drew sword and dagger. Che noticed him and was distracted. Before he could start thinking *hostage,* Megan butted him in the face and made her escape, grabbing up a knife from the table as she passed.

"Stay where you are, Che!" Wolf waved his dagger. "Join him there, Gustavo. Don't try anything. I am an expert swordsman."

Señor! What is the matter?" Che's lip was bleeding.

Seeing Gustavo furtively comparing his distance from the back door to his chances of dodging around the hearth without coming within reach of *Diligence,* Wolf said, "Don't even think it! I will slice you thinner than tortillas." The only advantage to having a face like his was that people did believe his threats.

Dolores walked in carrying her sword and a coil of thin rope. He felt safer with all three of them there, but he did not relax completely until they had made the two scoundrels secure. They sat them back to back on the butcher block, binding them to both it and each other, wrapping the rope around them repeatedly.

"Now!" he said, sheathing *Diligence.* "Now you will answer some questions." He emptied his pocket of mushrooms and laid them in clear view on the table. Turning to Dolores, he saw she was strung as tight as a longbow. There was a world of difference between taking lessons in how to do something—run a rapier through a man's skull, say, or torture a confession out of him—and actually doing it or even watching it done. "Er . . . Megan, would you take the first hour?"

"Happy to do so, Don Lope. We may need some gags."

"There's a towel here." He ripped it in half.

"They won't be necessary for a little while. When they start to break . . . Gustavo, why did you try to poison Don Lope and Dona Dolores?"

"I do not know what you mean, bitch!"

Megan sighed like a nurse about to administer a major enema. "Notch one!" Both men gasped in surprise as their bonds tightened. "If you tell lies or do not answer, I will continue until the rope cuts you in slices. Why did you try to poison them?"

"I did not intend to harm the *señor* and *señora*," Gustavo growled.

Apparently that was a true statement, because the women exchanged puzzled glances. "What would have happened if they had eaten the mushrooms?"

He tried to shrug. "Make them happy, see pretty things. Not worry. Put one in my mouth and I will chew it."

"And we wouldn't get anything more out of you tonight, would we? How long does the effect last?"

"A day? Two? It is harmless."

"Why did Estavan try to open the baggage this afternoon?"

"This is crazy!" Che protested. "Estavan never tried to— *Eeeeee!*" Megan had just called for notch two.

They resisted until she reached notch six, by which time the rope was biting deep. They were in pain, yes, but fear of what was to come troubled them much more. No doubt they were surprised, as Wolf was, to discover the fiend inside his sweet-natured foster-mother-in-law.

"Don Lope," she said, "in the name of mercy we should adjourn for a while to let them consider." She flickered a wink they could not see.

"I don't see why. Keep going."

"Their ribs will start popping soon and no blood is reaching their hands. The risk of gangrene—"

"It is their own fault for being stubborn. We haven't got all night! Pop all the ribs you want."

"*No!*" howled Pretty-Boy Che. "I will talk! I will . . . tell, but please give . . . me air, *señora*! I am dying!"

"Notch four," she said, and they sighed in unison. "You weren't dying. You can suffer much worse than that before you die. If you start lying again, I am going straight to level eight, for half an hour. Now talk. You were sent here to pretend to be servants?"

"*Si, señora.*"

"Truth, at last!" She sounded as relieved as Wolf felt. "Who sent you?"

"I do not know!" Che cried. "It is the truth, *señora*! We were not told!"

"Someone must have sent you."

"Pablo told us a man wanted this."

"Who is Pablo?"

"A man, another man. He pays well!" Che was almost gibbering. He was not going to incriminate Ruiz de Rojas. He could not. His trail would stop at the mysterious Pablo, and Pablo's trail in turn would lead only one more link up a very long chain. The *Alcade* himself stayed out of reach. "Please, please, *señora*! The cramps . . ."

"The cramps will get worse. What were you going to do when you got the trunks open?"

"Just steal, is all. Anything we could see that we—"

"Notch eight!"

Both men screamed as the air was crushed out of their lungs. Wolf was suffering too, for Dolores had her fingernails buried in his arm.

Che managed to croak, "Tell Pablo!"

"Notch five," said the motherly fiend, smiling sweetly. "Keep talking."

Pablo was waiting at the third villa north. He was to be notified when all three strangers had been drugged, bound, gagged, and blindfolded—and the trunks opened. Che and Gustavo had been sternly warned not to help themselves to anything, because the contents might be dangerous, but Señor Pablo, cautious soul, would stay away until all the booby-traps had been removed.

"And if we had refused to open the chests?"

Che's teeth started chattering. "We were to persuade you."

Wolf felt less guilty then—torture his wife, would they? Megan asked more questions, but obtained nothing except a vague description of Pablo. They had reached the end of the road.

"I think that's all they can tell us," she said in Chivian. "They're trash, expendable."

Dolores nodded agreement.

"Then why don't you reward them both with a nice feast of mushrooms? I'll be right back." Wolf strode around to the front door, which opened onto a courtyard decorated with flowering bushes and some palm trees. Theoretically it was well illuminated by the flames of seven or eight torches on poles flanking the path. Che had insisted that these were a necessary precaution in this wicked town, but Wolf had noted several places where trees blocked the view of the stockade from the house, so a limber and well-prepared intruder could shimmy over the top and approach unseen through the dense shadows of the shrubbery. He did not doubt that Don Ruiz de Rojas was aware of this.

Here the growl of the sea was fainter and the racket of Sigisa enjoying itself much louder. Wolf walked down to the gate, slid back the bolts, and opened the flap a handsbreadth. Revelers were singing their way along the road, and the grog shop directly across from him was doing an uproarious business, complete with drums and trumpets. Near his feet, a man sat on the dirt with his back against the wall, mumbling happily to himself.

A faint shadow solidified into deeper blackness, only the whites of his eyes showing.

"All well?" Flicker asked.

"Very well. And you?"

"All present."

"No other watchers?"

"There was one."

Wolf did not ask. "Bring them, then."

A few moments later, he stepped aside to admit Serpent-night, Heron-jade, Blood-mirror-walks, Pulse-obsidian, Duff, Hick, Peterkin, and Will. The last four were sailors he had bought away from *Glorious*. Flicker followed and shot the bolts behind him. All nine had enjoyed a night and a day ashore at Dark Chamber expense and brought a strong smell of rum with them, but Flicker would have kept them operational. Duff had been the man in the gutter. Heron-jade carried a limp form draped over his shoulder.

"Do we need to tie him up?" Wolf whispered as the eagle warrior slid his load to the grass.

"Maybe next week," Flicker replied, just as quietly. "Seems it's a point of honor to hit once and only once. Killing is regarded as shoddy work."

"Come then." Wolf led his troops into the house, avoiding the kitchen. Che and Gustavo might hear voices, if they were still capable of hearing anything, but they must not be allowed to see faces.

First in Chivian, then Tlixilian, he explained what had happened so far.

"And now what?" asked Blood-mirror-walks, ever the leader.

Dolores came in and smiled at everybody, but she still looked wan.

"How are they?" Wolf asked.

"Che is giggling happily," she said, coming close to him. "Gustavo is worried by the alligators. We gagged them both, just to be on the safe side."

He nodded and turned his attention back to the Tlixilians. "What next, you ask? The enemy will meet violence with violence. If we do nothing, then they'll wait until tomorrow night . . . probably. Unless someone panics and acts without waiting for the leader's say-so." He repeated that in Chivian for the sailors. "But since we now know where Pablo is, it would be easier just to go and deal with them there. What do you all think?" Again he translated.

The men's smiles were enough answer. Peterkin and Will were natural fighters, almost on a par with the Tlixilians for ferocity. Hick and Duff were less aggressive but enjoying the skulduggery so far.

"Wolf!" Dolores said. "No! Defending yourself against intruders is one thing. Storming somebody else's house is a crime. There may be innocent people there, too, Wolf! It will be murder."

He conceded the point reluctantly, for he had his dander up. "I cannot seriously believe that our friend Pablo is merely spending a quiet evening visiting friends, waiting for Che's message. But I suppose it's possible. There may be innocent people in Sigisa. Let us see if we can provoke the others into doing something stupid."

8

$\mathcal{A}$ band of revelers reeling along a street was a common enough sight in Sigisa. In this case one was so drunk that he was being carried by another, a very large man. When they had progressed three gates from their starting point, Wolf ran a golden key over the timbers and heard bolts click. He peered inside. The courtyard was dark, but candles glimmered in windows, and he thought he heard a rumble of male voices, although he could not be sure.

He stepped back and Heron-jade went in just far enough to unload his burden, who was starting to move and make noises. Che and Gustavo were allowed to proceed on their own, weaving and groping into the dark yard. Wolf closed and locked the gate.

"Let's hope they enjoy the party." He led his army home.

They were gambling that the unknown Pablo would panic. This was the second time he had failed and the hour was late to go crawling to his superiors for fresh instructions. He must be under pressure to learn what the insolent visitors kept in their well-guarded chests before they had time to hide it or spend it. Now they had annulled four of his men and made him look stupid. Working for an unscrupulous gang boss, he *ought* to be panicking.

Back at the hacienda, Wolf opened the weapons chest and handed out swords. The jaguar warriors accepted eagerly, but Heron-jade refused, scowling and holding up a cudgel he had acquired from somewhere. Why argue with results?

"Kill or take prisoners?" Blood-mirror-walks asked, trying a few swings.

"Take prisoners if you can."

"We can. You will claim their precious jewels?"

Wolf suppressed thoughts of the butcher block in the kitchen. "Not unless you can explain how it is done."

"Only acolytes know such things." The warrior's eyes were dark pools of distrust, and Wolf wondered if he had just failed a test.

"I'd better explain these," he said, pulling out a roll of tangle mats.

"They have been blessed?" Blood-mirror-walks demanded, but he put the question to Heron-jade.

The big man nodded, squinting at them suspiciously. "Spider webs."

"That's a fair description," Wolf admitted.

"Put them away!" Blood-mirror-walks said contemptuously. "You have warriors here. You do not need such trash."

"Very well. Then let's inspect our perimeter. Flicker, Duff, will you keep an eye on the front while the rest of us take a look at the ocean side?" Wolf led the way out to the veranda. There was no light there except the stars, but a faint golden haze on the horizon showed where the moon would soon rise. He waited a moment for his eyes to adjust. "I took a look at the stockade earlier, and I didn't see any weak places where—"

"I can see five already," Blood-mirror-walks said at his shoulder.

"No, I meant places where a man or a boy could—"

"I know what you mean, Wild-dog-by-the-spring. You see the footprints beside that bush?" He pointed at an inky patch halfway between the house and the beach.

"No." Wolf could barely see the bush.

"I do. Yours and a bigger man in sandals. Leave this fight to your jaguars. Serpent-night, inspect the fence. Pulse-obsidian, the bushes." His tone softened as he looked up at the eagle warrior. "Taker of Four Captives, to have you as lookout would honor us all."

"The honor will be mine, terror of the dark."

"What signal will you give us?"

"If they come by the street—" Heron-jade cheeped like a small bird. "Along the beach—" Two cheeps.

Wolf doubted such a signal could be audible far enough away to be useful, but Blood-mirror-walks said, "Is good."

The big man shrugged and went back indoors.

Wolf made a last feeble effort to exert authority. "Where is he off to?"

The youth shrugged his oversized shoulders. "You will tell an eagle how to watch?"

"No, nor a jaguar how to hunt." However nimble, a Blade was outclassed in this situation by true warriors spiritually reinforced. "Where do you want the rest of us?"

"You and your women will be bait. Laugh. Drink. Be seen. Keep your men inside the house, out of sight. They will not be needed."

"None of them?"

"None of them. They blunder around making too much noise. Also they smell like Hairy Ones."

"That leaves only three of you to patrol the grounds, front and back," Wolf protested.

"One of us would be plenty. Now go."

As it please Your Majesty! Wolf did as he was told, gathering Dolores, Megan, and some wine on the veranda for a make-believe victory celebration, trusting that the enemy would see them but did not know about their allies. Flicker and the sailors stood guard indoors, furious at being kept out of the coming fight. The moon was rising in splendor, unrolling a golden swatch across the ocean.

Wolf had trouble laughing convincingly when enemies with crossbows might be prowling the darkness. Even the wine helped little, because he was warded by the inquisitors' "party-trick" conjuration, which was a sash worn next the skin. It would hold off drunkenness but not alcoholic poisoning, so users who overindulged would learn so when they dropped dead. Its spirituality gave him a dull headache.

As the night wore on, bats whirled and squeaked overhead, the raucous revelry of Sigisa subsided, the sea drummed untiringly, and the bait saw nothing at all of their four Tlixilian defenders. Wolf struggled against growing worries that they had simply departed, abandoning the Chivians in some bizarre Tlixilian practical joke, or in revenge for some slight against their warriors' honor.

"Dawn can't be far off," Dolores said at last.

"I am ready for bed," Megan agreed.

"Or should we simply slide to the floor in drunken stupors? This partying won't be convincing if we fall asleep." Dolores yawned and her husband's jaw began to ache horribly.

"You're right," he said. "Perhaps the enemy is just waiting for us to retire so they can—"

A bird tweeted right behind him. He jumped and peered around. His companions were doing the same. There were no birds present.

"I think that was our sentry's signal," he said. "One quack means they are coming by land."

"Spiritual ventriloquism?" Dolores was alert again. "How does he *do* that?"

"Ask him when Blood-mirror-walks isn't around and he may tell you. A toast to victory!" Wolf poured wine. The bird tweeted twice more at his back, causing his hand to twitch and spill some, but this time he did not turn. "And they are also coming by sea."

Then it cheeped three times.

He raised his glass and they drank to victory. "Tell us another of those funny stories of yours, Megan."

She laughed tinnily. "I think my sense of humor just dried up."

"Then tell about the first time you set eyes on Dolores. How old was she?"

"Not fair!" Dolores complained.

They were all trying not to watch the lawn. It was bathed in moonlight, and the isolated puddles of shadow did not seem large enough to hide a rabbit. The stockade was a saw-edge of darkness against the silver ocean. Surely nothing could creep up on them unseen from that direction? What was happening at the front? And what had three chirps meant?

"A few minutes old," Megan said, "still bloody and crying. The midwife handed her to me in a blanket. I know nothing of her past."

"As long as I still have a future," Dona Dolores muttered.

"Well, as Grand Master always says—"

"If you mention that man just once more I will make myself a widow."

So they babbled. Wolf managed not to stare, but he thought he was keeping a fair watch out of the corner of his eye, yet he saw nothing untoward before he heard a half-stifled cry, only one, seemingly from behind a tree in the middle of the lawn.

"What was that?" Now they were free to look openly, but there was still nothing to see.

"Probably a bat," Megan said and stretched. "I did enjoy the party, Sir Wolf. We must do it again some time, but now I—"

Dolores said, *"Eeek!"*

Blood-mirror-walks walked up the step to the veranda dragging two bodies, his fingers locked in their hair. He dropped them at Wolf's feet like a cat offering mice.

"All done, Wild-dog-by-the-spring." He did not even seem out of breath.

"Excellent work, Taker of Three Captives. Just two of them?"

"Eight this side. Four at the front. This one"—he kicked the larger, older man—"they called Pablo. I only throttled him, so he will wake soon. In case you want to torture him. What shall we do with the rest?"

Pablo, it turned out, had divided his force into three squads of four. One band had climbed over the stockade on the street side and the other two had cut across neighboring properties to come in on the flanks. The tops of the logs were all sharpened, of course, making for a tricky climb, and by the time the first man in each squad had finished helping his companions descend safely, a warrior had been waiting in the shadows beside them. When the intruders started moving toward the house, the defenders followed, stunning them all before they even knew they were under attack.

Wolf was impressed. He had been judging the Tlixilians by the mass assault on Quondam. With the advantage of numbers and surprise, the invaders should not have suffered the losses they did, but whatever their problem had been, he must revise his opinion of Tlixilian warriors in general. Blood-mirror-walks and his band were not even the legendary knights, yet they had stomped four times their number like a line of beetles. The Distliards' problems in conquering El Dorado became more comprehensible.

Pablo was tied to a chair and left in a dark room to recover. The other eleven they spread on the lawn, trussing them securely also, although they had barely enough rope. It was then Wolf discovered that the Tlixilians' success had not been quite perfect, for one man was dead. Head wounds were notoriously unpredictable and what barely dazed one man could kill another outright, but Tlixilians prided themselves on their skill at taking prisoners. Pulse-obsidian hung his head in shame under his colleagues' angry glares. It was not the death that troubled them, it was his clumsiness.

"A minor matter," Wolf said, although he regretted it. "We may perhaps turn it to advantage."

Having made certain his wife was not watching, he cut off the corpse's left ear. Then he collected Dolores and went in to see the chief brigand.

Pablo was fortyish, flabby, and greasy, with streaks of gray in his beard and an ugly scar half-hidden in his whiskers. He screwed up his eyes and moaned when his captors arrived with lanterns.

Wolf held up his bloodstained dagger. "Dog! Why should I not kill you also?"

Pablo made a croaking noise.

"Speak, scum of the cesspool. Who sent you to attack our house?"

His only reply was a silent glare. Admittedly Pablo had few good excuses available under the circumstances. Wolf grabbed the man's beard and shaved one side of his jaw, removing some skin. He screamed.

"Who sent you?"

"No one!"

Wolf made the shave symmetrical, so he screamed again. The remaining goatee did not suit him. Dolores was not speaking and Wolf was not looking at her, but he could sense her disapproval burning hot. He hoped she knew he did not enjoy maltreating a helpless man, however despicable. He wiped his bloody hand on Pablo's shirt.

"Then I must complain directly to the *Alcalde*. Take him this." Wolf produced the ear. "You will bring Don Ruiz de Rojas here before sunrise, do you understand? So he can see the vermin who assaulted me— what is left of them."

"It is not possible!" Pablo screamed, ashen under his tropic tan. The thought of reporting to Rojas upset him more than the previous rough treatment.

"Then I will send one of the others, with both your ears. And perhaps an eye?" Wolf took hold of the prisoner's right ear and he howled in terror.

"I will go! I will go!"

"Before sunrise the *Alcalde* must be here, or I will start tossing pieces of your men over the wall. And I will not stop with ears."

They untied the wretch and threw him out the gate with an ear in his pocket and his hands still tied behind his back. He took off at a staggering run, unaware that Flicker was lurking out there to make sure he arrived at the correct destination.

Sick and trembling with reaction, the ogreish Don Lope made his way to the kitchen, where half his forces were tucking into a meal prepared by Duff and Peterkin. The others had gone to catch some sleep. He perched on the butcher's block, which was the only vacant seat in sight, and accepted a steaming cup of a local beverage he had taken to, called *chocolatl*.

"Which way did he go?" Dolores asked.

"Looking for a fast horse-sleigh to Skyrria." Wolf burned his mouth and swore. "He was last seen going north, anyway."

His challenge to the tyrant was proceeding amazingly well, but it was still a terrible gamble. Many violent men understood nothing but violence, so Rojas might fly into a fury and send his militia to storm the fortress, whatever the cost in lost prestige. He would certainly guess that the impudent newcomers had troops he had not known of, but he must suspect spiritualism by now. There were no octograms in Sigisa and probably no conjurers, so he had no source of conjuration to offset it. Unless he had access to some of the local variety, in which case the battles might grow even bloodier.

"This is good," Heron-jade announced. He was eating an entire ham, clutching it in his huge fists and tearing chunks out of it with his teeth. "What animal?"

"Distlish man-at-arms," Wolf said.

"Wolf!" Dolores shouted. "No, it is pig, Taker of Four Captives. An animal about this big." She gestured with a tortilla and a beaker.

The big man grunted and offered the ham to Serpent-night, who had been cramming beans into his mouth nearby but showed interest in the subject. He bit out a nugget, chewed thoughtfully, then nodded. He ripped off a larger chunk and passed the rest back.

"What did you think it was?" Wolf asked uneasily.

"What you said." Heron-jade grinned with his mouth full. "Definitely not local."

Dolores shuddered. "Really? You do eat people?"

He nodded as if surprised by the question. "It is my right. I am a taker of four captives."

Wolf said, "I thought captives were sacrificed so that their hearts could be used to summon the spirits."

"But we do not waste the rest of them," the giant said cheerfully. He flexed a bulging arm. "One day I will make a great feast for someone."

"You chatter like a girl!" Blood-mirror-walks stood in the doorway, scowling.

Heron-jade dropped his eyes like a guilty child. "May my lord forgive!"

At the moment they were not eagle and jaguar but a great lord and a lesser. All four of the Tlixilians were nobly born to some extent. They had explained that commoners served in the army but rarely rose out of the ranks.

"Use your mouth for feeding in future!"

"I am justly accused," the big man said.

Abruptly the youngster switched back to military forms. "Will you honor us blind ones by keeping watch until noon, sky traveler?"

"Until sunset," Heron-jade said. "I will keep the day. The night is yours, dread shadow." He raised his head and peered around. "The emissary went to a large house north of here and was admitted. The servant Flicker is returning."

Blood-mirror-walks bowed. "We are indebted to you for this lore."

Dolores's eyes shone. If she could smuggle *that* spell home to Chivial, the snoops would be able to snoop on anyone anytime. Even Wolf could hear the sound of gold clinking then.

9

Wolf did not seriously expect Rojas to come running before sunrise as instructed. He was prepared for more violence, or a conciliatory letter, or almost anything except what did happen, which was nothing. The sun rose and kept on rising. Rojas had called his bluff.

Having no intention of chopping more pieces off the corpse or vivisecting the ten prisoners, Wolf did nothing also. The jaguars had gone to sleep—curled up in corners, to his amusement. Will and Peterkin slept also. Big Heron-jade was working his way through the larder, eating indiscriminately, as if to redress weeks of slaves' diet and ship rations. He insisted that he was also keeping watch, but just leered when Dolores tried to charm him into discussing the conjuration he was using. His childlike amiability hid warrior flint. Eventually she gave up and went off to rest. Hick and Duff tended the captives, giving them water, untying each in turn for brief exercise, and making sure the three still unconscious were as comfortable as possible. Flicker reverted to his manservant personation and unpacked his master's clothes. Wolf just paced around, waiting for something to happen.

He was in the kitchen preparing a beaker of *chocolatl* when Heron-jade looked up from his stool and remarked through a mouthful of onion, "You have visitors."

The gate bell jangled.

"Who?"

He shrugged. "A Hairy man and a Real People woman."

"Is she wearing jewels?" Wolf asked, wondering how well an eagle warrior could see through several walls and trees.

He nodded, grinning to show he saw through the subterfuge.

"No snakes hanging on branches?"

"None."

With such spying ability available, it was no wonder that El Dorado was holding off the Distliards. On his way to the front door, Wolf met Flicker.

"Rojas and his wife. Tell Dolores."

Wolf opened the gate himself, expressing delight and honor at the visit.

Rojas returned his bow. "The pleasure is ours, Don Lope." He wore a sword and a gentleman's finery. Fortunata curtseyed demurely. She sparkled with gems and her gown would have passed at Court.

"The villa is to your satisfaction?" Rojas inquired blandly as they strolled along the path.

"The villa, yes. The servants, no. The neighbors, definitely not."

"You wish to lay charges?"

"What else can I do?"

The mayor shrugged. "Do anything you like with them, *señor*." Incompetent henchmen were of no more use to a gang boss than, say, a conscience.

"Our mutual friend Pablo?" Wolf inquired as he opened the front door.

"Pablo?" Rojas murmured, entering with his wife on his arm. "Pablo? I know many men by that name. I cannot be expected to remember them all."

Dolores appeared—miraculously relaxed, coiffed, and groomed, with only faint shadows under her eyes to hint at a sleepless, stressful night. The guests were made comfortable on the veranda. Flicker served fruit juices and cakes, then departed. With sailors and warriors safely out of sight, the villa might have been deserted. Conversation flitted like a forest butterfly, never touching on murder, torture, home invasion, or any such sordid topics. For a while.

Then Wolf found himself being studied by the coldest pair of eyes he had ever seen. The Blades' greatest killer had never faced such eyes in a mirror. Rojas had dropped his charm.

"Let us talk business, Don Lope."

"By all means, Don Ruiz."

"What do you want?"

"Knowledge, the secrets of Tlixilian conjuration."

"You would rip beating hearts out of men?"

"Never. My wife is the expert on spiritualism. She believes that the jaguar and eagle knights have skills we could apply without resorting to their murderous ways." Without looking at her, Wolf could sense Dolores disapproving of his candor, but Rojas was not the sort of man she could have studied in lecture halls, and he trusted his instincts. Rojas would never accept Wolf as an equal, but now he must take him seriously.

The snake eyes continued to stare unblinking. "Others have tried to learn those secrets and failed. Do you not think *El Caudillo* would rather have that knowledge than another five thousand men? Or that King Diego would not reward whoever supplied it?"

"Were I the Emperor of El Dorado," Wolf said, "I should not want Don Severo to have it, either. But Chivial is far away and harmless. King Athelgar is no friend to King Diego. Those in need must deal in whatever coin they have."

"And you? What coin do you deal in, *señor*?"

Wolf had fought mortal duels less stressful than this conversation. Rojas had the power to storm the hacienda, murder every inhabitant, and loot whatever he fancied. He need answer to no one for his actions.

"For the combatants—weapons, armor, war dogs, horses. Chivian horses are renowned. For others who aid our quest . . . King Athelgar can be generous, also."

That meant *gold for Rojas*.

For what felt like hours, Rojas just stared as if he had been turned to bronze. Wolf sweated it out, determined not to be the next to speak.

"If I could introduce you to persons having the sort of knowledge you seek?" Rojas asked softly.

"This would be a most valuable favor."

"Ninety thousand pesos."

The Chivians had more than that lying around the house, but only an utter madman would confess to owning such riches here. There were times when madness was the only sane policy.

"Seventy. And another forty if we obtain usable knowledge."

"The seventy without conditions?"

"Only that I am satisfied the other persons do possess the knowledge we seek and will negotiate seriously, whether or not we reach an agreement."

The charm flicked back—the *Alcalde* put his head back and laughed joyously. "It is a pleasure doing business with you, Don Lope! Enjoy your stay in Sigisa. This is the finest time of year. Allow me a month, even two . . . nothing happens quickly in these lands. Now, if you will excuse us, my wife and I have many urgent . . ."

As they all rose, Wolf said, "And the neighbors?"

"I find it easiest just to lay the garbage on the beach at low water— the tidal race is very strong along here. I trust you will experience no further disturbances, *señor.*" Or cause them, of course.

The moment Wolf closed the gate on the guests, his wife threw her arms around him and kissed him with great enthusiasm, while trying to jump up and down at the same time. Rojas was probably halfway back to his residence before she broke loose long enough to say, "Darling, that was wonderful. You were brilliant!"

"Wasn't I?" Wolf resumed the kiss so he would not have to point out that they might still wake up tomorrow to find their throats cut and all the gold gone. They would not beat City Hall so easily another time.

He sent the prisoners out the gate in threes and they departed without a fuss. If they had any sense at all they would be gone from Sigisa by nightfall.

10

The tyrant made no move in the next two days, while the Tlixilian warriors were still available to defend the villa. That was fortunate, because the four sailors all succumbed to the Sigisian variety of dysentery, which was notorious even within the Hence Lands. Duff recovered fastest; Peterkin was hit hardest; the inquisitors were protected by their conjuration. Wolf and Flicker were kept busy outfitting the ex-slaves for their trek home. Warm clothes and bedrolls were not the easiest merchandise to find in that tropical oven, and they tried to rent a canoe without provoking questions, although Wolf was certain the *Alcalde* would have spies watching.

On the last night, an argument broke out. The three jaguar warriors were ready to go, stripped down to loincloths and the local footwear, which was made from congealed tree sap. Their kit was packed, they had three days' rations—more than that would be a burden to carry—and they bore a Chivian sword apiece. Wolf would be lynched if the Sigisians learned he had given arms to cannibal warriors inside their town.

Heron-jade sat on the floor with his knees up, the *naturales'* favorite posture, for they never used chairs. His gear lay in a heap, ignored. The other three were shouting furiously at him.

Blood-mirror-walks was red-faced with fury. "It is your duty to the Emperor!"

Heron-jade just went on picking his teeth with a thorn. His amiable, almost dopey, expression meant he had made up his mind over something and would not be dissuaded. He had probably grinned like that while the slavers flogged his back to paste. "My duty is to my liege, soaring Sky-cactus."

"And how will you serve the great lord by staying here? By being a slave?"

"By being true to his will."

Blood-mirror-walks growled dangerously.

Wolf said, "Will you tell me why you do not wish to go?"

The big man's dark eyes studied him for a moment. "I have eaten your meat. You saved me from the slavers. I have not repaid that debt."

"But I asked you to repay that debt by defending me from the brigands, which you did, and by going home."

"I will not go."

"You want to repay the debt and I say you can repay it by going home and yet you say you will not go?"

"I will not go." The conversation was over.

The situation did have merit, because Wolf would undoubtedly weasel more information out of the eagle warrior when Blood-mirror-walks was not around to nanny him. That no doubt explained the jaguar's anger.

"You do not have to take the sword!" he said. "Lord Wild-dog-by-the-spring will not mind if you do not take the sword."

Heron-jade just shrugged. He had refused to handle one of the metal swords before. The raiders at Quondam had stolen no weapons. A pattern was emerging.

"You do not have to take the message!" Serpent-night said. "Lord Wild-dog-by-the-spring will not mind if you do not repeat his message."

"Yes, I would mind that," Wolf said. "Since I do not know why Heron-jade refuses to do as I ask." That earned him angry glares all round. Sometimes he despaired of ever understanding how their minds worked.

Eventually even Blood-mirror-walks gave up hope of making Heron-jade change his. The three jaguar warriors took their leave with polite speeches. Wolf was convinced that three minutes in the jungle, even in daylight, would see him dying of snakebite or sunk without trace in a swamp, but to them it was sanctuary. Their danger would come in a few days, they said, when they left the forest and began traversing the foothills. If they were caught in Allied territory they would find themselves dead or back in a chain gang, but Wolf was confident that they would reach El Dorado long before de Rojas's messengers did.

When they had gone, Wolf and Dolores took their voluntary slave out to the patio. They dined at the table. The big man sat on the floor and ate more than both of them, just to keep them company. While an unorthodox companion, Heron-jade was certainly an interesting one. Wolf plied him with rum to loosen his tongue and was amazed at the quantity he poured down his throat.

"If you feel you still owe me a debt, Taker of Four Captives, then there is a small task that you may perform for me. It is a very trivial thing to ask of so great a warrior, but it is dear to my heart."

"Name it," the eagle said with his mouth full.

"You see this jewel on my sword?"

"Blood–mirror–walks said it was the regalia of a knight."

"Yes it is. How did he know that, do you know?"

"Yes. I promised not to tell you."

Wolf said, "My mother bore another son who wears such a sword, and I believe he is on his way here. He may not come for a very long time, or never at all, but if you would consent to look at the men disembarking from each ship as it arrives, then this would put my heart at ease."

Heron–jade stared at him as if he were thinking, but that was just his way. "For how long must I search, Wild–dog–by–the–spring?"

"Until my brother arrives, or until you feel you have repaid the debt."

"It is a life for a life. I will do this. I can do it from here."

Dolores uttered a small gasp. "Your great powers impress us."

He leered drunkenly at her. "Noble Sky–cactus is generous with his blessings."

She said, "He *gave* you his ability?" Delegation of powers was another marvel.

"I would accept it from no one else!"

"Of course not."

He sighed. "My lord said I was the truest of his watchers."

"But this stone is so small," Wolf said, tapping *Diligence*'s pommel. "I would doubt that even the eagles flying among the peaks could see so tiny an object at such a distance."

The big man found that remark hilarious. "It is a weapon, borne by a warrior. You think I cannot see that? When I am *looking* for it?"

Well, yes.

"I will look in every ship," he promised.

"You will also warn us if brigands approach our house?"

"Of course! Fear not, Wild–dog–by–the–spring. I do not want to wear sky–metal regalia again!"

Heron–jade downed another half bottle before he explained his refusal to leave, which turned out to be nothing more than ordinary human stupidity.

"Only a coward fights on the back of a deer!" he proclaimed. "Dogs are for eating, not to turn into monsters to attack noble warriors. A true warrior uses his strength, his courage, the powers that come from the captives he has taken. With these he fights. He does not sully himself with the ways of his enemies."

That was that. El Dorado was split. Eagle knights were traditionalists and scorned anything that stank of the invaders. More pragmatic, the Jaguars would use steel blades and armor if they could get them. The Great Council was divided and the Emperor had made no decision yet. Until he did, Heron-jade would not tarnish his honor by carrying Wolf's offer to sell weapons, because the offer was insulting. Similarly, the eagle knights Amaranth-talon and Bone-peak-runner had agreed to transport Lizard-drumming's men to Quondam but had refused to bring back any of the demons' weapons. A matter of honor.

The party ended when Heron-jade laid his head on his knees and went to sleep. Wolf led his wife off to bed, feeling very pleased with himself. He had launched two birds and had nothing left to do except enjoy the lordly life in Sigisa while waiting for them to return to his wrist with the prize in their talons. That, and wonder where Lynx was and what he was having to endure.

VII

Birds of prey must be handled with respect

1

"The Fierce Ones met in formal session yesterday."

Basket-fox spoke offhandedly, as if commenting on something trivial, like the current shortage of captives, but Lynx knew him well enough by now, and was sufficiently fluent in Tlixilian language and customs, to guess that something important was coming. His throat tightened.

"My lord honors me with this confidence."

"I sorrow to report that my friends and I were overruled. The misguided majority hailed the imposter Flintknife as a lawful member of the order, successor to the mourned Plumed-pillar."

"And did the mighty ones make any decision about me?" Pass a death sentence, for example? Was that why they were climbing the pyramid?

Lynx's long and painful metamorphosis was complete, so a spectator would see two jaguar knights padding up the steps side-by-side. The older, Basket-fox, was magnificently arrayed in full regalia of feathers and treasure, heading for a ritual, obviously a big one, for many captives were already waiting below and guards were still bringing in more.

The younger Jaguar wore only a loincloth, a sword strapped on his back, and Plumed-pillar's regalia on his chest. At times Lynx rather fancied himself in his new form. His skin was tanned almost as dark as the *naturales'* and only his greater hairiness distinguished him from a true Jaguar in appearance. Although he could no longer wield *Ratter,* he was at least as fast as he had ever been and came armed with sixteen deadly claws, which Night-fisher kept as sharp as razors for him.

Basket-fox said, "They concluded that you were an imposter and must die, of course."

It was typical of the sly old cat that he would make this announcement in such a place. He strode confidently upward, not even breathing hard, although the steps were so caked with dried blood that even a surefooted jaguar knight must tread with care. They were also fiendishly steep, because they were crafted for Jaguar legs and paws, not human limbs. A squad of warriors preceded him in case anyone at the top thought of rolling anything down on him; there was no one behind him to catch him if he slipped, for even a slight stumble would be proof that it was time for him to retire.

Lynx said, "It would be an honor to give you my precious jewel, terror of the night." Relatively speaking, of course, for the scoundrel had been kind after his fashion. Better him than anyone else. Better still to keep Lynx's heart where it was.

The old rogue shot him a cryptic glance. "So it would, but I am ordered to send Plumed-pillar's regalia to Flintknife with you attached. Your jewel would then be his. I do not see why this must happen today, though. Unless you insist?"

The wind blew cold on his Lynx's sweat. "I will serve as my lord commands."

Celeste had warned him that something was brewing. They met every day at language lessons, and could talk freely in Chivian. She was now Basket-fox's senior concubine, tended by many servants, and she bragged that she had him feeling like a kitten again. Only this morning she had warned Lynx that their owner was planning something new for him: "He has been asking me about your life before you became a knight."

"What did you tell him?"

"That you are of noble blood, of course. I didn't dare make up too much because I didn't know what you'd told him. I'm trying to talk him out of getting me with child. He can control that, you know." Celeste could never think of much except Celeste for very long.

"You would probably be safer as mother of his kits than just a plaything," her Blade had suggested helpfully. She had screamed at him.

As they neared the top of the stair, Basket-fox said, "There is still hope, Bobcat-by-the-spring." That was Lynx's name when he was not Plumed-pillar Redux.

"The noble lords may reverse their decision?"

"No. Even if you were high-born in your own city, here you are nothing. And there is the problem of battle skill. However noble his blood, a candidate for knighthood must have won a glorious reputation in battle. Your scars prove that you can fight, but where are all the captives you have taken? You can no longer swing that sword you carry. How would you fare in battle now, think you?"

"You know how it goes on your practice grounds, lord." Lynx could win the mock battles nine times out of ten—he was a demon with paws. "Can I challenge Flintknife to single combat?"

"He would use the Breath of Night on you. You would stand there yawning while he ripped you to tatters."

"The prospect does not appeal," Lynx admitted. Understatement, that.

They reached the flat summit of the tower. The escort opened out on either side to let their lord advance, and a drum throbbed a salute. Some of the disgusting black-clad acolytes were fussing with the great brazier, making it burn hotter, and others were readying drums and conches, laying out knives. Ignoring these gruesome preparations, Basket-fox headed to the far edge and stood there, apparently lost in thought, while the wind whipped his feathered cloak and the plumes of his headdress. Lynx went with him, his stomach churning at the thought of what was going to happen to the wretches waiting down below.

He concentrated instead on the breathtaking view of the city, the bustle and activity, crowds milling along the streets, canoes plying the canals. With the rainy season over, the peaks encircling the green valley had shed their mantles of cloud and stood starkly white against a sky of flawless blue. The marshes where the peasants grew the city's food were even greener, almost painfully so, and the lake shone bright as silver. Many small towns dotted its shores, most of them too far off to see.

Suddenly Basket-fox said, "You remember the Battle of Blackrock?"

Now what? "Of course, great slayer. That was when the Zolicans' Eagles tried an ambush, moving two four-hundreds in behind the knoll on our right. You and I and—"

"Good. Point to your pyramid. Good. And Bone-peak-runner's?"

Lynx brandished a claw over the floating city. "There, on Four-Cactus Canal."

"And who is Moon-feeder?"

"One of Flintknife's senior warriors, a taker of ten captives, my brother by another of our father's concubines. He wears a jade labret in the shape of a swan and he has a jagged scar on his right thigh."

The Jaguar uttered his strange chuckle. "Your memory is returning, Plumed-pillar!"

Having spent hours every day for months being coached by Basket-fox's reciters, the illiterate keepers of Tlixilian history, Lynx could rattle off his pretended ancestry back for generations and list more than two hundred living relations. Recognizing their faces would be more of a challenge, and all that work was useless now, since the Jaguars refused to accept his claim.

"We will appeal to the Great Council to overrule yesterday's wrongful decision."

"My lord is gracious," Lynx said. "Will that work?"

"No, but it gains us a little more time. You are a warrior of the Hairy Ones."

"Not the same sort of—" He was stopped by a feline glare.

"Whose side are you on, Bobcat-by-the-spring?"

"Yours, lord." Lynx had known for a long time what his answer must be when this question came. "The other side would kill me on sight. Many on your side would too, if you sheathed your claws. But while you guard me, my heart beats for El Dorado and I will do all I can against the Hairy Ones." His real motive, of course, was that only thus could he be of any use at all to his ward. A dead Blade was no protection. He could never return to Chivial in his new shape, so he would not allow Celeste to do so either. Fortunately she had not realized this yet.

"Pretend for a moment you are the enemy. How would you attack this city?"

Blades were not military strategists, but one-legged Jorge had been a mercenary back in Eurania. Did Basket-fox not know that, or did his dignity not allow him to seek advice from a slave? Lynx was a slave in fact, but not by agreed pretense, and perhaps that made a difference in the old man's contorted thinking.

What had Jorge told him? That street fighting was the most vicious sort of battle possible and El Dorado was far larger than any city in Eurania. To take it house-by-house against determined resistance would cost thousands of lives; Jorge even doubted that it would be possible. Eastward the lake was wide and unobstructed. South, north, and west, three great causeways, straight as arrows, connected it to the mainland. Each causeway was broken at intervals by removable bridges, specifically to block an assault.

But Basket-fox was not after the obvious answers. What did he want?

"Have the Hairy Ones reached the lake yet, terror of the woods?"

"There!" Basket-fox aimed a paw at the far distance. "Seven Reeds, a town of cowards, a nest of traitor Tephuamotziner lackeys."

"Are the Hairy Ones building boats there, by any chance?"

The cat eyes shone brighter than *Ratter's* pommel. "So my Eagle friends tell me. Many of my brothers feel that we have enough canoes to counter anything they can make."

Now Lynx saw where the conversation was headed. "No, lord." He made some wild guesses as to what would be possible for the Distliards' shipwrights. "You could fight them with fire arrows and grappling irons, but otherwise it will be horses all over again. Their boats will be faster and far more agile than your canoes, and much less likely to tip over. Their boats will ride the wind, but not only in the direction the wind goes. They can move across or even toward the wind, also."

Basket-fox bared his fangs in what usually implied a smile. "Their knights bless them thus?"

"No blessing needed. Even I could do it, after a fashion. I am not skilled, but give me some workers of wood and I will show you roughly how it works." Lynx's life at sea had been brief, but he had seen how *Papillon* sailed into the wind, and Jorge could assist him.

"It shall be so." The big cat head nodded. A furry paw patted Lynx's shoulder. "It is strange! I trust you more than my own sons, for you have no friend but me. Even Night-fisher believes in you only because I told him to."

"I owe you my life, lord. I will serve as I can."

"Go and do so," Basket-fox growled. "Quickly, before the ritual begins. Order whatever you require. You speak with my voice."

Relieved that he would not have to watch the slaughter, Lynx ran to the top of the long staircase and started down. Night-fisher would be surprised to see him coming on his own two paws instead of rolling down as dead meat. Maybe next time.

Meanwhile, he must find Jorge. Put a sail on a dugout canoe and it would tip over in a twinkling. So tie two of them together for stability? Add a mast . . . a rudder and perhaps a keel board?

2

The workers in wood were probably slaves—Lynx did not ask, and it was an unimportant distinction in El Dorado. They tended to collapse and bury their faces in the dirt at the sight of a jaguar knight, but he cured them of that by threatening to kill them if they didn't behave. What else could he do? If he smiled, half of them fainted.

After some hours and several unexpected swims, he managed a successful maiden voyage on his ungainly craft, which he privately named *Celeste.* He strengthened the rudder, had his workers attach splash boards along the gunwales, and tried again. The moon was full, so he sent Jorge and the carpenters home at sunset and worked on through the night with a fresh team. Getting the sails right was the hardest part, and finding a satisfactory way of attaching the boom was almost as bad, but just before dawn he sent word to Basket-fox that he was ready to demonstrate sailing.

They had hardly left the dock before the old knight yowled with delight and insisted on taking the tiller. He learned the knack of steering in an astonishingly short time, as if he had an instinctive feel for the way the catamaran would respond. Soon he was running before the wind, tacking back, chasing down terrified paddlers in canoes, even deliberately ramming them just to watch them tip over. In high spirits he returned to his palace and summoned friends. Jaguars began arriving at the dock in canoes or palanquins or just appearing, sometimes accompanied by Eagles and sometimes with dusty feet, as if they had actually walked the streets. Seeing that *Celeste* was becoming dangerously overloaded, Lynx made his excuses and left them to it.

That night he was summoned. As he trotted through the grounds with Night-fisher at his heels, Basket-fox appeared ahead of him in what had been an empty patch of moonlight. That was not surprising. What was surprising was that he hailed Lynx with a formal greeting due a brother knight.

He added, "Your dancing canoe was a magnificent feat, Plumed-pillar!"

"It was a trivial trick, silent killer. I am happy to have amused you."

"A valuable amusement." The old monster chuckled deep in his throat. "I have given some thought to your entourage. A single stripling is not enough." He nodded at a nearby tree; a fully fledged warrior became visible in the shadows, complete with spear and shield, labret, and plumed headdress. "You remember Corn-fang, now a taker of one captive? A most promising warrior who has seen the shame of following the imposter Flintknife and will be overjoyed to serve the real Plumed-pillar again."

Who had been bribed, in other words. Astonished, Lynx thanked his mentor for this further generosity and spoke a suitable greeting for a knight acknowledging a taker-of-one-captive follower. Corn-fang came forward to touch the ground before his new-or-restored lord. By Tlix-ilian standards he was an impressive sight in his finery, although he would have driven whole armies hysterical back in Eurania.

Unless Basket-fox was being exceptionally devious, even for him, he would not donate followers to a man he intended to kill very soon.

Another knight materialized—an Eagle, his great hunched shape towering over them all, feathers shining in the moonlight. This time there were no flowery greetings. Ignoring warriors and Jaguar-imposter, the newcomer spoke directly to Basket-fox.

"We see few guards posted. None is blessed."

"No knights?"

"Not one."

The Jaguar bared his fangs in what looked like an enormous yawn, but probably was not. "Then we shall have sport!" He turned to Lynx. "Plumed-pillar, we go to Seven Reeds to find the Hairy Ones' boats and knock holes in them! The mighty Frowning-whisper, here, will carry us on the Spirit Wind—four Jaguars and three twenties of warriors. You wish to accompany us?"

Lynx dutifully said, "I shall die of shame if you forbid me."

The cat-man grunted. Moonlight shone on his eyes. "But you will come only to observe, not to fight. You will instruct Corn-fang and Night-fisher that they are to guard you closely, and are not to seek out captives, nor attack anyone who is not threatening you."

That seemed entirely reasonable to Lynx, who was already wondering what he was letting himself in for, but honor required a protest, so he protested.

Basket-fox cut him off with a snarl. "Jaguars' weapons are sleep and madness and mindless terror. When a knight chooses to close in battle and gather captives with his own hands, he must go unseen or the enemy will roll over him like an avalanche. You would be a stain on the grass before they even noticed you were a fake. You will come along only to observe, so that you can copy the Hairy Ones' work for us."

Oops! Lynx should have seen how the wind blew. And the Tlixilians were still thinking of dugout canoes, not planks. "Lord, knocking holes in the boats will do little harm. You should go prepared to burn them or steal them."

Growl! "Is it so?"

"Also, may I suggest that capturing the men who do the work would be advantageous? We could use their skills."

Any great lord might glare when contradicted, but few as effectively as Basket-fox. "Star skimmer, do you see where the workers sleep?"

The eagle knight clicked his beak a few times, whatever that meant. "There are shelters nearby. We can bring back captives on the usual terms."

"And tools!" Lynx said. "Anything made of metal, all or part." He knew no words for nails or spikes.

"No!" The Eagle's beak shut with a noise like an ax. The knights were divided between Traditionalists and Progressives, and most Eagles were Traditionalists.

Lost in a jungle of tangled values, Lynx saw he might as well push on as try to turn back. If he must risk his neck on some madcap sabotage raid, then he would prefer that it made sense. "To take the Hairy Ones' tools would be the hardest blow you could strike."

"Tools are not a matter of honor!" the Eagle declared.

"But let us hear how warriors of the Hairy Ones think," Basket-fox said. "Continue, Plumed-pillar."

Blades were not soldiers, but one thing Ironhall taught was the value of reconnaissance, and it sounded as if the Eldoradoans had not done theirs yet. "I don't know what we are assaulting, lord. If it were me, I would have the noble Eagle send a scout across tonight and leave the actual attack for another evening."

Basket-fox's talons flashed in the moonlight. *"You dare?"*

Frowning-whisper uttered a shriek that might denote either fury or amusement.

Lynx gaped in sudden terror and hurled himself to the ground, groveling. "I mean no disrespect to my lord! I know not how I have offended the most terrible one!"

Basket-fox snarled dangerously. "Stupid, ignorant foreigner! I will forgive your ignorance just this once. Rise." He retracted his claws with what seemed like an effort. "Your suggestion has merit, though, and I will allow you to accompany me. You will oblige us, terror of the dark?"

Frowning-whisper said, "I am humbled by your trust."

"Tarry a moment!" The old knight spoke to empty air. "Raging-stone, stand down the Furious and the Flesh Eaters."

Lynx was still shaking, hard put to keep his fangs from chattering. That had been a very, very narrow escape! He would never volunteer to go alone into an enemy camp, but his imperfect Tlixilian had been understood as an insult to Basket-fox's courage or judgment or something. Of course the mission would not be certain suicide if the enemy truly had no eagle knights at Seven Reeds, as Frowning-whisper claimed, but it still felt like going into battle armed only with fingernails.

The Jaguar turned to stare fixedly at him, and he felt a strange sensation that the moon was growing brighter, like a strange colorless sunlight. The bats and crickets and the frogs in the lake sounded louder. How long had the air born this rich medley of scents? Even its touch on his skin felt suddenly meaningful. He was being blessed.

"We are ready now, friend of stars," Basket-fox said. If the old cat felt scared out of his whiskers, as Lynx did, he was not showing it.

The moon lurched a third of the way around the sky. The air chilled, changing scents and sounds; the frogs' chorus barked louder and nearer. Yet Lynx experienced none of the giddiness he had felt the first time he rode the Spirit Wind. Sheer terror yes, dizziness no. He glanced around quickly, registering a sawpit and stacks of tree trunks and cut planks. The Eagle had set them down in a secluded spot . . . *them?* There was no sign of Basket-fox. Panic surged until Lynx realized that he had no shadow, so the moon was shining through him. Old Kitty-cat would be somewhere close.

With his heart still thumping like a drum, Lynx padded toward the nearest gap, moving as quietly as he could, although his steps on the dry clay sounded abominably loud. When an invisible paw touched his chest, he barely suppressed a shriek of terror.

Whiskers tickled his ear. "Mud!" said an anonymous whisper.

Lynx nodded. He was still shivering as he edged around the puddle.

In the next few minutes—which felt like weeks—he established that the Distliards were constructing a fleet ashore, but close to a canal leading into the lake. The boats were larger than he expected, capable of carrying forty or fifty men. Several were near completion and would burn nicely. Best of all, he found a well-built shed with a massive iron lock on the door, a device that must have come from Eurania. He paced out the building's dimensions, remembering that his stride was longer than human.

Then he set off to explore the rest of the site, occasionally being warned off some particular course by a touch of his unseen companion's paw. He found pickets, crouching around small fires that seemed painfully bright, like fragments of the sun itself, but the men were relaxed, and might just be keeping watch for thieves. He inspected the rough shelters where the workers slept, peering inside a few to estimate how many there were.

What next? He had a sudden hysterical mental image of his enormous, near-naked feline self dining at high table in Ironhall, expounding on his military exploits in the Hence Lands to the horrified candidates. Join the Blades and see the world. . . .

A paw detained him. He waited. It did not move. He began to feel alarmed. Another touched his other shoulder, turning him to look leftward. Still, for a moment, he remained puzzled. Then he saw a movement . . . another . . . and yet another. He almost cried out in terror as shadows transformed into misty outlines of warriors, a gang of them drifting silently through the shrubbery, crossing his path not ten paces ahead. The paws urged him farther around and he saw another squad. The whole camp was filling up with armed men.

The moon jumped again and he was back in El Dorado, right where he had started, with the old scoundrel Basket-fox himself and an Eagle. About a hundred armed warriors were kneeling around the area—*naturales* did not line up in rows like Euranian soldiers. To Lynx's shame, his front paws began to shake violently as realization of his narrow escape sank in.

"We are in your debt, star gatherer," Basket-fox said cheerily, looking up at the monster beak. "You will see that Frowning-whisper is properly reprimanded?"

"He will not live long enough to repent his shame." The eagle apparition vanished just as Lynx realized that it had not been Frowning-whisper.

"Return the men to the barracks, Taker of Seven Captives," the Jaguar said. "Tonight is not auspicious. Tomorrow, perhaps, they will get a chance to show their mettle." He thumped Lynx's shoulders with both paws, in a sort of half hug. "That was very well done, Plumed-pillar! I applaud your warrior courage!"

"I don't understand!"

"No?" Basket-fox rumbled a deep purr of amusement. "Your dancing boat upset the Traditionalists today. I knew the Tephuamotziners had at least four knights at Seven Reeds yesterday, so I was sure that Frowning-whisper was lying and would betray me, but without your daring offer I might have lost many men proving that. Fortunately I had the mighty Star-feather watching over us. What was that house you found so interesting?"

Lynx gulped and pulled his wits together. "My lord's words warm the world. That house must be where they keep their tools, lord. Stealing those, or at the least destroying them, will do more to slow them than even burning the boats themselves. They probably have sails and ropes in there, too, and those must also be stolen or burned."

"We shall discuss it later. Come, tonight we shall feast."

The attack was launched the following night. No less than six Jaguars and two Eagles had listened attentively as the imposter knight told them what should be done to inflict maximum hurt on the enemy. A flotilla of canoes set off just after sunset; another army rode the Spirit Wind after them when the moon was high.

Lynx was left behind. He protested both loudly and sincerely, because he had developed a proprietary interest in what was now his plan, but he had made himself too important to risk. Knowing how disappointed his two warrior retainers would be, he begged that they, at least, be allowed to participate, and again was denied. Around midnight he walked over to the pyramid and started up its evil, blackened stairs, still reeking of blood from the recent slaughter. Probably this was forbidden behavior, for Corn-fang and Night-fisher seemed much perturbed, but they followed in silence as good bodyguards should.

Lynx ignored them. In the small hours of the night, he sat in lonely misery on the top of the pyramid and stared out across the moonlit lake to a distant yellow star glowing near Seven Reeds. Thanks to him, the Distliards' shipyard was ablaze, their boats and materiel turned to fire and ash. He had postponed the Allies' assault on the floating city for months. He had, in a very small way, altered the course of history. If he did a good job as shipwright and grand admiral, he might change it even more.

He had no idea which side Athelgar favored in this war. It might be that Lynx was supporting his King's enemies, but his duty to his ward gave him no choice. It hardly mattered, because he would never see Chivial again.

Sheese, Ironhall, Quondam—Chivial had never been very kind to the former Alf Attewell, so why was he so bitterly homesick?

3

We are wasting time!" Flicker repeated furiously. "Rojas is singing lullabies until we drop our guard, so he can storm the house and take all the gold. The dealers he promised will never appear. Even if Blood-mirror-walks and the others do reach El Dorado safely, do you think the Emperor will send a jaguar knight here to bargain with you? You can stay here and rot if you like, but let me go inland!"

"You must learn to be patient," Wolf said in fatherly fashion. Flicker was an explosive mixture of ability, ambition, and impotence, needing to vent his frustration regularly. The Chivians held a conference every week and always had the same argument. They had been a month in Sigisa, but that was not long enough for their messengers to have reached El Dorado, let alone bring back a reply. Even news of the war was scanty, although rumors suggested that the new *Caudillo* was faring better than his predecessors.

"Besides, it's Long Night! Enjoy the festivities."

Nothing could be less like Chivian midwinter than a sultry tropical evening on a patio in Sigisa. Surf rumbled on the beach, palm trees waved their tresses in the trade winds. With the sun asleep behind the ranges, moths were swooping lovingly around the lanterns, and frogs were tuning up. Here Don Lope and Dona Dolores lived a lazy, rich-folks life, gathering gossip and seeking to learn more about this strange new world. The Chivians had shed their sea-voyage scrawniness, except for Flicker, who was as gaunt as ever, restless and impatient for action. They had a team of servants to pamper them; Hick and Will had even acquired live-in companions. All such outsiders were liable to be recruited by the *Alcalde*'s minions, but the inquisitors regularly identified the spies and sent them packing.

Amid the vice and squalor of Sigisa in general, the ever-charming Don Ruiz de Rojas ran a bizarre parody of high society. Wolf and Dolores were frequent guests at his soirées, mingling with many other interesting guests—smugglers, pirates, spies from Isilond and other Euranian powers, also gentleman adventurers who tended to die young in brawls or vanish upcountry, where they would doubtless leave their bones.

"Why don't you let Flicker go, if he's so anxious?" Megan asked quietly.

Mutiny? Flicker had never won any support before. Wolf glanced at Dolores, to see what she thought, and was surprised to see her wearing her dead-fish inquisitor face. Did that mean she was trying to hide surprise or was anxious not to take sides? Personally, Wolf would love to let Wonder Boy go blundering off into the jungle and get himself killed, but the interests of the mission must come ahead of personal feelings.

"Firstly, because the mainland is enormous and infested by warring armies that kill strangers with no questions asked. Or answered. Secondly, because we are already too few. We need Flicker here. It would be crazy to divide the team."

"Then let's all go!" Flicker said sullenly.

This sort of back-talk might be correct Dark Chamber procedure, but it rankled a Blade. Wolf said, "Why don't you let Peterkin show you the sights, sonny? Then maybe we'd get some peace."

Peterkin was the expedition's brothel expert. Flicker scorned to visit the houses and brought home no women of his own. He just mooned around the hacienda making calf-eyes at Dolores, lovesick brat.

He glared. "At least let me visit the coastal states. Yazotlan or Zolica."

"No. We've been over this a dozen times. If the rebel states need arms, they get them from the Distlish. If they were willing to trade their conjury secrets, they'd have sold them to the Distlish long ago. We deal with El Dorado or with no one. We need you here and I expect you to be loyal to the team. Now, if no one has anything else to—"

"If you were loyal to the team we would be halfway to El Dorado by this time."

Now both Megan and Dolores were looking blank.

"Meaning?"

"Meaning," Flicker sneered, "you're keeping us all here in Sigisa only because you hope to catch your thief brother on his way through."

That hurt, as Flicker undoubtedly intended. Yes, Wolf kept an eye on ships arriving and Heron-jade said he did, too. What else the eagle warrior did with his time, apart from eating and wandering the streets, only the spirits knew. He kept his slave scars hidden under a shirt, and he was too big to attract trouble he did not choose himself.

Meanwhile, to become angry would be to give Flicker a victory.

"That is not true," Wolf said calmly. "I do watch for Lynx, but I do not let my own priorities interfere with the mission, and you can tell I'm not lying. You reminded me of something, though. There's a Chivian caravel named *Sea Queen* in the river, unloading barrel staves and pig iron. I've spoken with the captain and he's willing to take mail Home for us. Mention that to the sailors, will you, Megan? Now, if no one . . . Yes, Duff?"

The carpenter had emerged from the house, looking unhappy at interrupting. "Note handed in, sir. Man says it's urgent."

Dolores beat Flicker to the message, grabbed it, and broke the seal.

"They've answered, they've answered! Oh, Wolf, they want to trade!" She tried to kiss him and show him the note at the same time.

The cause of her excitement was brief, neatly inscribed. *Alcalde Don Rojas requested the presence of Don Lope and Dona Dolores at their earliest convenience this evening, so that certain promises could be made and other promises kept.*

Wolf glanced inquiringly at Flicker, but now he was being inscrutable, of course.

"Isn't it wonderful!" Dolores said. "I have nothing to wear!"

"Chain mail might be safest." Bait in a trap should smell as sweet as this. "It's a very quick response, but possible, I suppose." Just plausible enough to be believed? "Will you be able to tell if the emissaries he produces are fakes?"

"Of course! If they say they're what they're not." Suddenly she turned coolly professional. "He's hinting he wants us to bring the gold along!"

"Over my dead . . . I mean, not yet."

The summons gave Wolf gooseflesh, and even Dolores was starting to look edgy, now the first excitement had worn off. "Why not let me go and you have a headache?" he said.

"That won't work."

"I'll take Flicker. He can do truth-sounding as well as you can."

"Flicker doesn't know an execration from an exaltation. Don't *baby* me!"

She was right. "Very well. Tell the man he'll have our reply in a moment, Duff." Wolf went in search of pen and paper.

He would trust a fer-de-lance ahead of Don Rojas. Whenever he and Dolores visited the hyena's den, he put everyone on alert in case they needed rescuing or the villa was attacked in their absence. Normally a couple of the sailors accompanied them to the *Alcalde's* door, while

Heron-jade kept watch from their own kitchen table. There was no question that the eagle warrior could see some things at a distance and, although he was never specific about which things or how he looked for them, he had never failed to dispatch sailors to escort them home again when they were ready to leave. Rojas's invitation had taken them unawares and Heron-jade was nowhere to be found. He might be carousing somewhere or he might already be floating in the harbor. It was worrisome.

An hour or so later the Attewells strolled arm-in-arm along the bustling street, with nightlife roistering around them and Will and Hick stalking behind. The gate to the mayor's compound was opened by the usual men-at-arms, but the guard in the torch-lit courtyard included a dozen *naturale* warriors in feathered headdresses. Most wore the usual embroidered cloak or mantle pinned at the right shoulder, but some were in padded cotton armor, while a couple of youngsters had not graduated beyond simple loincloths. Many carried feathered shields, and all were armed with spears and obsidian-edged swords. They outnumbered the Distliards.

"This is real!" Dolores whispered in Chivian. "He wouldn't fake all this."

Seventy thousand pesos would finance a fair scam, but Wolf was certainly not about to call these bravos imposters to their faces. How had Rojas smuggled such visions into the city? How had he *dared*? By entertaining his king's enemies, he was openly playing traitor.

The usual servants had vanished. The visitors were greeted at the front door by pox-faced Don Pedrarias, who was chief justice of Sigisa and as ruthless as the *Alcalde* himself. He looked them over coldly.

"You brought it?"

"No. If it is due I can easily fetch it."

The villain scowled, but he could not seriously have expected Wolf to drop a fortune at his feet. He led the way out to the main terrace and left them there.

The garden was dimmer than usual, with no moon so close to Long Night, and only a few small lanterns substituting for the usual flaming torches. Stars swarmed overhead, flowers loaded the air with soporific scents, and the surf beat its slow measure like a great heart, but there were no guests in sight, no servants, not even stools or benches. Dolores grinned and fidgeted with excitement, while Wolf grew steadily more tense. Truly, they were the world's greatest pessimist-optimist partnership.

Soon, though, a dozen men paraded out from the house. Other than Don Ruiz, they were all *naturales* in their glory—gems, gold, and feathers. Earrings, labrets, nose plugs, bracelets. They were almost all armed, but older men than the guards on the gate. The leader of the delegation, the sun amid this constellation of nobles, was the man on the *Alcalde's* arm. When those two stopped, the others spread around in a circle. Trapped, all Wolf could do was wait politely to be presented to the bull elk.

He was a smallish man made tall by pride, well-preserved but old enough to have stringy whiskers. The shimmering feather cloak hung loosely on his shoulders, like his headdress and jewelry, seeming at once less gaudy than most of the others' and more impressive. His eyes were rapier-sharp, deep-set in wrinkles.

"This is the foreigner, glorious one," Rojas said in halting Tlixilian. "And his senior wife. His name is Lord Wild-dog-by-the-spring. Don Lope, we are honored by the presence of Prince Hummingbird, Conch-flute of Yazotlan."

Yazotlan? All the arguments Wolf had thrown at Flicker earlier collapsed. Why Yazotlan? Yazotlan was a coastal state, a Distlish ally. His head throbbed as he tried to work out why it would want to buy steel swords from him. Did the Distlish charge too much? Or were the Yazotlans trying to buy more arms than Distlain would supply?—for both sides must know that all bets would be off as soon as El Dorado fell. Or perhaps precious spiritualist secrets were the Distliards' asking price also. In that case, the Yazotlans must prefer they go to a distant, unaligned power like Chivial than to one with an army already on the mainland.

And the *Conch-flute*! El Dorado was ruled by a Great Council composed of men of the imperial family. The man called Emperor by the Distlish and Fountain-of-swords by the Tlixilians was leader of the army and thus the most powerful, ranking first in the council without being paramount. Second in authority was his minister for foreign affairs, termed the Conch-flute for reasons lost in the mists of time. Apparently the arrangements in the city of Yazotlan were similar.

Wolf offered a full court bow and some sickly compliments.

Hummingbird's curt nod suggested he should lie prostrate and kiss sandals. Rojas frowned, perhaps wishing he had coached the foreigners in the correct etiquette. Of course all those obsidian swords might be making the tyrant's neck itch. Technically Yazotlan was a Distlish ally, but only the *Caudillo* would have royal authority to deal with its government, so Rojas was still playing a dangerous game.

The Conch-flute gestured. An attendant spread a mat behind him. The great man sat down. Everyone else at once dropped to their knees on the stones. Since Dolores had given no signal that Lord Hummingbird was a fake, Rojas had amply fulfilled his side of the bargain and now it was up to Wolf to negotiate. In that sticky tropical night, the prospect made him sweat rivers.

"Your women are most beautiful, Wild-dog-by-the-spring," the prince remarked politely, hugging his shins.

"So are yours, Highness. So are all women."

He smiled. "There speaks youth."

The courtiers' obedient little chuckles sounded like beetles dancing.

"The *Alcalde* tells me that your wives are callers of the spirits?"

"I am limited to one wife, Highness, but she is wise in the ways of the elementals. This is not unusual for women in our country." It would be in his. He must find Dolores's presence bizarre.

Again a thin smile. "Then she has great talent as well as beauty, and also fortitude, for I understand that journeying upon the waves is an ordeal to try strong men."

"It is indeed, but what man ever dared give birth to a baby?"

A thinner smile. "She has very pale skin."

In Wolf's opinion Dolores's visible parts bore a magnificent tropical tan. "Our land lies farther from the sun, Great One. That is why."

"How many days did you journey upon the waves?" His accent was not that of El Dorado as Heron-jade spoke it.

"More than half a . . ." The query had sounded like more chitchat politeness. Too late Wolf saw that it struck at the heart of the night's business. ". . . year."

The bargaining had begun and he had already stumbled.

"You speak with your King's voice, Wild-dog-by-the-spring?"

"Well, sort of. But he doesn't know it. I mean my King doesn't."

"Of course he does!" Dolores corrected. Everyone glared at her.

Wolf tried to recall his blunder. "I mean he's really on the side of El Dorado in your war, but don't worry about that." No, that was worse. His thumping headache was mashing his wits.

"And what war goods have you ready to trade?"

"Swords and spears and horses. Lots of horses and swords. Good swords. Not the best, like mine, but good enough to fool you."

"Fighting dogs?"

"You want dogs, I'll promise dogs."

"You have ships standing by? On their way?"

"Oh, no. You can fetch the stuff the way the El Dorado knights sent their warriors to my land last winter, can't you? Isn't your conjuration as good as theirs?"

"The world is a big place. How will you show our Eagles where to go?"

"I can't."

"So when could you deliver the weapons?"

That was the crux. If the Distliards overthrew El Dorado without significant Yazotlan help, Yazotlan would not share in the booty. Worse, if the Distliards gave up and sailed away, the allies it abandoned would face terrible vengeance from the triumphant Empire. The negotiations were urgent, but Wolf had already admitted that his homeland was farther away than Distlain was.

"At least a year, maybe two."

Old Hummingbird sat there unblinking and spat questions. He ignored mosquitoes landing on his face. He had a mind like a dancing scorpion and Wolf was making an utter fool of himself. It was worse than being shredded by Quintus.

The Conch-flute asked, "And what do you seek in return for these wonderful things you promise?"

Seeing a chance to let Dolores take over, Wolf grabbed it. "Wisdom, Highness. To explain that, I must ask you to hear the words of my wife." It was a great relief to stop talking and rest his aching skull.

But it was too late for Dolores to save the situation, and she fared even worse. Oh, she knew exactly what it was she wanted to learn about the knights' techniques, but the technical terms she had learned from Intrepid and her other instructors would not translate into Tlixilian. Even Wolf had trouble understanding what she was saying and any Blade knew a fair bit about conjuration—certainly more than the aristocrat-politician, Hummingbird, did. It began to seem that Tlixilian and Chivian views of what conjury actually did were worlds apart.

When she finished, the Conch-flute just sat and stared at her for a while without expression. Then he said, "Extraordinary!"

Rojas was seething. "I was misled, Highness. I am deeply sorry that you came so far to no purpose."

"Never fear, it has been instructive. But I do not think we can trust these strangers. What does the exalted Shining-cloud think?" The old man had not raised his voice, but the answer came in a screech out of the sky.

"The man was trying to cheat you, benevolent one. The woman is merely crazy."

Dolores cried out in shock. An eagle knight stood on the ridgepole of the house like a giant weathervane.

4

He was only a black shape against the stars—bulbous, as if he had muffled himself in a quilt from his ears down to his knees, with only the top of his head showing. The way he held his balance up there brought back memories of the giant talons that had marked the snow at Quondam.

"That the man was lying was obvious," Hummingbird said dryly, not looking up. "What was the woman trying to say, could you tell, lord of the skies?"

"It was babbling, baby talk." Shining-cloud's discordant croak was a knife on a plate. "She wants to pry into the sacred mysteries of the knights, but her reasons for this madness are more madness. Kill the man for insolence, but the girl is worth something. I will take her myself if you do not want her." His laugh was even more dissonant than his voice.

Wolf gripped his sword, aware that he was hopelessly outnumbered, even without counting the mighty Eagle. Much too late, he remembered what gave him headaches.

"Wait! Your Highness, this freak up on the roof sullies your honor! I am an emissary of a great monarch, entitled to respect. He used the Serpent's Eye on me! Is not an envoy sacrosanct?"

A surge of pain cued him to cry out and clutch his head. Sometimes it helped to dramatize.

"What is this?" The Conch-flute was frowning. "Shining-cloud, are you blessing the foreigner?"

"Certainly not, scion of heroes."

The pain eased, though.

"He was! I am sensitive to the spirits."

Hummingbird peered around his entourage. "Prickly-pear, what do you say?"

"I may have sensed some blessing, valiant prospect," one of the older men muttered unhappily. "But I am sure no more than would be prudently applied to disable treachery." A good courtier could straddle any fence.

"Shining-cloud does not want the great ones of Yazotlan furnished with sky-metal weapons!" Wolf said. "He hoards the secrets of his order, so he seeks to block an agreement between us."

"By your leave, mover of mountains," the Eagle said, "I claim his precious jewel."

"Wait." The Conch-flute was frowning harder now, but at Wolf. "You slander a mighty warrior, stranger, and the penalty for that is death."

Wolf saw he was on to something. "Is it slander? Are the eagle knights of Yazotlan different from those of the floating city—Sky-cactus, say, or Bone-peak-runner, or the great Amaranth-talon?"

There he scored his first real hit of the evening. That he could quote such names caused hisses of surprise and disapproval all round.

"You deal with our enemies also?" the Conch-flute said. Sudden death was now on the table.

Even Rojas, who had been having trouble following the Tlixilian chatter, had caught the gist. He was displeased, but perhaps mostly at the thought that a dead Chivian could not pay his commission.

"To deal with those I named is impossible," Wolf said. "They live in dreams of the past. Jaguar knights—like Lizard-drumming, say, the mighty son of Quetzal-star—are wiser, and wish their warriors to be well armed." He was gambling that Lizard-drumming was not known for conservative views. No one contradicted him.

"August ruler," said the thing on the roof, "I confess that I did cast a very slight blessing on the strangers. They came bearing many strange, outlandish blessings of their own, so they were first to breach the rules of negotiation. I feared those were evils that might imperil you. It is possible that I disturbed the aim of the man's thoughts a little, but I put no filth in his midden mouth. I made him less able to deceive you, that is all. The foulness he revealed was his own."

"Your powers are undoubted, wind rider."

"As for the sky-metal weapons and other abominations, I argued against them only until the Great Council in its wisdom made its decision. We are always loyal to the Council."

"Your loyalty has been proven times beyond reckoning," the Conch-flute admitted. "But the stranger's charge was true and I am shamed."

"I claim his precious jewel!" the knight repeated stubbornly. "Emissary or not, a commoner who insults a knight must make recompense."

"What does Don Ruiz say?"

The *Alcalde* was an unhappy man, anxious to collect his fee. "Our traditions are similar, Highness. We did invite this worm to a parley. However foul his words, in our ways he would be allowed to depart freely."

"In your house we shall be bound by your ways." Hummingbird raised his elbows and two men sprang forward to lift him to his feet. Everyone rose. "We have been honored by your hospitality, Don Ruiz."

The *Alcalde* doubled over in a bow. "Nay, my house is exalted by Your Highness's shadow on the floor. I deeply regret that your journey was in vain. I am unworthy of the noble gifts Your Highness brought me and humbly beg that I may be allowed to decline them without giving offense."

"No, no. Keep them for friendship." Prince Hummingbird pulled his cloak about him. "If the glorious Shining-cloud will favor us once again, we are ready."

In response the eagle knight overhead uttered an ear-piercing screech and . . . he did not exactly *spread his wings,* but he seemed to stretch out sideways and upward and continue to expand so that his darkness blotted out the sky and the stars. Wolf felt a blaze of pain as if red-hot irons had been thrust in his eyes. He staggered and cried out.

Then the stars returned, fading in from pitch darkness. All the Yazotlans had gone.

"Darling, you were wonderful!" Dolores embraced him. "I was so worried, and you saved the day. That monster churning our wits! I loved the way you—"

"Later!" Wolf detached her gently and turned to face their irate host. Pedrarias and henchmen had emerged from the shadows. Negotiations were not over yet. "We are grateful for your efforts on our behalf, Your Worship. It is regrettable that the other side did not play fair."

"It is more regrettable that you turned out to have nothing to sell, Sir Wolf." Bluster would have been easier to deal with than Rojas's icy charm, his calculated killer's smile.

"I do have the merchandise. We had a misunderstanding. I told you I wanted to trade with El Dorado, which has conjurers who could transport it. You never told me you were going to bring in the Yazotlans. Evidently they are not so skilled in the spiritual arts."

"Nobody is," Rojas said. "What you ask is impossible. You betrayed my trust and shamed me in front of the most powerful men I know."

"With respect, Excellency, they admitted that the fault was theirs. Else why would they have left you the gifts they brought?"

The *Alcalde*'s eyes shone like steel in the starlight. "What they left or did not leave is not your concern. My fee is. You will produce it now."

"It is a fair request," Wolf admitted, having no choice. Knowing that the Yazotlan Great Council was eager to obtain weaponry that the Distliards either would not or could not provide, Don Ruiz had performed his role of middleman admirably and expected to be paid by both parties. "Seventy thousand pesos. Tomorrow morning?"

"Tonight. One hundred and ten thousand. I will offer your lady wife some refreshment while we wait. Hurry back."

Wolf made a halfhearted effort to argue that the additional forty had been conditional on reaching an agreement; not surprisingly, he got nowhere. He had right on his side, but he had admitted having the additional money and Rojas wanted it. He offered a bodyguard for the journey. Wolf assured him that *Diligence* was sufficient protection.

As if the night had not yet provided enough failure, he now had to suffer the shame of leaving his wife behind as hostage. He was shown the gate and hurried homeward. The street was thronged with revelers, but he traveled warily, for the presence of witnesses was no guarantee of safety in Sigisa. A man could be cut down in the midst of a crowd without anyone seeing a thing. Women and drunks moved to accost him and he snarled at them menacingly.

"You pee in the water jar, Wild-dog-by-the-spring." A hand like a paving stone dropped on his shoulder.

He glanced up at the scowling face of Heron-jade. "What means that?"

"It means you don't know your friends from your enemies." He was panting, out of breath.

"But you told me it was cowardly and dishonorable for eagle warriors to use sky-metal swords. You told me the Yazotlans were dishonorable and cowardly. Why do you object if I try to cheat them?"

The big man screwed up his face as he tried to work out the correct response. "Shining-cloud is not the least of Eagles," he said grudgingly. "I recognized his shadow in Calero's."

Calero's was a long way south, reputedly the wildest, nastiest dive on the island. "What were you doing there?"

Heron-jade chuckled low in his throat. "Urging tranquility on the excited."

"Calero pays you for that?"

"He lets me eat all I want for nothing." Heron-jade had never asked Wolf for money. His feeding bills were so high that Wolf had never felt obliged to offer him any, and doubted he even knew what it was. It was amazing that the big man could be eating elsewhere as well, but his peculiar ideas on warrior's honor might see bouncer as a permissible occupation.

They walked in silence for a few minutes.

"Great and most trusted watcher," Wolf said at last, "speak of something near to my heart. If Shining-cloud or some other mighty eagle knight wanted to send me back to my homeland and then bring me back with a heap of valuable things, could he do it?"

The eagle warrior had been asked such questions before, but had always sulked and refused to answer. This time he chuckled as if he found such ignorance amusing.

"Of course not! If you told one of those rats in that corner to run to El Dorado, would it know where to go?"

Wolf could see no rats where he pointed. "But Amaranth—"

"Soaring Amaranth-talon and star-walking Bone-peak-runner went to rescue Plumed-pillar."

So Celeste's jaguar pin had acted like a beacon, and without that guidance, the Dark Chamber's plans lay in ruins. There was no practical way to import Chivian weapons into El Dorado.

At the villa, Wolf ran his golden key over the gate. Nothing happened. He cursed and rang the bell. *Many strange, outlandish blessings,* Shining-cloud had said.

Flicker opened the gate and stood foursquare in the entrance. "Where is she? What have you done with Dolly?"

"I sold her to the cannibals. You are between me and the ransom money."

He stepped back to let Wolf past. "I told you to take the money with you!"

"Bless the spirits I didn't!"

"What do you mean?" Flicker yelled, following. For once he had dropped his personation.

In the light of the first torch, Wolf paused to examine the three pesos he had been carrying in his pocket. Then he continued, now trailed by Flicker, Peterkin, and Heron-jade. When he reached his bedroom, they were joined by Megan and Duff, both anxious.

Wolf handed Flicker the key. "Open the box for me." He pulled off his sweaty shirt and reached for another from the closet.

"If you'd taken the money with you as I said, you wouldn't have had to abandon her to those criminals!" Flicker insisted, kneeling beside the great sea chest in which they stored the bulk of the money. In a moment he cried out in fury as the key slid from his nerveless fingers.

"Oh, sorry, Flicker," Wolf said. "I thought it was just me. I suppose you can all see my sash now, can you?" Fearing trouble, he had gone to the mayor's house wearing what the inquisitors, with unusual humor, referred to as his "war band," a normally invisible belt that not only provided some defense against poisons, including alcohol, but also contained many useful gadgets. In Chivial only a White Sister could detect a war band, but obviously Shining-cloud had. Now its contents must be worthless—enchanted bandage, infallible tinder, light-maker, stamina bracelet, and the rest. The twine stronger than a steel chain would be only string. For most of these Wolf had no replacements. He held out the fake pesos for the others to see, reverted to nasty, greasy lead. "It is good I didn't take all the money, or we would be in much deeper trouble. They had an eagle knight there. He disabled all our conjuries."

"No!" Megan said, wide-eyed. "No, that isn't possible, Sir Wolf! No Chivian conjurer could do that, certainly not without putting the conjurements inside an octogram. And not several different conjurements at once!"

"He did. He also used the Serpent's Eye on us, so we became twittering chickens when we needed all our wits about us. Did you expect them to play fair? Nobody does, here. Someone find the antidote for Flicker. I want his sword arm working when we go to deliver the money."

He took Flicker and three of the sailors with him when he carried the ransom to the Rojas mansion, but they met with no trouble. Dolores was alive and well, chattering with Dona Fortunata. It was a very civilized extortion. The odious Pedrarias accepted the bags and weighed the coins under the *Alcalde's* watchful eye.

"So where do you head now, Don Lope?" Rojas inquired as he ushered his guests to the gate, where their guards were being guarded by his guards. "Home to Chivial, or on to El Dorado?"

"I have not thought beyond falling into bed tonight, Your Excellency. Conjuration gives me a headache and your feathered friend packed a mean punch, spiritually speaking."

Rojas squeezed Wolf's arm in a sort of friendly menace. "The Distlish allow their allies to keep very few captives, so they are short of virtue. You made them waste a lot of it tonight. Do remember *Sea Queen,* in port just now. You could do worse."

"I have not been doing well recently," Wolf admitted.

"But if you prefer to tarry in fair Sigisa to spend the rest of your money, I am sure there will be those who can help you do so." The *Alcalde* smiled sadly—such a shame to cut a friend's throat. "Good chance to you, and to you, Dona Dolores."

They headed for home with his threats still ringing in their ears. Dolores bubbled with joy, as if she'd just been to a glorious ball instead of being ransomed from a monster's den. She had witnessed impossible things.

When Wolf broke the news about the conjurements, she laughed.

"That's impossible, of course."

"So Megan told me. It's still a blow."

"But that wasn't the only impossible thing Shining-cloud did!" she said. "Oh, Wolf, it's so wonderful! Let's have a conference the moment we get back."

They went straight to their bedroom; Flicker and Megan joined them. Wolf sat on the bed and nursed a seething anger; Flicker stood by the door and glowered, arms folded. Megan made herself comfortable with her knitting.

Dolores paced about, like Athelgar. "What the eagle knight did was absolutely incredible! Moving two dozen men from here to Yazotlan with a snap of his fingers!" She laughed excitedly. "If he has fingers. Then he deactivated all our conjurements—poof! Like that. No chanting. No octogram. All by himself! And there's more. He is not only the most incredible conjurer I ever heard of, but he's a sniffer as well!"

Megan frowned. "You sure of that, dear?"

"Yes, yes! He had to sniff out all our little gadgets in order to break them. We know," she said with a glance at Wolf that meant he might not, "that a conjurer can never be a White Sister or vice versa. You either push the elementals around or you stand still and watch them. Blacksmiths don't play lutes, is how Intrepid puts it. But Shining-cloud can do both!"

"I don't believe it," Flicker said. "He must just have a general conjuration to release elementals."

"That has *got* to be impossible!"

"I believe it," Wolf said grumpily, aware that he never missed a chance to disagree with Flicker. "The sniffing, I mean. Heron-jade told me he detected the eagle knight all the way from Calero's. 'Recognized his shadow' was how he put it."

"Now you're saying Heron-jade is a White Sister?" Flicker was rarely so witty. They all smiled.

"He'd look great in the hat," Wolf said. "But remember he saw the enchantment on our tangle mats? The jaguars didn't, but he did. They had an unnatural ability to see in the dark and probably other skills. An eagle knight, like his Sky-cactus, can *delegate* the ability to sniff out conjury to his followers. He must *conjure* them to do it! Try telling that to the White Sisters!"

Glum silence. Everything they had been taught about spiritualism had fallen apart in the Hence Lands.

"What does matter," Dolores declared, "is that the Eagles' conjuration skills are absolutely incredible and it's worth *anything* to get hold of them! What do we try next, love?"

"We go home. De Rojas told me to get out of town or he'd skin us completely. He even pointed out that there's a Chivian ship in port. He was giving us a five-yard start."

Megan's needles clicked softly. She was nodding to her knitting. Dolores stared in dismay at the crumbling of her dreams.

Flicker sneered. "You flee from threats, Wolf?"

"I learn from my mistakes, and tonight I learned that what we want to do is impossible. The mission has hit the rocks; all hands to the lifeboats. Firstly, we were relying on the eagle knights to fetch the trade goods. Rojas and Heron-jade both say that's impossible." He waited a moment in case his wife wanted to say Rojas had been lying, but she did not. "The Eagles need something to aim for, and without it they can't find Chivial. To ship arms by sea would take us years. Secondly, the Eagles and Jaguars will never reveal their secrets."

"They will if they are desperate enough!" Flicker said.

Wolf sighed. "No. I should have listened to my own advice. I told you, all of you, back on *Glorious*. I told you, 'The Jaguars and Eagles guard their secrets so closely that we could learn nothing if we were free to walk the streets of El Dorado.' "

"They were willing to trade tonight if we'd had trade goods ready!" Dolores protested.

"Hummingbird was, love. Shining-cloud wasn't. He and his flock had orders from their king to cooperate, but he found a way to wiggle out. That will always happen. You can bribe the rulers, or threaten the cities with massacre, but you cannot pressure the knights. Are you suggesting we tie the likes of Shining-cloud to a stump and start pulling out his feathers? You're thinking of them as conjurers, like old Grand Wizard and his fumbling fog of fogies. I'm telling you they're fighters, military orders like the Blades or the Yeomen. You could offer a Blade anything in the world for his sword and he would turn you down even if he were starving. Or try bribing a Yeoman to go out in public with mud on his cuirass. *We will never get their secrets out of the knights!*"

He was looking at three disbelieving faces. Even Megan probably just thought it was too dangerous to try, not that it was impossible.

"I should have seen this sooner," he said. "We all should. We are trying to exchange goods for knowledge and that is never easy. It's almost impossible in this case, because the *naturales* have no proper system of writing. They have no spell books we can buy." More blank looks. Wolf pressed on. "Listen! Suppose we offer a whole wagonload of swords just for one conjuration—say the one the Eagles use to teleport people. That can't be written down anywhere, because Tlixilians don't have real writing. But we have the swords, they have the know-how, and we agree to trade. We send them, say, Flicker, and the knights teach him the technique. They may grumble, but they obey orders from their king or emperor and they reveal their mystery. We hand over the swords, and they send Flicker back. Now they have the swords and we have Flicker and *both parties* have the information. You see the difference?"

"Then they kill me." Flicker's mind was as fast as his feet. The women were still puzzled but he was smiling, thin-lipped.

Wolf nodded. "With their powers, they could probably do that no matter what precautions we took or where you fled. You might cheat them by writing it all down quick, but I wouldn't count on even that. You'd be a dead man running. Then they still have the swords and we have nothing."

Even Dolores was frowning now, still reluctant to believe.

"Suppose we had not been unmasked tonight," he said. "Suppose I had managed to gull the Conch-flute into believing I did have a shipload of hardware on its way. We make a deal, so what happens? He certainly does not call Shining-cloud down off his perch to give Dolores a few tips in Tlixilian spirituality. No, he whisks her off to Yazotlan with him to learn the skills she wants at leisure. When I am ready to deliver the goods, I get my wife back in exchange. But for how long? I'm telling you that tonight was the luckiest failure of my life. I say we give up and go home."

Dolores jumped to her feet. "Darling, we can't! We mustn't! Chivial needs this. What if Isilond or Distlain gets these powers before we do? They could drop an army in the middle of Grandon. So what if it's dangerous? We knew this mission would be dangerous. You're trying to baby me again, Wolf! You are treating us like children."

"I am not trying—"

"Yes, you are! I did not come all this way just to turn around and run home with my tail between my legs."

Megan folded her knitting back in its bag. "Let's talk about it in the morning, Sir Wolf. It's a big decision and we should sleep on it."

5

The most important rule in a marriage was *Never take an argument to bed*. But there were times . . .

"You didn't listen to Rojas," Wolf said as he snuffed the candle. "He knows we're trying to deal with El Dorado. He can guess we have more gold. One night he's going to send an army here again. He more or less promised! And this time we don't have jaguar warriors to bash heads." He rolled over.

"Don't touch me!"

He rolled back again. "That won't help."

"Nor will what you want."

"It would, you know."

"No, it wouldn't."

"As you wish. Megan was right. We should sleep on it, not talk about it anymore tonight. Go to sleep."

"You don't love me." She saw triumph and fame being snatched away from her. He saw no chance of either. She saw her great adventure cut short for no reason. He saw both them and the people who relied on them dying nastily and soon.

"You think I came to this fever swamp to please Athelgar?" he asked.

Silence.

He was bitter. "Yes, you let it slip tonight, didn't you? I wasn't the only one babbling secrets under the Serpent's Eye."

"What do you mean?" she whispered, still with her back to him.

"*Put it in writing!* Remember? What you said to Flicker the first time I met him, in the Pine Tree Inn. Then you told me it meant he was to go away. But that's not what that means! That happens to be one scrap of Dark Chamber code I know. It means *The plan is going well, targets will be met or exceeded.* I hoped you were telling him we would catch Lynx. But you meant me. Had you slipped something in my food when I wasn't looking? Or were you just using feminine intuition to know you were going to land your fish?"

Silence.

Wolf sighed at his own folly. "Flicker took the news back to Grand Inquisitor and the Privy Council. Because no matter what Grand Inquisitor may say, the Dark Chamber would never dare launch a major international venture like this without approval from the Council. You confessed that tonight. You manipulated me into taking on the mission by telling me I was deceiving the King. I expect Grand Inquisitor persuaded the King to agree by letting him deceive me. Athelgar would have enjoyed that—not to mention enjoying sending me to somewhere far away and dangerous. They spun me a cock-and-bull story about Vicious threatening to resign."

Flicker must have been in on the joke too. That rankled.

Dolores's answer was half-muffled in the pillow. "I don't know what Grand Inquisitor does."

"No? Well I'm not interested in risking my life to give Athelgar or the Dark Chamber any more conjury than they already know. We're going home."

She rolled over. "No, we're not! I came here to make my name and fortune and I'm not ready to quit."

"Fortune? Fool child! You expect Athelgar to make you rich? The man's tighter than the axle nut on a millstone. If you go home with any Tlixilian conjury, you'll be locked up in the Bastion as a military secret weapon before you know what happens to you. Trust Athelgar? You're crazy!"

"And you're a quitter!" She rolled away from him again.

He lay and sweated in the airless heat. Mosquitoes shrilled in his ears, moths bounced off the windows. Little tropical things moved silently over the floor and walls. He went over the problem a million more times and found no new answer. He had nothing but lies to offer for secrets beyond price. If the inquisitors stayed in Sigisa, Rojas would skin them. Conclusion: Go away.

Eventually he realized that he was scratching. He slid out of bed and went in search of a candle. As he had feared, he was covered in mosquito bites. Shining-cloud had de-conjured more than the tricks in Wolf's pockets; he had also stripped off his personal enchantments, and that was very bad news indeed. Every advantage the Dark Chamber had given him had been wiped away. The knights' powers were terrifying.

He had next watch. Giving up hopes of sleep, he dressed and went to relieve Peterkin on guard. Then he could pace the house in silence, still seeking some safe way to keep Dolores's mad ambitions alive. A couple of times he almost stepped on a tangle mat, which would have wakened the household and exposed him to ridicule.

As the crescent moon rose from the sea to herald dawn, Flicker emerged from his room, fully dressed. He had drawn last watch and prided himself on never needing a wake-up call, but he looked more guilty than sleepy.

He regarded Wolf sourly. "Still planning on running away?"

"If you have a better idea, I'll listen."

"You never have before."

"Your personation is slipping."

"Not surprising. Go to bed." Flicker headed for the kitchen.

"I'm going for a walk."

Flicker spun around to stare at him, suspicion visible even in near-darkness. "Why?"

"Thought I'd hit a few brothels and grog shops. I may be gone some time."

"Brave of you."

"Takes one to know one." Wolf moved the tangle mat away from the front door. "Good chance. You'll need it."

Angry at having been transparent, Flicker growled, "Thanks."

"Don't forget to spread out this mat again." Wolf stepped outside and closed the door.

He climbed over the stockade because he could no longer bolt the gate from the outside. Dawn was his favorite time of day in Sigisa. The town was as quiet by then as it ever was, the insect population less trouble-some, the temperature bearable. He headed south along the beach, en-joying the sea's company and worrying at his problem. By the time he reached the southern end of the spit, where the river emerged from the jungle, the sky was blue and he had still found no way to reconcile love and common sense. (Was that a contradiction in terms?)

He began making his way back through the town, pausing once in a while to chat with drunks still able to speak. He often met interesting characters on his early-morning outings. He met dead ones, too, on oc-casion, but not that day.

His real objective was *Sea Queen*. He had spoken briefly with the master, Walter Wagge, agreeing on a price for taking mail home to Chivial. Shipping out seven or eight people was a different matter, and Wolf wanted to know more about Wagge, his ship, and his planned itin-erary. That problem solved itself, because *Sea Queen* had moved. It took Wolf awhile to find her at anchorage and when he did she was loading slaves. She would not be going home to Chivial with that cargo, and she would not be carrying him or anyone associated with him.

So the urgency had vanished. He might need days or even weeks to find a suitable vessel, and by then he could talk Dolores around. That as-sumed that Rojas would behave himself in the meantime.

He had to haul on the bell rope to gain admittance and the gate was opened by Dolores herself—Dolores in great distress. She threw herself into his arms so he staggered backwards. He had never known her drop a tear before, and now she was weeping helplessly. Muttering sympathy, he eased her inside the gate and closed it.

"So Flicker's gone?" he said. "I guessed he was planning it." In Flicker's eyes, he had wasted a month of precious time and most of the money. Flicker had always wanted to head straight inland.

Dolores continued to sob into his shoulder, mumbling incompre-hensibly.

"You can't be surprised!" he said. "I think he's crazy, but he's young and ambitious and . . . and *what* did you say?"

It took two more tries before she gasped out, "He tried to rape me!"

Wolf screamed, *"No!"* and pushed her back so he could see her. "You mean that?" There was a swelling red bruise on her cheek.

The very vehemence of his reaction seemed to sober her. She nodded. "Came into . . . bedroom . . . say goodbye. I tried to talk him out of it." She pulled back into Wolf's embrace again, burying her face against his neck. "He went mad. Said you were . . . called you terrible things. Wanted me to go with him. Oh, Wolf! Pulled sheet . . . away . . . had to fight him off! Really *fight!*"

Had a tearful farewell gotten out of hand? How far had she gone in trying to persuade Flicker not to leave? Wolf cursed himself for a jealous, suspicious fool. He must not try to imagine that scene. Any of it. The details did not matter. Nothing excused rape or attempted rape.

"Did he hurt you?"

Sniffle. "A few bruises. Oh, Wolf! Be all right . . . just shock."

Seeing that she was barefoot, Wolf picked her up in his arms. "Come along." He headed for the house. When a man had killed so many brother Blades, what would one more inquisitor matter? He wasn't even an inquisitor, he was a rat. "He can't have got far yet. Where's Heronjade?" It would be an execution.

"Went with him."

Wolf let rip with a few obscenities. The big man would be a far greater loss to the team than Flicker would. What had made him change his mind? Wolf's treachery in dealing with the Yazotlans, or just homesickness? Without the eagle's far-seeing skills, Wolf had no hope of tracking Flicker down and administering justice.

"Well I hope our eagle gets home safely." He hoped much more that the Tlixilians caught Flicker and roasted him alive. "I hope we do, too. *Sea Queen*'s a slaver."

"You won't wait for Flicker to come back?"

He laughed. "The next time I see Flicker, my love, I kill him."

"Wolf! No!"

"Yes. Did you invite him into bed?"

"No, no, no! I swear!"

"And he did try to rape you?"

She nodded.

"Then it doesn't matter if he comes back here before we leave or I run into him in Grandon ten years from now," Wolf said. "I will kill him."

6

*L*ife was always going to happen and never did. Young Alf Attewell had expected his life to begin the moment he escaped from Sheese into the real world. At Ironhall, Candidate Lynx had looked forward to life beginning as soon as he was bound. But the Guard had been cheated of his services and, as chief Blade to the King's doxy, Sir Lynx had enjoyed much less freedom than guardsmen did, and much less security, because in any kingdom the office of royal mistress usually had short tenure. It had seemed then that life would begin as soon as Celeste was dismissed; he had never foreseen anything as terrible as Quondam. At Quondam life had receded into the remote future, beyond the Baron's death. Now he was Bobcat-by-the-spring and life looked likely to end before it ever got started.

Under the million stars of El Dorado, the Grand Admiral's barge swept along the canal. Yes, it was only a dugout, but no horse-drawn carriage could compare with it for comfort. It moved as smoothly as a raindrop running down a windowpane, with no sound except the forced breath of the four naked paddlers as they stroked the silver water, speeding their lord through the night. Could this be life? He had expected it to feel more real.

Ruling the world had never appealed to Lynx. He would have always settled for a happy wife, well-fed children, and a few convivial friends—plus some useful and interesting way of getting from dawn to dusk, some task he could perform well enough to earn a little respect. Life could offer little more than that. Respect he had achieved, at least for now. He was a revered citizen of the floating city, with servants and handmaidens (pawmaidens?) and rich landholdings. But the happiest time of his life had been the month he had spent as Prime, at Ironhall. Then his job had been to keep a hundred boys happy and motivated, which for him had been no problem at all, and his reward had been praise from Grand Master. Overseeing three thousand men shaping planks with stone adzes just did not compare.

In El Dorado he had proved his loyalty and developed many useful skills. As well as being commander of the new imperial shipyard, he was Jaguar advisor on anti-cavalry tactics. He had taught the Tlixilians that horses had a terror of fire, and how to fight them with caltrops of obsidian flakes set in earthenware balls. He had assisted at the interrogation of prisoners, even managing to save a few from the altar stone, although he was not sure for how long. The Tlixilians feared and hated the Distliards' war dogs so much that he had suggested the Eagles drop poisoned meat in the pens; this had killed off two whole packs before the Distliards woke up to what was happening.

For that exploit Bobcat-by-the-spring had been formally honored in the Hall of Eagles. (Whatever would Grand Master have thought of that ceremony's barbaric splendor?) Such recognition of a non-Eagle was almost unprecedented, so the intent had been more to insult the Jaguars than to honor Lynx, but the Jaguars had countered by hailing Lord Bobcat-by-the-spring as a full jaguar knight and presenting him to the Emperor, the Fountain-of-swords, who had promptly granted him great estates. His former delusion that he was the revenant Plumed-pillar had been quietly forgotten, at least for now.

It was all make-believe. His vast landholdings lay in country currently held by the Hairy Ones, so he would not be able to visit them until after the war. Besides, however useful he might be as a wartime advisor, socially he was still an embarrassment that the Jaguars would likely dispose of as soon as the war was won. If it was lost, he would die in the carnage.

So if this was life, it was going to be short.

The Admiral's barge back-paddled to a stop alongside a quay where several other canoes were unloading important people. Lynx sprang nimbly ashore, without tipping his rowers into the water. Human attendants dropped to touch the ground in salute. He was respectfully ushered through a gate, into the grounds of the palace of Salt-ax-otter, a very senior knight, the Jaguar representative on the Grand Council.

The Admiral had been summoned to attend a meeting of a select group known as the Progressives. Old scoundrel Basket-fox called them the Peyote Eaters, although he had been one of their founders. They had first come together a year or so ago, not long before Lynx arrived in the floating city—some Jaguars, a few highborn officials, and two or three Eagles, about a score in all. Their doctrine had been that the Hairy Ones were a new peril and must be fought in new ways. Their opponents, the Traditionalists, had considered anything new to be dishonorable. Now the Traditionalists were discredited, thanks largely to Lynx's efforts. The Progressives had won the argument and the Emperor's approval, so he wondered why they needed to meet at all.

Not that the war was going any better, of course. Two bad defeats had cut off the supply of captives. The dwindling flow of virtue from the altar stones was hoarded so jealously now that eagle knights were traveling by canoe or palanquin.

As always, the members had assembled out-of-doors, standing under trees in an irregularly shaped area, so that there could be no arguments about rank or precedence. Many conversations were under way, but no one offered to chat with the foreigner. Untroubled, Lynx spread his lower paws, rested his knuckles—well, they *felt* like knuckles—on his hips, and waited for the meeting to begin. He thought everyone must be present . . . no, the host was still missing.

After a few minutes heads turned in Lynx's direction and Salt-ax-otter emerged from the outer darkness to stand near him. With him came a man who was certainly not a member of the group. He seemed short alongside a Jaguar, but was actually tall. Also young, highly respected, and a member of the Great Council. All conversation ceased instantly. Any other group would have dropped to its knees—and even these would if the guest were formally named, for he was the Emperor's brother, designated heir, and deputy, Two-swans-dancing, the Conch-flute of El Dorado.

Salt-ax-otter did not name him. He merely said, "Friends, you are welcome all. Honored Star-feather, we are curious to know how the Hairy Ones' boats are progressing." That opening was sufficiently unusual to convey that *we* meant *the Great Council* in this instance.

"They have four in the water," the Eagle said. "But only one has ventured out from shore yet. I estimate they will have ten complete within twenty days, and they have another eleven started."

Two-swans-dancing peered past his host. "And what can the skilled Bobcat-by-the-spring report on his progress?"

"We have four boats operational," Lynx said. He calculated quickly. "In ten days we should have another six or seven. We cannot go as fast as the enemy."

"Why not?"

"They have better tools." What else to say? Basket-fox's raid on Seven Reeds had destroyed the cache of equipment there, instead of capturing it as Lynx had urged, and the Distliards seemed to have re placed it all. They had steel saws and chisels, spikes and nails; they had hemp ropes and lathes to make pulley wheels. They had pitch for caulking, wedges to split logs. "And besides, er . . ." This group shunned all honorifics, but it felt wrong not to offer them to a prince. "And besides, we are about to run out of timber."

Trees had to come from the hills, borne on the shoulders of men until they reached the lake. Enemy forces were rapidly encircling the floating city—not so much by marching troops across the landscape as by perverting towns from their loyalty. Soon the whole valley would be hostile territory.

"We should attack Seven Reeds again?"

That was a major decision involving far too many factors for an upstart Chivian Blade to evaluate. The city rulers knew the boats' capability as well as he did, and they should decide whether to gamble their fleet now or save it to defend the causeway drawbridges in the assault to come. "Such choices belong to the Great Council," Lynx said stubbornly.

After a moment's ominous pause, Two-swans-dancing said, "True." He passed the meeting back to Salt-ax-otter with a nod.

"Friends," said the host, "today I had joyous news. My son and first warrior, whom we mourned for lost, has returned to us. He brings news you should hear. Have I your leave, friends?"

Who would argue when he had the Emperor's brother at his side? Out of the darkness strolled a solid young man wearing the grandiose trappings of a very senior jaguar warrior, a youngster Lynx vaguely remembered having seen somewhere—mostly because he had shoulders that would have impressed an ox. Quiet welcomes and congratulations murmured through the trees.

"Tell my friends your tale, Taker of Nine Captives."

"My lords do me honor . . ." Blood-mirror-walks related how he had been captured on the field of battle. He considered that he had been doubly unfortunate in having been taken by Distliards, who had sold him into slavery, instead of by the local Tephuamotziners, who would have had the decency to rip his heart out. Instead he had been transported across the stinking water in a floating house and offered for sale like cloth or pottery, but a strange Hairy One had ransomed him, blessed him to cure his injuries, and brought him back to the true country. So he had returned from the halls of the dead, trotting in along a causeway to report to his lord and father. The message he had brought explained the presence of Two-swans-dancing—this dissident foreigner on the coast was willing to aid El Dorado in its righteous struggle against the invaders, and would sell it all the war materiel it needed.

"His city is not that of the Hairy Ones we know," Blood-mirror-walks explained. "He is a knight among his people. His regalia is a sword bearing a jewel like a jaguar's eye, like unto one I saw once in the Hall of Jaguars."

All eyes had turned to Lynx.

A *Blade*! Here? Death and fire! But a Chivian should not want to aid El Dorado. Would he not rather seek to bring the Quondam killers to justice?

"And his name?" inquired the Conch-flute.

"It is Wild-dog-by-the-spring, mover of mountains."

Wolfie! Lynx bellowed out a laugh that must be a grievous breach of protocol. "A very ugly man, who looks as if his face had been stamped to mush in childhood and then chopped up by many obsidian blades?"

"It is he."

"This is my brother, lord, my own parents' son! And if he says he has brought the things we need to fight this war, then it is so."

"You vouch for him?" asked Two-swans-dancing, beaming.

"With my life!" Lynx cried.

VIII

The mort is sounded by one long call and several short

1

All his life, Wolf had detested failure. Dolores made fun of his compulsive boot polishing, but that was a small part of a much greater struggle, his determination to succeed at anything he tried. Some Blades did only what their bindings demanded, nothing more. Not he. He had served a master he despised to the limits of his ability, even killing men when that had been the right thing to do in the circumstances. Nothing he had done in all his years in the Guard troubled his conscience.

But the Sigisa mission had turned out to be far beyond his abilities. The fact that no one could have achieved what he had set out to do was no comfort, because he should not have taken on an impossible task. The knowledge that the inquisitors had tricked him into it only made him feel worse. He had not even managed to end it cleanly and run away. Sigisa had piled disaster on disaster.

Within hours after Shining-cloud nullified their spiritual protection, both Wolf and Dolores succumbed to dysentery. She recovered in a few days. He took much longer and was barely back on his feet, still as shaky as an autumn leaf, when he contracted tertian fever, another Sigisian specialty. He had never known a serious illness before, and was appalled at what it did to him. He burned. He thrashed and raved in delirium, ranting mostly about his brother. Every second day the fever would return, each bout leaving him weaker than before, but nothing in the medicine chest helped. He needed an octogram and eight competent conjurers, and those did not exist in all Tlixilia. He almost died.

The start of Secondmoon found him reclining on a portable bed on the patio, sipping fruit juice and watching unfamiliar stars play peekaboo between the romping palm fronds. Phosphoric breakers spilled up the beach. His fever had stayed away for several days, so he might be going to live after all.

Dolores settled at his side. He moved the beaker to his other hand and wound an arm around her.

"Peterkin's found a ship," she said.

That was good news, although Wolf doubted he could walk as far as the harbor. "Not a slaver?"

"No. Isilondian trader, outbound for Mondon the day after tomorrow."

The new *Caudillo* had been enforcing the laws against foreigners more strictly, and almost no non-Distlish vessels had dropped anchor in Sigisa in the last month. A Distlish captain would be within his rights in accepting the Chivians' money and then impressing the men into his crew. What might happen to the two women then did not bear thinking about.

Wolf studied his wife's face by starlight. "You will be coming with us, won't you?"

She nodded wistfully. "Of course. I was wrong and you were right." She lay down to snuggle against him. "Darling, I was so frightened we were going to lose you!"

He offered lips to be kissed. "Then it must be time I declared myself recovered. Tomorrow I shall strap on my sword and resume my old domineering ways. I think I can walk with it on if I lean sideways. Don't ask me to use it."

"Good. I feel in need of being domineered."

"Has Peterkin fixed a fare yet?"

"They're still bargaining."

Something about her tone alerted him. "How much have we got left?"

"Less than ten thousand pesos."

"What!?" That might not be enough to see all of them home to Chivial. "What has Rojas been up to, curse his smelly socks?"

"Well, first he tripled the rent on the villa. Now he wants to triple it again. When the sailors go out they get arrested on trumped-up charges and we have to ransom them from jail. You ought to see that jail! We must get out of here, love. Soon! Take over, please! We need you."

"I love you when you're humble like this!"

"Enjoy it while it lasts."

Their humor was a shroud to bury black thoughts. Even if the Isilondian captain was willing to take passengers, would Rojas let the Chivians escape with the clothes on their backs? Not until he had taken every last maravedí out of the pockets. They would arrive in Mondon penniless. Wolf wasn't ready to take up the battle again. He needed time to recover his strength.

"No word from Blood-mirror-walks and the boys?"

Dolores shook her head. "I don't think we're ever going to hear from them."

"Or from Flicker?" Wolf would certainly have heard if there had been word from Flicker. He had been gone a month. He might be dead or almost at El Dorado by now.

"No. And no sign of Lynx. We have been watching every ship, love."

Yes, it was time to go. "But we'll need to find some way of sneaking on board without Rojas knowing," he said glumly. "Let me sleep on it." Expecting his milk cows to make a break for it, Rojas would keep close watch on the foreign ship. He might even preempt their flight and send in his bully boys this very night.

She cuddled closer and said softly, "Wolf?"

"Mm?"

" 'Put it in writing?' " She was smiling, but he heard shadows behind the words. "I did lie to you that day, love, but not very much. And we weren't even betrothed then!"

"It doesn't matter now." What was done was done.

"It matters to me. So listen. It was the jaguar plaque I was after. You'd told me at Ivywalls that it was an active conjuration, remember? When Lynx refused to part with it, I guessed it was important. In the morning you and I delivered Lynx to the Pine Tree and went on to the palace. The plaque was the first thing I mentioned. Flicker and a couple of others were sent to the inn to keep an eye on Lynx. He'd skipped by the time they got there. Flicker dropped by when you and I were eating to tell me that they'd lost him."

Wolf said, "He said, 'Mother's looking for you.' "

She chuckled. "Well done! I'll make a snoop out of you yet. The code words are only hints, though. They can't be more than that or they couldn't be hidden in ordinary conversation. 'Mother' means bad news and 'Father' is good. If the team had been tailing Lynx he would have said something like 'Father's still on the road.' I told him we didn't know where Lynx was either."

"And 'Put it in writing?' "

"Meant I was working on it and didn't need any more help. I hoped we'd find Lynx with the tracker. If we couldn't, then there was nothing more to be done." She kissed him again. "And I honestly don't know if the King knew that Grand Inquisitor were trying to recruit you. I'm just very happy that they did and you married me."

"No regrets here," he said. He wished he believed more of what she had said.

Dolores punched him awake. "Wolf! Wolf! Burglars!"

He sat up, bewildered. One of the tangle mats was shrieking. Then another sounded off, even shriller, and now he heard thumps and human screams as well. He fell out of bed and dropped to his knees, not entirely by choice. It was his custom to lay *Diligence* under the bed at night, unsheathed, but during his sickness she had been pushed so far in, beyond easy reach, that he had to scrabble on his belly to find her.

Appalled at how heavy she was now, he reeled across the room to the door. Dolores was wrapping herself in a gown, but he did not worry about such niceties. He tumbled out in the corridor, bounced off the opposite wall, and headed for the din. The house was dark.

A tangle mat reacted to being stepped on by uttering an unbearable screech and closing around the trespasser's feet so he could not walk. If he fell over, as he usually did, the mat slithered up his body and enveloped his head. The man in the entrance hall had reached that stage. He was a naked, dark-skinned *naturale,* heavily built. Surrounded by the ruins of a bench, his loincloth, and a once-sturdy table, he was thrashing wildly in his efforts to tear off the suffocating bandage. Knowing the rug would choke him unconscious and then relax enough to keep him alive, Wolf ignored him. He headed for sounds of battle coming from the dining room.

Before he reached the door, a man staggered out backwards, contesting possession of a sword with another invader. The first was recognizable as Hick by his clothes and lurid sailor language. His opponent was another *naturale,* albeit a somewhat skinny one, who should not be giving Hick so much trouble. When Wolf scooped up a table leg and cracked it over his skull, he dropped, taking Hick with him. The other intruder had now lost his contest with the tangle mat, making two of them out of action and available for later questioning. So far so good.

Peterkin lay groaning and half stunned on the dining room floor. Another intruder was doing a mad one-legged sword dance against the starlit windows, trying to kill a tangle mat before it broke his ankle, but without cutting off his own foot in the process. The mutilated mat howled as if it were alive and in agony. The window it had been guarding stood open.

Whatever Ironhall tradition might say, there were times when the table leg was mightier than the sword. Wolf slammed his cudgel against the back of the dancer's knee, sending him toppling to the floor, screaming as the tattered mat scrambled for his face like a giant spider.

Something hurtled in through the window without touching the sill. It hit the floor with its front paws, spun over in an airborne somersault to strike the far wall with its back paws, twisting in midair so it was the right way up, and without ever pausing, launched itself at Wolf's throat. He glimpsed fangs and claws, but he already knew that if this was not an actual jaguar, it must be a jaguar knight.

Off-balance for an attack from that direction, he had no time to turn and bring *Diligence* into play, but his left hand still held the table leg and he instinctively parried at the open jaws. Turning its head aside to save its teeth, the monster slammed into him. They hit the floor in a tangled heap. Had he been his usual nimble self, Wolf might have made a better showing, but in his fever-weakened state the double impact almost stunned him. His throat was exposed; he expected to feel it ripped open.

The cat thing rolled clear and went to the aid of the man being smothered by the vengeful tangle mat. Back in Grandon the inquisitors had insisted a mat could not be forcibly removed without pulling the victim's head off, but they had never met a jaguar knight armed with eight finger knives. The remains of the mat fell silent. The gasping victim stopped thrashing.

All this had taken only a few seconds, and Wolf had barely managed to stagger to his knees. He was ages too slow to fight such a monster. Eyes glowing in the starlight, the Jaguar sprang, batting his weapons aside. They hit the floor together again, and this time he cracked his head so hard that flames danced before his eyes. Paws pinned his wrists, great fangs opened over his face. He heard a snarling cat sound. After a moment he realized it was human speech distorted into a yowl.

Not only that, the Jaguar spoke Chivian. What it said was "And whose turn is it to rub whose nose in the dirt now, brother?"

2

Before Wolf could collect his wits, light flooded the room. Help had arrived at last—Dolores, Megan, Hick, and Will, all armed with swords

and carrying lanterns. Dolores was out in front and reasonably so, because she was the best fencer. She came within half a second of running
her sword into a jaguar knight.

That was at least four-tenths of second too late, though. Lynx
launched himself upward again, almost crushing Wolf's wrists in the
process. He slapped Dolores's sword aside with his claws, spun her
around, and pinned her against him. Then he waved four black talons in
front of her face and the rescuer party froze.

"Stop!" Wolf croaked. "It's all right. He's on our side."

My brother the monster! Spirits save us!

"Oh, I wouldn't hurt my dear sister-in-law," Lynx yowled, releasing
her. "You are legally married, I trust? Give me a kiss, dearie?" He bared
his fangs and waggled a grotesquely long tongue at her.

Dolores screamed and reeled backwards.

Yes, it was Lynx. Wolf knew the scars, although they had faded from
red on pink to white on brown. He stood tall on his stilt feet; his head,
hands, and feet had been transformed, and he wore a Tlixilian-style loincloth, but his chest was hairier than any *naturale*'s. He carried something
strapped on his back. Seeing Wolf struggle to rise, he offered a paw. Wolf
gripped his wrist where spotted fur gave way to human skin and was effortlessly flipped upright.

"What's the matter with you? You fight like a grandmother."

"Fever. More important, what happened to you?"

Lynx chuckled—a sound not far off a purr. "Obvious, isn't it?
Where's my guide? Where's Blood-mirror-walks?"

Wolf recalled the husky invader out in the hall. He should have recognized those shoulders. "He'll be all right, as long as he doesn't struggle." He wrapped an arm around Dolores, who had been working her
way closer to him without going too near Lynx. "Megan, release him,
will you? And see to the other one?" Megan swept from the room.

"The other one's Night-fisher." Lynx seemed to be enjoying himself, but he was mistaken if he thought that exposing those frightful
teeth counted as a grin. He turned to the intruder he had rescued from
the mat. "And this is taker of one captive Corn-fang. Dread warrior,
greet my father's son, Lord Wild-dog-by-the-spring." Lynx spoke Tlix-

ilian haltingly, and with what must be a Chivian accent. He had learned the language the hard way.

"I kiss the feet of my lord's brother," Corn-fang said, making no move to do so and looking as if he would prefer to cut them off. "His glory dims the sun." The tangle mat had totally ruined his elaborate feather headdress and there was blood around his jade labret.

"I weep with shame that a valorous taker of captives should have been so maltreated in my house," Wolf said. "May we evermore fight in each other's shadow." He presented his wife and the sailors, whom he promoted to warrior rank.

"I want to know how Lynx got here!" Dolores whispered. She was trembling, almost in shock.

"Yes. Explain, Lynx."

"We can sing old songs later!" the cat-man said in Tlixilian.

Wolf was about to go and find some clothes, when in strode Blood-mirror-walks, clearly furious and wearing no more than he was. If a relative of the Emperor did not care, why should anyone? Behind him came the adolescent Night-fisher, limping and rubbing his neck. Then Peterkin and Don, and the room was crowded.

"Where is Heron-jade?" Blood-mirror-walks demanded. "Why did he not warn you of our approach?"

"The noble warrior went inland with Flicker about a moon ago."

The Tlixilians exchanged glances that Wolf found worrisome.

"Good chance to them," Lynx said. "We must hurry, Brother, but you should offer your guests hospitality."

The servants might be hiding under their beds or they might have fled to raise the population. Wolf asked Megan to inspect the outbuildings, and she went off accompanied by Blood-mirror-walks.

"You are welcome to all we have. What do you eat now? Raw meat?"

"Meat when I can get it." Again Lynx had answered in Tlixilian. His obvious reluctance to speak Chivian suggested that either he had learned a new respect for good manners or that his companions did not trust him.

"Should I butcher a gardener?"

He purred that peculiar laugh again. "No, I haven't gotten to that yet. It's good to see you again, Wolf!"

"And you, Lynx. But you are changed."

"No regrets!"

Could this night get any worse? "Then I'm glad for you. How is dear Celeste?"

"Very well. Much happier. I came to fetch you, Wolf. Your presence is commanded in El Dorado."

Yes, it could! Much worse.

"And me!" Dolores shouted. "And me!"

Wolf was appalled. He had been sure the mission was dead and could be written out of his life. Now it was alive again, he knew that he did not want it alive, did not want it to succeed. He wanted his brother to be a man, not a monster. He wanted to take his wife home, not squire her halfway across a continent of cannibals. He certainly did not want to acquire any vile conjurations for Athelgar and Grand Inquisitor.

He flopped down on a chair, feeling a hundred years old. "Listen, Lynx. I was relying on the Eagles to transport the arms we want to trade. I'm told that they can't do that—that they only found Quondam last year by homing in on that pendant. If that's so, then we'll need years to ship weapons here."

His brother scratched an ear with a claw like a fleshing knife. "Don't see a problem. Both Amaranth-talon and Bone-peak-runner have been to Quondam. Either of them can find it again for you."

Dolores squeaked with glee. The original plan was viable again! Life and incredible wealth were back on the table.

Wolf switched back to Chivian. "I have no weapons to trade. I was lying."

"Then you may have serious problems when you get to El Dorado. But you are coming to El Dorado if I have to carry you."

"So am I," Dolores said sharply.

Lynx curled his lip in the snarl that he considered a smile. "Then you carry him. Where's the kitchen?"

Wolf heaved himself to his feet and ripped a tapestry off the wall to make himself at least semi-respectable. He led the way to the kitchen shed, where the sailors were already preparing food for the visitors.

Megan emerged from the dark with a different escort. There were more intruders out there in the grounds, she said, but the servants were still abed and must have slept through the commotion. Fights were every-night occurrences in Sigisa.

Lynx ignored promises of beans and tortillas, demanded meat now, raw if necessary. He shrank to his old height when he sat on a stool with his cat feet under the table, and when he also tucked his forepaws out of sight he could almost have been a human being with his head inside a huge pard mask. The illusion disappeared as soon as he began to eat. Young Night-fisher held the meat for him and he tore off chunks with his side teeth, swallowing without chewing.

The object strapped on his back was *Ratter,* securely tied in her scabbard so she would not fly out when he performed the sort of gymnastics he had demonstrated earlier. He must be carrying her only as a talisman, for he had no need of a sword and could not have wielded one with both hands. Forepaws. *Oh, Lynx!* Did he not even *care* what they had done to him? Wolf wanted to scream.

The Jaguar consumed most of a standing rib roast, raw. Night-fisher was his squire, or possibly nursemaid, for he wiped Lynx's muzzle and chest to clean him up after the meal. Then the boy was free to finish his master's leftovers, which he did eagerly. It was common knowledge that the native diet offered little meat—venison, turkey, rabbit, and dog—and almost all of that went to the nobility. Human flesh was a privilege of the very highest, meaning the most honored warriors. Other intruders had been ransacking the larder and almost came to blows over some pork ribs they found there.

Leaving the feast in progress, Wolf went in search of Dolores and found her being helped into her traveling clothes by Megan. Obviously she was bound on going to El Dorado no matter what he said or did. A trek of eighty leagues or so over mountain ranges seemed utterly impossible in his condition. He doubted he could walk as far as the river bank. If the Emperor wanted him so badly, why didn't he send an Eagle?

He found a shirt and sank down shakily on the edge of the bed.

"You, my beloved, must stay here and see the others safely home to Chivial."

Before Dolores could protest, Megan bristled. She changed her posture, her voice, and her age, transforming into a lady. "Since the death of my husband the count," she announced haughtily, "I have decided to return to Chivial with my entourage. Do you imply that I am incapable, Sir Wolf?"

Dolores laughed. Wolf apologized and pulled on the shirt. In the next few minutes each one of the sailors appeared in turn, offering to go to El Dorado with him, but they spoke little Tlixilian and he refused to lead them into a stewpot.

"Flicker left us three stamina bracelets," Dolores announced. "You want one now?"

"I'll save them for later." What else did he need? "Medicine chest?"

"It's too big," she said. "And we can't know what we might need from it. Leave it all."

Probably only an hour intervened between the first tangle mat scream and the click of the gate being bolted behind them as they left the villa. Wolf took nothing with him except *Diligence*. He was too weak to lift a bedroll off the floor and knew better than to ask a warrior to be a porter. By then it had become obvious that the real leader of the expedition was Blood-mirror-walks, for it was he who assigned them positions—Lynx, Dolores, and Wolf in the center, six Tlixilians around them. However much Lynx looked the part, he lacked a knight's authority.

The eastern sky was just starting to brighten, but Sigisa never slept. As the expedition emerged from the hacienda, a sailor reeled past with his arm around a woman. Neither seemed to notice anything amiss. Nor did any of the other people they passed on their way to the river. A were-jaguar might be disregarded as illusion—mushroom eaters saw much stranger things than that—but feather-decked killers carrying obsidian-toothed spears and swords around in the middle of the night should be attracting suspicion.

"You are conjuring us?" Wolf asked.

"We have been blessed," his brother said softly.

There were always many dugout canoes moored along the river-bank. Their owners slept or even lived in them, for no one in Sigisa left anything of value unattended. The intruders had brought one of their own and left three men to guard it. Exhausted already, Wolf collapsed into the stern. Lynx shoved in behind him as if that were his place; Dolores went in front of him. The warriors pushed off and scrambled aboard without tipping the Chivians out, which was undoubtedly trick-ier than they made it look. Soon the craft was racing upstream, driven by powerful paddle strokes.

The sky over the treetops began turning blue, birds and monkeys were wakening in the forest. The Tlixilians began chuckling and crack-ing quiet jokes, as if they thought they had made a clean getaway. Blood-mirror-walks chirped once and silence fell. Sound traveled well over water, of course, and his caution was justified almost before they rounded the first bend. Another chirped order sent the canoe veering sharply to the right. It drifted in under trailing vegetation; strong hands took hold of roots or creepers and brought it to rest against the bank. Wolf tried not to think of snakes and poisonous spiders. Then he de-tected sounds the warriors had noticed much sooner.

A large canoe came into view, heading downstream. Paddles were much quieter than oars and no one aboard was speaking, but a man at the stern beat stroke with a maddening monotonous tap. There was also a muted clinking sound. The canoe swept past, clearly visible in mid-stream, carrying a cargo of prisoners, at least some of whom were being compelled to paddle their way to exile and slavery; the clinking came from their chains. Wolf expected Blood-mirror-walks to order an attack, for the slavers were few and could have been speared before they even knew they were being watched, but no one moved or made a sound, and the evil sight glided on its way unmolested. A few minutes later two more canoes followed it.

Some time after that, the warriors resumed their journey, but the luxury of effortless travel did not last long. Alerted by no landmark Wolf could see, they swung the canoe into the bank, passing under a leafy drapery into a tiny creek; also into renewed darkness, a fog of insects, and air ripe with vegetable odors. A paw tapped his shoulder and whiskers tickled his ear—

Lynx whispered, "Salt-ax-otter is royalty. Do not look at him."

Interesting, no doubt, if one knew what it meant. Wolf passed the word on to Dolores, who gave him an odd look, checking for delirium.

They passed within arm's length of logs that plunged into the water and swam away. A creeper extending downward changed its mind and slithered back up onto its branch again. The creek soon dwindled, grounding the canoe at the edge of a tiny clearing, not far from a tumbledown thatch cottage, well hidden from river traffic. There were no people in sight. Had the original owners of the boat been paid for its rental or just slaughtered out of hand? There had been law in that country before the Distlish came and might be some in the future, but there was none at the moment.

The travelers scrambled out and set off in single file along a barely detectable track, slick and ankle-deep in rotting leaves—huge leaves, like heaps of old clothes. The ground on either hand was mossy and fungoid, half hidden under fallen trunks and roots that coiled and looped as constant reminders of snakes. Life rioted amid the odors of decay, with every tree a colony of lesser plants, suckers and parasites, all draped with vines and constantly dripping in the steamy air. Far overhead the forest soared in shadowed vaults, inhabited by flocks of raucous, improbably colorful birds.

Wolf managed to keep up only because he was wearing a stamina bracelet, but it would not support him for long at that pace. He staggered and sweated rivulets. They came at last to a place that was a little more open, although not truly a clearing, and Blood-mirror-walks stopped without warning. He dropped. So did everyone else, and Lynx's great paw pressed hard on Wolf's shoulder. He crouched in the weeds like the others.

Blood-mirror-walks touched a hand to the ground and his lips. "I kiss the feet of my lord."

Only then was Wolf allowed to see the jaguar knight posed in their path. He had not been invisible, exactly, just hidden by a few trailing fronds and dappled shadows that should not have concealed anything at all. Back in Chivial the Dark Chamber's spiritual toolbox included an invisibility cloak, but it was unreliable and required long training in a type of mental gymnastics most people found extremely difficult. What Salt-ax-otter had just done did not seem any harder than blinking. There was another warrior behind him, holding spear and shield. And another off to the left . . . there must be at least a dozen of them.

The knight was magnificent, towering seven feet or more from his furry toes to the tips of his spotted ears. He wore an embroidered loin-cloth and a sumptuous full-length feathered cloak, which hung equally from both shoulders, exposing a jaguar pendant of jade and silver on his chest. Plumed-pillar would have looked like this before his battle with Fell and Lynx.

"Speak," he said.

"As my lord commanded, so it is."

"You are valorous and worthy, having been dutiful when there was no honor to be gained." The knight's voice was distorted like Lynx's, yet it carried resonance and power.

"Glorious are the words of my lord." Blood-mirror-walks rose. One by one his men performed the touch-ground-and-kiss-hand gesture, then stood up, keeping eyes respectfully lowered. And so, when it was their turn, did Dolores and Wolf. The only exception was Lynx, who had remained standing all along.

"This is my father's son, terror of the night," he said, "and his wife, the acolyte."

The man-cat did not answer. It must be Wolf's turn.

"We are honored to meet the dread Salt-ax-otter, and bring greetings from our king."

The Jaguar looked to Blood-mirror-walks. "We could hear them coming all the way from the river. Carry them both."

"As my lord commands."

Wolf flopped down on the soggy ground to rest. Dolores joined him and Lynx squatted on his heels, which left him as high as he would be on a chair.

"What *is* the problem?" Wolf asked.

Lynx growled. "Enemies everywhere."

"Those prisoners we saw—there has been a battle?"

"Many battles. Fighting's going on everywhere from the coast to El Dorado."

So much for Flicker and Heron-jade. This was no time for non-combatants to be wandering around Tlixilia.

"You can't just whistle up an Eagle?"

Lynx said, "Don't want to attract attention. The enemy has Eagles too."

"That's a good second reason. What's the first reason?"

Silence. Cat eyes stared at Wolf as if their owner was planning how to skin him. How much of the old Lynx was left inside the new Jaguar?

Unnerved, Wolf said, "Not enough prisoners, maybe?"

Lynx licked the back of a paw and wiped his whiskers. "Don't ask too many questions, my lord Ambassador. The Pirate's Son can't protect you here." He rose and stalked away.

Wolf looked at Dolores. She bit her lip and said nothing.

Four men were already weaving creepers and others had begun chopping down saplings with flint axes. In minutes they completed two hammocks, slung under poles for carrying. However humiliating the prospect of being treated as baggage, Wolf did not protest when he was ordered aboard. Lynx traveled under his own power on his grotesquely elongated legs, but this was not a noble moment in the history of the King's Blades.

3

For several days thereafter, Wolf saw nothing but walls of jungle enclosing the tracks the Eldoradoans followed. He knew they never strayed far from cultivation, because they could always provide an evening meal. Lynx insisted the food was obtained by honest barter, because otherwise the locals would report marauders to the authorities, and even if "honest barter" meant a gift to the headman and nothing for anyone else, that would ensure that mouths stayed shut. Their road zigzagged between Zolica and Yazotlan, in territory now loyal to the Distlish, in a steamy heat unbelievable by Chivian standards.

In the second week, the country changed from lowland jungle to foothills, with the great white peak of Sky-is-frowning looming ever closer. The weather grew more bearable and each day Wolf walked part of the way, managing better as his strength returned. At some point they began encountering patches of territory still loyal to the Empire and could spend nights in villages instead of huddled together in camps. Loyal and rebel villages formed an irregular patchwork, and even Lynx could not say how Salt-ax-otter knew in advance which was which. None of the settlements were large, usually just a dozen or so thatched adobe cottages, but the friendly natives were eager to serve. They provided shelter and bedding, plentiful beans, maize flour, and sometimes small amounts of dog meat.

Day by day Lynx told more of his story, but some questions he always parried. Obviously he was not the equal of Salt-ax-otter. Among the warriors, only Corn-fang and Night-fisher were his vassals and only Salt-ax-otter was wielding spiritual power. The Chivians rarely saw the knight, but the others spoke of him as if he were nearby, not present and invisible—jaguars were solitary hunters. That a lord of his stature should have come to fetch them in person was a huge honor, Lynx said.

In the villages the knight was never visible and even Lynx became strangely inconspicuous, so Wolf would jump when he spoke and realize he had been present all along. The locals either did not register his inhuman appearance or failed to notice him at all.

One night Dolores pointed out that a full moon was shining in through the doorway, so it must be exactly twelve months since the attack on Quondam. Lynx declared that this anniversary should be commemorated and demanded *pulque* from the villagers. The Chivians drank to the memory of the fallen and toasted Celeste's release from imprisonment. Wolf was not at all sure that he would have wanted to celebrate, were he in his brother's place, but Lynx had always looked at life on the bright side.

They had been assigned a hut of their own, surprisingly clean and spacious because the owners owned no furniture. Outside, in the moon-bright street, the locals were singing and dancing to honor their visitors. After Night-fisher had wiped Lynx's muzzle for him, Lynx dismissed him, telling him to go off and have some fun.

The youth said, "My lord is bountiful as the clouds," and vanished out the door, leaving the Chivians alone.

"You don't fancy striking up some friendships of your own?" Wolf asked. He felt much stronger now, and was anxious to demonstrate this for Dolores. It seemed a long time since he had been uxorious.

Lynx made a sound somewhere between a chortle and a cough. "I think one kiss would blow my cover." He lifted a gourd between two paws and slurped *pulque,* spilling as much as he drank. He had drunk enough to become jovial and talkative, which was rare for a bound Blade, but his ward was too far away at the moment for temporary fuzziness to matter. Or perhaps his shape-change had weakened his binding.

Dolores had noticed an opportunity to ask questions. "Tell me, how eager is El Dorado to buy our aid?"

He set down the gourd with care. "Very. The Distlish are gaining. If they can pen the Eldoradoans up in the floating city, they can starve them. Starve them of food, but also deny them captives. No prisoners, no hearts; no hearts, no power; no power, no defense except brute muscle. Oh, I think you can make a deal!"

"What are your plans?" Wolf asked.

The big cat eyes fixed their menacing stare on him. "Can you see me back in Chivial? A cozy cage in the Bastion zoo?"

There was no answer to that.

He uttered a chilling growl. "I stay with my ward. As long as Celeste lives, I'm bound to El Dorado. Why do you think I'm racing around the countryside instead of following her? Because this is the best thing I can do to defend her. And I do help! I'm Lord High Admiral. We must have boats to keep the invaders from bypassing the drawbridges on the causeways. But, burn it, Wolfie, I need tools! Lathes, pulleys, ropes. You get me some of that. And some shipwrights." He crouched to lap *pulque* directly from the bowl.

"You're not visible to the locals, are you?" Dolores said. "Warriors can see in the dark and move without making any sound, even see conjuration on things. How are these 'blessings' done? With ritual on the pyramids?"

Lynx sat up and wrapped his arms around his knees, his huge furry feet protruding in front of him. He favored her with his disconcerting silent stare for a while, as if he had to translate his thoughts into Chivian. "Depends. Some blessings are done that way."

"All the major rituals are performed on the pyramids?"

"You'll have to ask the acolytes. They're the real conjurers."

"Stow it!" Wolf had had enough. He knew what Dolores was after. She had already established from Lynx that the murders on the pyramids were committed by the acolytes under the eyes of the knights, but she suspected that the eating of human flesh was another part of the process. Granted that Lynx had been trapped into the change he called the Flowering without meaning to be, and had been driven to persist by self-preservation and loyalty to his ward, had he accepted more than the bare minimum needed to survive?

Wolf was not about to let his wife ask his brother if he was a cannibal. "I'm ready for bed!" he announced. "How about you, darling?"

Lynx took the hint instantly—his way of thinking might have changed, but he had not lost his wits. He purred his odd laugh. "Think I'll go and hunt some mice." He flowed out the door and was gone.

Wrapped in llama-wool ponchos, they made their way over a bleak pass where icy winds cut like a thousand machetes, under a shoulder of the great volcano, down into a wide and verdant valley that they traversed by moonlight over several nights. Beyond the next range lay the valley of El Dorado, but to cross that one they needed camping gear and villagers to carry it. By then Wolf's strength had returned enough that he could keep up with the plodding porters and no longer needed his litter. They spent two nights in a frozen desert, so high that it was impossible to sleep properly and everyone huddled together for warmth.

The next day the scenery changed dramatically. At dawn they plodded through snow and thick fog, trusting to Salt-ax-otter to find the trail. By noon they were shedding furs and descending grassy slopes, rocky and steep. A vast valley extended below them, speckled with white salt lakes and green farmland, and very far ahead—still days away, but visible as a brightness—lay the great lake of Tlixilia itself. Although weary from lack of sleep, everyone was jubilant. Even Blood-mirror-walks was cheerful. If they were not completely out of danger, he admitted, they were a lot safer now than they had been.

Soon heat was forcing them to strip down to bare necessities. They came to level meadowland dotted with clumps of strangely familiar trees—oaks, alders, and something Dolores said was cypress. One of the porters laughed and joked with Lynx, whom he must be seeing as fully human. Close behind those two, Wolf was walking with Blood-mirror-walks and having no more success at extracting information from him than he had back on *Glorious*. The warrior would neither admit that El Dorado had warships on the lake or deny that the Distliards did. He would talk about almost nothing except his forthcoming marriage and his bride's exalted ancestry.

Wolf's attention wandered, thinking of escorting his wife into the fabulous El Dorado a few days from now. Would they find a smug Flicker already there, negotiating the final details of a treaty? Or had Flicker and Heron-jade run into Distlish allies somewhere and ended up on an altar stone? The expedition was truly scattered now—Quin back in Chivial or at the bottom of the sea, Megan and the sailors perhaps hanging around Mondon trying to find passage back to Eurania.

As they were crossing a clearing he said, "My head hurts. That usually means—"

Blood-mirror-walks screamed a warning. An army sprang up out of nowhere. At least a hundred painted, feathered warriors came charging in on all sides, howling war cries and already hurling spears. They could not have been hidden by trees, for there were few trees close. Most of the porters dropped flat and played dead, but the one beside Lynx stopped a spear and there was nothing make-believe about his fall. Lynx himself seemed to blur, dodging two or three more spears and smacking a couple more right out of the air.

Drawing *Diligence* and his dagger, Wolf looked around wildly for

Dolores. Then the horde was on him and he had no time for anything but staying alive. Blood-mirror-walks yelled, "Guard my back, Wild-dog!"

"Guard mine!"

The warrior had only his shield and a spear, because the glass-edged swords were impossible to sheath and had to be carried to battle by squires. Salt-ax-otter's expedition was not equipped for full warfare and had been caught in sad disarray, as if some Eagle had been using the Serpent's Eye on them.

Wolf faced his first painted, shrieking, be-feathered monster, blocked a downward sword slash with his dagger and ran *Diligence* through the man's gaudy feathered shield into his chest. Before he even flattened grass Wolf parried a cut from another warrior with his dagger, surprising him, for that was not the *naturales'* way of fighting. Obsidian shattered. Wolf swung his sword and the shield went with it, so Wolf hit him with that. Then Wolf jerked *Diligence* free and, as he tried again, cut his opponent's knee almost through. Two more men came at him. There was no quarter in Tlixilian warfare; you died on the field or the altar stone.

He had been taught melee fighting at Ironhall, but had never expected to use it. He needed all his expertise just to stay alive, and did so only because he had Blood-mirror-walks at his back. With a glass sword taken from a corpse, the Eldoradoan made blood fly like rain. Footwork became tricky on ground littered with men—dead, dying, or pretending. Wolf just hoped that Dolores had had the sense to lie down, out of the way, but he knew in his heart that she would have drawn her sword and become fair game. He could hear wild animals snarling nearby and vaguely registered that Lynx was in an even wilder battle than he was, because the enemy would see him as a knight who must be neutralized before he could bring his powers to bear.

Two men rushed him with spears, holding them like lances to impale him at long range. He prepared to parry the first with *Diligence* and swing his dagger at the second, fearing it lacked the weight to deflect a pole properly. A renewed stab of pain in his head threw off his aim, but Blood-mirror-walks howled and crashed backward, knocking him flying, so both spears missed. One of them hit Blood-mirror-walks, but he was already as good as dead, pinning Wolf under him and fountaining blood over his legs. Helpless, Wolf looked up at a multicolored monster wearing a smile of triumph as he changed his grip to club his victim with the haft of his spear. Wolf had faced death often enough before and known terror, but now he felt only regret, a sense of waste that there was so much living to be done and he would not share it. He really did not want to be eaten.

Diligence slid from his fingers. The warriors dropped their spears. The world faded behind a sugary pink mist.

Somewhere a bird chirped in the mountain stillness.

After a little while Wolf struggled free, sat up, and peered around at the trampled, bloodstained turf. His temples throbbed. He could see more men on the ground than upright, but nobody was fighting anymore. They just stood there, most of them disarmed. This had to be spiritualism, he decided vaguely; men did not take time out in the middle of carnage.

A new force had appeared. Two or three score of men were striding over the battlefield in line abreast, methodically wielding the toothed clubs he had seen at Quondam, stunning the ambushers with brutal efficiency, knocking them flat without even breaking stride. The victims did not raise a hand to defend themselves. Survivors of Salt-ax-otter's party were just ignored, but as soon as the line had passed, they began to recover their wits. It took a few minutes for the sugar to dissolve and the sun to break through.

"Dolores!" Wolf cried, scrambling to his feet. He lurched two paces, then came back to retrieve his sword. "Lynx?"

Lynx was sprawled within a circle of ripped and bleeding corpses and turning the air scarlet with a profane medley of Chivian, Tlixilian, and infuriated jaguar noises. He was well spattered with blood, but if much of it were his own he would not be capable of such a tirade.

"You all right?" Wolf demanded.

"Twisted my pastern. Where's Night-fisher? Where's Corn-fang? Why did they take so long? What kept them? *You!*" he roared. "Why didn't you prevent this?"

Wolf swung around and found himself looking up at the bizarre and cryptic shape of an eagle knight, dark against the sky. Golden eyes glared down at him. The great beak opened, revealing a black tongue.

"If Salt-ax-otter and his whelp had kept proper military order," the monster croaked, "this would not have happened."

"You swore you'd keep watch over us, you oversized bag of feathers—"

"Eat dirt!" the Eagle shrieked. "But you did well, imposter. You were stunning them!"

"Of course I was stunning them!" Lynx raged. He flashed eight claws. "These are only good for skinning. I just thumped them." He paused and looked around. "How many did I get, anyway?"

The Eagle assessed the bodies. "Seven. Perhaps five will live to reach the altar stone. That is no mean feat, warrior."

"Right!" Lynx said, and calmed down. "Five *is* good, isn't it? In one skirmish? This is my father's son, Wild-dog-by-the-spring. Wolfie, meet terror of the skies Star-feather."

Not convinced that his wits were back to normal, Wolf bowed and said something polite.

The towering Eagle nodded, setting his feathered headdress to waving. "Your father bred notable warriors, Hairy One."

"Lord! Lord! You're safe!" Young Night-fisher came racing across the field with arms outstretched. He skidded to a halt on his knees beside Lynx, looking ecstatically pleased with himself. "I took a captive for you, lord!"

Wolf said, *"My wife! Where is my wife?"*

"Here." Star-feather stalked over the bloody sward, lifting and placing his feet like a giant rooster. Ashen pale, Dolores lay curled up very small within a terrifying puddle of blood. Her sword lay beside her, and there was blood on that, too.

"Flesh wound in the belly," the Eagle said. "Is the woman important?"

Wolf fell to his knees beside her. She was conscious, but overwhelmed by pain. Something inside him was shouting, *No! No! No!* in endless, mindless denial. Why had he ever let her come on this crazy, hopeless mission?

"Wolf?" she muttered through clenched teeth, her hand grasping for his. Her fingers were icy.

He forced his voice to remain calm. "Just a minute, love." He cut away the cloth and was both relieved to see how small the wound was—she had not been run through or disemboweled. It was a clean, obsidian-sharp stab, but blood was still flowing from it and she might well be bleeding internally as well; the blade might have broken off inside her. Abdominal wounds were excruciatingly painful and invariably fatal unless promptly conjured. Tlixilia had no healing conjury.

"We'll get you some help, love," Wolf whispered, then looked up at the monster. "She is very important. She is vital, if you wish to make a treaty."

She was vital to him, too. This must not have happened. It was impossible. He could not accept it.

"She is the emissary spoken of," growled a new voice. Another Jaguar had arrived, recognizable from Lynx's description—scars, slack body tone, ragged ears. He wore a flowing feathered cloak and a king's ransom in gems and gold.

"The dread lord Basket-fox, I presume?" Wolf did not rise.

The old knight snarled, showing his fangs. "This was unfortunate. We were not prepared for the foe to use such force against you. You should be proud that the Yazotlans sent four knights. Discretion requires that we quit the field. Cloud harrier, take us to the floating city."

4

Sunlight jumped, shadows shifted. The inevitable jab of pain made Wolf cry out and very nearly draw *Diligence,* in the fighting instincts of a swordsman. The air was hotter, damper, flower-scented, with macaws screeching nearby and drums rumbling in the far distance. He was kneeling on a rooftop, obviously in the center of El Dorado as Lynx had described it—white, flat buildings and a multitude of tapering towers.

Dolores lay bleeding on a mat, instead of grass, but she did not seem aware of the change. Only Star-feather and Basket-fox had traveled with them.

"I will find healers for your woman," the Eagle croaked, and vanished in another momentary headache. Having eagle knights dance attendance on a commoner, and a woman at that, was probably equivalent to a marquis delivering groceries.

Lynx flashed into view and yowled with fury, claws out. Evidently he had not expected the move. He was balanced on one paw and leaning on Night-fisher's shoulder. Another Eagle towered over them both.

"Where do you want me to deliver your captives, terror of the dark?" the monster inquired.

"Yawrg!" Lynx said. "Um . . ."

"I shall be happy to install them in my own pens until you are ready to take them."

"That is gracious of you, storm tamer."

The Eagle vanished.

Lynx bared his fangs, somehow implying that if he had a tail he would lash it. *" 'Terror of the dark!'* Did you hear that, Wolfie? That's like—"

"Congratulations. And just what are you planning to do with your captives?"

He said, *"Yawrg!"* again and glanced up at the nearest pyramid, which overlooked them, its long shadow stretched by the westerly sun. "I'll think of something."

Let it go! This was no time to start a family quarrel with a big-brotherly lecture on ethics. "Whose house is this?"

"Basket-fox's." Still supported on Night-fisher's shoulder, Lynx came hobbling over. "Sorry about this, Dolly."

Eyes closed, she did not reply, and her hand did not respond to Wolf's touch. She was unconscious, or narcotizing. Or dying. *Hurry, hurry, hurry!*

"Someone should . . ." Lynx said, "Ah, I hear them coming."

Wolf heard nothing. Four middle-aged women came scurrying up the steps, carrying bags, and still he did not hear them, because they were barefoot. They wore the same white skirts of maguey fiber he had seen on almost every *naturale* woman, plus loose white tunics. He had expected men, but women to treat women was reasonable.

"Are male healers better at treating wounds?" he asked in Chivian.

Lynx shrugged. "About the same." He meant *neither much good*.

The women clustered around the patient. Wolf moved out of the way.

"There is no octogram on the mainland, is there?" Condridad would be the closest.

Lynx said, "No. Don't know why."

Rojas had claimed that skilled conjurers refused to live in Sigisa, but there was probably some political reason. Dolores was going to die for want of a few minutes' conjuration. In the haste of their departure, they had left all their conjured bandages back in Sigisa.

One of the women rose and turned to Wolf, keeping her eyes lowered. She held a blood-stained probe.

"Speak!"

"Lord, the wound has penetrated the bowel. We could cauterize with red-hot silver, but she might die of shock. She would almost certainly lose the child."

"The child is of no importance." He had not known of it and doubted that Dolores had. "The woman must be saved." His mouth was so dry he could hardly speak. "Can you stop the bleeding? How long can she live?"

"The visible bleeding has almost stopped. We can sew the wound, but it may still bleed inside. We cannot answer the lord's other question."

She might die of loss of blood in minutes or hours, or of wound fever in days. No one survived an untreated stab in the intestines; pregnancy must make her even more vulnerable.

"Do not cauterize. Just keep her alive as long as you can."

Of course it was Flicker's child she carried. She could not have conceived before Shining-cloud stripped away her Cumberwell conjuration, and Wolf had succumbed to dysentery and fever right after that. For the next month he had been in no state to sire children. So Dolores had not told him the whole truth about Flicker's farewell visit to the bedroom. Now that the truth was out, Wolf saw how very improbable her story had been. Flicker was a martial arts genius; he would not fail in something as physical as rape. Or had she cooperated? Wolf shuddered away from the thought. No, she had been bruised. People could not deliberately bruise their own faces. That was impossible. And she had been genuinely distraught.

He turned to Lynx. "We must get her home!"

Basket-fox came padding across the roof on his big cat feet. "Your acolytes in Chivial could make her live?"

Hope surged. "They could. Can your Eagles take her there?"

"They can. We are told you come as spokesman for your King, noble lord, and he sent you to make a treaty with our Emperor."

"This is correct," Wolf said.

The Jaguar touched the floor in salute. "Emissaries should be lodged in comfort and treated with honor and ceremony, brother of my friend, but clearly the matter is urgent. If you would waive all such ceremony without feeling that you have been slighted, then we can discuss a treaty right away."

"This courtesy honors me beyond words."

"Spirit stalker, you will keep watch over your brother's woman for him?"

Lynx flashed fangs in delight at another compliment. "I will, terror of the forest. I'll stay with Dolly, Wolfie."

Wolf said, "I will be back very soon, love," but she did not answer. He bowed to Basket-fox. "At your service, mighty lord."

Lynx snarled, "Er . . . Wolfie, ambassadors do not go around armed. His sword is his regalia, dread slayer."

"He may retain the sword," the Jaguar said. "If you will be so kind, honored ambassador?" He beckoned with a paw.

Wolf had to run to keep up with the old cat as he hastened down the stair, and obviously everything had been foreseen. The first stop was a room where half a dozen boys waited with water and sponges and fresh garments. Wolf stood and endured while they stripped off the Distlish clothes he had worn since Sigisa—filthy, ragged, and now blood-soaked—then washed and dried and oiled him. He barely noticed. He could as well have been in a whirlwind or the bottom of the ocean, for he could not stop worrying about Dolores, and whether she would be alive when he returned. They garbed him in a loincloth and a larger, triangular cloth tied at his hip, then a feather cloak, a diadem of feathers, jeweled sandals, rings, bracelets, and flowers. All the time Basket-fox stood in the doorway urging them to go faster.

When they had done Wolf managed to curb his impatience for the moment it took him to thank the slaves, and the jaguar knight also. "Such finery overwhelms me!"

Basket-fox waved a paw dismissively. "Mere trinkets. Keep them to remind you of the day your footprint honored my house. If my lord is ready . . ."

Off they went across his private park, between trees, ponds, flowers. The sun had set but the sky was still blue and the air silky smooth. Dolores was dying. Lynx had said that the Tlixilians were anxious to make a deal, but the first rule of trading was never to seem too eager. Dolores was dying. Wolf must agree to any terms, like the commander of a starving city pleading with its besiegers. Dolores was dying. Dolores was dying. Cats play with mice. Dolores was dying.

"His name," his host announced, "is Two-swans-dancing. He is a member of the Great Council."

"I have heard the great lord's name and am honored beyond speech." Two-swans was the Conch-flute, so the Tlixilians must be greatly expediting negotiations, cutting through the protocol. An eagle knight on guard at the door of a gazebo of white stone stepped to one side as the newcomers approached. Basket-fox went to the other, and Wolf walked through between them.

The man he had come to meet was standing within, arms folded, smiling welcome. He was young and virile, sumptuously dressed in a full-length feather cloak over a beaded and embroidered kilt and golden sandals; the plumes of his headdress reached higher than an Eagle's. He wore gold and jade earplugs, gold plugs in his nose and lower lip, and he was wreathed in flowers. Wolf gave him the ground-touching salute. As he rose, the Conch-flute took his hand and led him to a pair of mats, the only furnishings in the pergola.

"Your troubles pierce us to the heart, Lord Ambassador," he said, as soon as they were seated. He had a magnificently resonant voice, too. "We sorrow that we failed to guard you well on your journey and that your senior wife has been injured. Let our agreement now make recompense for these sufferings." He turned to a tray beside him and poured *pulque* into beakers.

The Chivian ambassador mumbled some suitable retort, keeping careful watch for hints of headache.

"Let us negotiate like warriors," his host said, "cutting fast to the quick, not maundering for hours like gossipy old women. Already the sky-soaring Amaranth-talon prepares to transport you to the place he went a year ago, you and your wife. That is what you wish?" Two-swans-dancing had a personality to melt limestone. If Athelgar were in the least like him, there would have been no Thencaster Conspiracy.

"Indeed it is, lord. Or can he find a similar place a day's walk to the northeast if I described it?"

"No. He can go only to a place he knows or can see."

"It will suffice." Wolf hoped that the Great Bog had frozen again this year, bringing the Ironhall elementary within reach, but at least Quondam would have conjured bandages on hand.

Two-swans-dancing smiled an invitation: *Your turn.*

Wolf said, "The floating city is truly the wonder of all the world. What can it possibly lack that humble Chivial could offer to increase the happiness of your mighty Emperor?"

The Conch-flute had his answer ready. "Stags for riding and war dogs, also slaves who can teach ours to care for both. Swords and pikes and crossbows. Armor. The tools your brother seeks. Will you trade all these things?"

"We keep no slaves, lord." That was stretching a legal nicety, for many Chivian peasants were little better than serfs. "We could loan you skilled teachers, but would it not be better if you sent your men to our land to see how the animals are cared for? Then they can return with the first livestock. We can provide the things you ask if you can transport them across the great water."

"We can do that. We have many Eagles and Amaranth-talon can show them the way. What do you seek in return?"

So here it came.

"We would know your ways of conjury." Still no headache.

Two-swans sipped his *pulque,* cellar-dark eyes fixed on the stranger. "It would be easy for me to send some acolytes with you tonight, who can instruct your acolytes at leisure. But the other Hairy Ones abhor the use of sacrifice and seek to prevent their allies, the traitor cities, from putting prisoners to death. They think it kinder to sell them like fish in a market."

"But their allies still do use conjury! How else were we attacked today?"

The Conch-flute shrugged. "The Distlish allow it now only because we use it, so they say. Your people do not share their strange ideas?"

"We, too, disapprove of sacrifice, but my wife is an acolyte and hopes to combine our ways of summoning the elementals with your ways of controlling them."

Two-swans shook his plumes. "She will fail. Our rituals absolutely require the precious jewels of prisoners taken in battle. Unless those are offered, the god of battle will not bless our knights."

Dolores might be dying at that very moment, but so was El Dorado. These shaky negotiations with Wild-dog-by-the-spring offered the best, if not the only, hope for Two-swans and his people, and yet he was spurning a chance to hide behind a half-truth. He slaughtered prisoners like oysters, yet Wolf would trust him a lot sooner than he would Athelgar.

"You are a man of great honor, lord."

"I am anxious that both sides benefit from our trading. Can we not offer you gold instead? The other Hairy Ones have a great hunger for gold."

Wolf tried to imagine himself appearing in the bailey of Quondam Castle with a wagonload of gold—his mind rejected the image. Athelgar would be delirious with joy. No, gold was a distraction. Time was a-wasting, Dolores bleeding to death. It was time to make a specific offer, and it must seem reasonable.

"My wife and those who trained her are confident that your conjury can be made acceptable to our customs, great ruler. Tonight, let the great Eagle transport my wife and myself to the place he went last year. Let us take two wise acolytes with us. This is the rainy season in Chivial, and we will need time to collect great quantities of goods. Let the Eagle return on the first night of the new moon, and we shall have assembled there as much as we can of what you need. We shall return your acolytes, of course. If your conjurations seem of no value to us, then we shall happily accept gold. We can agree at that time on all details." New moon was nine or ten days away, so the timing would be tight but not impossible.

The Conch-flute nodded at once. "It shall be as you have spoken." He did not ask for hostages for the two acolytes' safety. He had Lynx and Celeste.

Negotiations are easy when both parties are desperate.

They sprang up together and embraced. Two-swans-dancing unfastened a lengthy gold chain from his shoulders and laid it on Wolf's. "Take this as a keepsake of our friendship, Lord Wild-dog-by-the-spring."

The weight was amazing. Every link was in the shape of a scorpion, each with claws joined through the looped tail of the next. It was an artistic marvel, but the gold alone, melted down, would make him rich. They had come to the Hence Lands to seek their fortune and here it was. Could he keep Dolores alive to enjoy it?

"This is generous beyond measure, lord. I have never seen such a wonder. If you would honor me by accepting this trifle, which is all I have of my own to offer." Wolf unfastened the scabbard at his right hip and presented the Conch-flute with his dagger of shiny steel. The Tlixilian exclaimed in joy. It was probably at least a fair exchange in Tlixilia.

When they had embraced again, and Two-swans-dancing had wished his new friend a good journey, he clapped his hands. Eagle and Jaguar appeared in the doorway to hear his orders.

"This was well done, ruler of the night. Choose four twenties from our pens. To my house, star fisher." Conch-flute and Eagle disappeared.

Tattered old Basket-fox touched the ground in salute. "Your father bred most noble sons, Wild-dog-by-the-spring. Between you, you will save our city from the Hairy Ones."

Wolf said only, "Chance may produce strange wonders, terror of the dark." This day was far from over yet.

5

$\mathcal{D}$olores lay propped up on cushions near where he had left her, a gaudy sheet drawn up to her chin. A slave girl kneeling alongside was fanning away insects, and two of the healers squatted within call, keeping watch. In a far corner, Lynx sat on the parapet with Corn-fang and Night-fisher. A bearded Euranian sat at their feet.

The indigo sky was growing starry, but the air was still warm, flower-scented. The moon would not rise for hours yet. Men carrying torches were climbing the stairs of Basket-fox's pyramid.

"Dolores?" Wolf took her hand. It was cold.

Her eyes seemed enormous in a marble-pale face. She tried to smile. "This was stupid of me."

"Don't ever do it again. But everything's going to be all right."

"Good."

"Are you in pain?"

"Not much. Gave me stuff to drink. How did the meeting go?" She was mumbling, either drugged or faint from loss of blood.

"*Put it in writing!* We're going home, love. They'll be here to fetch us in a few minutes. We'll ride the Spirit Wind back to Quondam and put some conjured bandages on that cut. They kept Lynx alive, remember, and his wounds were a hundred times worse than yours. Then we'll cart you over to Ironhall and the octogram. See this chain the Conch-flute gave me? We're rich already."

"No spell books?"

"Better than spell books. We're going to take a couple of acolytes with us, so as soon as you're healed you can start jabbering conjury with them night and day. And they'll have orders to tell you everything."

She closed her eyes and her wan smile faded off into sleep. Her grip on his fingers went slack, but her breathing was steady. He looked inquiringly at the healer women, who nodded reassuringly. Somewhere in the distance drums and conches made strange music.

Lynx was beckoning. Wolf rose and went across to the group. An armed man approaching their lord was enough to bring Corn-fang and Night-Fisher to their feet. The bearded man had only one leg and remained seated.

"What does 'Put it in writing' mean?" Lynx asked in Chivian.

Wolf had forgotten how acute his hearing was. "Inquisitor talk. Means the plan is going well, targets will be met or exceeded." He stared out at the fabled city he would never properly see.

"So this is goodbye?"

"At least for now. I promised Two-swans-dancing that we would start delivering materiel to Quondam at the new moon. I don't know how bad the roads will be, but we'll get something together by then." He forced himself to meet the deadly stare of the great cat eyes.

After a few moments, Lynx spoke softly, still in Chivian. "I've been trying to decide what to do with the prisoners I took today. With Night-fisher's I have six. That isn't enough to make anything spectacular, but I can probably trade them for several days' invisibility. Would be useful when the war gets here."

Wolf studied the last rays of the sunset. More men were climbing the pyramid stair.

"You don't approve, Brother Wolf?"

"No. But I understand better than I did this morning."

Lynx said, "Miaow, miaow! Transporting you home will take more than six hearts, Brother Wolf."

"I said I understand!" Wolf snapped louder than he had intended. He knew there must be sacrifices. He did not want to hear numbers.

Lynx's voice stayed soft, burning like hot cinders in his ears. "I don't know how many it took to turn Sir Lynx into Bobcat-by-the-spring. I did not ask. I did not protest. I took what was offered. I ate what I was given."

"I didn't pass judgment on you, did I?"

"But you thought it. Who's pot and who's kettle now?" It was impossible to read expression on the cat muzzle. The Lynx of five years ago would have been wearing a lackadaisical, almost foolish, grin, but that was before the exile to Quondam, and the massacre, and everything that had happened since.

"Needs must." Wolf's conscience reminded him that this was the excuse the Distliards used for allowing their allies to continue sacrificing prisoners—if the enemy uses conjury, then so must we, just for now.

"Must needs?" Lynx said. "The high moral ground isn't quite as high as it was, is it?"

"It isn't just me. There are more ways of being bound than Ironhall's, Brother. I'm doing it for my wife."

"And for Chivial, I hope?"

"Not especially."

The cat-man chuckled. His bodyguards stared fixedly at the stranger. Wolf's scalp prickled.

"What did you tender as the price of your ticket?" Lynx asked.

"Survival of the city. Weapons, horses, dogs, tools. Whatever you need to give the Distliards a boot in the cuirass. Drive them into the sea."

"Ah!" Lynx licked his fangs with a thick pink tongue. "And can you deliver, Ambassador? Will good King Athelgar really trade thousands of crowns' worth of war gear for a couple of stinking, blood-caked acolytes?"

"He'll deal. The Conch-flute will pay gold instead of conjury if he wants."

"That's better! The Pirate's Son likes gold." Lynx switched to Tlixilian. "Jorge, give him the list."

The Distliard held up what appeared to be a piece of paper. Wolf took it and peered at it, but he could not read it in the dusk. "Paper?"

"It's some sort of bark," Lynx said. "They make picture books from it. That's a list of what the navy needs. You'll be able to get most of it in Lomouth or Brimiarde. I need all that and the sooner the better. Hide it! Celeste's coming."

Before Wolf dared ask how he knew that, a woman came floating up the stair, closely attended by half a dozen maids carrying useful equipment, such as fans, sunshades, even a stool. They were dusky, she was the color of starlight. She gestured for them to wait there, then sauntered across the rooftop to inspect Dolores, ignoring the audience but aware of it. Watching her in motion, Wolf thought of she-jaguars.

"Why is she dangerous?" he murmured.

"Celeste is always dangerous."

She had started all this. Wolf strode over to join her at the sickbed. Dolores was asleep, or pretending to be so. Celeste wore only a knee-length skirt of white cotton and a scarf of the same cloth hung around her neck, with its ends dangling to cover her breasts, at least in theory. Even in two rags and barefoot she looked as if she were dressed for a coronation—her own.

He bowed. "Good chance, my lady."

"Hello, Ed."

"The years have passed you by."

Celeste decided Lady Attewell was no threat and turned to regard Wolf. She curled her pretty lip. "They have not been kind to you, have they? I understand that this will be a flying visit?" She had extracted the news from Basket-fox, no doubt.

"Regrettably. I must get my wife to an elementary."

Celeste smiled; the danger level rose. "Must you? Well, I want to know what you're really up to, Ed. If I don't like it, I'll put a stop to it. What game are you playing?"

Seemingly no one trusted him tonight except the Conch-flute. "No game. I am in a hurry to save my wife's life, certainly, but I am fulfilling my duties as emissary from King Athelgar."

"You? Athy wouldn't appoint you ambassador in a thousand years!"

True. "Men change, Amy. You have been away from Grandon a long time." But nothing had changed. He had to force himself not to stare at the twin roses glowing through the gauzy scarf.

"But for a year before that I had to put up with *dear* Athelgar's opinions of you. All night, every night!" She sighed. "Ranting about the beetle guardsman Sir Wolf, and what he'd like to do to you. Pathetic, it was."

What game was Celeste playing? All Wolf could do was keep parrying, wondering when the acolytes would arrive to take him to the ritual. Already a drum had begun a slow beat from the top of the pyramid.

"The Pirate's Son's never liked me, but—What did *you* tell him about me, Amy?"

She shrugged. "Well, he always wanted to hear how you deflowered me, of course."

"That's a lie to start with."

"And how virile you were, even as a boy. How no man could compare. He would quite wear himself out trying to better your feats. I may have exaggerated a teeny-weeny bit when describing your equipment. The King does not stand above all other men in that respect, you know."

So Celeste had fanned Athelgar's animosity toward him, just out of devilry. That might well be true. But what was she after now? Return to Chivial? Would Basket-fox let her go? Lynx would fight it, because he could not go with her.

"I don't believe much of this, Amy. I do have to leave shortly. Is there something you want of me, for old times' sake?"

Celeste floated closer to him—dangerously, intimately close. Her scent was sweetly tropical, her allure incredible, even yet, and her eyes reflected the stars. "Yes. I want to borrow the King's Killer. There is a matter of justice that needs be attended to."

"What are you talking about, Amy?"

"Justice," she said. "Justice for my murdered child."

Startled, Wolf glanced back to the cat-man sitting on the parapet. He had not moved since Celeste appeared.

"I thought your baby died. I had it on excellent authority, sworn in the presence of an inquisitor . . ." Ah, but that day back in Ironhall something in Lynx's testimony had rung false. Wolf's heart sank. He could not recall his brother's exact words but deceit did not always require actual lying. "What really happened, then?"

Celeste laughed coarsely. "The midwives pulled it out of me, cut it loose, dropped it in a blanket, and handed it out the door to my senior Blade, Sir Lynx. *And he killed it!*"

Wolf batted away the wheeling insects while he tried to think this through. If it was true, then the moral high ground had sunk to new depths. It was as hard to think of genial, easygoing Lynx murdering a baby as of Celeste being maternal, but a Blade must do anything necessary to protect his ward. She had been given years to brood over an injustice. Without raising his voice, Wolf said, "Brother, you are accused of murder."

Lynx yowled like an alley cat in heat, but he stayed where he was, sitting on the wall with his guards around him. "So?" he called. "So what can you do about it now, Wolfie? I'm *much* faster than you are. I carry eight blades to your one. Corn-fang is nimble, too, even at this range. Draw that sword and you'll have a spear through both ears."

Light glowed in the stairwell. The waiting maidens twittered and cleared a path for a mighty feathered warrior, who came marching across the roof with seven or eight men at his back. He thumped the butt of his spear down in front of Wolf.

"Lord Ambassador, I am taker of seven captives Raging-stone, son of Lord Basket-fox, who bids me tell you that the ritual is about to begin."

"We have a few things to settle here first," Wolf said. Infanticide, perjury, fratricide.

"We have brought you garments in the style of your city and blankets for your wife."

"That is very kind." Wolf turned to Celeste. "I don't believe you."

She shrugged again. The light of the newcomers' torches made her long hair shine like copper; her eyes were an intense green flecked with gold.

"Then I shall warn my dear old tabby cat protector that you are a notorious liar, Edwin Attewell. That you will betray his trust. That you do not speak for the King of Chivial, that the King of Chivial wants vengeance on El Dorado for the massacre at Quondam, and that you plan to torture the conjury secrets out of the acolytes and have no intention of delivering any weapons. Old Foxy will get one of his Eagle friends to lay the Serpent's Eye on you and out will come the truth. So if you're lying, Ed, you'd better kill that brother of yours for me, by hook or by crook."

Yes, she was dangerous. She was deadly. She had guessed that Wolf was lying and dared not face the Serpent's Eye.

"How long has she been like this?"

Lynx said, "She has some lucid moments."

"Maybe we should call for the Serpent's Eye for you, Amy Sprat, and get the truth about the baby."

"Yes, let's!" she said, but her neck muscles were tense. She was lying, too, somehow, at least slightly.

Maybe they all were.

"Brother?" he said.

"I didn't kill it," Lynx said. "The King had made it quite clear that he wanted no royal bastards running around. They endanger the realm. They get used by unscrupulous people. He promised me Celeste would be released if the child was born dead."

"You trusted *Athelgar*?" Wolf said. "How could you be so stupid? Oh, that was *really* stupid!"

"But we had no choice, did we? I found a good home for it . . . him. I had a wet nurse waiting. She knew that."

"I know what you said!" Celeste snapped. "But then you told me he had died. When Athelgar went back on his word, you wouldn't give me back my child!"

"Of course not!" Lynx said. "That would have been admitting to conspiracy. In ten minutes the old Baron would have been high-tailing back to Grandon babbling about treason."

Watched by the healers and grandiose Raging-stone, four slaves were lifting Dolores on her mat, to lay her on a litter they had brought. Wolf should be providing comfort and support, not engaged in this absurd quarrel.

"Oh, so now you tell me he's alive?" Celeste said, baring her teeth. "He's been dead for years and now he's alive. I want my son! Where is he?"

"You don't need to know."

"Eater of stars Amaranth-talon is waiting, speaker for kings," Raging-stone announced.

"We'll be ready very soon," Wolf said, "Is the child still alive?"

"A year and a half ago he was," Lynx said.

"What's his name?"

"Edwin."

"I'm flattered."

"Her idea."

"And there's no doubt it's the same boy and he's Athelgar's get?"

"I've watched him grow. Every year I delivered money for his board. His hair's as red as any I've seen."

"Where can I find him?"

"Brackyan. Remember it?"

"Brackyan!" Celeste practically spat. "A king's son *there*?" Brackyan was another mining hamlet, not far from Sheese and its equal in squalor.

The slaves had raised the stretcher and were carrying Dolores toward the stair. One torch-bearer remained, fidgeting. It was time to go.

"I know Brackyan," Wolf said. "It is no fit abode for a king's son. How can I know him? Who fosters him?"

Lynx chuckled. "Cob Sprat, her brother. He doesn't know Edwin's his nephew, though. The boy limps, has a twisted foot. The right one."

Drums throbbed in the sultry night. Torchlight danced.

"Should be able to find him," Wolf said. He braced himself to take hold of Celeste's arms, which was like embracing lightning. "Do you want him sent here to you, Amy?"

She hesitated, then shook her head. She was a slave in an embattled city. What future for her son here? All these years she must have been at least half convinced that the baby was dead. She didn't know what she wanted.

Wolf said, "Will you take my word for it that I'll find him a good home and see he is raised as a gentleman? I can, now. Two-swans-dancing made me a wealthy man tonight."

She studied him with those huge green eyes that he knew so well from so long ago. Every gold fleck in them he knew. "Will you tell him who his parents are?"

"Of course not. But I'll see he is educated and taught gentle manners."

"You will adopt him as your own son!"

Now, there would be irony! "If you insist." He had no time to bargain.

"You swear?"

Wolf nodded. "I swear. I swear I will do the best for him I possibly can. I will never hold his father against him."

Still she hesitated, but no man could tell when Amy Celeste Sprat was being real and when she was acting. "Kiss me, Ed."

"For Edwin," he said, and kissed her. Even after all the years, he knew the taste of her and the warmth of her breast in his hand. It was an incredible kiss; he let it persist as long as she wanted. They were both burning when it ended; she buried her face in his shoulder.

"Spirits!" she muttered. "We should have stayed in Sheese, you and me."

"Maybe we should have." He broke free. "I'll look after Edwin, I promise. Goodbye, Amy. Good chance." He set off toward the stair, the torchbearer at his side.

"Lucky man," Lynx said at his back. "I do miss kissing."

"So does she." Wolf sighed. "Were you telling the truth about the brat?"

Lynx chuckled. "Surprisingly, I was. Were you?"

6

Glimmering like mist in the starlight, the great masonry pyramid tapered upward into the night. Flames streamed from two great fires on the summit, where the drums now beat the double rhythm of a giant heart: *Boom-BOOM! Boom—BOOM!* Many people had gathered at the base of the pyramid steps, the low rumble of male voices like surf on distant reefs, wafted by flower-scented trade winds. There was a dreamlike quality to any big crowd in darkness, but Wolf had never felt that unreality as strongly as then. He saw a few Jaguar and Eagle heads towering above the others; he saw feather-decked warriors and slaves holding flaming torches, and a group of blackened acolytes went by him, trailing an unbearable stench.

Boom—BOOM!

He squeezed between guards and bearers standing around the litter and knelt to speak to Dolores. She opened her eyes and smiled briefly, but soon drifted off to sleep again. He hoped that was a good sign, meaning she was not in pain. Three of the healer women were in attendance, and nobody seemed to know what everybody was waiting for.

Lynx said, "If you're doing favors for Celeste and people, will you do one for me?"

Wolf stood up. "Of course. What?"

Night-fisher offered him a sheathed sword. *Boom-BOOM!*

"I can't wield her anymore," Lynx said. "I can never come home. When the city falls, I will die with it." *Boom-BOOM!*

"I've told you! The city is not going to fall. I'm going to send weapons and horses to save it for you."

"*Awoull!* Really?"

"Of course." In that sticky-hot tropical night, Wolf's body betrayed him and shivered as if he were cold.

Lynx purred a sort of chuckle. "I know you will do your duty as you see it, Wolfie. You always have. Even if you do save Tlixilia, the other pussycats won't tolerate me for long. Take *Ratter,* please."

Wolf said, "If you insist. I'll see she goes to the sky of swords—but not until I'm sure it's time."

"I'll write you as soon as I'm dead."

Wolf tucked the sword in under the blankets and warm garments that had been piled on the litter at Dolores's feet. She did not waken. As he straightened up he became aware of a new sound, a low moaning, a lament like wind in a forest. A long line of torches was emerging from the darkness. The leaders were armed men, men with torches, men with flutes, but behind them followed a line of prisoners, all naked, all tethered by the neck to a very long rope. Some staggered, some shuffled, and a few tried to march with their heads up. Some were moaning, while others sang softly or sobbed or just mumbled to themselves—the noise he had heard was the sound of the entire coffle, a weeping snake of doomed humanity. Guards walked alongside, carrying canes and torches. Any misbehavior earned a blow.

They went by from left to right and joined a score or so other prisoners sitting on the ground. As they sat down, slaves moved among them, untying and coiling the tether. But the vague wind sound continued, and to leftward the lights were still coming, flickering between the trees. How many?

Horror, most horrible!

"Lynx? These aren't all for . . . they're not just for us, are they?"

Lynx stroked his whiskers with a giant paw. "Who else?"

"How many sacrifices does an Eagle need to send four people to Chivial?"

"Hundreds."

Boom-BOOM! Boom-BOOM!

No! Wolf had not dreamed of massacre on that scale. A man might rationalize a few deaths because this was war and he was playing for great stakes and trying to save his wife's life. But *hundreds?*

"You never told me!"

Dolores was dying . . .

Lynx shrugged human shoulders. "Maybe thousands."

"All the times we talked about transporting weapons, you never once told us they sacrificed men on that scale!"

"It isn't exactly a pleasant topic of conversation," the cat-man said wryly. "I'm sorry if you bit off more than your conscience can chew, but it's too late to back out now, Wolfie-my-lad. Much too late. You shook hands with the Conch-flute."

Were two murders worse than one? Were nine hundred worse than nine? Why should the King's Killer—after offing an inquisitor, eight brother Blades, and possibly a stepfather, not to mention many traitors he had helped send to the scaffold—why should he trouble his soul over anonymous prisoners of war in what would shortly be a very distant country? Why did he feel a need to vomit?

Jorge had arrived, hobbling on his crutch, and now his harsh voice broke into the conversation. "You think we Distliards are driven by nothing but greed, Chivian? You think only love of gold makes King Diego squander his army's blood? We fight to end this atrocity!"

"Do you?" Wolf snapped. "But you use it. Your allies have eagle and jaguar knights. Your hands are bloody too."

"We use it so we can stop it!"

"Oh, isn't that a sweet rationalization!" But Wolf was doing exactly the same thing himself. And how could he not? Dolores was about to die. The torches in the night, the drums, wailing horns, the stench of men and fear . . . none of those mattered when Dolores was dying. He just did not know how to put that into words, though. Her life against how many?

All right! He was not doing it for Dolores. He was doing it for duty. Was that better?

Boom-BOOM! Boom-BOOM!

"It's not quite as bad as it seems," Lynx said. "They don't know what's going on. They're drugged stupid with peyote and other stuff. And they're all doomed anyway. If they don't die tonight for you, then they will soon, for some other purpose. And it's funny—if you threw open the gates a lot of them would refuse to leave. The Distlish would, of course, but not the *naturales*. It's an honor."

"Oh, thanks!" Wolf found little comfort in that. To learn that there might be Euranians among the prisoners should not make things worse, and yet it did. It was one more horror to deny. He jumped at the inhuman screech behind him.

"We are ready!"

He looked around and then up, up to the great cruel beak and ruthless eyes of an Eagle.

"So are we, lord."

"This is the sun-grazing Amaranth-talon," Lynx said.

The Eagle ignored him. "You would go to the beach, or the tower?"

"The tower, please."

"You will not interrupt the ritual."

Wolf said, "No, lord."

"It would be dangerous and give offense."

"We shall do as my lord bids." To interrupt an incantation could be disastrous even in Chivial, where the spirits were confined in an octogram.

The Eagle vanished like a bubble.

Boom-BOOM! Boom-BOOM! Boom-BOOM! The great heart beat faster.

Raging-stone, taker of seven captives, started barking commands. The bearers raised the litter. It was time to go. Wolf turned to say farewell to Lynx, who dropped his heels to make himself human height, and gave him a rib-bending embrace. He smelled of tomcat.

"Try not to watch," he said quietly, furry cheek against Wolf's ear. "It is horrible, but remember the victims don't know what's happening."

That was an admission of guilt.

"Thank you for that," Wolf said. "Good chance, little brother. If you ever get the opportunity, do give Celeste my love as well as your own."

Lynx purred a laugh. "That will be the day."

Wolf had never imagined so terrible a parting, in so terrible a place. He turned away with a pain in his throat, to find that he could not leave yet, his way was blocked. Raging-stone's men were trying to clear a passage through the endless line of victims shuffling past between them and the staircase. The soldiers cut the tether. The dazed and drugged prisoners ahead continued on their way without noticing, but those behind had to be halted forcibly, so the line bunched up in sheeplike confusion. There was much shouting and cursing, and the guards spread their spears like rails to make a barricade.

Then Dolores's litter could go through. Wolf and the warriors followed, and began to mount the great staircase.

7

The stair was very long, perilously steep, caked with old blood. Up ahead, the bearers carrying Dolores mounted sideways, two at each end of the stretcher, with the rear two having to hold their side head-high. Wolf hurried as much as he dared, trying not to imagine what would happen if they dropped the litter, or even if he stumbled. The drums grew louder. The steps reeked like an abattoir. Pale smoke from the braziers drifted overhead, sparkling with its own red stars. His head began to ache as he approached the center of spirituality.

When he drew his breath of relief on reaching the summit safely, he was facing the blackened altar stone, the heart of evil, flanked by two great braziers. His forehead ached, but not as badly as it had in the Forge at Ironhall—so far. Many black acolytes, busy as ants, were loading wood into the fires, and two were playing drums. He saw other drums and conches not yet in use, and dozens of flint knives set out on a stone table. How many other pyramids would he see from here if he came in daylight? How many tens of thousands died here every year? The city was dark and mysterious, seeming very far below, hardly a light showing. The slaves carried the litter around one of the braziers and set it down some way back from the altar; then they were herded away by a couple of acolytes.

Wolf knelt beside the litter. "We're on our way home, love."

Dolores was just conscious enough to ask, "How many . . . sacrifices?"

"I don't know. Lynx says they'd all die anyway, very soon." He must rationalize this atrocity somehow or he would go mad.

She pulled a face. The eagle knight appeared, plumage shining metallic green in the firelight. He took up position between them and the altar, fortunately blocking all Dolores's view of it and most of Wolf's also. More drums and a conch were joining in the music, if that was what it was. The four slaves who had carried the litter were drinking something, with acolytes fussing around them.

She smiled with bloodless lips. "So that was the famous Celeste?"

"You see why Athelgar was smitten?"

"What happens about her child?" Her voice was so soft he could barely hear it.

"I promised we'll adopt him. You don't mind, do you?"

"It won't matter what I . . ." She screwed up her face for a moment. When the spasm passed, she said, "I don't mind." Later she said, "I'll make this one a girl, then, all right?"

He laughed and kissed her. "Anything except kittens! Did you know before the healer told you?"

She shook her head, then murmured, "I wondered." She was drifting into sleep or coma, and the next few things she tried to say were inaudible under the thundering drums, the scream of conches, acolytes wailing incantations. Wolf remained kneeling by the stretcher and kept his face turned away from the altar stone, watching Dolores, or the lake, or anywhere. He must not think about the clean-picked bones of Cam Obmouth and Rolf Twidale on the rocks at Quondam. *Where is your outrage now, sinner?*

One of the ragged, revolting acolytes came to kneel at the end of the litter. His face was shadowed from the fires, a blank darkness with two eyes visible. Then he smiled, showing white teeth also. He reeked worse than a midden. Wolf looked away and found another at the other end. These two were to be his traveling companions, and no doubt they had their orders. Their hair hung in matted strings, never cut, their fingernails were long and jagged.

Drums boomed. Conches wailed.

The four bearers, now naked and thoroughly drugged, were escorted back from the far side of the platform. Three were stopped close to the litter, but the fourth was led on, around to the altar stone. Wolf guessed what was about to happen and quickly looked away. Perhaps the ache in his forehead grew a little worse, but he heard nothing sinister over the racket of drumming and wailing. The second slave was taken.

He would not watch. He could imagine.

Except that he couldn't. They *really* did not resist? Against his will, his eyes followed the fourth slave all the way around to the altar. The man went willingly until the last few steps. Then he tried to draw back, but four acolytes seized him and stretched him across the great stone, face up. Wolf's view was obstructed by Amaranth-talon's outspread wings, but he closed his eyes anyway. He thought he heard the hiss of the beating heart landing in the brazier.

The corpses were rolled down one side of the great staircase. The procession of captives came up the other side, the side Wolf could see. All were naked, all doomed, all drugged almost senseless. And they just *stood* there, a line of four men waiting like sheep between the uppermost step and the murder site. Then another body would be dragged away, another young man grabbed and thrown down. The rest would take two steps forward and a replacement victim appear at their backs.

How much was this done by drugs and how much by indoctrination? Once Wolf had sat on the anvil at Ironhall waiting for a sword through his heart, but he had known it wouldn't kill him.

None of the victims cried out, but they probably couldn't, once their chests were cut open. How long must this go on? He had lost count already. He wanted to scream at them to stop. But why? He was the King's Killer, wasn't he?

His head was throbbing now. The conjuration must be concentrated around the altar stone, but the ride on the Spirit Wind would hurt, as he knew from today's experience. Long journeys brought mental confusion, Lynx said—that was why he and Fell had managed to overcome Plumed-pillar at Quondam. Wolf must plan. He must be ready to act when he reached Quondam. Only if he knew exactly what he was going to do could he hope to be fast enough to overcome the Eagle.

Yet he could not tear his eyes away from the horrifying parade of drugged victims, could not help staring at them, wondering why they did not rise in revolt and at least try to die fighting. Most of them were appallingly young. Young or old, their faces were totally blank, their eyes dull as pebbles in the torchlight. Then came one who was paler than the others and had a straggly beard. He was Euranian . . . Chivian, in fact . . . his name was Louis, known as Flicker.

Without thinking, Wolf surged to his feet. The pain in his head clanged like a great bell, so he staggered—and then just stood there, staring, paralyzed.

There was no sign of Heron-jade, who ought to stand out because of his size, but he might be farther back, lower down on the long climb. No, he had to be dead, or he would have identified himself and called for his lord, Sky-cactus. A blood-caked swelling disfigured the left side of Flicker's face, perhaps a relic of the blow that had disabled him and led to his capture. Had it rendered him unable to talk, to explain who he was, or had his protestations just been ignored? Who would believe a Hairy One, trying to lie his way out of the abattoir pen? Had the Eldoradoans killed Heron-jade by mistake, or had he fallen to the Distlish forces and Flicker gone on by himself? There were a thousand possible explanations.

Another man died without a cry, another corpse rolled away down the staircase to the waiting butchers. Flicker was urged forward by an acolyte, and another man stepped up behind him. Now Flicker was only two men back from the stone.

What could Wolf do? However the Tlixilian prisoners might feel about donating their hearts, Flicker would not feel honored.

Nothing. Wolf could do nothing. He had promised not to interrupt the ritual, and the pain in his head was ample warning that elementals had been gathered in great strength. To release so much power at random would surely cause disaster. He could not save Flicker and why should he even want to? He had sworn to kill the rat. He was a rapist. Let him die now!

Another heart dropped in the brazier. Another corpse rolled over the brink and was gone. Flicker was only one man away from the altar stone. His unsteady gaze wobbled past Wolf, then returned. Something changed. He seemed to make an effort to focus. He frowned uncertainly.

Dolores began to fret and her eyes opened, as if the pain had returned. She could not see Flicker from down there.

But Flicker could see Wolf. Life began to shine in his eyes. He was struggling against the mind-numbing drug—perhaps even using some inquisitors' trick to resist it. The acolytes noticed his alertness and two of them jumped forward to grip him even before the previous victim had been completely processed. He shouted feebly and tried to struggle. He was turned around and dragged down on the altar.

Wolf knelt down to attend to Dolores. His head hurt less down there. "What's wrong?" He had to crouch close to hear her whisper through the thunder of the drums.

"How many? Wolf, stop this! Murders?"

Wolf kissed her. "Soon be over," he promised.

"Wrong!" she muttered. "Wrong, wrong!"

Not all wrong. Flicker had gone. All the waiting victims were Tlixilians. The rising moon was smearing the eastern sky with gold.

Wolf had fulfilled his oath—he had executed the rapist Louis Duteau, known as Flicker. Why should that bother him? The spirits knew he had slaughtered enough of his brother Blades in the line of duty, and this latest killing ought to bring him great personal satisfaction—and no small relief, because in mortal combat Flicker would have been as dangerous an opponent as any he had ever encountered. Was that why? Or because he had let others do his dirty work for him, like an Athelgar? Or because it might have been possible to save him with a whispered word to the Eagle? Or because he was not quite certain of Flicker's guilt? No, no, no . . .

How would Dolores feel when she learned that saving her life had cost hundreds of deaths and it had all been in vain, because what she wanted to do with the conjury was impossible, that Tlixilian spells would always require mass slaughter? Wolf was cheating her as much as he had cheated Two-swans-dancing. He was the King's Killer, but he would not rescue a culture so unspeakably barbaric that even Lynx could not discuss what underlay its power. Dolores was wrong. Jorge had been right. The Distlish were right. El Dorado must die.

He must have his plans clear in his mind, so he could act instantly when he arrived on the turret at Quondam. It would be dark, possibly snowing. If the sentries noticed his arrival at all, they would take a few minutes to react. He knew what the cold of a Chivian Secondmoon night felt like, and the Tlixilians did not. He must take the Amaranth-talon first, certainly, before the Eagle could use the Serpent's Eye on him. If he could kill the Eagle and the two acolytes and throw their bodies over the edge, to fall far down the cliffs below, then he might just get away with it. If he didn't, Athelgar could have the pleasure of deciding whether to hang him for murder or behead him for treason. Flicker would certainly have tried to stop him, but Flicker had met his just deserts.

The moon peered over the mountains. There were no more men waiting at the stone and the ritual had ended. Amaranth-talon raised his head to the stars and screeched in triumph. He swung around to face the stretcher, spread his wings. Wolf screamed at the explosion of agony in his head.

8

The world rocked. After the din of trumpets and drums, the bonfires in the night, he was plunged into blazing sunlight and a salty gale as cold as any icy torrent. And intolerable pain. Screaming, he drew his sword. The howling wind helped, making the Eagle stagger, and he was too big a target to miss, even in that sudden blinding glare. Wolf leaped over the stretcher. A slash might have been deflected by the tough feathers, so he lunged, withdrew his blade, and rammed *Diligence* into the monster again before it had collapsed on the shingle. He stabbed it a third time to be sure.

The sun was not far above the horizon, a brilliance in a hazy maritime sky. Surf boomed on the rocks, hurling up pillars of spray. One of the acolytes scrambled to his feet and Wolf felled him with a slash to the neck. The other screamed and tried to run, reeling and flailing on the loose shingle, but heading the wrong way, toward the sea. Wolf ran unsteadily after him. A breaker exploded on rocks directly ahead, hurling foam skyward and probably terrifying the Tlixilian out of his few remaining wits. Wolf caught up with him and killed him too.

By then the pain was almost gone from his head. He felt no guilt or regret as he hurried back to Dolores. Those three had been pitiless murderers on a vast scale. Compared to such butchers, the King's Killer was merely a naughty child. He removed Amaranth-talon's regalia and smashed it to fragments with a rock so that no other Eagles could come to see what had gone wrong. The only one who knew the way now was Bone-peak-runner, who had accompanied Amaranth-talon on the raid a year ago, but Wolf doubted strongly that the Eldoradoans would risk him. At the new moon they might. Not now.

It was a wild morning, but the damp in the air was flying spray, not rain. Impelled onward by the wind, he almost fell over the stretcher. Dolores made incoherent noises. He wrapped blankets around her.

"It's all right, love," he said. "We're home in Chivial. We'll have you to an octogram very soon." Not as soon as he had hoped. He had asked the Eagle to deliver them to the turret, but they were down in Short Cove. He wondered if he could have bullied one of the acolytes into helping him carry the stretcher. Probably not, and murdering him later would have been more difficult in the presence of witnesses.

"Why, why?" Her whisper was almost lost in the wind. Her pallor was terrifying. "Why kill them?"

"Because what you wanted isn't possible, dearest. Their conjury only works with beating hearts. The Distliards have tried to make it work otherwise and can't—Rojas told us, the Conch-flute says so, too. This horror must be stopped. I've stopped it. Now let's get you out of the wind."

She stared at him unbelievingly, tears in her eyes. "All those deaths? Why did you let them die?"

To get her home, of course. He raised one end of the litter and dragged it off the beach, into the grass, and there found her a sheltered spot in the lee of a boulder. He was still exposed to the gale, though, and it was a struggle to change into the Euranian-style garments that Raging-stone had provided. They were not Chivian style, but would seem less bizarre than his Tlixilian garb. The hose were two large for him, the shirt and tunic too snug. No doubt they had belonged to Distliards who had left their hearts in El Dorado.

He crouched beside her again. "I'll be as quick as I can, love. I'll run up to the castle and get some conjured bandages and some men and horses."

She was weeping, but perhaps that was just the wind. "You could at least have let me try to make the rituals work. Just for a few days, Wolf!"

No. To bring knowledge of the Tlixilian conjury into Chivial was to trust Athelgar, and to trust Athelgar was incredibly stupid, as he had told Lynx and Celeste. Oh, the beloved monarch would not start tearing men's hearts out right away, but sooner or later the public good would demand extreme measures. *Needs must*—so Wolf himself had argued. And Lynx had, too. In a jam, if the evil was available, eventually it would be used, just as the Distliards were using it now. As he himself had just used it to save Dolores. He would *not* let Athelgar have it!

And even if the floating city promised a mountain of buttery gold instead, he would not send them weapons. The city must fall. The secrets must be wiped off the face of the world.

"I'll explain tomorrow, love, when you're better," he said. "I have to run up to the castle. They'll have conjured bandages up there, and we'll come back with horses."

She tried to cling to him. "Don't leave me!"

"I must. I will go as fast as I can, I promise!"

Remembering Twidale and Obmouth, he covered her face to keep the gulls away, although they should find enough carcasses to keep them occupied. He set off as fast as he could go on rough ground, plunging through spiky grass. By now the Eldoradoans must know that Amaranth-talon was not going to return. Were they even now interrogating Lynx and Celeste?

He was appalled at how weak he still was from his long bout with fever. In no distance at all he had to slow to a walk. He looked up to orient himself on the single turret that could be seen from Short Cove. It was not there.

Spurred by panic, he ran down the shingle to the water's edge and looked again. From there he could just see a jagged edge of masonry, blackened by fire. For a moment his mind staggered from one absurdity to another, but finally had to accept the only possible explanation—the King had followed his suggestion and slighted Quondam. That explained why the Eagle had not done as Wolf asked—the turret was gone. The walls would be cast down, the buildings burned, and no doubt the bailey was a wasteland of rubble. There would be no one up there to help him, no conjured bandages, no horses.

He trudged back to Dolores. "It's me, dear," he warned her before he lifted back the blanket. "I think I'll have to carry you."

She looked even paler than before. She shook her head feebly. He had to make her repeat her words three times before he understood: "I'm losing the baby."

She was hemorrhaging. Nothing he could do would make any difference. He stretched out on the grass beside her and held her as she writhed in pain. He talked, barely knowing what he said—lies about help being on the way, probably—but soon she was past speech and probably did not understand anything he said anyway. He could not possibly carry her up the cliff path unaided. To make the attempt would kill her. Even if it did not, they would still be miles from the nearest help, perhaps days away from an octogram. Flicker's child was killing her.

Flicker was dead. So was Lynx, dead man walking. He had known what Wolf planned, had guessed, could have stopped him. So he had approved.

Later Wolf said, "When you're healed, we'll go and rescue young Edwin from Brackyan."

Later still, "We have to get out of the country fast, before Athelgar finds out what I've done."

And even later, "We did find our fortune, darling. We're rich now!"

He babbled on for hours, until he was too hoarse to speak, long after he knew that he was alone.

Half frozen, Wolf staggered across to the stream and drank. Then he began the long labor of gathering driftwood, dragging it across the shingle, and eventually the work warmed him and eased his cramped muscles. Knowing he lacked the strength to lift the body onto a pyre, he covered it with brush he cut with Lynx's sword and piled the heavier wood on top. When that was done he searched the beach in the fading daylight until he found a piece of flint to strike sparks. After much effort he made a flame, using an abandoned bird's nest as tinder. Once the fire was burning, he hauled the acolytes' corpses to the water so the tide could carry them away. The Eagle he left for the Tlixilians to find if they came looking.

He was tempted to hurl the priceless scorpion chain into the blaze as a final gift, but Dolores would have disapproved of such waste, so he didn't. As night fell, he started wearily up the path, burdened with riches and sorrows and his brother's sword.

Epilogue

The horseman rode up by the arroyo track and paused at the top to let the mare catch her breath while he admired the view. Workmen were burning brush somewhere, so a faint haze lay over the green hills that rolled away to a far glimpse of ocean. It was as fine a vista as he knew— grass and high rainfall and limestone, great country for horses. The mare snorted, as if in agreement.

He laughed and patted her sweaty neck. "Not far now, Malinda." He nudged her forward again. Many years ago, founding his stud, he had bestowed that name on his first brood mare, and he had kept the personal joke going ever since.

His own name had varied over his life. Originally he had been Hugh Byrd. For three glorious months, he had been Sir Eagle of the Royal Guard. Much later he had become Don Águila, but the locals had more often called him *El Chiviano* and still did, although there were two Chivian ranchers in the hills now. It was the other one he was on his way to visit. This new one, Don Lope, was generally known as *El Diablo*, but that was a comment on his looks, not his behavior. His workers adored him, for he paid them the highest wages on the island and addressed them in their own tongue. The only people who spoke ill of him were other ranchers who had seen their best hands disappear in his direction.

The man had ability and fanatical attention to detail. Felipe's hacienda had been a ruin when he bought it, and was now such a success that half the landowners in Condridad were trying to copy his methods. Riding in, Eagle noted improvements even since his last visit—the new roof was almost complete, the dam on the stream had been raised to turn a pond into a tiny lake, and the training ring had been much enlarged. Edwin was in there now, putting his pony over the jumps under his father's watchful eye.

Eagle enjoyed visiting his new neighbor and wished they lived closer. It was good to talk his mother tongue sometimes, to reminisce about Ironhall and hear tales of men he had known in boyhood: Panther, Hector, Stalwart, Shadow.

He had been seen. Wolf was waving a greeting. Eagle rode up to the rail and shook hands across it.

"You are indeed welcome, brother," his host said. "How long can you stay? Greet Don Águila, Edwin."

The boy began in Distlish and switched to Chivian. Then he grinned and repeated the welcome in Tlixilian.

Eagle thanked him in the same three languages. "You speak as well as you ride, master. Let me see those jumps again."

"*Sí, señor!*" Flushed with pleasure, the boy turned his mount, digging in his heels.

"I swear he grows a handsbreadth every time I see him!" Eagle said.

That was Wolf's cue to look pleased. "That's because you don't come by often enough. You should have seen what a starved little waif he was when I . . . by the way, I have a gift for you."

When Sir Wolf had passed through Mondon five years ago, he had been accompanied by a wife. The following year he had turned up again, with a son and no wife. The boy was almost certainly not his. Edwin was going to be very tall and his shock of screaming-red hair would not have shamed a pure-blood Bael. Whatever their relationship, man and boy were obviously very close.

"Indeed?" Eagle said. "And I have news for you."

"Good or bad?"

"Both."

They waited until Edwin had completed the circuit, then applauded as he rode past, triumphant. Hands arrived to take charge of the riding lesson and Eagle's horse. The two ranchers walked over to the house.

"Begin with the bad news."

"A great tragedy. Sigisa has gone."

"Gone? How?"

"Hurricane. Six days ago. *El Caudillo* barely escaped—he had sailed just two days before. They say the entire town has vanished. The sandbar was washed away. The river empties directly into the sea now."

Wolf walked for a while staring at the ground, then said, "The world is better off without Sigisa, but there were some innocent people living there. At least, I think there must have been. No survivors?"

"Oh, yes. Homeless, of course. And we shall have shipping problems from now on. There is no decent harbor on that coast."

Don Lope shrugged. "We're better off than the farmers."

"How so?"

"You can't drop cotton or beans overboard and expect them to swim ashore." He smiled, which required only a slight change in the permanent tooth-displaying sneer of his disfigurement.

Eagle laughed and said, "True."

Lady Attewell greeted the visitor when they reached the veranda. Wolf excused himself and disappeared into the house. Eagle presented the trifling gift he had brought for the lady—a seashell necklace—inquired after her daughter, chose a comfortable chair, and accepted a glass of cool fluid. He yielded to her entreaties and promised he would stay for at least two days this time. Wolf had chosen wisely when he bought this place. The view of the mountains was stupendous on one side, and the sea was visible on the other. Eagle could almost feel jealous.

El Diablo had done well in his choice of wife, too. Dona Novia was the daughter of a prosperous planter, Pascual Fombella. She had the striking dark beauty that often appeared in a first cross, and wit to go with it. Eagle told her about Sigisa and she duly expressed horror. He suspected she was pregnant again. That was not unreasonable, because Amy must be about two now. Wolf reappeared with a package which almost certainly contained a sword, but which he laid beside his chair unexplained.

Polite conversation floated in the evening air like dreams of butterflies. Novia asked what was to be done about Sigisa. Eagle mentioned a relief ship being organized in Mondon. Wolf promised a contribution. The problem was money, of course. Rich though ranchers were in land, hard cash was always short. Young Edwin came limping in to boast of his riding.

In a moment Dona Novia rose from her chair. "Come along, young man. Don Águila has business to discuss with your father."

Edwin aimed a worried glance at Wolf, who laughed.

"I haven't forgotten! Don Águila will come with us and teach both of us. He's a much better diver than I am."

Reassured, Edwin allowed himself to be led away.

"I am hopeless in water," Eagle protested. "I know nothing about diving. You should be teaching me."

Wolf grinned wolfishly. "Edwin will be pleased when he realizes that! Now, brother . . ." He produced a scroll. "When El Dorado fell, I had occasion to send a package Home to Ironhall, Returning a sword. Amazingly, it arrived safely. Equally amazingly, Grand Master's reply reached me, too. It came a couple of days ago."

Eagle laid down his glass and stared very hard at him. "Are you telling me that there was a *Blade* in El Dorado? That a Chivian *Blade* died in the assault?" And if so, how had Wolf obtained his sword? He had been here in Condridad when the long and bloody siege finally ended. There were fantastic rumors that he had visited the floating city the previous year and his first wife had died there. Eagle hoped to get the story out of him one day, Blade to Blade, but their friendship had not yet advanced to the sharing of confidences.

"It is a long story, brother, not all of which I can reveal, even yet." Wolf smiled wanly. "I'll tell you what I can, but yes, a brother did die in the fall of El Dorado, if not before. When I wrote, I passed on your thanks to Grand Master, as you once asked me to. And he sent this for you."

Eagle accepted the scroll reluctantly but made no effort to unroll it. The seal was obviously the royal signet of Chivial. He had seen it often enough. "The bitch?" he said.

Wolf chuckled. "Lord Roland wrote that, when he became Grand Master, he inherited some items of unfinished business. That deed, he told me, is a royal pardon for the former Sir Eagle, and accolade of knighthood in the Loyal and Ancient Order."

"The bitch!" Eagle repeated. The injustice still rankled, after thirty years.

"Durendal also pointed out that the document is dated very early in the reign of Queen Malinda. It must have been done on her first visit to Ironhall. I remember that day! Thirdmoon, 388, it was, twelve years ago. Hereward was Prime." When his guest did not comment, Wolf reached for the package beside his chair. "This, I am informed, is an exact replica of a sword named *Stoop*. The original was destroyed when you were expelled, of course."

"The nerve of the hussy!" Eagle muttered. "She was sixteen. Spoiled rotten. Arrogant. Oversexed." He had never told anyone the story, yet it had been common knowledge at the time and ancient history now. He sighed. "I suppose I wasn't completely innocent. We had to guard her, of course, and we played games with her. We'd take turns flirting. Just a glance or two would do it. She was lonely, insecure, daren't trust anyone around that snake pit Court of her father's, and he barely knew she existed. Blades could be trusted, though. All her life she'd been told that the Royal Guard could be trusted. We toyed with her. We weren't serious! Spirits, a bound Blade could collect more girls around Court in those days than he had hours in the day for!"

"They still can," Wolf said. "They still do."

"Not princesses, though. When Malinda went starry-eyed, we'd complain to Leader, and he'd reassign us. But then Durendal was promoted to Chancellor and Bandit took over. He didn't react fast enough. One evening she cornered me in the stable and kissed me. *She* kissed *me*! And in walked the snoops. They must have been watching her day and night."

"Sounds right," Wolf said. "That's exactly the sort of game they like to play." He sipped his drink. "Some of them."

"Ambrose wanted to cut my head off!" Eagle said bitterly. "You'd think I had raped her and sired triplets on her. I was cashiered, exiled, transported. Durendal arranged for me to escape and saw I had money."

"That's typical, too," Wolf said. "But remember that Ambrose married her off to a pirate, poor child. And if she took the first chance she got to try and make what amends she could, doesn't that suggest that she had been feeling guilty all those years?" He raised his glass. "To the Pirate's Wife!"

Eagle grunted wordlessly, but he did drink the toast. Wolf waved for the servant in the corner to come and refill the glasses.

Eagle unwrapped the sword. He had forgotten just how fine an Ironhall blade felt to handle, the damask, the perfect balance. "I suppose I can regard this as my due." He admired the engraving: *Stoop.* "Thank you. I will write and thank Grand Master."

"What was the good news you were going to tell me?"

"Oh, nothing to get in a froth over," Eagle said, squinting along the sword. "*El Caudillo* is in Mondon, Don Severo de la Cuenca himself! I told you they barely missed the hurricane. Even so, their ship got badly battered. He's on his way Home to fame and riches. The King has made him a marquis."

Although they were speaking Chivian, Wolf waited until the glasses were filled and the boy had gone before he responded. "I suppose he earned it. The world is certainly a better place without El Dorado. No more mass sacrifices, no more half-human monsters."

"Nary a one," Eagle said. "Not a building left standing in El Dorado itself, apparently, and he leveled every pyramid in the Hence Lands, so no more altars."

"And no survivors?"

"None in El Dorado, anyway. Except the Marquesa, of course."

"*Who?*"

Surprised by his vehemence, Eagle said, "The Marquesa. She's pure blue-blood Distlish, apparently. She'd been a prisoner in El Dorado and was rescued during the sack. *El Caudillo* took a fancy to her and now he's married her! The gossips barely pause for food or drink. A striking woman with red hair, I understand."

Wolf stared very hard at him. "A prisoner in El Dorado?"

"So they say." Eagle thought it over. "I don't know if I believe it, though." He chuckled. "Come with me next week and hear it from her own lips. Cuenca will be in Mondon for a few weeks; he and his wife. If you want to meet them, I can arrange it."

Don Lope seemed to be studying the sunset. A group of boys went racing past, kicking a ball and screaming at the top of their lungs in a mixture of Distlish and Tlixilian. In among them, fair-skinned and red-haired but as loud as any, went Edwin. Despite the awkward, lopsided gallop dictated by his twisted foot, he was keeping up. Only after the ball went bouncing away with the raucous gang still in hot pursuit did *El Diablo* turn to answer his guest's invitation.

"No! Thank you, but no! I have absolutely no desire to meet *El Caudillo* or his Marquesa. I'd be much obliged if you see I am not even mentioned—*brother*."

"Why ever not—*brother*?" Eagle smiled an *I-told-you my-story* smile.

Wolf scowled. "In confidence?"

"Upon my sword!" That was a good Blade oath he had not heard in years.

"Because if that Marquesa is who I think she is, she will take Edwin away from me."

"You're joking!"

"I am not joking!" Wolf's snarl was fearsome. "And nothing on this earth will make me give him up to the likes of her!" He drained his glass and banged it down on the table beside him. "That boy saved my life. I mean that, literally. I needed a reason to keep going and I found someone who needed me as much as I needed him. I came from the same sort of background myself, and I had forgotten just how terrible it was—houses like holes in the ground, food that would sicken cattle. I rescued him. And he rescued me, because he's why I'm still here."

After a moment he shrugged as if ashamed of his vehemence, for he was not a demonstrative man. "I'd made a promise, see?"

CB
11/05

MG 7/05

* NE 4/05

10/04

ML